To Hell You Ride
Carissa Hardcastle

HARDCASTLE PUBLISHING HOUSE

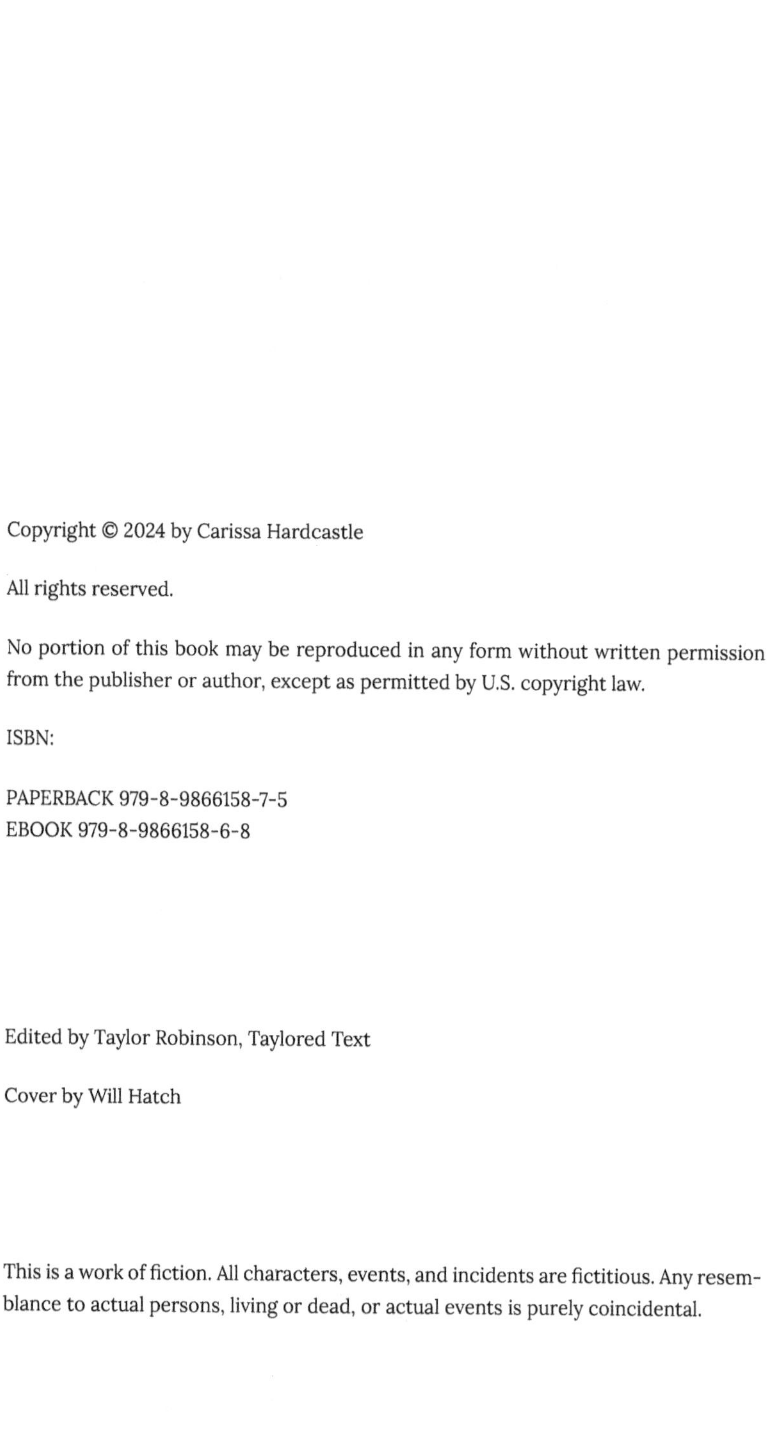

Also by Carissa Hardcastle:

Leaves May Fall
Mountains Will Crumble
A Code of Conduct: The Mercenaries' Tale

To Hell You Ride is a horror novel that contains violence, gore, strong language, sex, and recreational drug use.

For the ones who have always been
a little too curious for their own good;
May the resulting adventures always be worth it.

And for Murs, for always being down to chase the good nature

"The world is indeed comic, but the joke is on mankind."
H.P. Lovecraft

The introduction from an article by Dr. Kelvin Curtis found in *Science* (May 2024)

Man's folly has always been that he thinks he is at the top of the food chain; that, because he has figured out how to harness the power of the wind and the sun, and bend electricity to his will, he is somehow superior.

But nature is not that simple. Man, at the base of his existence, is weak. Intelligence has helped him rise to power, but were he to be stripped of his buildings and weapons, suddenly hundreds of species could easily kill him. Without his tools, man is soft, unprotected, and vulnerable to the rest of nature.

Because man has always thought himself superior, whenever fear of what lies beyond this planet and solar system has surfaced, it has always been of another humanoid creature, a race more technologically advanced than his own. The most terrifying form of an invader is the one with laser weapons, saucer ships, and bipedal gray bodies.

Man is extremely self-aggrandizing in this way. He thinks of a threat that reminds him of himself, but with greater tools, and decides that this is the fate he could never possibly overcome. A more inventive, industrious version of himself is surely the best evolution could ever do, despite the fact that man's survival is reliant on his own inventions.

Mankind is smart, yes, but intelligence has left it physically weak and unprotected.

Consider, for a moment, creatures that have evolved to survive without technology, modern medicine, and every other amenity and convenience that has made life easier for humans.

Even smaller, seemingly insignificant creatures have developed to live in the harshest conditions. Carcinization, for example, is a phenomenon being observed in the twenty-first century that shows trends of sea creatures developing the characteristics of crabs. Take away natural predators, and lobsters are practically immortal, even living beneath hundreds of pounds of water pressure.

This is not even taking into account the creatures whose only predator is man—or more accurately, man's weapons. Lions, cheetahs, grizzly bears, crocodiles, giant constrictor snakes, wolves, sharks, electric eels, giant jellyfish—the list of animals that survive the worst nature has to offer is almost infinite. Even dinosaurs are only extinct due to a cataclysmic cosmic event.

So consider the existence of an apex predator whose topmost instinct is survival, who has not only withstood every single hardship, but has also overcome it. Consider a creature who has developed not only physical superiority, but also cunning and critical thinking.

Now, put this predator up against man's technology and written communication and understanding of science, and it will not be man who comes out on the other side. Because this creature is not dependent on the things it has created. Everything about its being is geared toward survival by any means necessary. There is no bargaining with it. No flying in linguists to try to communicate with it and figure out why it is here. It simply wants to establish dominance, and it wants to eat.

Yet man still will not understand why that is more terrifying than a gray humanoid with a ray gun. And that will be his downfall.

Day 1

Thursday, 24 August 2023

1

0015 MDT//2hr 48min before arrival

In the cab of the control tower, one of Effie's hands hangs down in front of a space heater, fingers splayed out in the comforting draft of warm air. The sky over the Telluride Regional Airport and the surrounding mountains is clear, not a cloud in sight and nothing more than a gentle breeze drifting over the peaks. A *Nightmare on Elm Street 3: Dream Warriors* plays quietly on her iPad, easily drowned out when an aircraft keys up.

"Tower, Hawk762 flight with information foxtrot. Request VFR departure to the west." The call is choppy from the sound of spinning rotors in the background.

Effie pauses the movie and stands to glance out the window at the two helicopters on the ramp below her, tucking back a lock of bright blue hair that falls into her face with the movement. She grabs the handset resting on the console. "Hawk762, are you requesting flight following?"

"Negative, and we'll accept a present position departure."

"Roger, squawk VFR, departure will be at your own risk. Wind three-four-zero at seven."

"Hawk762." With that, the H-60s lift off, heading out of the mountains with their tail lights flashing.

Effie keeps her eyes on those rhythmically blinking lights before flicking her gaze to the radar display hanging from the ceiling to watch their data tag pop up. When it does, and she sees no other traffic on her screen, she keys up again. "Hawk762, frequency change approved. Safe flight."

"Have a good night, Telly."

Effie smiles at the nickname for Telluride, double clicking the handset in response before marking the departure information on the flight progress strip and returning to her chair.

Expecting it to be another slow, quiet night, Effie grabs her iPad and reclines back with her feet propped on the console. When her movie finishes, she stands up and stretches, glancing at the radar. Only a couple of targets make their way slowly across the screen, well above and away from her airspace, so she returns to her entertainment.

She loads up A *Nightmare on Elm Street 4: The Dream Master* and tosses a bag of popcorn into the microwave sitting on a window ledge, her eyes roaming the dark expanse of the mountains around her.

Effie has worked at Telluride Tower for just over two years. She'd been surprised to learn that the small airport even had a control tower when her cousin not-so-subtly hinted that she should apply for the job. The airport itself is public, owned by the Telluride Regional Airport Authority, but the tower is funded and operated by a private agency. She'd never been told who, and her curiosity around the matter quickly faded with most of her mental effort going into learning a new airspace, new airframes, and new operating procedures. While air traffic control itself was still the same, everything else about working in a contracted tower was jarringly different from the military environment she'd known before.

The ten-hour night shift sometimes feels long, but she only works Monday through Thursday, which more than makes up for it.

Though she loves her schedule, it does amount to a lot of time alone, and the traffic at night can be close to non-existent. To help the hours pass, Effie decided this summer she'd make her way through all of the old "cult classic" slasher films.

"An excellent use of time," her mother sarcastically commented when she heard during a phone call a couple weeks ago.

Effie had sighed, flicking the tip of her thumbnail against her teeth. She'd pulled her hand away from her mouth before she could bite it, a horrible habit that she'd been battling her whole life. The compulsion really only overtakes her now when she's stressed, uncomfortable, or talking to her mother. She doesn't care to evaluate what the latter means.

"I'm only saying you could be taking some college classes, using the time to get a degree or something," her mother elaborated. "You have the GI bill, you know."

"I don't need to get a degree." Effie tried to keep the irritation from her voice. There are many reasons people join the military, but she hadn't sworn in to the Air Force because she wanted a free ride to college. She'd just wanted a free ride away from home.

"You should always be trying to better yourself, Elizabeth. And you could do something fun, like get a degree in conservation. You've always loved birds."

Effie bit her tongue against the exasperated sigh that built in her chest. "There's a lot more to conservation than bird-watching."

"You know Laura has already enrolled for fall classes, and little man won't even be two yet," her mother continued, unphased.

"Yup." Effie was quickly shutting down. She'd already talked to her younger sister, who'd been excited to share the news that she felt ready to continue her education after the whirlwind that was new motherhood. Effie was happy for her, and proud of her for pursuing something for herself, but just because something was right for one of them didn't mean it was right for both.

A sigh came from the other end of the phone. "I'm not trying to compare you two, you know that, honey. I just don't want to see you waste your potential."

Effie hadn't bothered trying to explain to her mother that she was perfectly content where she was—that she didn't want to spend her life continually trying to claw herself higher. She'd found a cushy, well-paying job that allowed her to explore her own hobbies and interests, and she intended to stay in this cushy, well-paying job for as long as humanly possible. Her thumbnail had worked its way back to her mouth, and she jerked her hand back down to her lap, gripping the hem of her shorts. "I know, Mom," she replied. "I gotta get ready for work."

"Okay, honey. I love you, have a good night."

The beep of the microwave and the smell of artificial butter fill the small tower cab, pulling Effie back to the present. That conversation had been their last, and if she doesn't call her mother sometime this week, her stepdad will send her a text intended to guilt her for being a negligent daughter.

Effie reaches for a pen. *Milk* is scrawled across her left wrist, a habit she got into as a teenager in order not to forget things. Bored in school, she'd taught herself to write ambidextrous so that mundane things could go on her left wrist, but more important things could go on her right. She adds *call Mom* beneath *milk*, then tosses the pen aside to pull the bag of popcorn from the microwave and settles back down, ready to resume her nightly movie marathon.

To her delight, the fourth *Nightmare on Elm Street* installment is even cheesier than the third, and she leaves it playing while she gets up to grab a napkin from across the room.

On her way back to her seat, she glances out into the night. The airfield is still quiet and dark, the surrounding mountains solid black masses against a sky filled with stars. She takes a moment to admire the band of the Milky Way drawn thickly across the cloudless sky, a small smile of contentment pulling at her lips.

A brilliant flare of green draws her attention, quickly fading but movement still discernible, and she squints, peering out the window for a second before glancing up at the radar.

Her mouth drops open, head falling to the side as she watches what appears to be a small patch of precipitation barreling toward her airspace.

Barreling, because it's moving at the same pace most aircraft targets move.

Effie blinks, stepping closer to the radar. It must be a glitch, because there is no way a storm is moving that fast. She glances down to the display showing airfield information, where the wind reads a mere four knots.

Even while assuring herself that it can't be anything other than an error, she instinctively reaches for a pair of binoculars and scans the sky for any sign of movement.

An indiscernible shape is flying through the darkness. Effie is only able to track it thanks to years of prior practice watching fighter jets maneuver through the sky, but she loses it when it dips below the line of the mountains. Without the backdrop of glittering stars to accentuate its position, it's impossible to see.

The Dream Master continues to play in the background, quiet screams reaching Effie's ears but going ignored. She looks back at the radar, and sure enough, the precipitation has disappeared.

Tapping the pads of her fingers against her thumbs, Effie scans the tower cab as if it holds an answer for how to respond to strange things shooting across the sky.

A strangled laugh bubbles from her chest as she plops back into her seat, entirely unsure of what she just witnessed.

"That wasn't precipitation," she mutters, sure of at least that much. But with the lack of light to identify any sort of features, Effie has no clue what else it could have been, either.

Was it an aircraft that had gone down? Should she call out Search and Rescue?

She dismisses the idea before anxiety has a chance to take hold in her gut. There had been no targets on the radar, it couldn't have been an aircraft.

Another incredulous laugh spills from her with the realization that, whatever that thing was, for now it is an unidentified object.

Rolling her chair over to the small bookcase that houses regulations and publications, she quickly locates the thick binder labeled FAAO 7110.65 AIR TRAFFIC CONTROL and pulls it onto her lap. After a brief search through the table of contents, she flips to chapter nine, section eight: Unidentified Flying Object (UFO) Reports.

There is only one subsection: General.

Under that, an A, which dictates that persons wanting to report UFO or unexplained phenomena should contact a data collection center such as the National UFO Reporting Center and a B, which tells her that if concern is expressed that life or property might be in danger, she should report the activity to local law enforcement.

Effie scans the remaining regulations, grabbing the FAA AERONAUTICAL INFORMATION MANUAL. It, too, has a small section for UFO reporting, but repeats the information from the .65 almost verbatim.

Closing the binder with a snort, she slides it back onto the shelf and propels herself backward, coming to rest at the console. She taps her fingers against the Plexiglass covering little quick-reference bits of information pertinent to the airport and the airspace and looks at the watch supervisor desk, the computer monitor dark in sleep mode, debating whether or not to annotate anything on the daily log.

One of Effie's hands moves to her mouth, fingers trailing across her lips in thought before her pinky works its way between them. Her teeth close on the fingernail, the act triggering a small release of serotonin amidst the stress of the situation.

She bites at the nail for a moment before realizing what she's doing and rips her hand from her mouth. "For fuck's sake, Eff," she chastises herself. Finally deciding it's not that big of a deal and could have been any number of things, she scribbles a brief note for the day shift:

The radar glitched a bit last night. Looked like a patch of precip, but moving too fast. Only happened the one time, but keep an eye out just in case.

Short, simple, and only facts. If something comes from the situation, it shows she was paying attention. If nothing comes from the situation, she won't look crazy. The loudest alarm bell in her mind at this point is the knowledge that if she wants to keep her cushy, well-paying job, she can't give the airport's leadership any reason to question her competency or sanity.

2

0605 MDT//3hr 3min after arrival

Sunlight caresses the tops of the mountains, gradually edging out the cold of night. The world wakes—a flycatcher flits after its breakfast, pikas dart from rock to rock, and further up the ridge, a marmot toddles along, pausing in alarm when it notices the gigantic, oblong shape ahead, dark in color but shimmering brightly in the early morning light.

The marmot sniffs the air, but aside from a faint, chemical tinge of ozone, the thing smells of nothing, so it continues along.

The warmth of the planet gradually seeps into the smooth, translucent surface, waking the creature inside from her interminable hibernation. Slowly, her wings uncurl from around her, losing the form of the airtight cocoon they'd made. Dust drifts down around her, all that remains from the molt she underwent during her hibernation, jarred and disintegrated upon impact. The remnants fall into piles below her body as her wings stretch open, sunlight reflecting from the unblemished surface.

She flaps them, spreading the dust across the mountainside as she tests her muscles after the intergalactic journey. Eight legs, encased in the same rigid, gray-blue shell that covers her entire body, unfold from beneath her. Their sharp tips poke into the rockbed as, one at a time, the four eyes on her triangular head open, surveying the landscape around her.

The marmot stands a few yards in front of her, nose and ears twitching suspiciously as it tries to figure her out. A short shriek leaves its body, echoing off the walls of granite that surround them.

The sound vibrates through her, and she lunges on instinct, long, sturdy legs sliding free from their telescopic joints to propel her forward.

The little, furry thing darts to the side, but not fast enough to avoid the mandibles that lock around its hindquarters, and its squeaking cry cuts off when she gives a sharp shake of her head.

One raptorial forelimb reaches up to grasp the limp body, and she makes quick work of the animal, devouring it within seconds as her wings curl up onto her back to be tucked away beneath two thick plates of exoskeleton.

With her meal done, she turns and hisses at the sun, squinting a glare into the brightness over the horizon. The rays sear hot where they touch her, and a low-pitched, irritated cry escapes her. She scuttles over boulders and through the trees in search of refuge from the too-bright star.

Two antennae extend from either side of her mouth, scenting the air until she catches something dark and damp, and she lifts her head to better locate the mineral-esque smell that reminds her of home. With fresh motivation, she picks up the pace, moving like liquid over the mountainside.

A wooden door covers the entrance to a mine tunnel, secured by a thick padlock and heavy chain. She screeches at the audacity, dreadfully uncomfortable with the sun's rays at her back, and punches through the wood with a foreleg, hooking onto the door and flinging it off to the side. As she does so, a remaining section of her molt is dislodged from the spines that line one side of the limb and bounces over the rocks and down the hillside.

With a simple twist of her joints, her legs shorten, retracting into themselves to help her large form better fit in the tight passageway. She slips into the cool, damp darkness, a nictitating membrane flicking over her eyes as she scurries into the mountain.

The hard shell of her back scrapes against the rock above her, the vibrations echoing through her whole body, but also out along the tunnel around her, and she knows it's caved in several hundred yards ahead.

She taps the pointed tips of her legs against the ground, tilting her head to the side as her view of the tunnel fills into a crisper picture. Scuttling forward, she drags her middle legs against the walls on either side of her, outer two eyes watching for any hollow spots in the mountain as she nears the place where the old mine had been collapsed.

She doesn't know that scientists would be amazed by the biology behind her third eyelids that allows her to see even the most subtle vibrations, because she doesn't know what a scientist is. She just knows she wants deeper into the ground, and she wants to relieve herself of the heavy fullness in her abdomen.

There's a spot to her right where the tunnel wall is thinner, and she stops, tapping her legs against it to search out cracks and weak spots in the granite. A satisfied series of clicks sounds from her throat, and she leans against the far wall, giving herself space to kick repeatedly at the side of the tunnel, the sharp tips of her legs chipping away until rubble fills the passageway.

She sweeps the rock beneath her, blinking away dust as she continues digging. After crudely carving away at roughly ten feet of granite, she breaks free into an expansive cavern. If any light had penetrated the cave, it would glitter from floor to ceiling with chunks of raw beryl—another fact that means nothing to her, aside from the way the soft, subtle vibrations of the stone feel right against her exoskeleton. She tilts her head up, repeating a soft clicking noise from her throat as she looks around her.

There's a break in the rocks across the cave, and she moves toward it, the tips of her legs repeating an endlessly echoed *click-clack* against the floor. She crawls over the pile of rocks, calling softly into the darkness ahead until she can see the way forward, and she pushes through.

The top and bottom plates of exoskeleton that protect her body disconnect, shifting slightly off center and sliding into each other as she squeezes underneath an outcropping of rock into a tunnel beyond. Down, deep into the belly of the mountain, she crawls before pulling herself out into another cave.

This one is much more damp than the first, but warmer—a steady temperature that hasn't fluctuated in thousands of years. Tapping her front legs against the granite beneath her, she looks around before scuttling over to a smooth depression that rests at the base of a large column connecting floor to ceiling.

Much like a dog, she circles around the dip in the cave floor before crouching to let her belly rest against the ground, the two sections of her abdomen expanding and clicking back together. Her outer eyelids droop, more out of habit than anything. There is neither light nor irritants to block down here.

Her mandibles part slightly, antennae creeping forward and twitching as she scents the air. Ever so faintly, she can smell others, and that's the last bit of confirmation she needs to know that this cave, with its warm, humid air and many tunnels and crevices, is right. Her eyes squint further closed, and the muscles in her abdomen twitch, convulsing downward and forcing out the clutch of eggs she's carried and kept safe through her entire journey. The oblong cylinders, covered in a thin layer of mucus, drop to the floor with a soft splat. When the discomfort of their weight and the space they took up inside of her is gone, her whole body shudders in the semblance of a sigh.

She's hungry. Terribly, unfathomably hungry. But her voyage has been long, and she is tired despite her hibernation. With her eggs laid, she settles further against the ground, and the shell over her wings separates, letting them unfurl to cover the clutch behind her. Then she tucks her head back beneath her wings and sleeps.

3

0740 MDT//4hr 37min after arrival

Kel drains another water bottle and reaches over his head to drop it into the back seat. He's not in the habit of driving through most of the night, especially when towing, but he'd been way too wired to sleep.

He'd been camping on the outskirts of Gunnison National Forest, set up with his telescope and camera, taking notes on the stars, when he'd seen a flash of vibrant green burn through the atmosphere.

Kel has been staring up into space since he was a toddler, so he's seen more meteors burn through the sky than he can count, but this one fell *all the way down*.

And it had been *close*.

He'd stared in open-mouthed wonder for a single moment after it disappeared, then grabbed his equipment and ran full tilt back to his fifth wheel to pull the footage from the camera and plot its probable location, a giddy energy buzzing in his veins. With no other forethought, he packed up camp and started driving to Telluride. It wasn't until he stopped to fuel up in Montrose that he realized it was almost dawn, and he'd need to find somewhere to stay. After a quick Google search for campsites that would accommodate the fifth wheel, Kel was back on the road.

Just over an hour later, he pulls into a camping spot, leaning over his steering wheel to stretch his back out as he taps his fingers along to "Danger Zone." He turns off the truck, the rhythmic chugging of the diesel engine cutting out, and Kenny Loggins's imploring croon silenced as he opens the door. Grabbing a black ball cap from the dash, he rakes a hand through his hair to pull back the unruly, dirty blond waves and tuck them away before stepping outside.

The not-quite-silence of early morning greets him as he stands for a moment, pushing plastic-rimmed glasses further up the bridge of his nose and taking in his surroundings. The chatter of birds is accompanied by the rustle of aspen leaves in a breeze that carries with it the fresh smell of earth. It's all wild and quiet and beautiful, and it feels like the right way to start a discovery that could potentially alter his entire career—put his name on the astronomical map.

Exhaustion creeps in, tugging at his muscles and his eyelids as he walks to the front of the campground to fill out a pay slip, booking the entire weekend. With the last reserves of his energy, he unhooks his truck and levels out the camper before collapsing into bed.

4

Effie steps outside, wincing at the brightness, when her dad calls her. "Hey," she answers as she walks through the parking lot toward a bright blue Jeep.

"Good morning!" he says cheerily as she opens the door and climbs in, tossing her bag onto the seat next to her. "You headed home?"

"Hold on, you're going to switch to Bluetooth." After turning the key in the ignition, she pulls a pair of sunglasses from the center console and slides them onto her face while waiting for the car to verify her phone's connection. When it does, she shifts into gear and pulls out of her spot. Her eyes catch her left wrist, and she sighs. "Not yet. I've actually gotta run to the store first. Need milk and a few other things."

"Fingers crossed they've got your Lucky Charms."

Effie smiles, turning onto the road that leads down the mountainside. "I'll keep you posted."

"Well, I won't keep you. I'm actually headed into work; I just wanted to let you know that I finally mailed out that new bike seat, so it should be there in a few days. I'll text you a picture of the tracking number on the receipt."

"Ah, thank you!" She does a little dance in her seat, making a mental note to text Bethany and let her know. Effie had originally been the one to pull her best friend into mountain biking, a hobby she'd kept up with from high school, but Bethany had latched on with a fervor and was now the one dragging Effie out at every opportunity. Her dad is also into the sport, and recently bought a fancy after-market seat that he ended up not being a fan of and was thus gifting to Effie. "I'll keep an eye out and let you know when it arrives."

"Sounds good. I'll be looking forward to hearing how it works out for you. Get home safe and sleep tight, okay? Love you, bud."

"Love you, too. Hope you have a good day."

They say "bye" and she hangs up, feeling rejuvenated as she turns onto the main road, headed to town.

The burst of excited energy doesn't last, though. Once parked outside the grocery store, she turns off the car and tips her head back against the headrest, knowing she should make a full restock run since she's already here. But even just the thought is exhausting, not to mention having to put everything away once she gets home. "Milk and maybe cereal," she tells herself, glancing at her wrist with a sigh. *And then a call to Mom.*

She grabs the corduroy tote from the passenger seat, dumping her keys and phone inside, and marches in. The produce steers her off course, and even though the cost of plums makes her wince, she grabs three before moving to the cereal aisle. A squeak almost squeezes from her chest when she sees Lucky Charms on the shelf, spurring her to pick up her pace. Two boxes are plucked up and held to her chest like the beloved possessions they are.

Deciding this is a good omen, she practically skips to the dairy section to grab milk. Just one little phone call to her mom, and then she'll be able to have a bowl of cereal or two before going to bed.

With a gallon of whole milk completing her selections, she rounds a corner to the checkout and slams straight into another person, the breath leaving her with an audible *oof* as she clutches the cereal tighter, pressing the fruit to her chest and almost losing her hold on the milk. "So sorry, I—oh, hey." She steps back, an easy if not abashed smile pulling at her lips and her posture relaxing when she registers the man in front of her: Lance Sutherland, the chief deputy sheriff and also her cousin, who may as well have been her older brother growing up.

"Look who's up with the sun," he jokes, reaching out to take the gallon jug from her tenuous two-fingered grip.

"Yeah, well, there are a few things more important than sleep," she replies, punctuating the sentiment with the shake of a cereal box as she continues toward the self checkout.

Lance follows, still holding her milk. Setting her items down on the counter, Effie begins checking out, holding her hand toward him. When the cold press of the jug doesn't hit her fingers, she looks up, noting the bags under his hazel eyes and haggard pallor to his face. "Is everything okay?" Her brows pull together as she reaches to take the milk, watching him while she scans it.

He blinks as if pulled from a deep thought and runs a hand over his close-cropped beard, the same light brown as his hair but with slightly more gray peppered throughout. "Yeah, just tired. Had an early start this morning." The smile he offers her is just as tired as his voice.

"Oh?" That patch of strange precipitation flashes unbidden through her mind. She readjusts her grip on the milk, and the self-checkout beeps, asking her to please place all items in the bagging area.

Lance yawns, his gaze drifting before he pulls it back to her. "I should head over to the station. You get home safe, okay?"

He starts to walk away, but Effie grabs the sleeve of his jacket, his parting words sinking in her gut and sending up a wave of apprehension. "Lance, wait. Did something happen?" She lives on the back of his property, less than ten miles away. Adverse weather notwithstanding, he isn't in the habit of telling her to *get home safe.*

When he turns back around to face her, his expression is as open and easygoing as she's ever seen it. "No, no, I just know you've been up hours longer than me, and I'm already struggling. Came in to grab a coffee for that very reason. Seriously, I don't know how you do it."

She eyes him suspiciously, but if he's hiding anything more than exhaustion, she's equally too tired to find it. "It helps that I'm a vampire." She shoots him a grin and collects her purchases.

"Wait until you're my age, kid, and those night shifts might not be so fun anymore," he chuckles.

Effie rolls her eyes. "Later, Lancelot."

Her stomach growls as she climbs back into her car, and she pats it placatingly. "Just a few more minutes," she promises, pulling out onto the street and cranking the radio up.

A handful of alt rock songs later, she's turning into the paved driveway of a large, ranch-style home. She drives past the main house to a casita out back, exhaustion flooding her bones the second she pulls under the metal carport. Without giving herself the chance to become overtired and stare listlessly out the windshield for minutes on end, she quickly collects her things from the passenger seat and heads inside, tossing her keys onto the counter and immediately pouring a bowl of cereal.

The milk and plums make it into the fridge, but she leaves the two boxes on the countertop and moves to the living room to sink onto a comfortably worn couch, legs tucked underneath her.

The first bite settles something in her soul, and she sighs, leaning back into the microfiber cushions to eat.

Her eyes catch the writing on her wrist, and she groans

around a mouthful, realizing she forgot to call her mom. Cereal bowl in hand, she hauls herself up to dig her phone out of her bag.

A text from her dad distracts her, the promised picture of the tracking number, and she plops heavily onto a bar stool, setting the bowl down in front of her as she shoots a message to Bethany.

Beth2nd: Bike seat en route!

The reply comes only a few minutes later, and Effie reads it as she drinks the
sugary, leftover milk, cereal finished.

Beth1st: This means we need to plan one last big ride this weekend as a non voyage to your old one then, right?

Beth2nd: Twist my arm. Sunday?

Beth1st: Bon*

Beth1st: Perf. I'll pick a good trail

Beth2nd: I expect a full report by the time I wake up

Beth1st: Sleep tight, my little creature of the night

5

Lance Sutherland sits in his department-issued SUV and finishes off the bottled frappe he bought from Clarks Market in five large gulps. He almost shivers at the cloying sweetness of caramel that lingers on his tongue, but he's counting on the sugar just as much as the caffeine for energy.

He glares at the bottle, knowing its contents will do nothing for the slowly building headache in the back of his skull. It's been years since he quit, but the need for a cigarette is overwhelming.

For the past three years, Lance has been working for the San Miguel Sheriff's Department, placed on special assignment by an outside agency, but operating on a regular nine-to-five, doing typical work found in most remote sheriff's departments. If it weren't for the quarterly reports he copy/pasted to send in to HQ, he could imagine that he'd never even taken the assignment and instead ended up in Telluride by completely organic circumstances.

But his phone had rung in the wee hours of the morning, and now he sits, exhausted, terrified, and trying to convince himself that he knows what he's doing. He sighs, shifting in his seat and pulling the seat belt over his shoulder to buckle in, but before he can shift into drive, a text pops up on his phone.

Hal Phillips: Expecting a report within the hour.

He scowls the entire ten-minute drive to the sheriff's office, annoyed by the reminder. Regardless of whether or not this is his first "incident," Lance knows the procedure, and the implied questioning of his competence is grating.

"Good morning, Chief!" the administrative assistant greets from the front desk, black hair piled in a messy bun atop her head.

"Morning, Morgan," he replies, trying to hide some of his tiredness behind a smile. "Been nice and slow for ya?"

"Nothing to report yet," she assures him, her focus already returning to the screen in front of her, where she has a game of spider solitaire loaded on one of the screens.

Relief washes over him more palpably than he expected, and he struggles to keep the emotion from his face as he walks past her and into his office. No reports. No calls. No unusual occurrences.

That's good.

That means whatever fell last night went underground like it was supposed to and shouldn't be a problem.

With a heavy sigh that makes him feel at least a decade older than forty-one, he sinks into his chair and boots up his computer, ready to send off the report to the agency that's feeding his kids' college funds.

6

2104 MDT//18hr 1min after arrival

"Okay, it's south of Silverton on the million dollar highway—Molas Pass? There's an overlook there we can park at, then ride to ... fuck, I forgot. Emerald Lake? No, that's not right. Maybe Elder?" Bethany's voice is accompanied by the sound of running water as Effie rinses her face.

She turns off the faucet and grabs a towel before answering. "How long is it?"

"Eh, roughly twenty miles round-trip."

Effie pulls the towel away and shoots a pointed look at her phone, propped against the mirror.

"What?" Bethany crosses her arms defensively, but laughs. "I swear it's not longer."

"Uh-huh," Effie concedes, dropping the towel on the counter in exchange for a small tub of lotion.

Bethany pulls the length of her dark, unruly curls over a shoulder, examining the ends as Effie moisturizes her cheeks. "If you count the hike to the lake, it's over twenty, but barely."

Effie releases her hair from the clip holding it back from her face, short blue strands sweeping her shoulders, and ruffles the roots before deciding that dry shampoo isn't a necessity. "Let's do it, then. We can bring some drinks for the lake." She plucks her phone up and carries it into the kitchen to pack some snacks.

"Perfect. You drive and I'll provide the alcohol?"

"You shouldn't drive if you're drinking," a small voice pipes up.

Fighting back a laugh, Effie looks over her shoulder to where Izzy, the younger of Lance's daughters, sits at the breakfast bar, scribbling notes on a pad of paper.

"You're right, kiddo," Bethany says, speaking up. "Which means it'll all be for me."

"Don't tell her that or she'll lecture you about moderation," Effie warns.

"As long as we can record it to play back to her after her first high school party, let's hear it."

Izzy rolls her eyes without looking up. "I'll be in college when I'm twenty-one, not high school, right, Effie?"

"Absolutely correct," she affirms, holding back another laugh.

"Derek just pulled in, so I'll let you go," Bethany says. "Have a good night."

"Later." Effie blows her a kiss before hanging up and pocketing her phone.

"I figured out what I saw today!" Izzy pushes up on the counter, standing on her knees on the barstool and wiggling back and forth.

"What did you see?" Effie grabs a plum from the fridge.

"A snowy egret," the younger girl proclaims proudly.

Setting a single-serve frozen lasagna on the counter next to her plum, Effie walks across the kitchen to read the paper Izzy slides across the counter. Looking over the two columns of large, messy seven-year-old writing labeled "graet egret" and "snowy egret." A few characteristics underneath great egret are crossed out, and snowy egret is circled heavily. "Check out that sleuthing!" she compliments.

Izzy beams, glancing down at her list with pride. "Where are you driving with Bethany?"

"We're planning a bike ride Sunday." Effie packs the food up in her bag before wandering around the living room in search of her iPad.

"Can I come?" Izzy asks hopefully, and Effie realizes the child has it in front of her, looking up information about birds.

"Not this time, Iz."

"Is Katie going?" She pouts, not wanting to be left out of anything her older sister gets to partake in.

"No, just me and Bethany," Effie assures her, and she sighs like being a child is the world's heaviest burden, locking the screen and handing the tablet over. Effie runs a hand over the back of her head in sympathy, fingers trailing down the girl's light brown braid. "I need to head out a bit early tonight, so let's get you home."

"Why do you have to leave early?" Izzy hops down from the barstool.

"I need to stop by the store." Effie slips the iPad into her bag.

"Why?"

"Gas and Red Bull."

"Mmm," Izzy hums thoughtfully. "Daddy says energy drinks are *not* a good choice."

Effie ushers her out the door. "Well, when you're my age, sometimes you sacrifice a good choice to get through the work-day."

"So in twenty-one years I can make bad choices?"

Effie pauses, mouth open. "Uh, not ... I wouldn't put it that way exactly. But you will have the autonomy to make bad choices if you want to, I guess."

"Autonomy," Izzy repeats, as though trying the word out for size, then grins. "Awesome." She turns without another word, running across the back lawn toward the main house.

"Oh dear," Effie sighs, watching until Izzy opens the back door and disappears inside. With an amused shake of her head, she climbs into her Jeep and heads to work.

I saw a meteor last night!

Sorry if this isn't the place to post this, but I'm way excited and want to see if anyone might have been stargazing and found a picture. This was in the dead of night, and truly I should have been asleep, but we've got a newborn at home so we keep odd hours.

Anyway, I was wondering how to go about finding information about the thing. It fell full through the atmosphere, I'm sure of it. Did anyone else happen to catch this?

Replies:

u/constellationbeanz: check your local facebook groups and news outlets! sometimes they get caught on security cameras.

^u/fullchinchilllin82: good idea, I'll look into it!

u/federalhomie333: sometimes things look like they make it through because of the arc of the sky, but honestly, dude, it's more rare than you think. Probably just a run of the mill shooting star, but still cool you got to see some sky magic!(:

^u/eatmy_sawsage: You got a source for that, buddy? There's a lot of shit that makes it earthside.

^^u/federalhomie333: "A lot" is subjective, bUdDy

u/butimalibra0: we should all be spending more time looking at the stars tbh. meteor showers are so gorgeous but most of us are too busy staring at a screen to ever notice them ...

^u/federalhomie333: I'm not even going to point out the irony here.

^^u/eatmy_sawsage: I bet you're a lot of fun at parties.

^^u/butimalibra0: idk if you know how time zones work, but it's daylight for half the world rn.

u/eatmy_sawsage: check out the American Meteor Society! They keep pretty good track of all this stuff.

^u/fullchinchillin82: amazing, thank you!

Day 2

1

0009 MDT//21hr 6min after arrival

Deep beneath the mountains to the south of Telluride, the alien creature stirs. She's disoriented at first, startling awake and standing tall to tap her legs against the stony ground. The sound moves through the space around her, giving her a clear picture of the cave, and she relaxes, extending her antennae to smell the air as she tucks her wings away. Her clutch of eggs rests behind her, and she turns, antennae flicking over those on top. The tiny lives within twitch in their sleep, and her fuzzy feelers retract, satisfied.

They will be safe here, and, now that she's rested after her voyage and labor, hunger overtakes every other instinct. She moves back through the mountain, toward the world above. The entrance is dark, free from the bright sear of ultraviolet light, and she pokes her head out, antennae extending from her mouth again as she emerges from the mine.

The scents of this world are strong and vibrant, and her antennae twitch animatedly as she scurries over the rocks, chasing the smell of warmth, life, and iron—blood. Contained, but easily accessible nonetheless.

She crawls over the ridge of the mountain, each leg punching down into the shale, crushing it beneath her weight. Hunger drives her, and a soft series of satisfied clicks, almost like a purr, rattle in her throat as she spies her prey. Her antennae retract, and she moves swiftly down the mountain, her steps eerily silent.

2

0029 MDT//21hr 26min after arrival

The San Miguel Mountains are home to many picturesque alpine lakes, three of which are located near an abandoned mining outpost. Despite the pothole-riddled, winding dirt road to reach them, Alta Lakes is a wildly popular camping destination and is known to fill up fast, especially around holidays.

Tonight, though, there are only a handful of campers getting an early start to the weekend. At this late hour, most are tucked away in their makeshift beds—all of them, really, with the exception of two.

"Casen!" Julie whisper-squeals, following her boyfriend across the muddy shore. It's her first time camping, and with a boy, no less. Her parents don't know, but she's a junior in college now, and she doesn't need their permission. Besides, Casen loves her, and she's going to end up marrying him. Probably. Maybe.

The surface of the lake ripples in the wind, waves slapping the muddy shore. "We're going to get leeches!"

Casen turns with an insolent grin, grabbing both of her hands and walking backward through the water. "There aren't any leeches here, babe. They can't live this high."

There are, and they can, but Julie doesn't know any better, and she giggles, shrieking when the cold water laps at her toes. He steps closer to her, wrapping his arms around her, and she relishes his warmth, his skin against hers, before his arms tighten and she realizes what's about to happen. "Casen, no!"

But it's too late. He throws himself backward, her with him, and icy water engulfs them. She splutters, forcing her way out of his arms and back to her feet as she gasps for air after the cold steals her breath. "God, I hate you," she laughs, brushing water out of her eyes and checking that her messy bun is still intact.

"Mmm, no you don't." Casen stands, pulling her back close and trailing kisses along her neck. "Come on, sit."

"It's muddy!" she protests.

"Sit on my lap," he offers, his hands lowering to her hips and hoisting her closer to his budding erection. "Or better yet ..."

"You're shameless." Julie swats at his hands, but lets him pull her down, his mouth still on her neck. She shivers as the water laps over her thighs. "And this water is gross."

"No one's gonna see anything," he promises, fingers slipping into the waistband of her bikini bottoms.

"Casehhhhn," she draws his name out beseechingly, but drops her hand to palm him.

He grins, moving to slip his trunks down, freeing himself to the cold water, half his butt in the slimy mud. The warmth of her hand and the hormone dump that is young adulthood keep him from going soft in the water's chill, and he's overly eager to be inside of her before that chill wins out.

As he pulls the crotch of her bottoms to the side, a larger

wave splashes against her stomach, and she shivers, trying to draw herself closer as he pokes around at her entrance. Another wave hits her skin, and her eyes flutter open. She intends to look down in a naïve attempt to help him get past the awkward difficulty of underwater insertion, but her gaze locks on a shape behind his shoulder first.

Julie screams, thrashing to unlock her legs from around Casen's waist and scrambling backward, her feet and hands sliding in the mud.

Casen hardly has time to turn around, much less register the creature behind him when her head dips, mouth closing over his skull and ripping him from the lakebed.

His shorts still hang halfway down, erection flopping in the air as the creature gives him a firm shake that snaps his spine before slamming him back down against the water. A foreleg pierces his abdomen, sticking fast from the tines along one side, and the monster jerks her head up, tearing his body in two. A string of intestines connects the pieces, blood and other guts spilling out into the water with a loud splatter.

Julie would think the sound was disconcertingly similar to that of vomit landing in a toilet if she weren't too busy screaming to hear it.

The creature lowers herself in the water, dropping Casen's upper body and pinning it with another crab-like leg to tear him into smaller pieces. His shoulder goes first, arm flopping from her mouth as she breaks up bone with a wet crunch, tipping her head back to swallow like a bird.

Julie screams, tears and snot streaming down her face. The sight of her boyfriend being eaten temporarily freezes her muscles—her hands, feet, and ass buried in the soft mud. A leech latches onto her thigh before her basic motor functions finally snap into place, and she shuffles backward out of the water, pushing clumsily to her feet to run toward the trees.

The creature narrows her eyes, the constant shrieking rattling around in her skull. She emits a low sound like slowly tearing paper and shakes the boy's body from the narrow point of her forelimb before giving chase. She catches Julie with ease, slamming one leg straight through the girl's lower back and pinning her to the ground.

Julie is still screaming, but now the sound is garbled, blood filling her throat. Her legs have lost the ability to move and a bolt of fire burns up her spine, but she throws her arms forward, fingers clawing at the dirt in an attempt to pull herself away. Mud cakes under her fingernails, a few starting to pull free from their beds. "Help," she chokes out, coughing up more blood.

Then the creature's jaws close around Julie's head, and brain matter squirts from between the moving parts of her mandibles with the force of the cracking skull.

A blank silence fills the night, even the soft lapping of waves against the shore seeming to fade out for a few moments before returning, soon accompanied by the rustle of wind in the trees and crickets chirping.

In a tent further from the shore, a child wakes, heart pounding. A noise machine whirs at the foot of his sleeping bag, drowning out distant sounds. But ... had that been someone screaming? Or was it just an animal?

No, surely animals can't make noises like that. The child shivers, reaching over to wake his father, who snores loudly, rolling over and settling deeper into his own sleeping bag. The child lies back down, clutching a worn stuffed dog to his chest. "It's just bad dreams, Wolfie," he tells it, squeezing his eyes shut and attempting to return to his dreams.

The only other campers are a couple sleeping in their van, an action movie playing from a laptop propped at the foot of their air mattress, blue light flickering over their faces as they sleep soundly through gunshots, yelled expletives, and the dying cries of Julie.

3

0036MDT//21hr 30min after arrival

The predator standing over her kill emits a soft, contented series of clicks from her throat as two joints on each leg retract to lower her belly to the mud. The spines along her forelegs help to hold the body in place as she methodically tears it apart, piece by piece. The bones are annoying, but the marrow that leaks from them coats her tongue and throat with a delicious, silky warmth.

When all that's left of Julie is a swimsuit, half a torso, and the shredded upper husk of skin (too chewy, and she wasn't a fan of all that hair on the scalp), she raises her head, antennae sliding out from the corners of her mouth as she tests the air. She doesn't remember the dead boy in the water behind her until she smells the metallic tang of his blood mixing with the moist musk of the lake.

She lifts herself from the mud with a wet, sucking squelch, turning around to where the two halves of his body have washed up on the shore, still connected by that single string of intestine. Hooking the upper half, she drags him more fully from the water before consuming most of him as well.

With her belly full, she climbs with fluid ease back up the ridge. The sky is still dark, and she's eager to explore her new domain before that dastardly bright star returns.

4

0230 MDT//23hr 27min after arrival

Effie sits at the watch supervisor desk, chin propped in her hand and computer light reflecting in her hazel eyes as she scrolls through yet another interactive display on the American Meteor Society website.

It had all started when she looked up the bike trail after the scheduled traffic had departed for the night. Her and Bethany's destination, she'd discovered, is actually Eldorado Lake, and she promptly located it on Google Earth to build some familiarity with what terrain and elevation changes to expect from the ride.

After that, she'd moved to AllTrails to look up recent reviews for the trail they'll be biking and Ophir Pass, which is both the shortest route to get them to the other side of the mountains and also Effie's preferred route of travel. She makes any excuse she can not to have to leave the encompassing safety of the mountains. Once she realized how held she felt when surrounded by them, the thought of going back to open landscape was a stone's throw shy of appalling.

Reports of the pass said that the road is good—no rock slides or major obstructions to be aware of—and that should have been that.

But then she'd glanced up at the radar, a habitual look to make sure no one was headed near her airspace, and it had shaken free the memory of that weird glitch from last night.

One thing led to another, and over an hour later, here she sits looking through different 3D models of meteor showers that are both expected in the future and previously tracked. The whole site is in depth and there are so many links to other sections of information—most of which goes entirely over her head. She's just in awe of how much there is to *know*, and she gets a little lost in it.

She navigates back to the current active meteor shower, Perseids, sitting up straighter and plucking a half-eaten plum from its resting place on a napkin by the keyboard. "*Active* is pretty subjective, guys," she mumbles to the American Meteor Society, taking a bite. Peak activity isn't expected for a few more weeks, and best she can tell, none are expected to make it through the atmosphere, nor are they typically so brightly colored. She watches the model play out again anyway, finishing the fruit and wiping her hands with the napkin.

This is all a moot point, because even if the flash of green she'd seen had been some weird trick of light, the radar wouldn't have detected a meteor. With a disgruntled sound halfway between a sigh and a groan, Effie pushes away from the desk, grabs a pair of binoculars, and heads down a few stairs to the door leading out onto the catwalk.

The concrete ledge circles the entire tower cab and is enclosed with a four-foot-high chain link railing, which Effie leans her elbows against to steady her hands as she raises the binoculars to her face. The bulk of the mountains is dark against the bright expanse of the sky, but they aren't so shadowed that she can't discern the individual peaks or their depth.

Lowering the binoculars, she closes her eyes and replays her memory from the night before, trying to conjure exactly where she'd lost sight of her weird green meteor. Then she opens her eyes, sidestepping until she has the angle right, and looks back through the binoculars.

Effie may have only lived in Telluride for a couple of years, but she's spent so much time in those mountains—whether in her Jeep, on her bike, or occasionally on foot—that she's almost certain she can guess where that thing might have ended up if she can figure out which peak it disappeared behind.

A cool breeze picks up, blowing her hair across her face, and she brushes it out of her eyes, doing her best to ignore the shiver working its way up her spine. Pulling the sleeves of her flannel lower over her hands, she crosses her arms over her chest and heads back inside, wind pushing the door closed securely behind her.

The space heater gets dragged from her usual spot across the cab and set up next to the watch supervisor desk, where Effie pulls Google Earth back up and looks at the mountains south of Telluride. She's latched on to the possibility that something landed out there, and now her brain spins with scenarios of space rocks and radioactive materials and—"You need to let it go," she advises, cracking open a can of Red Bull and taking a long sip.

It's one thing to be the lady who works nights and has blue hair. It's another thing to be the lady who works nights and has blue hair and also claims to have seen things falling from the sky.

5

Honest to God, Effie tried to let go of whatever anomaly had happened early Thursday morning. She did. But she couldn't sit back and lose herself to campy horror movies. Instead, she'd spent over half the night digging through conspiracy sites (mostly Reddit) and reading about the confirmed (and unconfirmed) things that have made it to Earth's surface from outer space over the years.

Now, Effie's head is tilted back against the headrest as she stares blankly ahead, sitting in the parking lot at the airport. She's tired. She can feel it in the way her whole body sags into her seat, but curiosity nips at the back of her brain, ever-insistent.

You know you'll never sleep without taking a look, it tells her.

"I can just as easily go *after* some sleep," she argues, turning the key in the ignition.

But it will be so hot then. Do you really want to hike around in the heat of the day? Getting all sweaty, irritated, your snacks warm from sitting against your back—

"Jesus Christ," she grumbles, resigned to her fate, and pulls out of the parking lot to head down the mountain.

As soon as she's on the road away from the direct route home, she relaxes, the tired pull of her body slithering away as excitement takes its place. There's a few off-road trails she can look around near here, and if she doesn't find anything that seems out of place, she'll let it rest.

And if she does see anything strange, she can tell Lance. He'll know—

Her thought process is completely derailed as she pulls up to the turnoff for Alta Lakes. A cruiser is parked sideways across the road that leads up the mountain, blocking any traffic.

Effie slowly pulls in, parking in front of a trail map and hopping out. She rakes her shoulder-length hair into a ponytail as she walks up to the blockade, relieved when she sees one of the officers on scene is none other than Derek Griffin, who happens to be dating Bethany. "Morning!" she calls brightly, dropping her hands to her hips once her hair is secured.

"Morning, Effie," Derek greets, giving a friendly wave. "The road's closed," he states unnecessarily.

"What happened?" She crosses her arms over her chest and peers up the road.

"There was a—" He's cut off as his partner slaps the back of his hand against his chest.

"Sorry, Miss Blake, we're not cleared to share any details about what happened." Sgt. McCurdy narrows a glare at the younger officer before casting an artificially apologetic glance in Effie's direction.

"No worries, Sergeant," she replies, shuffling her feet. The hiking trail head is right behind her, and she can feel it staring at her back. *Come, discover the secret secrets I hold!* it implores. As lucky as it is for Derek to be here, it's equally unlucky for McCurdy to be present. He's a grumpy, no-nonsense man, and Effie has always detected a bit of bitterness from him in regards to Lance being an outside hire.

As Effie wracks her mind for a way to get more information out of them, the crunch of tires over gravel sounds behind her, and she pivots to watch a second Explorer pull into the turnout. She tucks her lips against the grin that wants to spread across her face, backing up to stand closer to Derek as McCurdy walks up to greet Lance, barely giving the chief time to open his door.

"Y'all have an Elizabethany trip planned this weekend?" he asks quietly. The nickname, a mashup he uses to teasingly imply that the two are so often a joint unit, sounds strange with the concern in his voice, punctuated by the dry rasp of his feet shifting in the dirt.

"Don't worry, I'll have her back before curfew." Effie nudges him with an elbow, leaning back against the cruiser to watch Lance and McCurdy. Her ears strain to pick out words from their hushed conversation.

Derek shifts again, pulling her attention. "Reschedule it, yeah?"

Her stomach drops as she looks up at him, his coffee-colored eyes worried and serious. "What happened?"

He presses his lips together below the thick brown mustache that Bethany both loves and teases him about as the other two walk up.

"There's been some bear activity," Lance says, adjusting where his utility belt sits on his hips.

She looks at him skeptically. "So you're closing the road up to Alta?"

"Some campers were mauled."

"What?" She blinks, and her heart thumps a steady rhythm in her ribcage as thoughts rush wildly through her head. "A bear *killed* someone?" she repeats, forcing her gaze to refocus on her cousin. She searches his face, trying to find her footing in the conversation.

"We're not releasing any details to the public yet, out of respect for the deceased and their families," he says, clearly expecting it to be the end of the conversation, and reaches out a hand to pull her away from the cruiser and back to her car. But she sidesteps him, shaking her head.

"But that doesn't ..." she hesitates, shooting a glance at Derek and McCurdy. Her thumb sneaks up to her mouth, and she bites at the side of her nail, her mind calming. Changing tactics, she nods, letting him escort her away from the others.

"I saw something the other night," she says, keeping her voice low. She peeks up at him, gauging his response.

Lance's gaze narrows, but Effie can't read anything solid in the expression. "You saw something? What does that mean?"

She chews on her thumb again before pulling her hand away and folding her arms to trap it. "I saw something fall from the sky." Her voice gets stronger at the end of the sentence, solidifying her confidence in what she knows. "I saw something fall from the fucking sky, and last night I looked up a bunch of stuff about meteor showers, and I think whatever fell made it all the way down."

Something flashes across Lance's face—apprehension, maybe?—but it's gone before she can get a good read on it. "I don't see what that has to do with anything."

"If a bear really killed people, what if whatever I saw is what's making it act out—"

"No," he cuts her off, and a little kernel of indignation flares to life in her chest. He must see the change in her expression, because he holds his hands up placatingly. "I'm not trying to be an ass," he soothes. "But I've been up here dealing with this since well before the ass-crack of dawn. We've had a whole slew of people—coroners, Fish and Wildlife, my own deputies—checking the scene and dealing with clean-up. If there was anything out of place or weird, don't you think one of us would have noticed?"

Effie shakes her head, not in answer, but frustration. "But what if ..." She trails off, not sure exactly what road she's about to go down. Lance is still watching her, waiting. "How do you *know*?" It's a demand disguised as a plea, because the need to chase down what she knows she saw bleeds into a strange apprehension at the fact that someone is *dead*, and she really wishes she hadn't spent the night reading conspiracy theories. An indiscernible tremor runs through her chest as a result of the confrontation and the niggling feeling that something is *off*.

Lance pulls a tin of citrus Zyn out of his back pocket, cutting her a glare as he tucks a nicotine pouch into his cheek. "If I start fucking smoking again, I'm blaming you. Come on, before I change my mind."

Curiosity calms some of the agitation in Effie's blood as she follows him back over to the others, and she files away his renewed tobacco use in the back of her mind for later examination. The sergeant watches their approach with unveiled disapproval, but Derek looks relieved, which scares her a little bit.

"You got a tablet handy, Griffin?" Lance asks, and the deputy nods, ducking into the cruiser to grab one and hand it over. Lance taps on the screen a few times, pulling up what he wants before tilting the device in Effie's direction.

Her brow furrows, unsure of what she's looking at. The picture is of a Douglas fir, a few boughs broken and hanging. He swipes, and the next photo is closer, showing deep furrows carved into the trunk.

"Those are bear markings," he tells her.

Effie looks at him skeptically, reaching up to swipe again, but he pulls the tablet back before she can reach.

"You don't want to see any of the others," he warns, voice soft.

She bites her tongue against the childish retort that threatens to spill from her lips. He's already given her more information than he owes her as a citizen, but she's still not pacified. The fact that they're closing down the entire road rather than just cordoning off the area where the incident took place feels suspicious. "When will the road be opened back up?"

"I'm not sure, but definitely not any time today or even this weekend." He's looking at her like he's trying to see into her thoughts, which only serves to further feed the feeling that she's missing something big. A sigh escapes him, and his face softens. "Go home and get some sleep, Eff."

Unsure what else she can accomplish here with her thoughts in such fatigue-addled disarray, she nods, casting a parting wave to Derek before walking back to her Jeep.

A white pickup truck pulls in behind her as she makes her way to the driver's side. Maybe it's because she's already tired and in a mood from feeling like there's a part of the picture she's not seeing, but she gives the driver inside a look of "don't even bother" and loosely gestures in the direction of the clearly marked county sheriff's vehicles blocking the road.

On par with everything else that's happened this morning, the man behind the wheel surprises her by grinning, and she stays standing with one hand on the handle of her door as he turns off the truck and hops down.

"Do you know what happened?" he asks, covering a mess of dark golden waves beneath a backward ball cap and walking to the edge of his bumper. He's in hiking boots, worn jeans that hug his thighs when he stuffs his hands into the pockets, and a black hoodie with a star logo printed on the chest that she vaguely recognizes. His face is guileless, light eyes friendly behind plastic-rimmed glasses, and maybe that's why Effie leaves her door and walks to her own bumper.

"They closed the road up to Alta," she informs him.

He glances over the hood of his truck to where the officers

are chatting. "Because of whatever fell?"

Her mouth drops open. "You saw it, too?"

"It was probably a meteorite, but it's wild that it made it this close and no one saw it coming," he says, shaking his head in apparent confusion. "I was hoping to take a look."

"I don't—no, the road is closed because there was a bear attack."

His eyebrows shoot up, scrunching his forehead under the closure of the hat. "Damn, that's ... wow." His inability to find an appropriate response makes a smile tug at the corner of Effie's lips. Clearing his throat, he pushes his glasses up the bridge of his nose with a knuckle. "I'm guessing they already denied you access to try to find whatever's up there?"

"You're very astute," she says wryly, leaning forward to peer around the back of the Wrangler. "But, look, if you want to try to talk them into letting you past, you're more than welcome. I'm just glad you confirmed I'm not crazy for thinking I saw something the other night."

The smile he gives her is bright and genuine, and she feels it in her belly. "I can assure you you're not," he promises, and, after a brief pause, takes a step forward and sticks out his hand. "I'm Kel."

"Effie." She shakes it, returning his smile because this whole situation is absurd. "Good luck," she tells him, then retreats to her car.

The whole ride home, that last interaction sticks in her mind. There's a lot about the morning she needs to mull over, but after she tosses her keys into their little bowl and sets her bag on the counter, she grabs a pen and scrawls his name onto her right wrist.

6

After the girl departs in the blue Jeep that almost perfectly matches her hair, Kel turns back to his truck to grab a business card from the center console.

The three officers watch him approach, and he looks between all of them, unsure who to address until the one with a close-cropped, light brown beard steps forward and says, "Sorry, sir, this area is closed."

"That's what I just heard." Kel gestures with a thumb back toward the parking lot. "But I was wondering if I could speak to whomever is in charge."

The officer rests his hands on his hips, the front of his shirt pulling tight over the bare beginnings of a beer belly. "I'm Chief Deputy Sutherland with the San Miguel County Sheriff," he introduces. "I'll be happy to help where I can." His sunglasses are dark, and Kel hates that he can't see the man's eyes.

"I appreciate that, sir. My name is Dr. Kel Curtis; I'm an astrophysicist with Lockheed Martin. I saw that meteorite come down the other night and wanted to know if I'd be able to drive or hike up to the impact site and take a few samples and pictures." He holds out his card. It's hard to tell due to his facial hair, but Kel is almost positive the officer's jaw tightens.

Sutherland takes the card and looks it over briefly before handing it back. "I'm sorry, Dr. Curtis, but I don't know anything about a meteorite. There was an animal attack last night up at the lakes, so the area is closed until we're able to ensure it's safe."

Kel slaps the card against his open palm a few times, trying to think of anything else that may persuade them to let him through. "Okay," he finally says, mouth pulled into a smile he's sure is much tighter than he intends. "Well, thank you, sir. But if anyone does happen to find anything that looks a little out of the ordinary, would you mind giving me a call?"

Sutherland's lips press together for a moment before he nods, reaching out to accept the card again. "If we see anything, we'll let you know. You enjoy the rest of your day, okay? Stay safe out there."

"Thank you, sir, I really appreciate it." Kel turns back to his truck, rubbing a hand over the back of his neck as he quickly remaps his plan for the day.

The drive into Telluride takes him about half an hour, and he calls up a friend from his doctoral program when he gets into cell service.

"Well, if it isn't the prodigal son himself. You finally coming back to California?"

"Not a chance, but it's good to know I'm so missed." The smile on his face echoed in his voice.

A *tsk* of disapproval comes over the line. "Give a guy a fancy contractor job and suddenly he thinks he's too good for the rest of us."

"Never too good for *you*, Daph." After graduating, he'd taken a part-time gig at UCLA while looking for something with a more practical application. Academics were fun, but had never been his passion, and he had no desire to go back to his alma mater.

"You just don't like competing to be the smartest person in the room," Daphne accuses teasingly.

"Damn, you found me out."

She hums, appeased. "So why are you calling at this ungodly hour? Because if it's just to say you miss me, you could've sent a damn text."

Kel glances at his dashboard clock. "Seven is ungodly?"

She scoffs, and Kel can picture her eye roll. "I'm an hour behind, okay?"

"Nah, dude, that's *your* time."

"Then, yes, seven is ungodly. Was there a purpose to this call or not?"

"I was wondering if you could pull some data for me," he starts. "I saw a meteorite around three o'clock Thursday morning, and I'm pretty sure it landed somewhere south of Telluride. Probable copper makeup, because it burned a pretty green upon entry. Anyway, I'm out here trying to hunt it down, so anything you can find—thermal, radar, satellite—and send my way would be great."

"A meteorite, you say?" Her interest piques. She's currently working under a grant that covers an in-depth study of the solar system's meteor showers, so if anyone has data about debris making it Earth-side, it's her. "Do I get dibs on pictures and samples?"

"Obviously."

"Alright, Dr. Curtis. Give me a moment to wake up and get to the office, and I'll see what I can find."

"Much obliged, Dr. Folarin." Kel hangs up, scanning the street for a place to park. The stars seem to be on his side today, because he finds a spot to squeeze his truck almost directly in front of a coffee shop.

After grabbing his laptop bag from the passenger seat, he heads inside, orders an iced vanilla latte, and settles in to work while waiting for Daphne to collect and send the data.

An hour later, he's just about ready to send off an updated spreadsheet to the lead engineer he's working with on a satellite project when his phone buzzes on the table, lighting up with a text.

Daphne: You free to talk?

Kel: Should the fact that you're offering scare me?

Kel: But yes

His phone lights up a couple minutes later. "Hey," he answers.

"You're sure it was Thursday morning you saw something? As in yesterday?" Daphne asks without preamble.

"Positive."

"None of our cameras, Earth-side or orbital, caught anything."

"Wait, what?" Kel pulls his hat off, tossing it onto the table and running a hand through his hair. Had he been too tired? Misread the image on his own camera? Maybe he'd seen a plane or a glare on a lens? "No," he insists, remembering the girl with the blue hair—Elfie? *Effie.* "I'm not the only one who saw it. Something definitely fell out here."

"Hold on, let me ..." She trails off, humming over the sound of keystrokes in the background. "Well, what in the half-assed hometown farmer's market," she mutters softly before continuing at normal volume. "According to one of the radar read-outs ... Dude, what the actual fuck? There's one report that something roughly thirty-five feet long and almost eight feet wide entered the atmosphere yesterday morning, but it's there and then just ... gone."

"That can't be right."

"I know it can't be right," she scoffs. "But that's what I'm seeing. How ... where did it go?"

Kel taps his fingers on the table, sitting up straighter. "Do you remember the Chelyabinsk meteor?"

There's a pause. "Oh, shit. That was even bigger, right?"

"And nobody saw it coming because it was too close to the sun," he continues, already being pulled down this new train of thought. He'd still been an undergrad when a giant meteor had remained undetected until entry almost a decade ago. The circumstances here were different in many ways, but his analytically trained mind was connecting the similarities to better make sense of what he was looking for out here.

"Did you say you found anything?"

"I haven't had a chance to truly look yet." He'd wandered around near a tiny little town called Ophir yesterday but hadn't seen anything definitive, though he suspected he'd need to go deeper into the mountains and was unsure about taking his truck up some of the rougher, less established trails. "I was hoping to get more of it done today, but the road I need access to is closed."

"Fuck, right. If this is something big like Chelyabinsk was, and it's since gone undetected ... there haven't been any reports of seismic activity? Power outages? Injuries?" Daphne asks, a worried edge to her voice. "It should've made national news by now."

"Something is off here," he agrees. "Send over whatever data you do have. I'll try to hunt down any anomalies from Thursday morning and also take a look into the systems I have access to. Maybe I can grab something more concrete about this thing before trying to hunt down any remaining pieces of it. If there's one thing we know, it's that nothing that fucking big disappeared without leaving *something* traceable."

"I'll send you what I found, but I'm telling you, dude, it's a bunch of nothing." There's a few clicks as Daphne throws the reports together for him. "Let me know if you find anything or if there's anything else you need my help perusing."

"You got it, and thanks. You're the best."

"Don't forget it, either."

After she hangs up, Kel downloads what she sent and opens up a spreadsheet. Then he begins methodically working through all the information he has and all the information that's missing, starting with what's easiest: aftermath.

Or, it should be easiest, but he soon finds that there is no reported aftermath. No reports of explosion, disruption to any form of satellite service, earthquakes, or structural damage on any public forum or website he can find, which is beyond weird. So far beyond the realm of what should be possible that it makes his brain hurt.

Running a hand over his mouth and cupping the lower half of his face, he changes tactics (and makes a mental note to shave, stubble scratching uncomfortably against his fingers and palm), and logs into the systems he has access to thanks to his certs from work. But after another forty-five minutes of searching through satellite images and rough program data captures, he's even more frustrated. There's absolutely no trace of it.

He takes his glasses off to rub at his eyes, knowing he's been staring at the computer screen too long, and sits up straight, arching his back and rolling his shoulders in an attempt to counteract the slouch that had only grown worse the deeper he'd fallen into his search.

Replacing his glasses, he stares at his coffee, long since empty aside from the slowly melting ice, then moves his gaze out the window, roaming over the different storefronts and mountainside beyond to give his eyes a little break. Sunlight streams through the window, warm against the black cotton of his sweatshirt.

He pushes the sleeves up to his elbows without thinking, but the motion pulls his attention down to his arm, and he rotates it, letting the heat sink into his skin. An idea is forming, slowly taking shape and bouncing around all of the images and timelines he's looked at today.

It's worth a shot.

Instead of looking through the various satellite and telescope images, he pulls up the radar information, throws it to one side of the screen, and pulls up thermal readings, starting with geospace and moving out as far as he can.

"Oh," he whispers, sitting up straight as he zooms in on a reading taken at the same time as the radar data. "Oh … my God."

He opens a new Excel sheet and starts typing in different readouts, locations, temperatures, and surface areas. His fingertips are buzzing, and he's doing his best to keep his mind on task when his thoughts immediately want to take off and chase down a thousand different possibilities.

Kel doesn't even realize that a full hour has gone by until his laptop flashes a low battery warning at him. He glares at its neediness while digging a power cord from his bag and plugging it in. Settling against the seatback, he looks at everything he's compiled, placing a hand on top of his head, fingers splaying through loose, hat-flattened curls as a slow smile stretches his face. "Holy shit," he whispers.

He saves the file, copying it onto a thumb drive for extra security, then fires out a quick email to Daphne, attaching the file there as well.

To: dfolarin1@ucla.edu

From: kelvin.curtis@gmail.com

Daph,

Looks like our missing meteorite is camera shy. Maybe the same thing that makes it deflect heat makes it deflect light in a way that tricks the telescope images? I've pulled together what I could to track its progress (data attached). If you've got some spare time, do you mind seeing how far you can follow it? Maybe we can figure out where it came from.

I'll move my search back to land. A piece of something this big can't be that hard to find. Will keep you in the loop! Also, it might be prudent to get someone better versed in meteoritics on board (not Hughes) to get a head start on any samples I'm able to collect. We'll only have a short window to get a jump on this after I call in anything I find.

Cheers,

Kel

Email sent, Kel sits in front of his laptop, finally letting his mind spin off. Thermal imagery shows that the surface of his missing meteor seemed to deflect any sort of heat rather than absorb it. It's strange that nothing else picked up on such a large object hurtling toward Earth, but his current hypothesis is that the meteorite's makeup also made it harder to view with telescopes or satellites. His working theory had been that it's partially copper because of the way it burned, but maybe it also contained some other element previously unknown to humankind.

It's this thought that he latches on to, the possibility of large-scale scientific discovery buzzing in his veins. He could be on the brink of becoming one of the largest names in astronomy, and the prospect alone makes him a little dizzy.

He knows reporting procedures for objects that have entered the atmosphere and impacted Earth's surface, but, for now, it's all speculation, and it's this technicality that he's running off of. Until he—or some random hiker—actually sees the meteorite, its existence is imaginary. Once he finds it, he'll report it to NASA so they can log it, extract it, and do the hundred different things required by their governing laws and procedures. But until they arrive on site, there'll be no one to stop him from taking samples and photos for his own study.

A flash of giddiness runs through him with the thought that he could soon be holding an outside piece of the universe in his hands.

Speaking of hands, he frowns down at his as he packs up his laptop. If this thing does contain a previously unknown element, he'll need to prepare for the chance that it's possibly unstable or radioactive. Which means he'll have to make a pit stop at his camper before heading out into the mountains to continue his search. The Geiger counter in one of his drawers was a complete impulse buy a few years into his doctoral program, but he figured it would probably come in handy one day.

He'll stop by camp to grab it along with a few other supplies, then cross off another grid on his map. With a plan set, he gives a friendly wave to the barista on his way out, ready for a packed day of off-roading and hiking.

7

1645 MDT//1d 13hr 42min after arrival

Effie had woken up that afternoon antsy as all get out, and the feeling didn't ease until she'd decided, over a bowl of Lucky Charms, that she would spend her night hiking up to Alta Lakes under the cover of darkness to explore for herself.

When Bethany had sent her a "u up?" text and asked if she'd be down for a quick little late afternoon bike ride, she'd been more than willing to accept the invitation and burn off what remained of the nervous energy.

There are a few notable attractions in Telluride that keep the town a popular tourist destination outside of ski season, such as the cascading grandeur of Bridal Veil Falls at the head of the canyon, the blooming wildflowers that blanket the mountains, and the idyllic little downtown strip. But Effie's favorite—and a probable favorite of all avid mountain bikers—is the free public gondola that travels from Telluride into Mountain Village, allowing for convenient and easy access to the ski runs that become bike trails in the off season.

"What are the chances you want to call in sick tomorrow and go exploring with me tonight?" Effie asks as she and Bethany walk their bikes up to the gondola station.

Bethany arches one perfectly manicured eyebrow. "Why do I feel like you're asking me to do something illegal?"

"What's the point of sleeping with a deputy if you're not

going to take advantage of the get-out-of-jail-free card?" Effie responds with a shameless smile.

"And where would this nepotistic adventure take us?"

"Alta."

Bethany shoots her a suspicious glance. "Derek was out there this morning. Didn't they close the road for bear activity?"

"Technically, yes. But I think something else might be going on, and I really want to check it out." Effie launches into a brief explanation about seeing something fall, her successive deep dive into meteorites and conspiracies, and the guy who'd also been there to investigate.

"I don't know." Bethany's nose scrunches up as she considers. "Ordinarily I'd be down to go space treasure hunting with you, but wandering around in the dark when there's been a wild animal attack? That's asking for trouble, Eff."

"I take it that's a no to joining me, then?" Effie asks as they get in line for the gondola.

"Why can't you just wait until the road opens back up?" Bethany reasons with her, letting her bike rest against her hip while she twists her dark curls up into a low bun.

"Where's the instant gratification in that?" Effie pouts. She knows her friend's logic is sound, and certainly the safer option, but she can't snuff out the niggling feeling that something is wrong.

"I'll figure out what exactly Derek knows," Bethany promises, knocking her shoulder into Effie's. "If there was anything out of place, he'll have seen it."

It's their turn to board, and the women secure their bikes to the back before climbing inside, a solo rider sliding in across from them as they begin the ride up the mountain.

Effie leans her head against Bethany's shoulder and watches

the trees pass beneath them. "I love when the aspens are green like this," she sighs. "They just look so happy to be here."

"You should see them in a few weeks," the boy sharing their car, who looks to be in his early twenties at most, interjects. "The whole mountainside will be all gold and orange. It's absolutely unreal."

Effie blinks at him, sitting up and exchanging an awkward glance with Bethany.

He shifts in his seat to face them fully. "You know aspens share a root system?" He asks it like he's sharing confidential information.

"Yeah, they're pretty nifty that way," Effie answers before turning to Bethany in what she hopes is clear dismissal. "I looked up that lake you told me about," she says. "It should be gorgeous if the wildflowers are still out."

"Have you ever been to New Mexico?" the boy interjects. "Now *that's* some of the best nature around."

Bethany snorts, quickly covering her hand with her mouth, and Effie barely holds back the bubble of laughter crawling up her own throat. "I mean ... sure, if you like ponderosa pines," the former offers. "But desert's not really our thing." They'd both been stationed at Luke AFB in Arizona, Bethany in finance and Effie in air traffic, and had spent plenty of their downtime off-roading and camping in every forest within reasonable driving distance. The desert has its own unique beauty, but there's a reason both of them now live in Telluride.

"Nah, the mountains there are unmatched," he insists, apparently oblivious to all social cues. "It's not really desert, though, not in the mountains."

"M'kay," Effie responds, not caring enough to argue with him. They're approaching the summit—thank God—and she starts to gear up, clipping on her helmet and shrugging on her backpack. Bethany does the same, and they're both ready to go by the time the gondola doors open, grabbing their bikes off the back and heading out onto the mountain while their new friend is still struggling to get himself situated.

Bethany tosses her leg over her bike. "Hurry, before he follows us the whole way down," she whispers with dramatic intensity, her dark eyes wide, and Effie laughs, following her away from the station.

8

2207 MDT//1d 19hr 04min after arrival

Outside of scenic attractions, Telluride also holds allure for those with more of an inclination for the extreme. From the via ferrata to off-road trails to the 14,000ft peak to the north of town—adrenaline can be found year-round.

Though he's visited multiple times, especially during snowboarding season, today is Colby's first time mountain biking in Telluride. He's new to the sport, but it's given him an excuse to travel and done wonderful things for his physique, if he says so himself (he does.)

He thinks back to the girls he met earlier in the day, lamenting yet again that he failed to get either of their names. The one with the blue hair had been more talkative, but her friend with the bronze skin and wisps of brown curls escaping her bun is who he wished he could get to know better. By the time he'd grabbed his bike and gotten his things together, they'd already moved on, and he hadn't seen them since.

He sighs, pushing the interaction from his mind. It's been a good day of riding, so much so that he feels confident enough to tackle a night ride. He hasn't done one yet, and it feels like a rite of passage to truly call himself a mountain biker.

"I'm so ready," he says to the empty gondola car, psyching himself up.

All too soon, it's time, and he's pulling his bike from the back of the gondola and heading off into the night.

He trembles with adrenaline, maneuvering across the mountain by the light of the moon and his headlamp, which, admittedly, isn't as bright as it could be. But he's *doing* it; he's out here conquering the mountain with only the stars to witness, and it's every bit as exhilarating as he expected it to be.

This is probably why, when he reaches the end of one trail and sees the sign for a new run beginning, he pedals past without slowing, much less giving it any real thought. He ate dinner in town before heading back up, so his belly—and water bottle—are full, and he feels unstoppable in this moment.

Colby races across the mountain, wind whistling in his ears and buffering the sound of Måneskin coming out of his small handlebar-mounted speaker. He sings along, half-breathless, as he maneuvers the trail, wishing he'd splurged on a GoPro to capture all of this.

He's so consumed by the ride that he doesn't notice the creature that spots him up along the ridge shadowing him from a distance.

A half-buried boulder rises on the trail in front of him, and he pulls up on the handlebars as he rolls over it. He didn't see that the trail dips sharply down soon past it and gets more air than he'd intended. His stomach floats up into his chest as he plunges toward the ground, and he tightens his grip on the handlebars, unintentionally leaning forward as he braces for impact and throwing off his center of gravity. When the front wheel hits the ground, the back end starts to lift higher. Momentum carries Colby forward, and his only thought to fight it is to turn the wheel.

The bike tips, throwing him down the trail. He rolls twice before sliding to a stop, shock keeping the sting of his shredded arms and legs at bay for only a moment before pain flashes across his brain, lighting up each area that made contact with the ground. His knee is hot and wet and throbbing, brighter than the gravel-chewed skin slowly beginning to ooze blood across the majority of one arm.

"Ow," he mewls when he's finally able to suck air back into his lungs. As he tries to push himself into a sitting position, more of his body complains. It hurts to suck in a breath, and he thinks he might have cracked a rib. He reaches up with shaky hands to unclip his helmet, tossing it to the side and crying out as the motion sends a sharp lance of pain through his chest. "Fucking fuck," he mutters, tears pricking his eyes.

His headlamp was attached to the helmet, so he's just lost his light source, and the stupidity of the action is almost enough to force the tears to fall as he gently prods at his knee. He can tell both by the warmth and the glistening reflection of moonlight that blood is dripping down his shin from a large gash. The joint itself is quickly swelling, and his teeth chatter when he tries to bend it.

The wave of agony the action sends down to his toes and up into his stomach is so intense his vision blurs, and his entire abdomen clenches, trying to eject his dinner. Colby swallows against the urge to vomit, grunting as his leg relaxes. "*Fuck,*" he repeats in a whimper, blinking rapidly. But the tears leak out of his eyes anyway.

He slowly tries to slide on his butt back up the trail where his bike came to a rest, Måneskin continuing to blast the background music to his crawl for help. If he can reach his phone, he'll be fine.

Colby is so focused on the overwhelming pain, his body seeming to thump in a steady rhythm with the music, and his goal of reaching the bike that he doesn't notice the curious clicking sounds that filter through the trees.

His pulse pounds in his ears, another lightning-bright bolt of pain searing through his chest as he twists to reach his hand out toward the pouch on his handlebars.

And then he feels the tickle of something brushing through the blood on his leg. He kicks his foot to dislodge whatever it is, crying in both agony and relief as his fingers close over canvas.

The next series of clicks comes from so close that they rattle in his bones like the bass from a quality subwoofer. Colby's breath catches in his throat, every inch of undamaged skin rippling with goosebumps as he feels another brush against his leg and realizes with sudden certainty that he is in grave danger.

Swallowing past the lump in his throat, he slowly turns his head. At first, he only sees the two fuzzy-looking antennae dancing over his leg, then the mouth they lead into, with sideways mandibles opening and closing in anticipation as a string of drool drips to the dirt. When he meets the creature's eyes, his bladder releases, piss trickling down the trail toward the monster.

She doesn't click this time, instead emitting a horrifically low, grinding roar that has Colby's stomach clenching again as undiluted fear empties a final reserve of adrenaline into his bloodstream.

He lurches away with a high, throat-shredding scream. The pain in his knee makes his stomach fully convulse, but he doesn't have time to register the bile surging up his throat as immense, blindingly hot pressure boils from his leg.

He can't move.

His earlier meal is forcefully evicted, and as he retches, he's screaming and crying with snot dripping from his nose, but he can't move because the gargantuan *thing* behind him has speared one of her legs through his.

More pressure builds in his groin, followed by a wet *rip* and a definitive *pop*, and then he can move again, and he resumes dragging himself up the trail by his arms.

Colby is so delirious with pain and fear that he doesn't even realize he's roughly thirty pounds lighter, nor that the rippling agony from his knee has been replaced by a fast, steady stream of blood from the gaping wound below his pelvis.

It doesn't matter, though, because the creature has lifted her prize of Colby-hock to her mouth. It takes only one bite for her to know that she wants the rest of him.

Colby is terrified, but overtaken with the drive to live, to survive, and is determined to keep pulling himself forward.

Then his head is torn from his body, and he is eagerly and methodically consumed as BAD OMENS screams tinnily in the background.

James Dawes: Howdy folks! I'd planned to take my kids on their first extended camping trip this weekend, but when we woke up Friday morning, there were some folk from the Sheriff's office who told us we had to pack up and leave. Apparently there was some bear activity in the area? I'll admit I'm not an avid camper, and this was at a "dispersed" campsite with no reservation system or anything. Is it normal to have areas shut down because of predators?

Comments:

Peter Markson: I'm sorry, what? No. Where were Fish and Wildlife? A sheriff can't just shut down a campsite.

^**James Dawes:** Hmm, thanks. I'd thought it was weird but wasn't going to argue.

^**Peter Markson:** I'd go back and set up camp again, personally. Unless they're going to give you a legit reason you can't be there, it's public land.

Dawn Burns: Which campsite were you at? That seems very strange. There's wildlife activity around most remote campsites. Did you have proper food storage?

^**James Dawes:** This was up at Alta Lakes, and yes, we had everything in a bear box!

Lily Morris: You're such a good dad for taking your littles out for the weekend! Sorry it didn't pan out this time!

Jeff Rye: I've never been asked to leave because of wildlife in the area, but I have been notified by rangers to be extra cautious because of it. I'm sure there was a good reason they asked you to clear out, though. Stay safe!

Kyle James: Lol that's some bullshit. No, this isn't normal

Day 3

Saturday, 26 August 2023

1

0012 MDT//2d 21hrs 09min after arrival

Effie stands in the brush, hands wrapped around the straps of her backpack as she watches the county sheriff's Explorer parked in front of the yellow police tape that crosses the road up to Alta Lakes. The deputy inside has his phone propped up on the steering wheel, his face bathed in a blue glow from its screen.

The crunch of gravel sounds behind her, and she whips around with a gasp. The man across from her is just as startled, leaping back and dropping his unlit flashlight to the ground with a clatter.

Her heart returns to her chest from where it had jumped into her throat, and she peers into the darkness, something about the man vaguely familiar. The reflection of moonlight off his glasses clicks the recognition in her brain, and her right wrist tickles where his name is written. "Kel?" Her voice is marginally above a whisper.

He squints in the darkness. "Effie."

Satisfied she's not in immediate danger, she glances back through the trees, but the deputy's eyes are still glued to his phone, arms folded loosely across his chest. She breathes a sigh of relief, stepping into the center of the trail. "What are you doing out here?"

"Same thing as you, I bet." He bends down to retrieve his flashlight. Covering the end with a palm, he clicks it on, the light turning his hand a glowing pink around the dark shadow of his bones. Satisfied that it's not broken, he shuts it off, meeting her eyes in the dark with a lopsided smirk. "Bear hunting?"

"I didn't see your car." The accusation comes out without much forethought, but she's struck with the sudden knowledge that she's alone in the woods with a stranger.

"I'm staying at Sunshine, so I walked."

"Oh, right." The name of the campground just across the road is familiar, and her hand lifts to her mouth to chew on the edge of her pinky nail as an internal debate takes place in her mind.

Fact: She really, really wants to investigate what happened up at Alta Lakes.

Fact: Hiking in the dead of night with a man she doesn't know is really, really stupid.

Potentially really, *really* stupid. She mentally amends the second fact, the part of her determined to discover the truth trying to appease her sense of self-preservation. Plus, Bethany knows where she is, so there's an extra layer of comfort that at least someone is aware should she not check in come morning.

Kel watches her, an intent furrow between his brows. He seems to understand her struggle, because he tucks the flashlight into his back pocket, holding both of his hands out in an unthreatening manner. "Remember when I told you I saw something fall out of the sky?" he asks, slipping his backpack from his shoulders. It catches on the flashlight sticking out of his pocket, which makes him roll his eyes as he swings the pack around to the front.

"Yeah." She pulls her finger away from her mouth, shoving her hands into the pockets of her vest. "I saw it too."

He unzips the front, reaching in to grab his wallet. "I'm a scientist," he explains, hooking the backpack over one shoulder and holding two IDs out to her. "An astrophysicist, to be more specific. My life is basically the stars, and I'm *really* fucking interested in whatever came down the other night. That's the only reason I'm out here, and my only intention is to find the crash site and whatever might be left of the meteorite and collect some samples."

As he talks, Effie glances down at the cards in her hands, reading them by the light of her phone screen. She recognizes the logo from his sweatshirt earlier. "Lockheed Martin, huh?" The employee badge identifies him as *Dr. Kelvin Curtis, contractor* over his picture.

"I work in Lone Tree, but was mapping some stars—just as a personal side project—out in Gunnison when I saw the meteor."

She flips to the second card, a Colorado driver's license. He's only a handful of years older than her, and she can almost hear her mother: *a doctorate, Elizabeth. You could be in a similar position, too, if only you applied yourself.* Effie fights back a scoff, pushing the thought away. "What's the middle name, Dr. Curtis?"

"Don't have one."

She lets out a little hum somewhere between thoughtful and appreciative and hands the IDs back, self-preservation appeased. "Effie Blake." Then, in a show of solidarity with his transparency, adds, "Legally, Elizabeth Catherine."

"A pleasure to officially meet you." Kel takes the cards and returns them to his wallet.

"You should know I'm carrying bear spray. And a knife."

"I did clock the blade on your thigh. Very vigilante," he says, one corner of his mouth canted upward as he reshoulders his backpack.

Effie pats the hilt of the hunting knife, the sheath strapped to her belt and tied around her leg. "No point having a weapon if it's not accessible, right?" The can of bear spray is hooked to the outside of her backpack, also within easy reach.

"Your logic is definitely sound. All my protection is a little buried," he admits.

With one last peek through the brush to look at the cruiser, she heads up the trail, watching the ground beneath her feet. "Underneath all of your nerdy science stuff?" she tosses over her shoulder.

"Priorities," he answers with a full grin and follows.

After a few steps further into the trees, Effie clicks on her headlamp, illuminating the trail ahead. "So, astrophysics?"

"It's not everyone's passion, but it's mine."

"How many stars can you name?"

Kel laughs, an easy, open sound. "Hundreds, though most are just designated by people who first published about them, like Wolf 359."

"Really?" she asks with a slight huff, her body warming up to the exertion. "Do you have favorites?"

"Of course." She's thankful to hear that he's also struggling for breath a little bit. "Doesn't everyone?"

She frowns, tilting her head up to look at the sky. "I don't, but now I feel inclined to choose one."

They continue the steady march upward, gravel and mulch crunching softly beneath their feet the only soundtrack until Kel clears his throat. "So, do you live out here?"

She nods, the light bobbing with her head. "I moved up about two years ago. My cousin is the chief deputy, and I fell in love with the area the first time I visited him. Once I got out of the military, it didn't take much convincing for me to follow."

This sparks more questions from Kel—what she did in the military (air traffic control), where her parents are from (El Paso, Texas), how does she like it here (she's never been happier), and it all feels so genuine, like he's asking because he's actually interested in the answers. Effie is completely at ease, not a wall up around her thoughts or a filter over her words as she responds with unbridled honesty.

"I love it here, more than I know how to really express," she tells him, pausing to catch her breath and take a drink. The tube from her water bladder rests over her shoulder, and she fiddles with it after satiating her thirst. "I don't like to leave the mountains, and I know a lot of people probably say that, but I mean, I *really* don't like to leave the mountains. There's something about how they're so close here that just ... they make me feel held, like I'm free to experience the full depth of all my emotions, to let everything go and not hold back and it's okay, because they hold it all for me. I won't float off and disappear. I take Ophir and Black Bear—they're mountain passes—if I ever need to be on the other side of the range because the thought of driving out onto the plains sometimes feels like too much. It sucks in the winter when they're closed, but ..." she trails off in a shrug.

Kel caps his water bottle and replaces it in his bag. "I was up by Ophir yesterday. That's a pretty intense road."

She continues walking, shooting a quick glance over her shoulder. "It's slow going, but I'm not in a rush."

"I can appreciate that," he says, sounding sincere.

"Did you head into Silverton?"

"Huh?"

"Ophir pass. Did you take it down to Silverton?"

"Oh, no. I was looking for the crash site. I came back down the same way I went up."

Effie considers this for a moment, setting one foot in front of the other at a steady pace, watching where each step lands. "You said you were in Gunnison when it fell, right?"

"Yeah."

"How did you know it would be here? I saw it pass into these mountains from, like, four miles away at best as the crow flies, and I'm still second-guessing if I'm right about where I saw it go down."

"It's just a bit of simple math, really," he answers modestly.

Effie snorts. "Oh, really?"

"Okay, no, I guess it is a bit complicated when you dig into it," he laughs. "But it's fun math all the same."

"*Fun* math?" she asks incredulously, but intrigued by the excitement in his voice.

Kel adjusts his hat, clearing his throat. "Yeah, just compiling different equations together to find the information you want. It's cool being able to figure out how the world works that way."

"That's ... actually way cool. What equations?" she requests.

"Well, there are formulas for trajectory and distance traveled, right? They get a little muddied without solid data for all of the variables, like angle and velocity and mass. However—" he draws the word out, and the way he's gearing up to tell her something exciting makes her smile. "Even though the stars move, they're so far away that the naked eye can't track it, which is how people were able to use them for navigation back in the day. I applied that same principle based on the time of the fall and the meteorite's path across the sky from the footage I managed to grab—which unfortunately doesn't show much more than a dark mass. My camera settings were all wrong for it. But there was enough dimension to at least plot out its probable arc against which stars it passed and use those coordinates to plug into the other formulas."

"And that led you to Telly?"

He rests his hands on his hips, pausing for a moment to catch his breath before responding. "I have a five-ish mile radius to work with, but yeah."

He starts walking again, and Effie follows. "You said it was a meteor?"

"*Was* a meteor, became a meteorite when it survived the journey through the atmosphere." There's still too much open enthusiasm in his voice for the explanation to come off as condescending.

"Huh, I didn't know there was a difference." She tucks her thumbs beneath the straps of her backpack, and Kel launches into a half-breathless explanation about the life cycle of a meteorite before moving to a tangent about dwarf planets. Effie doesn't mind. If there is a bear wandering around, the constant stream of conversation should keep them from startling it and, hopefully, keep it away from them, and Kel's passion for the topic is refreshing.

She stops for another breather, turning to face him as he continues, one arm out to brace against a tree as he catches his breath. "So, Haumea's been my favorite since about 2006, even when it wasn't officially recognized as a dwarf planet yet. You have no idea how cool it was when they discovered it has *rings*." He smiles, sheepish now that he notices her watching, and removes his hat to wipe the back of his forearm across his brow. The front of his hair is only a few inches long, and it flops forward onto his forehead when he drops his arm to replace his hat, trapping the burnished gold waves beneath the velcro closure.

The backward ball cap somehow multiplies Kel's boyish charm tenfold, and Effie has to force her eyes from his face up to the sky, scanning the stars as she takes a drink of water. "I've always liked Pluto, I think just for the fact that he was downgraded. It made me feel sorry for him." She shrugs, the beam from her headlamp flashing across his glasses for a moment when she looks at him again. "Granted, I didn't know other dwarf planets existed. It makes me feel better knowing he's not alone."

Kel laughs at that. "Do you know where it is? Pluto, I mean." When she shakes her head, he steps back onto the main trail, tipping his head back and spinning in a slow circle before motioning her closer. "Turn off your light and give your eyes a second to adjust."

She does as instructed, going as far as closing her eyes for a moment before looking first at him, then back up to the sky.

"Do you see those stars?" He points, and she leans in to better follow his line of sight to a constellation right next to the dense band of the Milky Way. "That's Sagittarius, and that super bright one is Kaus Australis. Those eight stars around it make up the Teapot." He waits, giving her time to locate the group.

"I see it!" She smiles at the twinkling lights. "It's almost like it's pouring out into the Milky Way."

"Exactly," he agrees, and she can feel his warmth against her cheek from how close they are. "Now, you can't see it because it's too far away, but Pluto is currently just off to the left."

Effie shifts her focus to the blank space, suddenly hit with a sense of how small they are against the expanse of the universe. "It's incomprehensible, isn't it?" she whispers. "Even the solar system is just a speck in the galaxy."

"And our galaxy is half the size of its neighbors," he affirms just as softly, wonder tracing the edges of his voice.

She turns to look at him, surprised to find his face so close to hers. It's *adorable how much you love this*, she thinks, knowing there's no way she can say the words to a stranger without sounding demeaning. Warmth flushes her cheeks, and she pulls her gaze back to the sky. "What about Haumea?"

He straightens and takes a step away before shooting her a grin. "It's currently hanging out in Boötes, which is off the handle of the Big Dipper."

She peruses the sky, turning slowly until she spots the familiar constellation and follows the arc of its handle to the next bright bundle of stars. "Is Haumea closer than Pluto?"

"Yep, you can actually see it with a good telescope." He watches her, tilting his head to the side. "Maybe I can show you sometime."

She's thankful for the dark when her cheeks warm again, and she tucks her thumbs back under the straps of her backpack. "Maybe, if you're lucky."

Kel just smiles, clicking her headlamp back on as he steps past to continue up the trail, shining his own flashlight on the path ahead. "So, miss feels-sorry-for-Pluto, what other big choices have you made because you've pack-bonded with an inanimate object out of pity?"

"Sounds a bit judgemental for a guy who seems to have pack-bonded with almost every heavenly body," Effie fires back in good humor.

"Out of *interest*, not pity. There's a difference, Blake," he says in a mock-serious tone.

She bites her lip, thankful he can't see the stupid smile on her face. She's been referred to by her last name more times than she can count, but the address feels flirty coming from Kel and sends a nervous flutter through her stomach.

Physically shaking away the thoughts, she hums in contemplation. "Pity is the defining qualifier here?"

"Pity for an inanimate object," he reiterates.

She follows, unconsciously making a game of trying to place her feet in his footsteps. His legs are longer, but he's less accustomed to the altitude and incline, so she's doing okay. The rote movement, step after step, helps her mind focus as she digs through different memories. "Oh! Here's one. When I lived in Arizona, I had a favorite cactus. He was half off a north-facing cliff and didn't get as much sun as the others, and he was the only saguaro, surrounded by angry little jumping cholla, so I couldn't even go say hello and sit with him, which would have been nice, considering all the shade. Cacti may love the sun, but God, it was way too fucking hot there."

"Did you name it?"

She looks up from her feet to stare at his back, almost losing the thread of conversation when she realizes two oblong alien eyes embroidered in silver thread are watching her from above the bill of his hat. *Fucking. Adorable.* "What makes you ask?"

"You're calling it 'him,'" he points out.

"PB," she admits, pausing before adding, "Poor buddy. Most things are dubbed buddy, though."

As they continue on, Effie talks more in depth about her time at Luke and the different interactions and scenarios she's encountered in air traffic. The irony is not lost on her that their roles of enthusiastic subject-matter-expert to captive, if not willing, listener have been reversed.

When they finally exit the end of the trail onto the dirt road that leads up to Alta Lakes, she's forgotten that he was a stranger a mere two hours ago. Which probably explains why she takes a couple steps closer to him, the front of her shoulder brushing the back of his arm as she crosses her arms over her chest. Now that they've stopped walking, the night is completely silent save for the chirping of crickets and the occasional rustle of leaves in the breeze. Ahead of them are the ruins of Alta mine, dilapidated buildings sunken and thrown into strange shadows by the light of the full moon.

"They're a lot creepier at night," Effie says, eyes roaming over the old wooden structures, following the beam of Kel's light as it flashes over the DANGER: DO NOT CLIMB signs.

"You got that bear spray handy?" he asks, illuminating all the spots a large animal could be hiding.

She reaches a hand around her side, patting the can. "Yep." The confidence she'd felt in the light of day that there was no real danger up here has dissipated now that she's surrounded by shadows and so far from help.

After looking around for a moment, lips pursed, Kel nods to himself and slips off his backpack. Dropping to a knee, he removes a tablet and powers it on. Effie takes a curious step closer to peer over his shoulder, and he shifts to give her a better view, pulling up a downloaded map.

"Here's the probable crash zone," he says, pointing as she clicks off her headlamp to remove the glare on the screen. "I'd really like to get into this basin here, on the opposite side of Alta Lakes. The meteorite was big enough that, even with breaking up in the fall, it would've caused a good amount of damage on impact. If a bunch of people were tromping around the lakes all day, it's unlikely they wouldn't have noticed, and I'd rather not spend all night wandering around."

"You're putting a lot of faith in the situational awareness of people whose primary focus was a couple of bodies ravaged by an animal," she points out.

Kel chuckles, shrugging. "You might be right, but I still want to check out this other area first." Pausing, he looks up at her, pushing his glasses back up the bridge of his nose. "What's your agenda here?"

Her brow pulls into a glare, and she takes a defensive step backward. "What do you mean?"

Keeping the tablet out, he zips up his backpack and stands, swinging it over his shoulder. "What's your game plan? I know you didn't expect to see me here, and I don't want to steamroll right over anything you had planned."

"I ..." she trails off, her thumb working its way to the corner of her mouth. "I needed to see what happened, that's all." Pulling her hand away, she shakes her head with a frustrated sigh, mostly exasperated with herself. "I didn't really have a plan. I couldn't shake what I saw and needed to check it out, just for curiosity's sake. But then I showed up yesterday and was told, no, there was a bear attack and don't come back. And then you showed up at the same damn trail, also looking for something that fell out of the sky, which further grounded my suspicion that something weird is happening. I just needed to come up here to look at things myself." She finally stops, taking a breath and meeting his gaze. "These mountains are my home. I don't like not knowing what's happening, and I just want certainty, one way or the other."

"I can respect a healthy sense of curiosity." He clicks his flashlight back on, and they continue walking down the road together. "If you want to investigate the crime scene, we can go there first."

She blinks, the offer catching her off-guard. "Don't you have your space stuff to do?"

"Safety in numbers, right? I mean, something killed someone

out here last night. We at least know that as a certainty," Kel says with a little shrug.

Effie surprises herself by shaking her head. "It's okay. There's a lot of ground to cover—it makes sense for us to split up. Plus, I planned to be up here alone, so I'm prepared to make myself an uninteresting choice for any potential predators. Accessible weapons, remember?"

He looks at her for a moment before giving a perfunctory nod. "Split up it is. Do you know what you're looking for?"

"Anything that looks out of place, right?"

"Essentially, yes. If you do see anything weird, don't touch it. Some of this stuff can be radioactive, and if it—" he stops, readjusting his words, his hands moving in front of him like he's searching for a way to explain. "There's no telling what sort of alloys and minerals this thing is made of."

"Look with my eyes, not with my hands." Effie wiggles her fingers in front of her, saving him the struggle of having to over explain. "I'm a quick study." She smiles, then digs her phone from her pocket, opening up the contacts menu. "Service is shit right here, but it's decent enough to get a text out in Gold King Basin and parts of the lakes. If I find anything, I'll let you know."

After exchanging numbers, they split off where the road forks. "Good luck," she calls with a small wave before turning around to hike up the road. She's driven it enough times to know to keep her eyes on where she's stepping. Potholes litter the dirt, and the last thing she wants to do is hike all the way back down on a sprained ankle.

She pauses periodically to check her surroundings, though, the beam from her headlamp working with the light of the full moon to give her a decent view of the landscape.

A soft wind curls around the side of the mountain, ruffling

the water's surface and brushing across the back of Effie's neck. She suppresses a shiver, turning to look up at the mountainside to her right. Everything looks as it should until she reaches the lowest of the three lakes.

Her head tips to the side, ponytail bobbing happily with the movement. She squints, lips pursed, then takes a couple steps to the side, moving away from the mountain to get a better view of it.

There's a trail of scattered pockmarks leading from the road to the ridgeline, like someone had tried to posthole for telephone poles. Her brows pull together as she studies them, turning over different possibilities in her mind.

She struggles to come up with even one reasonable explanation and settles for snapping a few photos. Maybe Kel will have an idea of what they could be. She walks over to the one closest to the road, peering in and taking another picture. It's about a foot deep and roughly as wide across, tapering gradually as it sinks into the rocks.

When she squats down to get a better look, she notices the bottom of the hole is dusted in a fine powder, and she pinches some, rubbing it between her fingers and bringing it closer to her face to examine. She glances from her fingertip to the rocks, some of them broken off into a completely smooth edge. "That's not normal," she tells them.

Look with your eyes, not with your hands, they reply.

"Aw, shit." Effie quickly dusts her hands off on her pants, standing and stumbling backward a few steps. There's no strange feeling in her fingers, so she snaps another picture, focusing on one of the cleanly broken rocks, then moves down the road toward the lakes and campground to investigate further. Something echoes over the mountains, barely perceptible over the lapping of the waves hitting the shore and the louder, closer sound of gravel crunching beneath her boots.

She pauses, holding her breath and slowly tilting her head as her eyes roam the valley.

And there it is again, reminiscent of a screech, but at a much deeper pitch. The hairs on the back of Effie's neck stand on end, goosebumps breaking out over her arms.

The familiarity of the sound finally clicks, and she remembers Izzy's list. *Probably just a snowy egret. Startled ... in the dead of night.* She swallows, reaching around to touch the can of bear spray at the side of her backpack. There are none of the birds around, but maybe that bear found wherever they'd gone to roost for the night.

The noise doesn't repeat itself, but Effie stays alert to any other sounds as she continues around the lake.

2

0223 MDT//2d 23hrs 20min after arrival

Kel is awestruck by how close the stars look from this elevation and how insanely bright without any major sources of light pollution. His eyes travel over the familiar constellations, picking out the pinpricks of light from stars he can usually only spot through a telescope.

Before he can get fully lost in the sky, he forces his attention back to the task ahead and moves toward the back of the basin, scanning the mountainside for any signs of disturbance.

The piercing shriek of a marmot makes him jump, and he turns toward the small lake, his flashlight just catching the large rodent dropping back to all fours and retreating beneath a rock. An answering cry is echoed across the water, and Kel smiles, giving a friendly wave in the general direction. "You haven't seen anything extraterrestrial around by chance, have you?" he calls.

The marmot cries out again, like a smoke alarm with a low battery.

"Didn't think so, but it was worth a shot," Kel sighs. "Thank you for your time, anyway."

The dark opening of an old mine shaft yawns up ahead, and he can't help feeling spooked by it. Something about it feels off, and he changes his trajectory to take him closer, climbing through the loose scree to get a better view.

The entrance to the shaft isn't boarded up, which feels like an oversight and a hazard. Is this where the bear has decided to make its home? He raises up onto his tiptoes, stretching his arm out to give the flashlight as much range as possible.

Another cry from the marmot, and he fights the urge to glance over his shoulder.

There's a mess of broken wood littering the mine entrance, and he frowns. A bunch of kids trespassing on a dare or out of dumb curiosity? Or could a wild animal have broken through for shelter in a storm? He weighs the pros and cons of calling out. If there is an animal inside the mine, he doesn't want it to be surprised by his presence, but he doesn't want to provoke it, either.

Deciding against any unnecessary noise for the time being, Kel continues up toward the ridge. His hope is that if the crash site is nearby, he'll be able to see it from higher up.

A metallic glint in the rocks stops him in his tracks, and

he walks over for a closer inspection. "What the fuck are you?" he asks, squatting down. It's a deep grayish blue, and convex, allowing it to throw the light.

He slides his backpack off to dig the Geiger counter free, clicking it on. The granite composing the basin around him immediately sets it off, but the meter only registers marginally higher when he passes it over the strange shard. With a satisfied nod, he shuts the device off and stows it away.

Pulling his jacket sleeve over his hand, he reaches out, surprised to feel how light it is as he raises it to eye level and rotates it in the beam of his flashlight.

The shard is roughly the size of his palm, maybe an inch thick, but it weighs almost nothing. The edges are smooth with sharp angles, like it's been broken off of a larger piece, and the back side is textured with small bumps and ridges while the interior is smooth.

He's never seen anything like it.

Kel grabs a Ziploc bag to store the piece and gives it another thorough once-over from inside its plastic prison before plucking a small, powerful magnet from a side pocket. Running the magnet along the object doesn't appear to affect any changes, and he hums thoughtfully, replacing the magnet and dropping the strange object to the top of his backpack. "Now where the hell is the rest of you?" He sets a bright red plastic marker over the discovery location and stands, scanning the immediate area before continuing a slow, precise sweep up and across the mountainside.

Less than an hour has gone by when Kel's phone buzzes in his pocket, and he chokes on a laugh when he sees how Effie labeled herself in his phone.

> **Pity for Pluto: headed back your way. Any luck?**

> **Kel: found a shard of something, but no crash site. Looking for more. You?**

> **Pity for Pluto: Fingers crossed! Just some weird holes that could be nothing. Took pics to show you**

Kel pockets his phone and continues his measured steps, losing himself again to the search.

The flash of Effie's headlamp across his back throws his shadow out in front of him, alerting him to her presence some time later, and he turns, offering a wave before his attention goes back to the mountain.

She walks up next to him, hands on her hips. "What are we looking at?"

"An endless sea of granite chunks."

"Oh, how exciting." She claps her hands together, holding them in front of her as she peers intently at the ground where his light is pointing.

"Enthralling. You said you have some photos?"

She nods, pulling her phone from the pocket of her vest. Once the pictures are loaded, she holds it out to him, letting him swipe through the different angles. "Do you know what could have caused something like that?"

Kel frowns at the phone screen, zooming in on one of the pictures. "It looks almost like something punched into the side of the mountain. Jury's out as to what, though, but it had to hit hard enough to pulverize the scree into powder."

"Like debris from the meteorite?"

"I don't think so." He shakes his head. "Where would the

rest of it have gone? Unless the sheriff's department removed it, which would breed an entirely new set of questions." His gaze flicks up to her face as he hands her phone back.

She takes it, chewing on the edge of her thumbnail, her brow furrowed beneath the band of her headlamp. Her eyes meet his, a worried gleam in the hazel depths, and she pulls her hand down to her side, tucking her thumb into a fist. "No, I don't think so." Her gaze unfocuses over his shoulder, and then she gives a definitive shake of her head. "I know those guys. Remember when I said the chief was my cousin? I'm closer to him than my sister in a lot of ways, and the deputy that was there is dating my best friend. I've been to more burger burns and family days with the department than I have with my own coworkers. When I mentioned seeing something fall, no one gave any indication that they knew what I was talking about. If they'd removed a bunch of weird rock, they would have mentioned it or at least shown some sign of recognition." She places her hands on her hips, moving past the thought. "You found something, though?"

Her faith in these people catches him off guard, his brow furrowing as he turns over the notion of that sort of community. Her question takes a moment to register, and he pushes the errant thoughts to the back of his mind, nodding as he gestures down the slope. "It's in my backpack if you want to see it, Ziploc right on top. I will warn you, though, it probably doesn't look that exciting."

Effie rolls her eyes. "I'll be the judge of that," she says as she walks off. He's only moved another few feet when she returns, examining the bluish chunk intently. "So, what about this buddy caught your eye?"

"The color first. None of the rocks up here are tinted that way. It could almost be copper, but the blue is too true."

"Can you really tell in the dark?" she asks, her tone genuinely curious.

"The flashlight actually makes it a little easier," he explains. "Copper ore tends to pull more green, especially under harsh light."

She nods, headlamp beam bouncing up and down as she pushes the object around in the bag and flips it over to examine the other side. "The texture is really weird, huh?"

"It is. I've never seen a natural break go that smooth, and the curve of it is interesting, too."

"Do meteorites break apart like this?"

"None that I've seen, but it could be the different metals and minerals that are in this one created veins that broke apart easier under stress."

"Relatable," she sighs, and Kel lets out a bark of laughter that echoes back to them from across the basin. She looks up at him through her lashes, a coy tilt to her lips. "You're good for my ego, Kel no-middle-name."

"And you've made this rock hunt even more enjoyable than I expected it to be," he replies honestly.

Her responding smile borders between shy and pleased, and she drops her eyes back to the object in her hands before scanning the scree field around them. "Did you need help?"

Used to working on his own, he shakes his head. "I appreciate the offer, but you don't have to. Anything subtle will be pretty easy to miss if you don't know what to look out for."

"I'll leave you to it, then, Dr. Curtis. Holler if you need me." She spins around, rocks crunching beneath her boots.

"You don't have to wait," he says, watching her retreat. "I don't know how long I'll be out here, and I'm sure you must be tired."

She turns to face him, hands tucked into the pockets of her

vest. "I don't mind sticking around. I work nights, so I'll be up regardless. You may also be happy to know that, despite any earlier misgivings, I've decided you're not going to attempt to kill and-slash-or otherwise attack me, so ..." she trails off with a shrug. "As long as you don't mind the company, of course."

"I can't promise to be a great conversationalist when I'm on task, but if I do find anything else, you have my word I'll alert you and share probably too many details about why it's exciting," he jokes.

"It had better be too many details, or I'll be severely disappointed." Effie grins, then leaves him to his search.

He scours the mountain, lost in focus, until a rhythm of sound pulls him out of his thoughts. Kel looks over his shoulder to where Effie sits at the top of a gravel slope, tossing rocks into the small lake below. The stars would be perfectly reflected in the water's surface if not for the ripples from her continued assault, and the vaguely musical plops as the surface tension is broken become a steady background song.

He continues sweeping his flashlight slowly back and forth as he moves around the area and imagines brushing his thumb over the smooth side of that small chunk of plating, the rougher, textured side pressing against his palm. He wants so badly to sit and examine it with all the wonder of a child, but he won't risk contaminating it.

Plop.

If he can just find a few more pieces, a larger chunk of the meteorite, he can justify keeping this one for himself. Or, at the very least, letting himself mess with it on the hike back down.

Ploop.

Without realizing it, he's been timing his steps to Effie: perusing the area, then taking a step forward when he hears another rock drop into the water.

Ploink.

Click-acklick-clicklick.

Kel straightens, a cold chill running over him as his survival instincts recognize what his brain stutters against acknowledging: that sound came from something big. Even more disconcerting, it's followed by the unmistakable sound of scree clattering down the mountainside.

Slowly, he turns to look at Effie, an illogical part of him hoping that maybe she'd grown tired of the water and started launching rocks across the basin instead. He stares at her for longer than necessary, watching her so that he doesn't have to look up at the ridge. She's standing now, back to the lake with her arms hanging at her sides. Their exact position is hidden by the oversized flannel beneath her vest, one large swath of fabric in the dark. Her short, blue ponytail looks simultaneously darker and more ethereal in the moonlight and hides nothing of her face. Even from her profile, Kel can tell her eyes are glued to the ridge.

That deep, hollow clicking sounds out again, and Kel forces his feet to turn as a knot of hot dread tightens in his stomach.

The sound of his boots shifting the rocks beneath him seems ridiculously loud, but all self-awareness leaves his body when he finally registers the creature at the top of the mountain.

It's impossibly large, even bigger than his truck. Eight crab-like legs sprout from its body, and its triangular head is perched atop a thin neck. Two fuzzy-looking appendages slowly creep forward from its mouth, which opens both sideways and down, revealing a maw filled with little teeth. *Built for chewing,* his brain supplies unhelpfully. It has four dark, glittering eyes, and they're all focused on Effie, who stands in open view almost directly across from it.

Just as Kel is truly processing what he's seeing, understanding that everything he thought was possible or probable has just been proven or disproven, the creature tilts its head down, mandibles pulling wide as a horrible sound similar to tearing paper reverberates through the basin.

It drops from the ridge, moving with impressive speed over the loose rocks toward Effie.

She has nowhere to run, so she plants her feet. In one hand, she holds her knife, the other raised high to make herself appear larger. It's clear that she's had wilderness safety pounded into her, because she's treating this thing like a mountain lion or a wolf, trying to seem like too much of a hassle to be easy prey. "No!" she screams at it. "Stay back!"

But it's not a mountain lion. It's not a wolf. And it charges toward her, another shredding bellow ripping from its throat.

Kel sprints to his backpack, biting back a yelp as his knees hit the rocks when he falls in front of it. At the very bottom is an emergency kit, and he grabs the whole thing, pushing back to his feet and launching back into a run as he struggles with the clasp.

Effie has stopped screaming words at the creature, her face pale in the moonlight as she crouches low in a defensive posture, keeping her grip on the knife steady.

He dumps the kit as soon as the flare gun is in his hands. "Get down!" he shouts, cocking the release.

She takes only half a second to look at him before dropping, arms wrapped over her head.

He shoots, the flare ejecting with a flash of bright light and a piercing shriek.

The creature whips its head around at the sound and, just as it starts to move toward him, the flare smacks into its chest. It emits another ripping sound, much angrier than the others, and scrapes a foreleg across its front that knocks the flare to the ground.

Two segments of its back lift, letting large, billowing wings slide free. They ripple outward like two dark shadows, one curling forward to block the heat of the flare as the creature focuses on Kel, who keeps the gun trained on it in a full bluff. Its eyes narrow on him in a moment that seems to stretch for an eternity before it turns, skittering across the basin toward the open mine. The wings retract, and the upper and lower halves of its body seem to slide into each other as it ducks into the entrance and disappears.

Kel keeps the empty gun aimed until it's out of sight, holding his stance for a few torturously slow seconds. When it doesn't reappear, he releases a shaky breath and jogs over to where Effie is rising from her crouch. Her eyes jump from the flare to the mine to Kel, wide and unblinking.

"Are you okay?" he asks.

"You saved my life," she says at the same time.

He doesn't know how to decipher the way she's staring at him, mouth slightly parted, but he's overcome with the protective desire to grab her and crush her to his chest, to let himself feel that she's alive. His fingers twitch before the impulse is halted by his realization of it and the unsettling flood of confusion that follows.

He offers half a grin, then tears his gaze away and looks back at the mine. "I wasn't sure it would work," he admits.

"Thank you." She takes a step closer and crosses her arms over her chest, hiding her hands.

Kel pretends not to notice how much they're shaking, almost dizzy with the foreign urge to provide physical comfort. He removes his hat, gripping it in one hand and running the other through his hair to keep them occupied.

"What ... what was that thing?"

He shakes his head slowly, gripping his hair for a moment before replacing his cap. Then he sinks into a squat, elbows on his knees and hands together, resting against his mouth. For the first time in his life, his mind was shying away from discovery, and his awareness of her had kept him from having to acknowledge the glaringly obvious. He shakes his head again, swallowing. "Either we just discovered a new species of mountain-dwelling crustacean, or that was a fucking alien."

3

0338 MDT//3d 0hr 35min after arrival

The wind picks up over the mountains, rustling through the boughs of pines and rippling across the surface of the alpine lakes. But deep below, where the creature has made her den, the air is still and warm.

She seethes as she tends to the wound in her chest. Her next molt is still several weeks out, and the spot where the flame burned her will be softer, weaker until then.

It's not pain that fuels her anger, but the fact that damage was able to be inflicted at all. She should be superior—she *is* superior—to her soft-skinned prey in every way.

With an exasperated huff, she dribbles saliva onto the area, hoping that it will help harden it enough to avoid any further damage. Then she stops dwelling on the encounter, turning instead to take inventory of her young.

She sits next to her eggs, antennae dancing over them as she sniffs out which ones have been fully fertilized by the males who have access to this cave from other tunnels.

Of the thousand or so eggs in the clutch, seventeen have been fertilized in her absence. This isn't required for an egg to grow and hatch, only changes how the young inside will develop. These will be egg-layers, queens like her, and larger than their unfertilized counterparts. Three of the unfertilized are no longer viable, their scent indicative of lack of life. She eats these, lest they spoil and contaminate others.

As she tucks in to sleep, she thinks of the settlement she discovered earlier: a whole swarm of those soft-bodied, hot-blooded little beings just milling about in a crevice between two mountains.

She requires a more substantial diet than those of her kind who came before her, and if she had the mind for it, she would think herself lucky to have landed so close to such an abundant source of food. As it is, she only knows that she is eager to discover more of this place and sample everything it has to offer.

4

0330 MDT//3d 0hr 27min after arrival

Effie's mouth drops open in disbelief, but she can't dispute Kel's statement. Has she ever seen anything even close to resembling that monster? Has she ever even heard of anything like it outside of fiction?

Her mind can't process any of what just happened past the point of her realization that she was probably going to die a painful death. When she'd heard Kel's command, she'd dropped without fully registering what he'd said, her body operating on instinct alone.

I could have died. I almost died.

She digs her nails into her sides in an attempt to pull herself out of the cloud of her thoughts, but there's too much adrenaline in her system for the slight pain to truly register.

Letting her legs go, she sinks down next to Kel, but her balance is off and she falls ungracefully onto her backside. "An alien," she says dumbly, clasping her arms around her knees.

Kel glances at her, falling back onto his own ass with slightly more grace and tucking a leg underneath him. "Whatever it is, we need to tell someone that it's not a bear."

Effie wants to stand, but she's not sure her legs will hold her. Her body feels buzzy and uncoordinated, and she's very aware of her breathing. Is this shock? No one would blame her for it. She was almost breakfast for a giant ... what was it, even? Its legs were crab-like, but its mouth and forelegs were like a giant mantid. And its body ... its eyes ... *What the actual fuck.*

For his part, Kel seems to be taking everything in stride, but content to let her have whatever time she needs to process everything. She wants to be annoyed that she's so visibly shaken when he's not, but she can't stop stealing glances at his profile. Loose curls spill from beneath his hat (which is missing a set of eyes for accuracy), and his lashes are so long they almost brush the lenses of his glasses when he blinks. His tongue pokes out, wetting his lips as his gaze drifts from the mine entrance to the sky.

He saved my life. She's suddenly thankful it's dark, because she's pretty sure she's blushing.

He cuts her a look, a self-conscious smile playing at the corner of his mouth. "What?"

"Nothing, sorry." She averts her eyes, brushing her hands off on her pants. "We should get moving before that thing decides to come back out."

"Right." Kel pushes to his feet before stretching a hand to help her up, and she refuses to focus on the warmth of his fingers on hers when she takes it.

The hike back down is much quieter than the ascent had been. Effie is stuck in a continuous loop: replaying the attack, trying to make sense of the creature, reaching for her phone to call Lance, wondering what she's supposed to say to him that won't sound crazy or get her in trouble for crossing police lines (is that a felony? He'd never arrest her anyway. Right?), needing to cancel the ride with Bethany tomorrow because there is an *alien* living in the mountains, and she'd almost been eaten by it, which starts the loop back over again.

And every single sound makes her jump. She's stumbled into Kel's back multiple times trying to look behind her. He's taken that in stride, too, making little jokes each time, but he's also mostly silent, and Effie can't even begin to imagine what all must be going through his space-obsessed brain.

When they finally make it back to the trailhead, the sky is lit the dusty purple of pre-dawn, and Effie feels dead on her feet, bone-weary like when she first transitioned to the night shift.

Clicking off her headlamp, she peeks through the trees to find the deputy asleep behind the wheel, arms folded over his chest and head tipped back against the headrest. They easily sneak past, heading down the road to where Effie parked her car.

"You didn't have to walk me back," she tells Kel, opening the door to toss her backpack into the backseat.

He shrugs, kicking lightly at a tire before meeting her gaze. "I used my only flare to save you. Figure I might as well make sure you don't get mowed down on the side of the road, ensure a little more return from my investment."

"Ah, make sure I get buckled safely into my thousand-pound box and hurtle down the road without issue?" she laughs, though it comes out breathy and nervous, and leans against the frame.

"Exactly." He smiles, pushing his glasses up the bridge of his nose with the knuckle of his pointer finger. It shouldn't be that damn cute.

Effie pulls the cuffs of her flannel over her thumbs, making sure her hands stay low, as far away from her mouth as possible. "So ... what do we do now?"

Kel rests one hand against the top of the roll cage, eyebrows pulling together in contemplation and gaze flitting over her shoulder as he thinks. "Who do we report an alien to? Local law enforcement? Fish and Wildlife?"

"The nearest astrophysicist?" she offers with a cheeky grin.

He snorts. "An astrobiologist would be even better."

Effie presses her lips together, nodding seriously. "You're right. Pity they seem to be in such short supply this season."

Kel chuckles in agreement, then turns his head into his shoulder, stifling a yawn. "Let's start with Fish and Wildlife. What time do you think their office opens? Eight?"

"Probably." She pulls out her phone to check the time—close to 5:15—and groans. "Not too far off, I guess."

"Don't worry about it. Go home and get some sleep. I'll give them a call once they open up," he tells her.

"You need sleep, too, spaceman."

"I appreciate the concern, truly, but I'll be up for a little bit anyway trying to figure out more about that piece of … that shard I found," he assures her.

"Okay." She fiddles with her keys. "And you'll let me know what they say?"

"Promise."

"Cool." They both stand there for a moment, looking at one another, and Effie wonders if his eyes are truly gray or just such a light blue that they appear that way in the breaking dawn.

Then Kel moves closer, reaching around her, and her stomach performs a whole series of somersaults in that single span of time. He pops the driver's door open behind her without dropping eye contact. His hoodie smells fresh, like laundry detergent, and she's so aware of it that she almost misses when he tells her, "Get home safe, Blake." Then he steps back, out of her space. "I'll text you."

"You'd better," she replies without thinking, hopping into the driver's seat and buckling in to hide the heat she feels in her cheeks. With a final wave, she heads toward home.

Effie keeps a firm grip on the steering wheel the entirety of the short drive, fingers constantly shifting with nervous energy. Now that she's alone, she can't rid her mind of images of that creature, and she's more rattled than she wants to admit.

When she gets inside, she drops her backpack next to the front door and plops down right in the entry to untie her hiking boots. After kicking them off, she folds her legs and runs her hands over her face, pressing the heels of her palms to her eyes as a shuddering gasp wracks her body.

The events of the night feel less real in the light of day, surrounded by the familiarity of her home. She pulls her knees up, wrapping her arms around them, and stares blankly across the room. "It happened," she murmurs. "There's an alien living in the mountains."

Pushing back to her feet, she tosses her vest and flannel over the back of the couch and plods to the bathroom. "It's okay, though," she says, meeting her tired eyes in the mirror. The blue of her hair makes the hazel appear more green than brown, and the dark, puffy circles directly underneath only further add to the contrast. "You're alive, and you'll figure out what comes next."

She eyes the shower, but ultimately decides it can wait for later in the day, and hops up to sit on the counter while she brushes her teeth, too tired to remain on her feet. Texting Lance is the obvious next course of action, but she's still unsure how to broach the subject, too tired to decide if she wants to accuse him of knowing what was up there or try to warn him about an unknown danger, so she leaves it alone for now. That can wait until after sleep. She does need to check in with Bethany, however, and at least let her friend know she made it back home. Holding her toothbrush between her teeth, she taps out a text, typing and deleting multiple times before finally settling on wording.

> **Beth2nd: Made it home. Derek was right, though. We should rain check tomorrow. I need to sleep but I'll call you when I wake up to talk about it.**

Setting her phone down next to her, she finishes the task at hand in a weary daze, sliding back to the floor to spit and rinse.

As she leans down to wash her face, her eyes catch on the faded writing across her left wrist—*call Mom*—and she groans. Another thing to figure out after a solid nap. But her gaze slides to the opposite, and she bites her lip, another shiver working its way down her spine. If she'd known just how important Kel would turn out to be when she'd scrawled his name there ...

Her phone buzzes on the counter, startling her so much she splashes water everywhere. Grabbing a towel to dry her face and hands, she glances at the screen, little wings fluttering in her stomach with the thought that it might be Kel checking to make sure she made it home.

To her surprise (and is that … maybe a little disappointment?), it's Bethany.

Beth1st: EFFIE NO

Beth1st: The bear will be on the opposite side of the range from our trail.

Beth1st: Besides, you know we can outpace any old bear.

Beth1st: Where's your sense of adventure, you hag.

Effie rolls her eyes, some of the unease in her gut unwinding in light of Bethany's familiar teasing.

Beth2nd: If I'm a hag, you're a troll

Beth2nd: What are you even doing up?

She chews on the edge of her thumbnail, debating whether or not to mention the monster now or leave it. But she still doesn't know what to say, and honestly could use a distraction from the events of the night.

Beth1st: Gonna go get an early morning ride in before work.

Beth1st: Gotta stay warmed up for TOMORROW.

Beth2nd: Orrrr...you can postpone the ride and hear about the guy I met.

Beth1st: je'scuse?

Beth1st: where?

Beth1st: And WHEN, you weird anti-sun goblin.

Satisfied with her success in distracting Bethany from continuing to argue about Sunday, Effie tosses her phone onto the bed and peels off the rest of her clothes in exchange for a cami and a pair of cotton shorts.

Beth1st: You don't get to drop a bomb like that and leave. I will come over and drag you out of bed if you've fallen asleep.

Beth2nd: Remember that guy I mentioned, after Lance and DG warned me about the bear? He showed up at the trailhead last night.

Beth1st: I don't know whether to be glad you weren't out there alone or to slap you upside the head for hiking AT NIGHT WITH A MAN YOU DONT EVEN KNOW. Jesus woman what good is Criminal Minds as a comfort show if your decision making skills are that lax.

Beth1st: Picture?

Beth2nd: I know I know, but give me a little credit. He's a scientist, showed me id and credentials. I

> would've split if the vibes were off. Give me a sec, I'll try to stalk his socials for you

"You'd better have an online presence, Kelvin space-nut," she says, opening Instagram and typing his name into the search bar. His profile is easy enough to find, but it's private, so she copies the link and taps back to messages.

> Beth2nd: Is it creepy to send a follow request? instagram.com/kel_on_starwatch/

> Beth1st: Depends on how much snooping you had to do to find his profile.

> Beth1st: Kel, huh?

> Beth1st: The backward hat profile pic is a choice. Of course it doesn't have his face in it...

> Beth1st: Request him or I will. I'm curious now.

Effie moves back to Instagram, chewing on the side of her pinky, and hits Request.

> Beth2nd: Done. I'm going to sleep now. Brunch tomorrow instead of a ride?

> Beth2nd: Pretty please with a cherry on top? We'll have a lot to chat about.

Without waiting for her friend's reply, she puts her phone on Do Not Disturb and leans over the side of the bed to plug it in before rolling over.

Despite her exhaustion, sleep doesn't come immediately. Effie is in her third imaginary run-through of telling Lance what happened—Kel with her as backup in this scenario—when she finally drifts off.

5

0542 MDT//3d 2hr 39min after arrival

Kel sips on a mug of hot coffee, looking at the little baggies of scrapings from the shard he'd found now spread across the table in his camper. Most of the hike back, he'd been preoccupied about that ... creature.

Even though he already told Effie it was an alien, he hesitates to let the label stick in his mind only to avoid the disappointment if it turns out this is just some sub-surface dwelling relic from the Cretaceous period previously thought long-extinct.

Disappointment may be a strange reaction to discovering a new species, but he so desperately wants this thing to have come from space. If it has, if it is actually *alien*, the possibilities that would open up, not just for him but for the entire world of astronomy—he takes a deep breath, piling the sample bags together and pushing them off to the side.

Peeling the pair of black nitrile gloves from his hands, Kel pulls his hat off and tosses it to the table to run his fingers through his hair, then removes his glasses, setting them down more gently to rub his eyes. His vision has gone blurry with exhaustion, but his mind is racing. Images of that creature's strange, shelled body, its powerful legs, play on a constant loop. It was dark, so he can't be sure of anything, but he would almost bet that what rested in front of him was no rock at all, but a piece of that creature.

With that thought in mind, he secures the small bags into a gallon ziplock, sealing it tight before placing that in a bubble mailer to send off to Daphne. Then he's left with his chunk of ... Shell? Armor? Exoskeleton?

He's collected a decent amount from it and taken a plethora of photos from multiple angles, but the thing is still largely a mystery to him. He puts his glasses back on and reaches for a fresh pair of gloves (who knows what kind of microscopic mites or bacteria may be living on the foreign thing) before skimming his fingers over the surface, smooth and unadulterated aside from the places he used his tools to scrape it.

Out of curiosity, he grabs it in both hands and flexes, trying to push the two ends together, maybe snap it. But it has no give at all. He even places it on the ground inside a baggie and stands on it. When it doesn't snap under his weight, he bounces a bit, but when he leans down to pick it up, the only damage is where the edges of it slightly bit into the linoleum flooring.

He gives it a contemplative look, turning it over in his hands a few more times before finally setting it aside. There's still work that needs to be done. Before powering on his laptop, he tosses the gloves and disinfects the table.

Kel's intention is to find authorities to talk to, but, of course, almost every office is closed on weekends. After going in circles for a few minutes between ranger stations, fish and wildlife agencies, and a few official reporting sites for meteors and the like, he finally decides on calling the general USDA number in hopes that he can get help from there.

"Thank you for calling the United States Department of Agriculture. For English, press one. *Para español, presione número dos*. If you know your party's extension, please dial it now," a pleasant pre-recorded voice tells him, and he presses one. "Please listen carefully, as our options have changed." He waits patiently as nine different options are listed before choosing the one for forest inquiries.

A different voice comes on the line. "The USDA contact center is currently closed. The hours of operations are eight AM to five PM Monday through Fri—" Kel hangs up, scratching at the stubble on his cheek as he stares at the search results on his laptop screen.

In a change of tactics, he tries looking through different parks that require permits or passes to enter, in hopes that they'll have someone on duty. Unfortunately, none of them are close by, and he groans at the impossibility of it all.

He can feel his cognitive abilities waning, exhaustion tugging at his eyes, and tries one more search with slightly different wording. Digging through those results brings him to a ranger station nearby in Norwood with hours listed as 24/7, but no phone number, and he sighs contemplatively.

Knowing he's too tired to drive all the way out there before some sleep, he grabs a black bag from the seat next to him. His mind is still spinning, and he needs to relax. He pulls a pipe from the bag, packs a bowl, and lights up, cracking a window to blow out the fragrant smoke. A couple of hits later, he feels much less riled up, and relaxes into his seat when his gaze locks back onto that scavenged bit of something.

No, not *something*.

Alien. He forces the thought, wrapping his mind around the idea. Everything looks different in the light of day, but as the sun sneaks through the cracks in his blinds, he knows that nothing of that size could stay undetected for long. It's simply not possible in the modern world.

But alien or not, Kel is on the verge of collapse. He considers calling the sheriff's station to report the attack, but they've already got an eye on the area and are keeping everyone out, so he lets it rest.

After a quick stint in the bathroom for the bare necessities of hygiene, he kicks off his pants and pulls off his shirt before falling into bed. His intention is to set an alarm, but he gets distracted by a notification over his folder of social media apps.

He opens Instagram to see a follow request from a foxtro t.echo. The tiny profile picture bubble next to the notification features a blue-haired girl standing next to a waterfall and holding up a peace sign, and he smiles, accepting the request before moving to her profile to send a message.

> kel_on_starwatch: Stalkerish behavior there, Blake. Almost makes me second guess having spent all night in the backcountry with you.

He hesitates, debating the teasing, but eventually sends it. If the seven hours he spent with her is any indication, it's the right approach. The next several minutes he spends looking through her profile, learning more about who Effie presents to the world. After scrolling through several photos of the airport, mountains, wildlife, and her—both alone and with a handful of recurring characters that include two young girls, another woman about Effie's age, and the chief deputy—Kel realizes he's looking for signs of a relationship or other potentially serious (or messy) attachment.

Get a grip, dude. Closing out of the app, he sets his phone aside and rolls over to sleep.

6

Lance places a hand over his face, trying to disguise a shaky inhale behind the guise of smoothing down his beard.

"Chief?" Derek Griffin asks, his eyes glued to the forensic team taking the photos. "Don't Fish and Wildlife want to be out here? This is ..."

Lance nods, clapping Griffin on the shoulder. "Go ahead and go back to the station to start filing the report. I'll give them a call and wait around for them."

Griffin, who looks a little green around the gills and eager to get away from the grisly scene, agrees, and Lance watches him walk back up the trail toward his cruiser before he catches the eye of the lead forensic tech, gesturing that he'll be back momentarily.

He takes several steps up the trail before dialing, pacing in a tight circle as the line rings.

"Sutherland," Hal Phillips, his main contact with the agency, greets in a forcefully cheerful tone. "This isn't protocol."

Lance grits his teeth. "Fuck protocol. I've got another dead body up here. Give me a reason I shouldn't be calling in the feds, because all my guys are getting antsy, and to be frank, so am I."

"First of all, there's no cause to throw professionalism to the wind. I expect to be treated with respect, same as I give you. Second, nobody's calling anyone. We're sanctioned. I assure you, your report has already been routed up the proper channels. Now, what's this about a dead body?"

"A mountain biker—a *kid*—was torn apart last night. Most of him is just … gone." He turns, making sure no one is coming up the trail. "There are markers, too. Depressions in the dirt, trees knocked over—"

"It will settle soon," Phillips interrupts. "A trip through space will take it out of you. Once it's got its strength back up, it'll disappear underground, just like every other one we've seen."

"*Three people* are dead on my watch." Lance barely keeps his voice level. "What am I supposed to tell the people I'm sworn to protect? Hell, what am I supposed to tell the sheriff and my deputies? They're too smart to believe this was some rogue bear or mountain lion. Someone's going to put together all of the weird little pieces, and probably sooner than later." Effie's inquisitive, accusing stare runs through his mind, and he pushes the image away, hoping she will heed his advice to stay out of it. "What am I supposed to do? How do I keep it contained?"

"Like I said, it will settle down soon. You won't even see any sign of it again once it finds its way below ground." Phillips sounds annoyed, like he's placating a child who insists there's a monster in his closet.

Lance grinds his teeth together, but he's got a whole county to take care of, including this town where he's made his home, and that has to be bigger than his ego. "And we're not at all concerned about these things finding a way to congregate down there? Form packs? Reproduce?"

"They're not an issue," Phillips reiterates. "From what our scientists tell us, they're all males. They just dig around and root out pests, and our orders are to let them. *Monitor.* Not control, not guide, not interfere. Do you understand, Sutherland?"

"Heard," he grits out, pinching the bridge of his nose.

There's a long pause before Phillips speaks again. "Listen, I get that this is your first. That's always hard, a little frightening, even. It's one thing for us to tell you aliens exist; it's another altogether for you to know without a doubt that there's one living right under your feet. So, I'll tell you what—why don't you come visit and see how we monitor things up here? It might put your mind at ease. We can have a charter plane down there by the afternoon." The agency is headquartered in Eagle, Colorado, but Lance has never so much as met another member in person, much less been invited to tour the main operation.

He's suddenly thankful that the call is voice only, because he knows his shock and, more concerning, his relief, are stark on his face. "I'd really appreciate that, Mr. Phillips."

"All right, then. I'll have that set up and email you the specifics within the hour. If you have any other questions, we can talk about them face to face."

That simple promise further settles Lance, and he nods, adjusting his campaign hat. "Okay, I'll keep an eye out for it. Thanks."

"We're the good guys here, Sutherland. Remember that," Phillips says before hanging up.

Tucking a citrus-flavored Zyn into his cheek, Lance walks back to the crime scene to let the forensic team know he'll be headed back into town. A perimeter has already been set up, as well as lines at both the top and bottom of the trail to close it off, so there's not any real need for him to stick around anyway.

It could be the nicotine or the release of endorphins from the short hike back up to his cruiser, but Lance's earlier misgivings have dissipated. The agency knows how to handle these things. They'll help. He already feels more capable knowing he'll be able to voice his concerns in person and see firsthand what information they have and what sort of damage these creatures are capable of. Then he can put contingencies into place, help protect Telluride and the rest of the towns in his jurisdiction should his alien decide it's not content with staying in the old mines.

Because it's a weekend, there's no one manning the front desk, and the station is empty aside from Griffin, who looks up from his computer in the bullpen when Lance walks in.

"I didn't expect you back so soon," the deputy remarks.

Lance reads the slight suspicion in his tone and deliberately ignores it. *Last night was the last one. No more death,* he assures himself. "I need to get some paperwork done this morning, and then I'll be out of town all afternoon."

"On duty?"

Lance nods. "Gonna see what there is to do about our ... hungry nuisance of a friend."

This appeases the younger man, who turns his attention back to the computer for a moment before speaking again, his tone tentative and unsure. "Hey, Chief? Should we—have you, I mean, called the sheriff? Let him know what's going on?"

The sheriff takes a three-week sabbatical every summer, going up to a remote location in Alaska to deep-sea fish and otherwise unplug. His wife goes with him, and they're completely unreachable for the duration. This is Lance's third summer in the department and the only one where something noteworthy has happened while he's been left as the department head.

"I sent him an email with a link to access the reports filed, but he doesn't have service at the cabin, and there's no guarantee he'll check it before he's due back." And thank Christ for that. Lance will have time to get everything sorted before then.

Griffin nods, but a frown pulls at his mouth as he smoothes over his mustache. "What do you think is really out there, sir?"

Lance sighs, leaning against the empty reception desk and folding his arms over his chest. "It's nothing like I've ever seen before. But whether it's a territorial bear or a rabid pack of wolves, we'll find it soon," he answers without answering.

"God, I hope so." It seems to be enough. "I've almost got this report done, then I'll send it your way."

"Thanks, I appreciate it." Lance heads into his office, but keeps the door open as he runs through some of the day-to-day tasks that he's fallen behind on with taking over the sheriff's responsibilities.

When his flight information is emailed, he calls his wife, Danielle, to let her know he'll be needed out of town for the afternoon. Griffin forwards the report to him a short time after, and Lance sends him back out on patrol.

The rest of the morning passes by quickly, and soon enough, he's driving up to the airport.

His phone chirps with a text message on the way there, and dread sinks in his stomach when he sees Effie's name.

He wants to believe that she's simply notifying him that she's raided his pantry, or maybe borrowed some of his tools to work on her bike. Hell, maybe she's even backed into a fence post and it'll need mending ... but no. He knows—with every bit of a cop's intuition, he knows—that she's been poking around.

And he's going to have to lie to her again.

7

1154 MDT//3d 8hr 51min after arrival

When Kel wakes up, his brain is foggy, and he lies there for a moment, blinking in the dark without moving, unsure of the day or the time. Details come back to him all at once, and he throws his hand out, patting the blanket to look for his phone.

He squints at the brightness of the screen, reading the time before tossing it away again with a groan. After a long stretch to wake up his muscles, he rubs his eyes, then runs his hands through his hair, mussing the dirty blond waves and rolling out of bed for a quick shower.

Clean and dressed but still feeling slightly less than human, he moves to the kitchen for coffee and food. While a frozen breakfast sandwich cooks in the microwave, he pours a cup of cold brew, pre-mixed with milk, sugar, and vanilla.

Kel's finished half of the coffee by the time his food is ready, which he eats standing in the kitchen, giving his brain time to wake and wander before what's bound to be a long day.

Predictably, where his mind wanders is right back to yesterday. The possibility of attaching his name to this discovery feels more solid in the light of day, and the thrill of potential rolls through him, ballooning in his chest. The urge to share his excitement catches him off-guard, and he frowns down into his now-empty coffee cup.

Kel is the only child of two very career-minded people. His father has a doctorate in chemistry and his mother a masters in civil engineering. Though they always encouraged him to follow his passions, the support was always tainted by a note of ambition. Whatever he did, they subtly drove him to be the best. Mediocrity was never an option, and forging meaningful friendships was difficult when every peer was potential competition.

That's not to say that he never had friends or doesn't know how to make connections, he's still fairly close with several of the people from his doctoral program and spends some of his off time with his team at Lockheed, but he's used to being on his own, to keeping himself entertained. As a general rule, he truly enjoys solitude, which is why the sudden desire for companionship, to bring someone else in before he has anything concrete to show, is startling.

Setting his cup to the side, he methodically cleans the lenses of his glasses, holding them up to the light streaming through the kitchen window for inspection before sliding them on and picking up his phone.

He checks his email first, finding a reply to the work he sent yesterday, but no further findings from Daphne, so he moves to Instagram, where a message is waiting.

> **foxtrot.echo: Hardly the backcountry, and didn't we decide that the only reason you were there was because you were stalking me?**

> **kel_on_starwatch: Yes, that's right. Couldn't think of a better use of my time.**

Her reply comes before he's even finished pouring a second cup of coffee.

> **foxtrot.echo: I'm flattered. Speaking of, did you get anywhere with reporting that thing?**

> **kel_on_starwatch: No. I found a ranger station in Norwood that appears to be 24/7, but the phone number hasn't been updated. Planning to drive up there in a few to try to talk to someone.**

> **foxtrot.echo: Want me to come with? Might be more credible coming from two eyewitnesses**

> kel_on_starwatch: No obligation, but if you want to, I'd enjoy the company. Where are you in relation to Norwood?

> foxtrot.echo: You said you were at sunshine campground, right? I'm between you and there. I'll text you my address. You'll drive past the main house to the casita out back. I can be ready in 20?

> foxtrot.echo: Ish

> kel_on_starwatch: That'll work. See you soon.

Effie heart reacts to the message, then it disappears, and a saluting emoji takes its place.

Kel finishes getting ready for the day before opening his text messages to copy Effie's address, then grabs his wallet, keys, and hat from the counter. The latter is slapped onto his head, bill to the back, as he considers grabbing the samples to mail off to Daphne. But a quick search shows him the post office out here closes at noon on Saturdays, so he leaves the parcel behind.

He texts Effie to let her know he's headed her way and pastes her address into maps. Just over ten minutes later, and he pulls into a long dirt drive, following it all the way down to where a blue Jeep is parked under a metal carport. Definitely the right house.

Parking behind the Wrangler, he walks up to the door and knocks twice. There's a faint scuffle from the other side, and a few moments later a deadbolt clicks, and Effie throws open the door.

"Hey," she greets, a little breathless, hair wrapped in a towel. "Come in, I'm almost ready. Sit wherever." She walks as she talks, grabbing an empty cereal bowl from the counter and setting it into the sink before disappearing back into the bathroom.

Kel takes a seat on a barstool, curiously looking around a space that is undeniably Effie's, even with how little he knows her.

The decor is entirely eclectic, splashes of color everywhere. One wall of the open living room has a series of Ansel Adams prints, the only monotone thing he can see, another dominated by a picture window with a gorgeous view of the mountains, and the other a tv and a bookshelf.

He wanders over to peruse the titles, a smile stretching his mouth at the mix of thrillers and historical romance. The bottom shelf is all nonfiction: a variety of field and stream books, survival handbooks, and bird and plant identification guides.

"See anything you like?" Effie asks, head tipped to the side as she scrunches her hair with the towel.

Kel pulls out *The Total Outdoorsman Manual*, turning to face her as he flips through it. "You big on primitive camping, Blake?" he asks, cocking an eyebrow.

Her teeth sink into her lower lip for a moment. "With the amount of off-roading I do, it's only smart to be prepared for the worst." She walks over to him, tossing her towel to hang over the couch on the way. "What do you read, Mr. Judgy-pants—sorry, *Doctor* Judgy-pants." The green in her hazel eyes is bright as she meets his gaze with a playful smile.

"I'll give you three guesses, and the first two don't count," he says, sliding *Total Outdoorsman* back in its place.

She laughs. "No, Kel. You do *not* read physics books for fun."

"Not *just* physics," he defends with a grin. "All sorts of science *and* also sci-fi." He crosses his arms over his chest with the last part.

She tilts her head to the side, giving it a little shake and curling her lips inward against a grin.

"What's that look for?" he asks, heat flushing around his collar. He pulls his gaze away from hers, tucking his tongue into the corner of his mouth because he realizes that he's blushing, but he can't drop his own grin.

"Nothing," she replies, grabbing a corduroy bag and a flannel from a peg by the door. "Come on, science man, let's go report a … well, let's go report."

They climb into his truck and set off for the ranger station. Kel has an old rock playlist on, but before he can ask about her music preference, Effie adjusts her seat belt, turning to face him and tucking a leg underneath her.

"Did you believe in aliens before all of this?" she asks.

"Of course, I grew up in Denver. Aliens run our airport." His reply is met with a snort and an eye roll. "No, but seriously, I'm not sure belief is the right word for it. It's just the acknowledgment that the probability of other life is too high for it not to be out there. It's the Fermi paradox, right? The universe is huge in an almost incomprehensible way—ask me when I'm high and I'll go on a full tangent about the absurdity of how far a light year actually is—but the odds of us being alone are substantially lower than the odds of something else existing."

"What about Area 51? Roswell? Did you follow all of that stuff?" she asks, digging around in her bag.

He can't hold back another sarcastic reply. "I've been obsessed with outer space since I was three, Blake."

"Fair enough," she laughs, scribbling onto her wrist with a pen she'd found.

"What's that?" he asks.

"Don't worry about it." She grins at him, replacing the pen and dropping the bag back to the floorboard. "Anyway, do any of those guys—Area 51 and Roswell incident experts—have any helpful anecdotes for how to actually handle alien contact?"

"Aside from calling in the national guard to round up every bit of potential evidence and cover everything up so the general public can't prove anything?"

"Preferably, yes."

"Then, no."

"Do you think," she starts, but pauses, chewing on her pinky nail and staring out at the road ahead. "I mean, let's just say for a minute that the Roswell incident and everything like that actually involves aliens. You just said the government comes in and rounds everything up, hushes everything before people are able to figure out or, like, *prove* what happened. So, I mean ... If that's the expected response, where does that leave us? What happens to the people who see things they aren't supposed to see?"

Kel doesn't answer right away, taking the time to turn the concern over in his mind, examining it and following the threads that extend from the corners. "I have a piece of the creature. Not only that, I know who to take it to to prove what it is. Once I mail off those samples, it's done. Even if some higher authority intends to keep it all under wraps, irrefutable proof from a reputable source is pretty hard to silence. All that to say, they can try to make us sound crazy or keep us from talking, but they can't shut down the entire scientific community."

Effie sighs, tucking her hair—now dry and pin-straight—behind her ear and dropping her hand into her lap. "So as long as we make it to the post office before anyone gets ahold of us, we're potentially safe. Easy enough, I guess."

They're both lost in their own thoughts after that, silent until they reach the ranger station.

"How do you want to play this, then?" she asks when they park.

Kel shuts off the truck and cracks his knuckles. "We just go in, try to build a little credibility, and then we tell them what we saw."

"Right. Just a normal, average Tuesday." Effie nods, releasing her seatbelt.

"A normal, average, weekend Tuesday," he agrees.

As they walk through the parking lot together, Effie raises her hand, back of her fist to him for a bump. "For what it's worth, I'm glad we're in this together, creepy stranger from the woods."

Kel taps his fist against hers, grinning. "Right back at you, internet stalker." He opens the door, holding it for Effie and following her inside.

He blinks, his eyes taking a moment to adjust to the diminished light as he walks up to the counter. Effie wanders the small lobby behind him, one hand tucked into the pocket of her shorts and the open, red and black flannel falling off one shoulder as she peruses the various brochures available.

Kel peers over the counter, looking around for a ranger. There's a bell, but it feels rude to ring it despite the note telling him to do so. Then Effie is next to him, reaching to tap it without any hesitation. Her shoulder leans into his as she studies the map underneath the Plexiglass in front of them. He's unsure if it's a show of support for him, a comfort to her, or completely unintentional, but either way, he appreciates the contact.

The nerves knotted in his stomach double when two forest rangers walk out from the back office, finishing up their conversation and chuckling softly.

"How can I help you folks?" asks the elder of the two, hiking up his belt. A brass badge flashes on his chest, shined to perfection and perfectly accompanying his crisp, impeccably clean uniform. Kel's gaze flicks down just long enough to read it—Stafford—before meeting the man's eyes.

Effie's pressure against his arm increases just slightly, and Kel plasters his best professionally friendly, standing-in-front-of-the-board smile to his face. "Hi, we have a report to make about something we saw up by Alta Lakes last night. I wasn't sure who to bring it to, so I'm hoping you guys can help."

"That's what we're here for, son," Stafford says, and Kel's smile twitches at the hint of patronizing tone.

"Well, you know about the bear attack that happened a couple days ago—"

"Bear attack?" the younger ranger, Jones according to his badge, interrupts, raising an eyebrow. "Did you have your food stored properly? Was there any property damage?"

Kel blinks, mouth stuck partially open in confusion, and exchanges a quick glance with Effie.

"It wasn't—did the San Miguel Sheriff's office not get in contact with you?" she asks, pulling the flannel over her shoulder when the older ranger's eyes drift from her face.

"No, outside of our typical run-ins, we haven't talked to them in, oh, a few weeks or so." Stafford crosses his arms over his chest.

Kel feels Effie stiffen beside him, and she squares her shoulders, lifting her chin against his impudent gaze. "People were killed in an animal attack at Alta Lakes two nights ago. The chief deputy would have called it in. Is it possible that you missed that news in a pass-down brief or something?" Her tone is cool and even, leaving no room for argument.

"We've been here all week," Stafford replies just as cooly. "Is it possible that you were misinformed?"

This encounter is going downhill fast, and while Kel doesn't fault Effie for the heat rolling from her, they still need the rangers to listen to them, and he quickly regroups, interjecting himself between them. "The chief deputy himself is the one who told us, but that's moot." He waits for both of the rangers to look at him before continuing. "I have a doctorate in astrophysics, and early Thursday morning, I saw something fall from the sky." As he talks, he pulls out his phone, pulling up the satellite images he saved that show the thermal rejection of the mass. He explains, as simply but thoroughly as he can, about the data he'd sifted through that cemented his hypothesis that a meteorite had indeed made impact. Then he glances at Effie, letting her cut in to add what she'd seen move across the radar screen.

Stafford looks skeptical, and Jones looks almost begrudgingly interested, but Kel powers on, glossing over the supposed bear attack. He can tell he's losing them, so he only briefly mentions the shard he found, showing them a few of the pictures he took while collecting samples, and goes for it.

"We were attacked by a creature last night. The best I can describe it, it was like a cross between a mantid and a crab, but huge—roughly the size of—" he flounders, searching for something equatable.

"Just smaller than a Lakota—a UH-72 helicopter," Effie offers.

"I think what I found is a part of its exoskeleton," he finishes.

Jones looks to Stafford, who hikes his belt up again and clears his throat. "So you're telling us there's a monster in the mountains?"

Kel nods, relief flooding him. "Yes, I don't know if it came from the mines or from space, but it's big, and it's mean."

"How'd you get away, then?" Jones asks.

"I shot it with a flare."

"And you didn't get any pictures or video?" Stafford asks.

Effie scoffs. "I was a little too busy worrying about being eaten, and he was too busy saving me to worry about pulling out our cellphones."

"Settle down, there, little lady. No need for hostility." Stafford holds his hands up.

Effie visibly bristles. "Excuse me if my tone is unsuitable to you. We were attacked by some sort of monster, and now we're here asking for help before someone else gets hurt, and it feels like you're not taking us seriously."

"Have you brought these concerns up to the sheriff's department in Telluride?" Stafford asks.

"They think it's a bear," Kel reiterates, expending more effort than he should to speak normally instead of through gritted teeth.

"Aren't you guys a higher authority?" Effie shoots back at the same time.

Kel surreptitiously touches a hand to her back, a show of support but also an attempt to reel her back in. Her stance relaxes marginally, and she takes a breath, her hands unclenching, palms flat on the counter. He meets the rangers' eyes. "Please, at least take a look for yourselves," he implores. "It went into the old mine in Gold King Basin. It might still be there, or there could be signs of it at least."

Stafford looks at the younger ranger, one eyebrow raised. "Well, Jones, why don't you go write all this down so we can have an official report on file." He turns back to Kel and Effie, giving them a placating smile and pushing over a pad of sticky notes and a pen. "You leave us a good number, and we'll give you a call if we need any more information after that."

Kel holds eye contact, ignoring the pen and paper. "So, you're going to check it out?"

Stafford sighs, clearly over the encounter. "Of course, son."

"Great, did you want me to show you where I found the shell fragment or email you copies of the trajectory data that I have?" he asks pointedly.

"No need for all that. We'll put it on our schedule to go look, but like I said, if you'd like to leave us a phone number, we can give you a call if we need any more information."

Kel knows that the rangers don't understand the severity of the situation, and even as his heart sinks into his stomach, anger heats his blood. *Lazy, simple-minded*—he cuts off the thought, drawing in a deep breath. "Yeah, sure." He takes the sticky pad and writes down his contact information.

After sliding it back across, Kel folds his arms on the countertop, leaning forward to study the map with his lips pressed together. He raises his middle finger, smoothly pushing his glasses up the bridge of his nose before lowering his hand back to the plexiglass and giving it two perfunctory taps. "Okay. Thanks, ranger." He pushes off from the counter, grabbing Effie's hand as he turns and pulling her out the door.

A smile tugs at her lips as she follows him out into the bright sunlight, and she laughs as soon as the door swings shut behind them. "Kelvin Alien-watch Curtis, did you just flip off a US forest ranger?"

He drops her hand to retrieve his keys and unlock the truck, looking straight ahead with a shrug. But her amusement is infectious, and a smug smile works its way free. "Alien-watch?" He cocks an eyebrow as she slips around to the passenger side.

"It's on a trial run with a few other potential middle names," she tells him, buckling her seatbelt.

"Do I even want to know?"

"You'll hear them eventually, regardless." She beams, but

grows serious as Kel pulls from the parking lot, heading back toward Telluride. "Where do we go from here?"

He lets out a slow breath, contemplating. "They aren't going to check it out without proof. At least not until a few more people die. The way I see it, we have three options." He pauses, sliding a look to Effie, who's picking at the cuticle of her thumb.

She stops, twisting in her seat to face him. "Shoot."

"First and most obvious, I drop you off at your place. You go to work Monday like nothing has happened and let the government eventually take care of this problem."

She's shaking her head before he even finishes. "Not happening. We're a team now. Consider us Mueller and what's-her-name until this is all over."

"Mulder and Scully?" He gives her an incredulous look.

She waves him off, rolling her eyes. "I was always more into *Criminal Minds*, but Morgan and Reid don't fit the situation as well. Regardless, you're stuck with me. It's Curtis-Blake from here on out."

He keeps his eyes on the road, something warm expanding in his chest. He tells himself it's her gumption he likes and not the fact she's calling them a team. "You're putting my name first?"

"I have no delusions about being the one with the greater input in this situation," she replies. "So tell me what the plan is, star-boy."

"Two options for Curtis-Blake, then." He adjusts his grip on the wheel and pretends not to catch the smile Effie shoots him. "Option A: irrefutable proof. We go back and try to get it on camera, bring that back to Fish and Wildlife, and maybe they'll get their shit together and call in some help. Option B: takedown. We still go back, but with the intent to kill it."

"What's the likelihood that Option A turns into Option B?"

"If it spots us?" Kel clarifies. "Highly probable."

Effie begins chewing on the edge of her thumbnail. "Can two civilians access the kind of firepower needed to take out an alien?"

"This is America, Blake, and you're asking the wrong question."

"What's the right one?"

He props his elbow on the center console, cracking his knuckles. "Can an Air Force vet and an astrophysicist figure out how to *create* enough firepower to take out an alien."

"And the answer?" She pulls her hand away and glares at her thumb before looking up at him.

"We're about to fucking find out."

8

1320 MDT//3d 10hr 17min after arrival

Effie isn't quite sure how she ended up here. The logical part of her brain, where her self-preservation lives, hasn't quite caught up to her emotions and sense of adventure.

"So, are you also predisposed to reckless abandon, or are you just looking for a reason to spend more time with me?" Kel asks, one-handed grip shifting on the wheel.

She twirls a lock of bright aqua hair through her fingers and crosses her legs primly. "Oh, buddy, you're about to learn hard and fast: reckless abandon is my middle name. As we've already established, you're the brains of the operation. I'm the guts."

Kel laughs. "They do say no guts, no glory."

"I think we should tell my cousin," she says suddenly, forcing the thought she'd been debating all morning into the open. "The rangers aren't going to help, but ..." she drifts off, remembering the worry in Derek's face when he'd asked her to cancel the bike ride. "If the sheriff's department knows what's out there, maybe they can help."

"It's worth a shot." He surprises her by agreeing without hesitation, and her shock must be clearly written on her face because he shrugs, rotating his hat around so that the bill is shading his eyes from the sun. "They've got a more vested interest in what's going on, and it can't go any worse than it did with those assholes back there."

A sound somewhere between a huff and a snort escapes her. "I'm not saying that I'm not used to people's first impression of me being ... skeptical, but that older guy was a fucking prick. Gave me big 'women are hysterical' vibes," she says, pulling her phone from her back pocket and sending a quick text to Lance, asking to talk.

Before Kel has a chance to respond to her, her phone vibrates, screen lighting up with a picture of her, Lance, Danielle, and the girls from this past Easter. Izzy is holding up a chocolate bunny with an over-exaggerated expression closer to a grimace than a grin, Katie smiling sweetly with her arms around Effie's waist. "Well, that was fast." She slides her finger across the screen and raises the phone to her ear. "Howdy," she says, her tone infinitely more nonchalant than she feels.

"I'm driving. What did you want to talk about?" There's an uneasy edge to Lance's voice.

"Are you headed home?" she asks, picking at the hem of her shorts.

A heavy sigh. "Unfortunately, no. I'll have a pretty full day and won't be back until late."

"Oh ..." Effie glances at Kel, and he gives her a reassuring nod that ends with a shrug. She takes it to mean something along the lines of "might as well tell him." "There'ssomethinginGoldKingBasin," she blurts.

Silence.

She waits, holding her breath.

"Elizabeth," Lance says, the word dripping with the kind of disappointment only a father can conjure.

"Lancelot," she replies, tone just as serious.

"I could arrest you for trespassing."

"It's public property."

"Not when you have to cross police lines to get there. The road's been blocked around the clock."

She fights the urge to mock his rhyme. "But the hiking trail was open as hell." She loses to the impulse.

Kel gives her an amused look, mouthing *hail?* for the way she drawled the final word to force the rhyme.

"That was sloppy work," Lance snorts.

She shrugs. "It was a long night. And I'm serious; the trail from Sunshine to Alta was fully open, and if you didn't know to peer through trees to look for the cruiser, you'd never see it from there. Not in the dark, certainly."

"I should raise your rent."

"I should charge you to babysit."

"Apparently I should be babysitting *you*," Lance grumbles.

The pattern of banter they've fallen into is familiar and comfortable, and now that the strange edge has faded from his voice, Effie pushes forward. "There's something up there, Lance. It ran into the old mine in Gold King, and—"

"That's the one where the road branches off from Alta?" he interrupts, immediately all business.

"Yeah," she answers. "We tried to tell Fish and Wildlife, but they said they haven't gotten any reports from you guys about anything happening up there."

There's a long pause before Lance talks again. "I'll double check that all the filing went through, but Effie, I mean it, do not go back up there. Just stay out of the mountains until we find it, okay?"

"You're not listening to me," she insists. "It's not a bear."

"It's a wild animal." His tone is firm and final. "And it will be removed by the end of the week. Stay off the trails until then."

Irritation simmers beneath her skin at being blown off yet again, but Lance speaks before she has the chance to respond with something heated.

"Shit, there's another call coming through. I have to take this. Don't poke around, Eff, I mean it." And then he hangs up.

She drops the phone into her lap, rubbing her face, then pulls down the visor, checking in the mirror and wiping a few flakes of misplaced mascara from beneath her eyes. "I swear his head isn't usually this far up his own ass."

"I take it we're still on our own here?"

She flips up the visor and collapses back into her seat. "Looks like we'll be operating off brains and guts alone."

Kel is quiet as they turn onto the highway back to Telluride, then asks, "Do you like sandwiches?"

"What?"

"Like, cold cuts. I have some stuff back at camp. Figure if we're going to be planning how to prove an alien's existence, we probably shouldn't be sitting in a restaurant on a Saturday afternoon in one of Colorado's most popular tourist destinations."

He pushes his glasses back up the bridge of his nose with a knuckle. "But that's just a thought."

Her stomach chooses that moment to let out a quiet gurgle. "Sandwiches are great."

Once back at the camper, Kel pulls his hat off, tossing it onto the counter with his keys before running his hands through his hair. He toes off his shoes, leaving them by the door before moving to the fridge to pull out ingredients.

Effie stands in the doorway, looking around the combination kitchen/dining room/living room. "I like it," she says.

"Thanks. Make yourself at home. Bathroom's up that way if you need it."

She slips out of her own shoes and sits at the table while he brings over an array of ingredients, setting them down and dropping into the seat across from her.

Effie tucks her feet underneath her, then helps herself to the spread. She's focused on what she's doing until she sees Kel dump a handful of barbeque potato chips onto his sandwich before placing the top piece of bread. "Dude, what?" Her nose wrinkles with a laugh.

"Dude yourself," he replies, pushing the bag over to her. "You're telling me you've really never put chips on your sandwich before?"

"That's not a normal thing."

"Sure it is." He takes a big bite, then leans down to grab two bottles of water from a case under the table, sliding one over to her.

"Thank you," she tells him.

Both tired and still reeling from, well, everything, they eat in comfortable silence for a while. When Kel finishes, he packs up all the cold stuff, returning it to the fridge before settling back down and grabbing a small canvas bag from the seat next to him, plopping it on the table.

Effie watches as he removes a plastic container, a grinder, a pipe, and a lighter, lining them up methodically before pulling the top off the grinder and popping open the canister.

The heady, floral smell of marijuana fills the air, and her eyes stay trained on his hands as he grinds a couple buds to a fine powder, the muscles in his forearms flexing with the movement, and then pinches up the powder to pack the bowl.

She doesn't realize she's staring, or that he's watching her staring, until he extends the pipe and the lighter out to her, and she looks up to meet his gaze. "Oh," she says, sitting back. "Oh, no, sorry, I can't." She waves her hands as her face goes red. "I could get tested."

"Ah, gotcha." Kel reaches out to crack the window before taking a hit, blowing the smoke out through the screen.

"You don't?" she asks, remembering his work.

"Huh? Oh, nope. The perks of being a contractor rather than a permanent employee," he answers with a lopsided grin.

"The chips on the sandwich make a lot more sense now," she smirks.

"Wooow," he laughs. "I didn't expect this kind of judgment from a fellow Colorado resident." He gives a disappointed shake of his head, a few bronze curls flopping over his forehead as he takes another hit.

"Not judgment," she clarifies, popping a chip into her mouth. "Just observations and clarifications. I'm learning new things about you."

"I'm an open book, Blake." He holds his arms out to demonstrate his point.

"Science-man, space enthusiast, stoner: a Kel Curtis story."

She grins.

"There's a start." He beams, then straightens, folding his hands and placing them on the table in mock seriousness. "Now, I believe we've business to attend to."

Effie tips her head back with a hopeless groan. "Where do we even start?"

A laptop is produced from the seat beside him, and he flips open the screen. "I sent a couple things to a colleague. Let's see if she's gotten back to me yet." He clicks on a few keys, then motions her over, scooting down the bench to make room for her.

She slides in next to him and tries not to snoop too heavily at his inbox, but most of them are from lmco.com or .edu addresses and contain subject lines that go way over her head.

Kel sighs, the act lifting his shoulders enough to make his arm brush hers. "No dice." Minimizing his email, he opens the file containing all of the information that he's already compiled. "So, here are some of the things I'm sure about."

Effie expects him to keep going, but he's just staring silently at the screen, an intent little furrow in his brow as he raises his hand to cup his chin. She looks from his face back to the screen. The spreadsheet is well-organized, with some readable calculations like size, speed, and times, but none of it means anything to her. "Ah, yes, these things." She nods sagely. "Which are …?"

He rolls his neck on his shoulders, sitting back. "Well, put simply, a whole bunch of nothing useful."

"Oh," she says. "Perfect."

"I sent some pictures of that piece of its shell, but even if we overnighted the samples, nobody would be able to do anything with it in the timeframe we're trying to work with." Kel runs his fingers through his hair, holding his hand at the top of his head, the other drumming against the table. "So we operate off what we *do* know." He looks at Effie expectantly.

She cocks her head, unsure for a moment, but then she turns over the memory of last night, and it's the first thing that flashes through her mind. "It hates fire."

Kel holds up one finger.

Her eyes slide to the tabletop, other facts coming more quickly. "It's holed up in Gold King Basin."

He holds up a second finger.

"With all of the attacks happening at night and its affinity for the old mine, it can probably see well in the dark."

Another finger.

Her brow furrows, lips pressed together as she thinks.

"Based on the way it came after you, it's not scared of humans, or at least is territorial enough not to care about picking a fight," Kel supplies, wiggling a fourth finger.

"Even if it's intelligent, it's not humanoid. It's probably not using tools or anything sophisticated like that," she adds.

He sticks out his thumb. "That's five things, which I'd say is a pretty solid foundation and a hell of a lot more than we had yesterday."

His confidence bleeds into Effie, and she reaches in front of him, fingers resting against the keyboard before she remembers herself. "May I?"

"Be my guest." He slides the laptop over.

She minimizes the spreadsheet window and fights back a smile at the picture of a nebula on his home screen. *Predictably adorable.* She bites her tongue to keep from voicing it. Clicking the shortcut to Word, she opens a blank document and types out their list, labeling it "5 facts about Gordon."

"Gordon?" Kel asks, taking another hit.

"What feels more like something you'll live through: trying to kill a monster or trying to stop Gordon?"

He holds the smoke in his lungs, considering, then slowly blows it out the window before turning back to her. "Okay, there might be logic there. But where did Gordon come from?"

"Isn't that supposed to be your area of expertise?" she shoots back.

He levels her with a look, and she presses her lips together to keep her grin from widening. "The name, smartass."

"Well, Zoidberg wouldn't work, because that calls too much attention to the fact that it's an alien and the whole point is to gloss over that little tidbit. But what if it's not An AlienTM, what if he's just Gordon? Have you ever felt threatened by a Gordon?"

"Ask every contestant who's ever been on *Master Chef* or *Hell's Kitchen*."

Effie's brows pull together, then she finally makes the connection and sighs dramatically, propping her chin on a fist. "What are the odds our Gordon will just hurl a few insults our way instead of flaying us for dinner?"

"Are you actually asking?"

"Do you actually know?"

"Considering the only data we have—which are all still somewhat uncertainties, none of which are quantifiable—no, I don't know the probability of Gordon leaving us with nothing more than bruised egos. But I'll give you an educated guess anyway and tell you not to bet on those odds."

"Figured as much," she says resolutely, turning back to the document. "Now that that's in order—" She presses enter a few times and makes two more title lines: "how to prove he exists" and "what to do about him." Then she sits back, cracking her knuckles.

"Well, as point number one suggests, fire," Kel offers.

Effie taps her fingers against her chin. "He's only come out at night so far, so it's pretty safe to assume he sleeps during the day, right? What if we go in there with a couple bottles of lighter fluid, spray him down, light, and run?"

Kel shakes his head. "Do you really want that thing running at you covered in flames?"

"Ah, well, no. Something more sophisticated, then."

"If we're banking on Plan A, that could be as simple as hiding out up there and waiting for it to come out. Snap a few pictures, take a video, and we're done." Kel slaps his hands together like he's dusting them off.

Effie types Plan A into the document. "Okay, so if we are the world's luckiest two individuals, we'll be able to sneak all the way up there before sunset, grab a recording that can't be disputed, and head back down without any trouble. And I'm fine with hoping for that."

"But?" he prompts.

"But I think not having a backup plan or at least preparing for the worst-case scenario will end terribly."

"I can't disagree with your logic. So what's Curtis-Blake's Plan B, then?" he asks, and they begin to strategize as clouds roll in, a storm brewing over the mountains.

9

1413 MDT//3d 11hr 10min after arrival

Lance steps down from the citation, holding onto the lip of

the door as he descends the few steps to the ground in hopes that he'll be able to get the noodle feeling out of his legs before they have to support his full weight. He's never been a good flier, and none of that anxiety was soothed by his hurried conversation with Effie.

It's hotter in Eagle than in Telluride, and the wind buffets his face with an uncomfortable, blanketing warmth as he looks out to see Mr. Phillips making his way toward the plane, sunlight reflecting from his scalp beneath sparse, buzzed hair.

"How was the flight?" the older man calls over the droning of the engines, the tails of his suit coat flapping in the wind as he walks up to the aircraft.

Lance wipes his palm against the side of his pants, stepping forward to meet him and offering his hand. "Can't complain," he says, despite wanting to. "That's a nice plane you've got," he compliments, unsure of where to drive the conversation.

Phillips waves a hand dismissively and ushers Lance toward the hangar. "It gets the job done. One of the smaller birds in the fleet, but it's such a short flight from Telluride. No sense burning up the fuel for anything bigger, am I right?" he says with a boisterous chuckle, and Lance smiles politely. "Now, I know you've got a lot of questions and concerns, Sutherland, and I just want to say how much I really do admire that about you. You're a man that cares, and that's not as easy to come by as it used to be."

Lance's jaw clenches, and he adjusts his sunglasses in an attempt to hide the irritated pull of his brow. If he'd had any question about whether this trip had any purpose but to placate him, the overly friendly verbiage is a solid indicator.

"I hope your visit today will help soothe some of your anxiety," continues Phillips as he leads Lance through the bay to the interior of the hangar.

"Is this ... standard?" questions Lance, pulling off his sunglasses and tucking them into his chest pocket. "It wasn't presented as an opportunity when I was recruited."

Phillips snorts, the sound small enough that Lance assumes he wasn't supposed to have heard it. "It wouldn't have been. We have people keeping an eye out all over the country, most of them the same as you were last week: paid to sit pretty and tell themselves the agency is full of crazy conspiracy theorists, and if they're lucky, they'll spend the rest of their lives that way." He stops abruptly, Lance narrowly avoiding colliding with his back. "You gotta use the facilities? It'll be about a half hour drive, and it's a bit bumpy."

"I'm fine, thank you."

"Good, good." Phillips continues walking, moving them briskly through the building. "We do, however—" he picks up his previous spiel seamlessly "—always offer a visit to our people in your position, especially if they're having a bit of a harder go of it."

Lance squints as they step outside, donning his sunglasses again as he follows Phillips to an unmarked white truck with a thick layer of dust coating the bottom of the carriage. The heat and imposing glare of the sun further exacerbate his annoyance. "You're telling me most people take it all in stride without any qualms?" he asks as he buckles himself in. "Do these things usually not cause as much trouble, or am I truly overreacting here?"

Phillips starts the truck, a blast of icy air immediately flowing from the vents. "No, Sutherland, not at all." He adjusts his glasses and smooths down the front of his suit—the same light gray as his hair—before pulling out of the parking lot. "It's perfectly normal to panic when you get your first Azathothlin, and I assure you, we're here to help."

"Azathothlin?"

Phillips gives another dismissive wave. "It's a name our techs gave to the creatures, some sort of mythology connection, I guess." He rolls his eyes as if to say "kids, am I right?" even though he's just used the name himself. "Their official classification is SCP38-1875."

Lance redirects the vent so that it's no longer blowing directly on his face. "How long have they been here?"

Phillips shakes his head, sliding him a look that makes him think the older man couldn't be happier to have privileged information. "Sorry, Sutherland, that's need-to-know."

Lance's brows pull together, but Phillips doesn't give him a chance to question it.

"The fewer people that know all of the agency's secrets, the better. However, since you've got an Azathothlin of your own to monitor now, it's in our best interest to let you see how we've made it work all these years and remove any doubts you may have that this thing is a threat to your community. It's no more dangerous than a giant squid—stay out of the depths of the ocean and it'll never bother you."

"Last time I checked, Colorado is landlocked."

"It's called an analogy, boss."

"Boss" is even more condescending than the overuse of his last name, and Lance runs a hand through his hair, gripping the short brown locks at the back of his head and pulling, letting the pressure keep him from giving over to annoyance. "I'm just supposed to keep everyone out of the mountains, then? You do realize Telluride is a tourist hot spot."

Phillips laughs, going as far as to slap the steering wheel a couple of times. "Don't be absurd, you just need to keep everyone out of the old mines. Azathothlins don't do sunlight. Once they make it here, they find a way underground and stay there."

"But this one—"

"Trust me, Sutherland, the techs will be able to answer all of your questions and quell your fears. Just hold on to everything until you can see it with your own eyes, okay?"

Lance does, happily letting silence take over the car ride. Unease churns in his gut, further aggravated by the bump of washboards in the dirt road and Phillips occasionally clearing phlegm from his throat or tapping his thumbs along to the old-school country playing quietly over the radio.

They eventually pull up to a gate, where Phillips rolls down his window, waving a badge over an electronic sensor. There's a long beep, then the gate shudders and begins to pull back. A guard sitting in the shack close by looks up from his monitor, nodding at Phillips as they drive through.

He stops a few yards inside, waiting for the gate to start its lumbering path back across the road before continuing.

There's only one building out here, constructed right up against the side of the mountain. The small parking lot is almost full, but Phillips pulls to a spot up front marked *Reserved*. "Let's head in and get you all squared away, then," he says, giving Lance a winning smile.

Lance nods, following him out of the baking heat and into the building, where they move through a security checkpoint before arriving at the front desk.

"Welcome back, Mr. Phillips," greets the receptionist, looking polished and professional and so at ease that it only serves to further unsettle Lance. "And you must be Mr. Sutherland. I've got some forms for you to fill out right quick, then I can get you a visitor's badge, and you'll be all good to go."

Lance takes the clipboard she slides across the top of the desk, filling in his name and position on the front page before flipping through the various documents, NDAs, liability waivers, and even a form that asks if he's been sick or suffers from a variety of different illnesses. Phillips stands by patiently as he skims through everything. Once he's initialed and signed everywhere indicated, he hands it back, and the receptionist gives a quick look to double check it all.

Satisfied, she hands over an ID badge. "Clip that where it's easily visible, please."

Lance Sutherland, Telluride, CO it reads next to the picture of him that's posted in the sheriff's office back home. He clips it to the flap of a chest pocket.

"Alrighty, now if you'll just hand over your cellphone—no worries, I'll keep it in this little lock box and you can hold the key on your person—just please make sure it's turned off, so it's not ringing or buzzing away up here while you're visiting." She smiles at him, pulling what looks like a cash box from the floor beneath her desk and opening it before holding her hand out expectantly.

Lance does as requested, and she places it in the box, locking it, tucking it back under the desk, and ceremoniously handing him the key. "Perfect." There's slightly too much emphasis on both the *p* and the *t.* "Don't forget to check back in before you leave," she instructs before turning back to Phillips. "You're all set, sir."

"Thanks, hon," he tells her, leading Lance away.

The door to the hall requires a keycard for entry, every movement logged and nothing left unaccounted for. There are cameras at each junction in the hallway, and Lance's eyes keep drifting up to them, wondering if he's being actively watched or just recorded.

They've been walking long enough that Lance knows they

must be beneath the mountain now, and the thought raises the hair on the back of his neck. He shakes it off as Phillips opens a door at the end of the hall.

The room is dim, filled with the eerie glow of computer screens. New age metal is playing from one of the desktops, and the smell of popcorn permeates the air.

Phillips clears his throat, loud and pointed, and three heads pop up.

"Oh, Mr. Phillips, hey!" greets a young Asian man with a shock of black hair falling over his forehead. He looks at the clock on the other side of the room. "I guess you're right on time. Is this the newbie?"

Phillips's grin is tight, more forced than it was at reception, and his nose wrinkles slightly in distaste. "Yes, this is Mr. Sutherland, who oversees San Juan and San Miguel counties."

The tech, who looks roughly Effie's age if not younger, pushes back his chair to stand and walk over. "You're stationed out in Telluride, right?" he asks, brushing his hair back and offering his hand.

Lance shakes it. "That's right."

"Cool. I snowboard out there sometimes. Do you winter sport?"

"Not much time for it, I'm afraid, but I do go sledding with my girls most weekends during the season," Lance offers.

"Aw, cool, cool. I bet they love that." The kid offers him a genuine smile, his eyes crinkling.

Lance's gaze flits down to the badge on his lanyard, but its clear protector is covered in overlapping Dutch Bros stickers.

Phillips raises his arm to pull back his sleeve and glance at his wristwatch in an overly important manner. "I've got some things to attend to," he says, clearing his throat again. "They'll take good care of you, Sutherland." He claps Lance on the shoulder, then looks at the tech. "Give me a call when you're through, and I'll escort him out."

"Will do, sir." His face slips into a more serious expression as he nods.

Phillips stares at him for a moment before returning the nod and heading out.

A string of laughter erupts from all three of the techs as soon as the door clicks shut. "Show me a guy who's got his own head further up his ass, right?" The one next to Lance rolls his eyes. "I'm Jaron, by the way, and that's Kylee and Tommy. We're part of the analyst team up here. Kylee and I are bio, Tommy's geo, and we all do IT for Phillips and the rest of the names."

"It's what we call the upper office folks." Kylee grins, looping Lance in on the joke. "Every single one of 'em has a first name as a last name."

"It's part of the qualifications when hiring new staff for their tier," Jaron adds. "Capable of acquiring at least a Top Secret security clearance? Check. Willing to travel-slash-relocate for work? Check. Last name Shumaker?—*Errr!*" He makes a sound like a buzzer. "Resume straight to the trash."

"Or, if you're lucky, you get offered a grunt job like the rest of us," Kylee finishes, popping her gum.

"Grunt job," Tommy snorts. "Like we're not the only ones who are required to use our brains around here. They may look fancy and know how to play with the big dogs, but this whole operation would go down without us." He tosses a handful of popcorn into his mouth, propping his feet up on the desk. "What's your surface job?"

"My surface job?" Lance asks.

"Yeah, what do they have you doing out in Telluride that

explains why you're there?"

"Oh, law enforcement—Chief Deputy Sheriff, if you're into specifics."

Tommy nods, grabbing another handful of popcorn from the bag. "My guess was something more like Fish and Wildlife, since they had you all the way out there."

"Federal positions are always harder to make placements in, though," Kylee says. "I tried to tell him as much, and that's why I wouldn't take his bet." She holds her hand up to her mouth like she's telling a secret, despite not lowering her voice. "He's already in the hole from the last few."

Tommy tosses a piece of corn in her direction, missing widely.

Lance realizes his shoulders have lost most of their tension, and the nerves in his stomach have settled. Their banter is comfortable, and they seem like happy, well-rounded people.

Happy, well-rounded people don't sit by and let aliens take over their planet, right?

"So, Mr. Sutherland, you're out there because you've finally got yourself an Azzie?"

"Lance, please," he insists. "What is it you call them?"

"Azzie—short for Azathothlin," Kylee offers, attention returning to her computer.

"We named them after a Lovecraftian god," Jaron explains, everything about his posture open and relaxed.

A shiver runs down Lance's spine, and he rubs his hand over the back of his neck in an attempt to hide the reaction. "Nothing like a little eldritch horror to humanize the alien creatures setting up shop under our feet."

Tommy laughs, looking at Lance with a grin. "I like you, Mr. Sutherland. A sense of humor is hard to come by from agency outposts."

"He's not lying," Jaron says, moving to the door and motioning for Lance to follow. "You'd be surprised how many sticks-in-the-mud the agency tends to hire on the outside."

"Nice to meet you," Lance tells Kylee and Tommy before moving back into the hallway with Jaron.

"For real, though," the biologist continues as they walk, "I know Mr. Phillips is a bit of a prick, but I'm sure he's told you not to worry too much, and he's right. I've been here for five years now and have never once seen or heard of another one venturing back aboveground. Give 240 a chance to settle in and I promise it won't bug you anymore."

"Two-forty?" Lance questions.

"Your Azzie's official name, SCP38-1875-240."

A chill winds around his spine. "Am I allowed to ask if that means there are 239 that you already know of?"

"You're allowed to ask anything you'd like," Jaron answers with a wry smile, stopping outside of another door. "We're just not always permitted to answer." With that, he flashes his badge over the keypad next to it, and the door unlocks with a mechanical click. He opens it, stepping through and holding it for Lance.

Jaron leads him down a staircase that descends only a few floors before leveling out to a long hallway. Their footsteps echo softly off the bright, shiny flooring as they walk.

"This is kind of creepy, isn't it? How bright and clinical it all is, I mean." Lance's voice feels loud in the silence.

Jaron laughs, hands tucked into his pockets. "I think their intention was to make it so bright we'd forget we're underground." He raises his eyes to the fluorescents lining the hall. "I don't think anyone bothered to look into white versus warm—light is light."

Lance resists the urge to look behind him, feeling like they've walked for miles even when he knows it can't have been more than a few hundred yards. He blames it on the intense lighting and lack of windows, but his nerves are back to buzzing uncomfortably beneath his skin.

"And here we are." Jaron waves his lanyard in front of the pad beside an unmarked, nondescript door. But it's the only one on the left side of the hallway, so Lance supposes it doesn't really need any markings. The lock clicks open, and Jaron swings the door inward.

Lance steps over the threshold into a small room. Once the door is closed behind him, the overhead lights go off, and the area is illuminated by strips of red lighting along the floor and ceiling. Within moments, a door on the other side of the room unlocks, and Jaron pulls it open, more red light flooding the space. "Welcome to the Az-trium."

Lance blinks, momentarily disoriented by the extreme change in lighting. The air also feels different, balmy and humid, like the inside of a cave.

"The observation deck is separated from the rest of the facility by an air lock, both to limit light pollution and to avoid any major fluctuations in temperature. I'm sure you know, but conditions below the Earth's surface tend to stay pretty temperate and don't really fluctuate much. Our goal here is to limit the Azzies' awareness of us as much as possible."

"Because they're dangerous?" asks Lance, gaze traveling around the room. It's little more than a large cave cut into the side of the mountain, wooden support beams crossing overhead and shoring up the walls. The entire opposite wall—spanning roughly a hundred yards—is glass, with benches sporadically spaced. Red lights hang from the rafters, casting just enough light to see, all lined against the back wall.

"Huh? No—well, not no they're not dangerous—no, that's not why," Jaron answers, walking over to the observation wall. "Our whole job here is to monitor, right? Observe. Record. All that fun science stuff. If the Azzies were constantly being reminded that we're here staring them down, we could hardly expect them to behave normally, right? It's a change in variable."

"They are dangerous, though." Lance holds on to that confirmation. "You said it yourself."

Jaron laughs, waving Lance over to the glass. "I wouldn't go spelunking down there, no, but I've no fear of them crawling out from under my bed to eat me in the night."

Lance steps up next to the tech, peering into the darkness. The bottom of the observation deck is also lined with red lights, illuminating the system of tunnels below. He studies the shadows, watching for any movement amongst the sharp angles of rock.

"They stay below the surface. Once they find a way below, they don't leave." Jaron's voice is quiet, his eyes also searching.

"But mine did," Lance says, feeling like a stubborn child. "Twice."

Jaron looks at him, and Lance is very aware of the tense set of his shoulders and the wrinkle in his brow. But the younger man's expression shows only understanding and compassion. "Do you know what time it landed? These guys don't do well with any sort of UV. As soon as they wake up, they try to find a way below the surface, but once they know where safety is, they set out for food. The trip seems to take almost everything out of them—which is fair, because it's long as fuck—but after that initial refuel, they really aren't trouble at all."

Lance searches his face for any signs of deception, but he seems wholly sincere. "You've seen this enough to know it for fact?"

"You're 240, remember?" Jaron smirks, red light shining off his dark hair.

Lance huffs a laugh, nodding and folding his arms over his chest. They stand there silently for a moment before he speaks again. "What do they eat, then?"

"What d'ya mean? When they land? Or after?"

"Both, I guess."

Jaron scratches his cheek over the bare beginnings of a five o'clock shadow. "Whatever they can find, really. When they first land, they always take down something big. A deer, a goat—hell, I heard one of them out in—" He catches himself, waving both hands as if to remind both Lance and himself that he can't divulge unnecessary details. "One of them grabbed a whole ass *cow* before going to ground. A handful end up ... well, there's no sugar-coated way to say it, but they end up eating people. Once they've had that one filling meal, though, they don't seem to need much extra sustenance. They'll eat whatever wanders their way, of course. Rodents, bats, an unfortunate cat or two that ends up straying into old mines, but they aren't really hunters in the sense of tracking and actively pursuing prey."

"So," Lance starts, trying to sort through the information and place it against his understanding of the world. "They're not apex predators? Just ... invasive species?"

Jaron's head tilts side to side, as if waffling through how to respond. "I wouldn't say they're *not* apex predators. We've pushed a few of Earth's most deadly into the tunnels before, to see how the Azzies would respond. Even one is enough to take down a cougar. But they really don't bother anything that doesn't enter their space."

Lance frowns. "And it's not concerning to anyone that their

space is actually *our* space?"

Jaron holds his hands up placatingly. "Hey, man, I totally get you, trust me, I do. Scientist, right? It's my job to look at these things from all angles. But these mines aren't even in use anymore. Most of them are sealed off long before these guys find their way in, then they just connect them via cave systems that already exist beneath the surface."

"They connect them?"

"Yeah, dig through the rock until they're able to reach the central caverns. There's something about the rock composition that they seem to really like, though Tommy's more apt to explain that part of it."

Lance takes a breath, trying to wrap his mind around everything. "I just ... I don't ... How strong are these things? They dig through fucking mountains and kill cougars, but they somehow crawl around in abandoned mine shafts? What kind of—kind of—" he stutters around the word *alien*, as though refusing to say it will somehow help his situation.

"Wait," Jaron saves him from finishing. "You haven't seen one?"

Lance shakes his head. "Only the aftermath of what it can do to a person."

The weight of that statement seems to go right over Jaron's head, because he throws his hands up in the air. "Well, why didn't you lead with that, my guy?" he asks in excited exasperation. "Come on." He leads Lance over to a door at the side of the room, waving his card in front of the keypad to unlock it. "This is the main tracker lab. We have some others with more in-depth diagrams and experiments and data and shit, but, well, confidentiality and all. Anyway."

Lance is listening, but his eyes move to the large monitor set in the opposite wall, dozens of little green dots moving across the screen.

"Are those ..."

"Meet the Azathothlin colony of Eagle County, Colorado," Jaron gestures proudly.

"You implanted them with trackers?"

"Yep. I helped engineer the coating we put on the chips to try to keep them from being fully digested. We stuck 'em to rats and sent them off into the mines. There's a few that hit double, but when we notice them staying too close together like that, we just disable one. Same for if it goes dormant for too long. Figure it might've gotten dispelled, so we stop following it."

Lance finally moves his gaze from the screen to take in the rest of the lab, and his jaw actually drops. He steps forward, walking to a large poster. It takes up most of one wall, depicting an Azathothlin at least eight feet tall and fifteen feet long. Various parts of its body are labeled, pointing to segmented legs that apparently have the ability to shorten and lengthen as needed, an abdomen that can slide into itself to fit through narrow passages, and antennae covered in fuzzy little hairs that sense both movement and scent.

But there are two things that really catch his eye and chill the blood in his veins. First is its mouth, mandibles that open sideways and down to show rows of razor-sharp teeth. Second are the two pieces of shell on its back, similar to a ladybug's, that protect its wings. But the Azathothlin's wings unfurl in a wide arc, double the size of its body. The information listed next to them state that the wings are of a material previously unknown to mankind and are thought to wrap completely around the Azathothlin's body, folding together with a tight seal that creates a protective capsule they hibernate inside during their journey to Earth.

"I know, right," Jaron says, watching Lance's reaction. "They're fucking *wild*, man. The most insane, terrifying, beautiful, perfectly evolved thing I've ever seen."

"Are they ... is this to scale?" Lance asks dumbly.

Jaron nods, pointing to the legs. "This is about the average height when fully extended. It can differ about a foot either way, but never much more than that. They can make themselves pretty short and skinny, though. And that exoskeleton is tough as fuckin' nails. They use the tips of their legs to break through the rocks and have even demolished a few of the mini rovers we've sent down there.

"But those wings ..." Jaron trails off, and Lance looks over to see the biologist's eyes following the depiction on the wall. "They're something else entirely. I've never seen anything quite like them." There's an awe in his voice, so deep and almost reverent that goosebumps erupt over Lance's arms. He can't tell if it's a secondhand response to whatever Jaron is feeling or a sense of danger for that sense of worship.

"Have you ever killed one? Or found a dead one to examine?" Lance asks, moving around the room to where different low-light pictures of Azathothlins are posted.

"We've examined one, yeah. That's how we know they'll never threaten us. They can't survive extended exposure to UV."

"So they just live in the dark, then?"

"They've adapted well," Jaron says deferentially. "They don't need light to see."

Lance is about to ask what the fuck that even means when Jaron shakes himself, tucking his hands back into his pockets and giving Lance a tight smile. "Well, that's about all I can really show you. Does any of this make you feel better about your new neighbor?"

Lance spies a workstation on the desk in front of a smaller observation window. It looks like a log of activity and location, but Jaron steps in front of it before he can get a good look. Lance points at it anyway, meeting Jaron's gaze. "In all the time the agency has known about these things' presence on our planet, they've never resurfaced? Not once?"

Jaron blinks, lips pressed together. "Never."

Lance frowns, still not appeased. "And you aren't at all worried about harboring them? If they've no natural predators, what's to keep them from making enough offspring that the tunnels can't sustain them anymore?"

"There hasn't ever been an indication of reproduction. These things are either all male or asexual, but nothing we've seen has ever led us to believe in the existence of eggs or any form of young."

Lance swallows. He believes the tech doesn't think the Azathothlins are a threat, but he's so young. How much can he truly know? Was he even alive when most of these things first got here?

"Look, man," Jaron says, hands resting easily on the lip of the desk behind him. "I can get you a tracker for 240, send you updates on its whereabouts until your mind is at ease."

"You can do that?" Lance asks, failing to keep the surprise from his voice.

Jaron does that head tilt motion again—hemming and hawing, Lance's folks would've called it. "Offer you a tracker? Yes. Offer you updates? Not teeeeechnically," he draws out the word. "Not without cause, at least. But I like you. You seem like a guy who really cares about his community, and I can spin putting your fears to rest as due cause for a week or so." Jaron again uses his keycard to open a supply closet, filled with all sorts of different tech. He pulls a small plastic case from a drawer, flipping it over to read the back and marking different numbers on a form attached to a clipboard resting on top of the cabinet. He pauses, looking up. "You do know where your Azzie's holing up, right?"

Rubbing the back of his neck, it's Lance's turn to hem and haw. "I have the area mostly pinned down, but not the exact mine." *Unless Effie really did see it last night.*

Jaron starts to roll his eyes, but catches himself, returning to the paperwork. "Take a gander, sometime when you've got a lot of sunlight left. If you're really looking, it won't be hard to tell." He hands the plastic case to Lance. "There's an adhesive strip on one side of this. Once you know which tunnel is 240's, stick that to the back of a mouse or other small warm-blooded critter. The scruff seems to work best. You can touch it with your bare hands, just make sure you wash with soap first before you eat or touch your face too much. If you do want to use tongs or anything to work with it, that's fine, but nothing metal."

"Nothing metal, got it," Lance repeats, slipping the case into his chest pocket.

"Don't worry, man," Jaron assures him as they head back through the observation deck to the brightness of the hallway. "Give it a few weeks and you'll basically forget it's even there."

Lance nods, but there's a prickle along the back of his neck, an intuition that tells him not to count on it.

10

A summer storm rolls over the mountains, dumping rain until the rocky ridgelines are slick with water, runoff trickling down to gather in ravines and gulches. Wildlife take to bed, marmots and stoats returning early to their holes, owls and bats roosting away from the downpour.

Beneath a mountain that the storm has not yet reached, the alien wakes up hungry again, which irritates her. While no longer insatiable, she can still tell that she's drained from her travel and laying her clutch. She chitters in the darkness, voicing her displeasure at feeling weaker.

There's a commotion of scuttling to her right, and she stands, looking around the rocks to see two males crawling away from her and the eggs. She clicks at them, antennae reaching forward to smell them out. One of them still carries the faint scents of old home, not having shed since his arrival. The other is older, smelling of nothing but the mineral tang of the Earth's tunnels.

Both lower their heads to the ground in a show of respect, and her legs lengthen to stand over them. They're silent in her presence, and she clicks her approval to them.

Their legs tap against the floor, creating more than enough sound for all of them to see by. She taps each of them lightly on the head with the sharp tip of one of her forelegs, but makes no other vocalizations as she sinks back down, segments of her legs sliding back into one another to allow her to crawl through the more narrow tunnels between caves.

It's time for her to hunt, and she is very much looking forward to it.

Cool, clean air rushes through the entrance to the mine, heavy with moisture. Gordon, as she has unknowingly been named, crawls from her cave, stretching her legs to their full height. Her head tilts up to the sky, four dark eyes blinking curiously at the lack of stars. There's a distinct chill in the air, but she barely registers it through the hairs lining her antennae, the wind breaking easily over her shell.

Pulling the waving appendages back into the sides of her mouth, she begins up the mountain, anchoring herself in the scree without issue.

The wind whistles over the ridge, creating just enough noise for a fuzzy picture of the landscape to be a constant. She taps the tips of her legs against the rocks when a more defined visual is necessary, but is otherwise happy with the development.

The sky opens up, fat droplets splashing around her, sporadic for a moment before falling in heavy sheets. She pauses, antennae sneaking out to taste the air. This phenomenon is new to her, but the sound of rain hitting the ground lights up the world, the entire mountainside crisp and clear before her.

She lets out a series of satisfied clicks, pleased at the many things this planet has to offer her and her offspring, and continues, water sluicing off the curve of her shell and sliding in rivulets down her legs as she moves with ease over the terrain.

Buried within the sound of the rain is the roar of running water, and she follows a swift-moving river to an even more thunderous sound, where the water spills over the side of the mountain and crashes onto the rocks below.

She stands at the cusp of it, moving toward an old building. It's hard to tell in the rain, but the smell of it is stale, devoid of any of the warmth and vibrancy that this planet's main population seems to create. She lifts a leg, about to knock down several of the wooden planks regardless, when a flash of light from below grabs her attention.

Abandoning the building, she drops her front two legs over the cliff's edge, easily finding a hold, and scuttles smoothly over the side, stepping down the sheer incline toward the source of the light.

Cutting through the noise of the rain is the idle purr of a car's engine, and she tastes the air curiously. The rain traps the acrid bite of exhaust low to the ground, allowing her to easily scent the flesh and blood hiding beneath it.

Gordon steps gracefully down from the side of the mountain where the road levels out next to the waterfall, each leg moving separately from the others, instinctually keeping her balance on the slick and uneven terrain.

Two segments of her front legs slide into each other, giving her a better angle to view the car. She can see by the sound of rain pattering against it that it's a hard material, but mostly thin. Nothing she can't break through, and she examines the structure for the best spot to peel it open.

A brilliant flash lights up the world, and she whips her head up to see where it came from when a shuddering boom splits the air. The combination of bright light and the thunderous noise momentarily blinds her, her entire body vibrating with the echo of it.

That streak of lightning is also bright enough to throw her into contrast against the rocks, and the two humans in the car notice her standing there.

There's a soft click, then a repetitive *ding ding ding* as the car door is opened, a man stupidly stumbling out to peer into the darkness, positive his eyes have fooled him.

The warm, salty musk of his flesh invades Gordon's senses now that he's out in the open, and her attention snaps back to him, saliva dripping from her mouth as she again lowers her front to the ground.

A chittering series of anticipatory, eager clicks tick from her throat as she eyes him, watching him as he slowly makes sense of the shape looming over him in the dark.

There's another flash of lightning, and his mouth drops open with a shrill scream, quickly drowned out by another clap of thunder.

Without hesitation, he leaps back into the car, slamming the door shut behind him.

As Gordon shakes off the resonance of the thunder, the other person in the car screams commands. "Drive, drive, drive!" The sounds filtering out of the vehicle mean nothing to her, and she watches with something akin to fascination as the tires spin against the wet rock before finally catching, tossing loose scree back at her as it lurches forward.

The rocks pelt her legs, small taps of pressure that she ignores, never taking her eyes from her prey.

The vehicle bounces noisily over the road, creaking and groaning as it's forced over the rough, uneven surface.

Gordon pursues, legs lengthening and shortening as needed to keep her body level as she follows, quickly gaining. Reaching forward, she spears one raptorial leg through the back of the car, metal shrieking as she tears through it.

Her other seven legs are firmly planted, and the tires squeal, engine roaring as the car tries to pull free. She lets out a low, short cry, happily adding to the noise of the hunt, and the screams of the humans inside accompany her.

There's a great pull against the joint of her leg, and, enjoying the thrill of finally having something to toy with, she wrenches the limb free, letting the car lurch forward.

But the man driving it has either lost control or can't see through the pouring rain, and the car careens over the side of the road. They crash down onto the next level of switchback, landing unevenly and almost tipping over before slamming with a heavy crunch right-side up.

Gordon effortlessly follows over the edge. The front axle has snapped, one tire bent completely underneath the car, and Gordon realizes within seconds that the chase has ended. She stands back, waiting to see what her prey will do.

The door opens again.

"What the fuck are you doing?! Don't go out there! Don't—"

The man ignores the pleas coming from the passenger as he lunges over the rocks, slipping and stumbling in the rain as he races toward freedom.

Gordon steps over the car, swinging one of her front legs out to knock him against the wall of the mountain. The satisfying crunch of his bones is almost drowned out by the rain and his anguished screams, and he crumples to the ground.

Gordon nudges him with a leg, flipping him onto his back, and he raises his arms in front of his face, kicking and screaming.

She catches his foot in her mouth, rows of strong, pointed teeth tearing through skin and shattering bone as she pulls it free. Her jaws work quickly around the inorganic material of his shoe and sock, separating them from the flesh and bone and spitting them back out.

Pushing the tip of one leg against his skull, she breaks through bone, spilling gray matter onto the rocks and silencing his wails of terror and agony. Then she lowers her body and begins to eat.

Gordon is aware when the passenger closes the car door, both the clicking of the lock and the ceasing of the *ding* pulling her attention. The eye closest to the vehicle watches as the passenger—having stopped screaming—sinks down out of view, hands slapped over her mouth.

Gordon continues watching through one eye as she strips the man of his flesh, consuming him in large greedy bites. As she eats, the wet crunch of his breaking bones grows ever louder as the torrential downfall of the rain slows.

By the time Gordon finishes with him, the wind has pushed the clouds away, and the moon illuminates enough of the world that she is able to slide back the nictitating membranes from her eyes. One at a time, she raises her front legs to her mouth, licking them free of blood and bone marrow before turning her full attention to the car.

The passenger is cowering against the floorboard, silent as can be. Gordon taps the tips of her front legs against the hood, creating an almost musical tinkling sound. She steps onto it to investigate the glass of the windshield, and her legs pierce through when she shifts her weight to them.

Something in the engine grinds against her exoskeleton for a moment before stuttering to a halt. The metal below her is hot, transferring quickly through her shell, and she yanks her legs free, stumbling back and emitting that deep, shredding tear from her throat—her version of a hiss, or possibly a growl.

She scuttles around to the back of the car, punching her legs through the roof just enough to grab it and wrench it back with the sharp, angry screech of metal.

The passenger inside has started screaming again.

Gordon rises to her full height, peering down into the vehi-cle. With one front leg, she pulls down the side, crumpling the passenger door so that she can lower her head in. Her mandibles open, latching around the passenger's head and lifting her from the vehicle.

One quick, sharp shake snaps her prey's neck. As Gordon sinks back to the ground to eat, she kicks out with the two back legs of one side, pushing the car off the cliff for having the audacity to burn her.

It tumbles, crunching and rolling off another embankment before settling in a wasted heap, and the only sound left in the night is the howl of the wind, the roar of the waterfall, and the wet snapping and tearing as the alien eats.

11

2048 MDT//3d 17hr 45min after arrival

They hadn't meant to plan a full attack, but once Kel got going, Effie took everything he said and ran with it, asking questions and bringing up not only potential problems, but also possible workarounds. Before they knew it, they were sitting there, staring at one another with the realization that they were really capable of taking down a monster.

They're easily sidetracked as they put together a shopping list of everything they'll need to accomplish the plan, taking every rabbit trail and tangent that comes up in conversation.

When they finally have everything finalized and compiled, Effie scans over the document in front of them. Their plan contains multiple steps, but is simple nonetheless. Tomorrow, once Gordon leaves for the night, they'll go into the mine and find where he's been nesting, so Kel can try to collect whatever samples and information possible. Then, on the way out, they'll set up a series of homemade explosives. Step one is melting styrofoam down in acetone, which will create something similar to napalm that they'll use to line the tunnel. Step two is to create an improvised bomb by partially filling plastic bottles with bleach, then carefully dropping test tubes of ammonia into them. The bottles will be sealed, one set against each wall, and wrapped with a length of fishing line to create a trip-wire. When Gordon returns, they will wait for him to get deeper into the tunnel, then repeat the setup at the entrance of the mine, but knock over the bottles immediately and run for it. The two explosions should, theoretically, bring the mine down on the alien, burn him, or otherwise trap him. They will also bring a couple more flares as well as an arsenal of bangers and screamers—pyrotechnics used at the airfield to scare away birds—as back-up, long-range weapons.

"This is fucked," she decides, sitting back. "We're fucked."

"Yup, probably," Kel agrees, his shoulder brushing hers as he twists the top on his grinder.

"But we're the only ones who are going to do anything about it."

"Mmmhhmm." He pinches up some of the flower to pack a fresh bowl.

Effie watches him, head cocked to the side. "It feels like there should be professionals for this, people who know what they're doing and how to, like, trap and exterminate."

Kel glances up, not pausing his movements. "In a perfect world, the national guard would already be here."

Effie rolls her lower lip between two fingers in empty, anxious thought as she watches him light up. His chest expands as he pulls the smoke into his lungs, holding it there as he catches her eyes and offers the pipe. "Fuck it." She releases her lip to take it as he blows smoke into the air above their heads. It's thick and fragrant, making her mouth water.

"Hell yeah, Blake, that's the spirit." Kel flicks the lighter on, holding the flame as she draws in a deep breath. The smoke goes straight to her head as the sparkle in his gray eyes goes right to her stomach. She blows out slowly, fighting against the itch in her throat as a pleasant tingle spreads from her head through her body, melting seamlessly with whatever had been pooling in her core and turning it to heat.

The storm rages in full force outside, the camper shaking with a clap of thunder.

"Do you like storms?" Effie asks, watching him take another hit.

He shrugs, passing both pipe and lighter her way. "I guess it depends on what you mean by 'like.' I'm intrigued by how weather phenomena are created in the atmosphere and the physics behind it and the chaotic chemical changes that make them so hard to accurately predict. I don't at all enjoy driving in a rainstorm or having my clothes soaked through."

She snorts, which turns into a harsh cough from the smoke just released from her lungs. "God, you're such a nerd." She knocks her shoulder into his as she says it, and doesn't pull back all the way.

"What, and I suppose your answer is simple?" he asks, playfully tugging on a lock of her hair.

"Yes, actually, it is." She pauses as more thunder rumbles over the mountains. "I find them soothing. The smells, the sounds, the way they wash everything away and leave it glistening ..." She bites her lip, tilting her head to meet his gaze and feeling a warm buzz of satisfaction to find his own on her mouth. Tentatively, she reaches up to trace the scant beginnings of stubble along his jaw, watching his Adam's apple bob as he swallows. "Tell me, doctor science man, what are the odds that out of everyone out there, we were the only ones to see Gordon fall and then harbor enough curiosity to go look for him?"

His lips quirk, and he pulls her hand from his face, bringing it down to the table to fidget with it, tracing her fingers with his, drawing shapes against her palm. "I'd love nothing more than to calculate them for you, Blake, but I'd need to know a few things first."

Her head is light, her body is buzzing, and her chest is tight with the effects of that innocent touch. Not to mention the way her stomach dips when he calls her by her last name. She watches, teeth sunk into her lower lip as he concentrates on their hands. "What things?" she prompts softly.

Those gray eyes—hued such a pale blue—flick up to her, a wickedly charming grin pulling his mouth before his attention falls back to his study of her hand. "Easiest would be to calculate the number of people who are close enough to have seen or predicted the area Gordon landed and able to make it out here in the allotted time frame. More difficult, we'd need to figure out how many of those people would have a) been awake at three in the fucking morning, and b) looking at the sky."

"Ah, so simple enough then," she replies, unsure if her mouth is dry from the pot or the way his leg has shifted to press against hers.

"Or you could always take the stance that, mathematics aside, fate would have assured that we were both at that trailhead Friday night. That team Curtis-Blake was always our destiny, if that's your brand of philosophy." He peeks up at her again as he says it, and she knows he's being sarcastic.

Rolling her eyes, she pulls her hand away to grab a bottle of water and take a few sips, somehow managing to spill, and drags the cuff of her flannel across her mouth before waving her hand dismissively. "Oh, I'm more of an absurdist."

Kel laughs, grabbing his own water bottle, which he drinks from much more neatly, followed by a handful of chips. "Absurdist makes sense for you."

"I'm choosing to take that as a compliment," she replies, taking another drink of water, able to keep it all in her mouth this time. "What about you?"

"Would I take being labeled absurd as a compliment? Hmm." He strokes his chin in mocking contemplation.

"You're a smartass, you know that?"

"Takes one to know one, my dear Elizabeth." He taps her on the nose, and she pretends to try to bite him for it, her teeth snapping together with an audible click. He grins, dropping his hand back to the table. "I'm a scientist, which means I'm some unfortunate mix of practicalist and theorist."

She pats his cheek and pouts in sympathetic agreement. "So unfortunate." Her fingers curl around his jaw.

In a mimic of her move, he dips his head, and his teeth close around the heel of her hand with a light pressure that sends a somersault through her belly. His eyes stay locked on hers until she pulls her hand back, and he tracks the movement, curiosity replacing the heat in his expression.

He takes her hand again, pushing down the cuff of her flannel with his thumb. His head cants to the side as he reads the old, faded writing. "Call Mom."

Effie giggles, slapping her free hand over her mouth. "I forgot again. That's been on my list all week."

His eyebrow lifts along with a corner of his mouth. "Your list?"

It takes her longer than it should to answer the question, because she can't pull her attention from his lips. "I write things on my wrists so I don't forget them. Paper is too easy to lose track of, and palms get washed too thoroughly too often."

"Light year?" He reads the words she'd scrawled in the truck earlier.

Her cheeks heat. "You said to ask you about it when you're high. I didn't want to forget."

He searches her face, head still tilted, and her eyes flit to those burnished gold curls that she wants so badly to run her fingers through. "You didn't want to forget to ask me to explain how wild a concept five-point-eight trillion miles is or the fact that our closest galaxy neighbor is 25,000 of them away?"

"Yeah." She bites her lip again, giving in to the impulse and reaching out. His hair is soft and warm, and the tips of her fingers brush against his scalp as she combs through it. "It sounded like something you're really interested in."

His lips twitch, and he raises his hand to her wrist, wrapping his fingers around it so that they rest over her pulse point but not moving her away. "Keep touching me like that, Blake, and see what happens." He says it lowly, evenly, with his eyes on hers, and her heart is stuck somewhere between her throat and her stomach. She can't ascertain which, she only knows it's no longer where it's supposed to be.

But the challenge in his voice sends heat pooling in her core, and she's not really thinking of anything other than the aching need building low in her core when she brings her other hand up to run the backs of her fingers down his cheek with a smirk. "Don't threaten me with a warning."

Then his hand is no longer on her wrist, but the back of her neck, his fingers tangling in her hair as he pulls her mouth to his. Her fingers twitch, holding him there, and she sighs.

Kel's other arm wraps around her back, pulling her with him as he turns, leaning against the wall so their legs are draped over the bench seat. His tongue is in her mouth, and she slides hers across it greedily. His lips are soft and taste faintly of weed and barbecue, and her fingers tighten in his hair in an effort to pull him closer. Every nerve ending in her body seems to be tingling, and a stifled, needy whimper crawls up her throat with the want for *more*.

Then his hands are on her ass, and he raises one of his legs, wedging it between hers as he pulls her closer and slides his hands under her shirt. Effie grinds down against his leg, biting on his lip as she gasps softly and releases his hair to roam his body as he does the same to her.

He groans when her fingers skim his waist, hips flexing up to meet her touch. The sound runs straight to her center, and she's hungry to hear it again. She fumbles with his belt, prying open the button on his jeans, and that strangled groan rewards her as soon as her fingers make contact with his skin.

His hands tighten on her hips, his own fingers curled into her waistband. He sits up, nipping her neck as she palms his length. "I have a bed," he starts, pulling away.

She grins, removing her hand and using the newfound leverage to roll her hips against his erection. "Congratulations, that's an impressive accomplishment," she says breathlessly before leaning forward to kiss him.

"Who's the smartass now?" he asks, biting her lip.

"Takes one to know one," she tosses his words back to him, wiggling a little less than gracefully from his lap.

He leads her to the bedroom, then rifles around in a drawer for a moment before setting a box of condoms on one of the shelves in easy reach of the bed. Then he steps back in front of her, and every beat of her heart sends anticipation and need coursing through her.

She doesn't know who kisses who this time, only that their lips and tongues are connected as Kel lowers her onto the bed, then their hands are roaming and their clothes come off and she bites his shoulder to keep from begging.

His hands are in her hair, and she clutches his face, and he's thrusting into her, groaning and cursing and whispering her name. Every nerve in her body is alight and aware of every place he touches her, and how deliciously *full* she is, and she doesn't know if what's tumbling from her mouth are words or unintelligible noises, she just knows that she doesn't want him to stop because everything in her is ignited, sensations intensified by her high, and she willingly loses herself in him.

Neither of them notice when the storm ends. It's not until Effie is lying on her side, facing Kel as his fingers drift through her hair, the blankets pooled around their waists, that she realizes the patter of rain no longer dominates the background. It hits her so suddenly that she stops midway through her lecture on cryptids and the possibility that maybe they're also all aliens. "The rain's gone," she says, pushing herself up to peer through the window. Stars twinkle back at her through a patchwork of clouds, confirming her suspicion.

She turns to look at Kel, whose gaze rakes unashamedly down her exposed body before raising back up to meet hers. "You know what that means?" he asks when she slides back down next to him. "It's time for the best part of the night—hold on, no." He holds his hand up before she can say anything. "I mean, it's the best part of the night when I'm high by myself. Obviously we're working on a much different scale here."

Effie laughs, motioning for him to continue. "I promise my ego is fine. What is it time for?"

"Snacks and stargazing." He grins, pushing his hair back from his forehead.

His excitement bleeds easily into her. "Well, what the fuck are we waiting for?"

12

After they clean up, Kel is standing at the stove in a pair of sweatpants, backward hat securing his hair. He's just finished packing another bowl when Effie exits the bathroom. She's also in a pair of his sweats and a faded NASA crewneck with the sleeves pushed up to her elbows. Aside from his hat, he's never been overly sentimental about clothes, but he decides then and there that sweatshirt is his new favorite.

"So what's the snack?" she asks as he lights up, grabbing a bottle of water before hopping onto the counter. He offers the pipe and she accepts, inhaling as he gets a pan heating on the stove.

When she hands it back, he takes another hit and then taps out the embers, setting the pipe on the windowsill and gesturing to the ingredients on the opposite side of the stove from Effie. "How do you feel about quesadillas?"

"Solid choice, Dr. Curtis," she compliments before taking a long drink of water. Then she eyes the bottle, holding it up to the light. Kel is about to ask if she sees anything, concerned, when she finally speaks again. "Did you know that pee comes from your blood?"

It's the last thing he expected to hear from her, and he can't keep the smile from stretching his mouth as he generously spreads butter across tortillas.

"All the liquid you intake is absorbed into your bloodstream," she continues without prompting, tucking her hair behind her ears and kicking her feet lightly against the cabinets. "That's why things like alcohol are measured by blood-alcohol content."

"Huh, I'd never even thought about it before." He looks from the movement of her feet to her face. She looks carefree, happy, and it instantly soothes his initial discomfort at the tap of her heels against the doors beneath her. Seeing her so at home in the space he curated specifically for himself—a place that was only his and not influenced by any outside opinion—should feel foreign, but it doesn't. Realizing he drifted off, he throws one of the tortillas into the skillet, grating the block of cheddar over it and tuning back in to the conversation.

"All your blood runs through your kidneys," Effie tells him confidently. "Your kidneys filter out all the extra liquid that your blood doesn't need and send it to your bladder, thus, pee is just excess moisture from blood."

"They teach you that in air traffic control school?" He sprinkles a fajita seasoning mix over the cheese and then tops it with another tortilla, letting it rest for a moment before flipping it with a spatula.

She rolls her eyes. "Spaceman's got jokes."

Leaning a hip against the counter on the other side of the

stove, he cocks an eyebrow at her. "What other fun body facts do you know?"

Effie purses her lips, eyes floating up to the ceiling as she thinks. "So, you know how cannibalism is okay?"

He chokes on a laugh, transferring the quesadilla from the skillet to a plate and starting the second cooking. "Do I want to know where that introduction is going?"

"Not that it's *okay* okay, I mean okay in that your body can process human muscle meat just as easily as any other animal," she persists. "But humans *cannot* eat the brains of another human, which is what makes zombie lore so fun. Human brains will royally fuck up your nervous system."

"No brains in a survival situation, then. Duly noted." He continues cooking in silence, gradually becoming aware that she's watching him, and he cuts her a curious glance. Her face flames red, and she turns her attention to her lap, fidgeting with the hem of his sweatshirt. Her hair falls in front of her face when she dips her head, the blue contrasting starkly against the flush in her cheeks, and he suddenly realizes how much the color suits her. Effie in a natural hue just wouldn't feel right.

He takes a breath, preparing to tell her as much, and smells the food, catching it just on the cusp of overdone. Quickly turning off the stove, he plates the second quesadilla and cuts them both into quarters, then pulls a bottle of salsa verde from the fridge, drizzling it over one of them before looking to Effie in question.

"Sour cream?" She slides down from the counter and accepts the second plate.

He shakes his head with a scoff. "Not in this camper."

"What kind of self-respecting person eats quesadillas without sour cream?" she asks indignantly.

"Blake, it's *sour* cream," he emphasizes. "Why would you ever put *soured* cream on anything you want to enjoy?"

"Because it's tasty as fuck." The "duh" is missing from the end of her sentence, but heavily implied by her tone as she takes a hefty bite.

Kel shakes his head at her in fond amusement. If everything goes to shit, he's glad to have met her before it happens. "Come on." He walks to the door, handing his plate to her as he slips a hoodie over his head. After readjusting his hat, he reaches for his truck keys, making sure it's unlocked.

"After you." He holds the door open for Effie, then follows her out and grabs a tarp and a thick woven blanket from the back seat of the truck, tucking it under his arm and walking over to the tent pad.

He spreads both tarp and blanket on the ground and helps her down. "Sit tight, I'll be right back," he tells her, returning to the camper to grab his telescope.

"You are nothing if not predictable," she informs him happily, watching as he sets it up.

After making all the necessary adjustments, he settles next to her, close enough that their arms touch, and she leans into him. The air is crisp, chill from the passing storm, but with virtually no wind. "You wanna see something cool?" he offers, gesturing to the eyepiece.

She sets her plate aside and situates herself to peer through. "Holy shit," she breathes. "Kel ... it's beautiful."

"Saturn's in opposition with the sun right now," he tells her, his own gaze drifting up to the sky. "You can actually see its rings with the naked eye tonight and tomorrow."

"What's opposition?" she asks, briefly looking up with a curious smile.

And so he ends up explaining planetary rotations and the

order of the solar system as they eat, trading off looking through the telescope. He shows her how to adjust it, letting her explore the stars. The campsite is void of light pollution, the few other campers already asleep or shrouded by trees and brush. Despite the scattered clouds, the night is perfect for it.

Kel occasionally glances at her, something soft and unnamed warming in him at her undiluted awe and the way she eats like a raccoon, the quesadilla clasped in both hands, bringing it to her mouth to rip off each bite. A smile pulls at the corner of his mouth.

As if she can feel him watching, she pulls away from the eyepiece. "What are you smiling about?"

"I enjoy you," he answers simply, setting his empty plate aside and lying back on the blanket, an arm tucked under his head as he looks at the bright, crowded band of the Milky Way.

Effie lies next to him, using his arm as a pillow. "I enjoy you, too," she breathes, so soft he almost doesn't catch it, and it wraps around his chest like a vise.

Silence settles over them, and they watch as more of the sky slowly becomes visible, huddled together under the light of the moon. Kel names the stars in his head as Effie uses her pointer finger to trace her own patterns in them, lost in her thoughts.

She turns to look at him, and when he does the same, their faces are so close their noses brush. Her chin tips up so that her lips ghost across his, and she cups his cheek, her fingers like ice as they trace the line of his jaw.

"You're right," she whispers, her breath warm against his skin. "Sex was good, but this is magic."

And he knows that there's not a single other person on this Earth he would rather team up with in the face of certain peril.

"What's up, mountain dwellers? Welcome back to Adult Daycare with Dan and Darcy, where we're going to play you all the best hits to go along with your night and bring the party. As always, we're gonna kick off the hour with some what-to-expect. How are things out there, Darce?"

"Well, I hope you've all been enjoying this gorgeous Saturday afternoon we've been having, because there's rain in the forecast, and those clouds are rolling in. This might be for the best, though, because from what I've heard, there's been some trouble out in Telluride."

"Trouble? You know we love some trouble here."

"Not that kind of trouble, Dan. I'm talking about the kind that comes with flashing lights and sirens."

"Uh-oh. What's going on?"

"Well, that's just the thing: no one really knows. What I can tell you for certain is that the road up to Alta Lakes is completely blocked off, so I hope no one was planning to do any fishing or hiking up that way this weekend. But word around town is that one of the mountain biking trails was also roped off at some point this morning, closed to all traffic."

"Could just be routine maintenance. Maybe the trail got washed out?"

"That's not what people have been saying. Depending who you ask, the two incidents are connected and there's something to be afraid of out in the mountains."

"Ha, that sounds like a bunch of conspiracy mumbo jumbo to me, but what do you guys think? Call in and let us know if you've seen anything weird around here! In the meantime, enjoy a few minutes of uninterrupted music, and as always, thanks for listening to 97.1 KSOC, your number one alt rock radio destination."

Day 4

1

Despite his exhaustion, Lance is up with the sun. He dresses in plainclothes, then drops a kiss to Danielle's forehead.

His wife stirs, grabbing his hand. "What time is it?"

"Early," he says, rubbing his thumb over the back of her hand.

"Mmm. Will you be gone all day?" She peels one eye open to meet his gaze.

"I hope not. My goal is to be back by lunch. Dinner for sure."

Her eye slips shut, and she nods into the pillow. "Let me know."

"I will. I love you."

"Love you, too," she mumbles, giving his fingers a final squeeze before going back to sleep.

He checks in on the girls before he leaves, each sleeping soundly, and his heart clenches. He's doing this for them. Better to know what's out there, so that he knows what he needs to protect them from. He holds that thought fast in his mind as he backs down the drive, heading toward the city of Montrose to find an offering for the Azathothlin.

An offering—like sacrificing a feeder rodent will keep the alien named after a cosmic god from leaving the bowels of the Earth. Lance snorts, half a smile tugging at his mouth at the absurdity of both the thought and the situation.

Two and a half hours and an uncomfortable prick on his conscience later, he's turning off the road to the base of Alta Lakes with a cardboard carrier in his passenger seat. He can't remember who was on schedule to monitor the blockade, but he's never been happier to see Griffin's curious face behind the wheel of the parked cruiser and sends up a silent prayer of thanks that it wasn't McCurdy he'd have to try to explain himself to.

Leaving the car running, Lance throws the gearshift into park and steps out. "Morning, Griffin," he greets.

The deputy wipes the back of his hand across his mouth, brushing free crumbs of what looks like a ham and egg croissant from his mustache. "Good morning, Chief. Aren't you off today?"

"Wish it worked that easy," he chuckles. "There's something up at Alta I need to check for Fish and Wildlife." He waffles around with what to say, but finally decides to stick as close to the truth as possible. "I guess they got a report that one of the mines up in Gold King Basin had been busted open. I just want to poke around and see if maybe that bear isn't holed up in there."

Griffin's eyebrows raise. "Oh, no shit?—Shit. Sorry, sir—No kidding, huh? Want company?"

Lance knows the deputy is eager to move, not prone to waiting around all day, and he feels for him, even as he shakes his head. "I appreciate the offer, but it's best if you stay down here, especially with it still being a weekend. Can't have anyone slipping by."

"Right. Well, hope it goes well."

"If I find anything interesting, I'll radio you," he offers, knowing he'll do no such thing but wanting to see the younger man's countenance brighten regardless.

It works, and Griffin smiles. "Thanks, Chief." He starts the cruiser, backing up to give Lance room to drive by. With a final wave of thanks, Lance heads up the pitted dirt road that will take him up to the alien's supposed lair.

The drive up the mountain is ominous in a way he knows is just in his head. Even the glare of the morning sun feels like it's trying to warn him, and he struggles to brush off the feeling.

He pulls through two large boulders that sit on either side of the road at the basin's opening, following the dirt track around a small lake to the base of the scree-fall, staring up at the dark mouth of the mine.

His gaze falls to the cardboard carrier in his passenger seat as he turns off the car. "Sorry about this, bud. Just know it's for the greater good."

He fits a rubber glove over his hand before sliding the plastic case containing the tracker chip from his jacket pocket.

There's an open bag of sunflower seeds sitting on the center console next to the cup holders, and he grabs a couple with his non-gloved hand, carefully popping open the top of the cardboard box and dropping them in.

The rat inside peers up at him suspiciously for a moment before stepping forward to munch on the offered treat. Lance moves his attention to the slim plastic casing, prying it open with a fingernail and popping the chip free. It's smaller than his thumbnail and about as thick as a credit card. Holding it carefully in his gloved fingers, he pinches the small portion of hanging backing to peel the paper from the adhesive. Dropping a few more seeds into the box to keep the rat occupied, he reaches in to press the chip at the nape of the rat's neck.

This causes the rat to jump around with a grumbling squeal, and he tosses it a couple additional seeds for the trouble. "My bad, bud. Looks like it's pretty secure, at least." He closes up the top, slips off the glove and tucks it into the door, then steps out of the car, carrier in hand.

His steps sound loud in the stillness of the morning, setting him on edge, but the sun beating down, bleeding warmth through his jacket, offsets any chill his mind creates. When he arrives at the entrance to the mine, he reaches for the Maglite on his utility belt before remembering he's not wearing his uniform. His sidearm, though, is a comforting weight on his hip, an accessory he's almost never without.

Lance peers into the gaping hole that leads into the mountain, shading his eyes in a vain attempt to see further inside. The plywood that had previously been blocking the entrance was thrown several feet away, a hefty padlock lying useless, still locking two ends of a chain together.

He takes only a couple steps into the entrance, then kneels, popping open the cardboard box and gently tipping it onto its side as he sets it down.

The rat jumps free before the box touches the ground, landing in the dirt and spinning to look at Lance, little nose twitching. Then it turns and scampers off into the dark, taking the little tracker chip with it.

He stands, brushing dirt from his pant leg as he walks back to the car, and tosses the carrier into the back seat. He glances at his watch, eager to be back home and spend the day with his girls.

As soon as his tires hit level ground, he can feel the muscles in his shoulders finally relaxing, and he tilts his head back against the seat rest.

Then his work cell rings, cutting straight through his easy demeanor. He waits for the car's Bluetooth to pick it up, eyes flicking to the dash display to see who's calling.

McCurdy.

He sighs. Of course the day couldn't be that easy. "Chief Sutherland," he answers, already reaching for the canister of nicotine pouches in the side of the door.

"You'd better get up to Bridal Veil, Chief. There's been another attack."

2

0951 MDT//4d 6hr 48min after arrival

Effie stretches in her sleep, and her foot brushes against something warm and solid. Awareness floods her as her heart lurches into her throat until she remembers where she is, and she settles back into the mattress, bringing her hands to her eyes to help clear them of sleep.

Kel is already awake, scrolling on his phone with an arm tucked beneath his head, and she rolls over to face him, inadvertently pressing her leg against his.

He glances over at her with a soft, "Morning."

She offers a sleepy smile in return, admiring the rumpled disarray of his curls and the voluminous length of his eyelashes, highlighted by the scant light slipping past the blinds.

Heat blooms across her cheeks when he notices her staring, but he just tilts the phone screen toward her in offering. "Want to see what's new in science this morning?"

She nods, and he pulls his arm out from under his head, holding it open so she can wiggle closer, laying her cheek against his chest.

While lazily drawing his fingers through her hair, he explains the Reddit thread he's currently viewing, comments underneath an article about radio waves detected from some distant galaxy, but her mind doesn't attach to any of it. She's too focused on the solid warmth of him against her, the gentle rise and fall of his chest, the gravelly timbre of his voice, still thick with sleep. It's all so insanely grounding, the reality of last night's planning still dark and fresh, but less terrifying in the light of day, lying in Kel's bed.

The knowledge that this moment is fleeting—that soon they will have to start putting their plan into action—is nipping at her, threatening to chase away the peaceful perfection of the morning, but she refuses to let it. Instead, she hooks one of her legs over his and drags her hand up his chest to rest by her face. She smiles at the way he chokes on his words at the touch, but then she starts asking him questions about the article, prolonging this moment in time for as long as possible.

As he talks, his hand gradually glides from her hair to her shoulder, then down her arm to her side, tracing intentional lines that make her shiver. She tips her face up to nuzzle his neck, drawing her hand down his belly to the front of his pants. He grips her side when she draws her fingers over the fabric, feeling him grow hard, and she slips beneath his waistband, palming him and nipping at the base of his jaw.

Kel makes a strangled sound, his hips rising to meet her. Then his phone is gone, and his hands are on her waist, hauling her on top of him. Effie sucks in a breath, grinding down onto him, aware only of his touch roaming her body, rolling her nipples, gripping her ass. Her shirt is quickly discarded, and she raises up on her knees, allowing him to slip out of his pants, then shifts to discard her own.

Then his hands are back on her waist, fingers digging into her hips as she rocks herself against him, watching the wild light in his eyes as he looks at where they're pressed together. She leans over to grab a condom from the shelf, raising only long enough to slip it over him. Slowly, she lowers herself until he's seated fully within her, and everything after that is heated and heavy as they move together, chasing their pleasure.

When it's over, Effie collapses next to him, sweaty and panting from both exertion and release. Kel presses a kiss against the top of her head, and she burrows into him, tipping her face up to lick some of the salt from his neck.

He shivers, shifting away from her with a laugh. "I knew that cannibalism factoid should have been concerning."

"Had to get you comfortable and off your guard before I made my move." She flashes him a smile of mock satisfaction as he brushes her hair back from her face. The low lighting gives his eyes more of a blue hue, and there's a softness in them that almost makes her feel self-conscious, like she wasn't aware of the intimacy of the moment until she saw it reflected there.

"We should get ready for the day," he says, angling his face down to brush his lips against hers.

She lets the kiss linger, fingers curling into his chest. "Gordon's an inconvenient little bastard, ain't he?"

"Most wonders of the universe are," he agrees, sitting up and running his fingers through his hair. "You can have the shower first, if you want it. I'd offer to share, but it's hardly big enough to turn around in."

"I might just shower at home, since I'll need to stop and change anyway, but give me a moment to clean up." Effie clambers out of bed, padding to the tiny bathroom to freshen up as much as possible before moving back to the bedroom to pick up her clothes and dress.

While Kel is in the shower, she grabs a bottle of water and sits at the table to call Bethany.

"Well, look who's awake before noon," her friend answers.

"Please, I'm not that bad," Effie defends. "But listen, I'm gonna have to rain check today."

"Woman, you're killing me."

"I know, I know, but I ended up spending the night with Kel—" she pulls her phone away from her ear when Bethany squeals. "Chill out, psycho, I'm still with him," she chastises lightly.

"Rain check approved. But you'd better send me a fucking picture—as soon as you hang up—and then I need *details* the moment you're on your own again."

"Okay, I promise," Effie laughs. "Later, Beth."

"Stay hydrated, Beth," Bethany teases before hanging up.

True to her word, Effie grabs a quick screenshot from Kel's Instagram account to send, then types out a text to Lance.

> Effie: Are you home? I really want to talk

> Effie: I'm person

> Effie: In*

When she hears Kel leave the bathroom, she straightens, giving him a few minutes to get dressed before she joins him. "Want to do breakfast at my place and head into town from there?"

He's pulling a shirt over his head, hair a light molasses color with moisture that leaves damp spots around the collar. "Yeah, that works for me. You ready?"

"Whenever you are."

It takes him a few moments to collect his things and pack his laptop into a bag, then they're out the door.

Effie glances at her phone as Kel drives, but the only notification is from Bethany.

> **Beth1st: I approve. And I expect a full dissertation of a run-down later.**

But not so much as a read receipt from her cousin.

"I texted Lance," she says, hoping that, on some metaphysical level, talking about him will make his ears burn so that he checks his phone. "If he knows that we know—if I can talk to him in person—maybe he'll finally stop trying to pretend that this is just a feral animal and offer some real help."

"Do you trust him?" Kel asks.

She pinches at her lip. "I've looked up to him my entire life. Truly, I can't remember a single time he wasn't there for me. I at least trust him enough to take me seriously."

"He seemed to blow you off pretty quickly yesterday," Kel reminds her softly.

"Phones are different from face to face. Plus ..." She drifts off with a shrug, unsure if she wants to voice this line of thought. "It's the fact that he *did* blow me off that I keep coming back to. He didn't even ask what I thought I saw up there."

"You think he knows something?"

"At this point, I'd be more shocked if he doesn't." She frowns at the trees. "The real question, then, is why he hasn't tried to bring in a higher authority to help." The thought sits heavy in her stomach, accompanying her the rest of the drive and lingering even after her shower.

She sits at the breakfast bar, methodically working her way through a bowl of Lucky Charms as Kel looks through more data on his laptop, a plate of mostly finished eggs and toast to the side. She'd offered to cook, thinking that something more substantial would be a good start to the day, but as the eggs simmered in the pan, the knot in her stomach wound tighter, and she'd decided to default to comfort food instead.

Kel looks more frustrated than anything. Daphne has finally emailed him back, but it's mostly just a list of what looks like a lot of math, so she's content to let him sort through it on his own.

Her phone vibrates on the counter, startling her, and she drops her spoon into her bowl with a clatter, splashing a few drops of milk over the sides. It's her mom, and while she doesn't really have the bandwidth for it today, she knows she can't decline the call.

"Hi, Mom."

"Elizabeth, it's good to hear from you, honey. If it weren't for your aunt passing me reports through Lance, I'd worry something might have happened to you."

"Sorry. I meant to call a few days ago, but you know how it is with the night shift."

"Well, there's not much new here. Your step-daddy and I are still planning on visiting sometime in the fall ... unless you're planning to make the trip out here?"

Effie sighs. "Probably not this year."

"What's new with you? Do you think we'll be meeting a boy when we come to visit?"

"Mom, what? No." Her cheeks flush red. Kel looks up at her, which only makes her face heat further.

"What about any of the guys you work with? No one catches your eye?" There's a needling hope in her mother's voice.

Don't shit where you eat is what Effie wants to reply, but her mother wouldn't appreciate the phrasing. "I don't really get to interact with other people much with my schedule."

"You know, you might attract a nice man easier if you don't wear men's clothes all the time. They might all think you're a lesbian, honey. Not that we'd have a problem if you were, of course. I just mean that might be why they don't approach you."

"*Mom*," Effie groans, but can't refute the statement. The green flannel she's currently wearing open over her sports bra is a purposefully oversized men's XL. "My clothes are fine. They're comfortable, and you need layers up here."

"I know, I know. I'm sorry, I don't mean to nag, you know that. And I think you look cute no matter what you wear."

"I kinda dig the flannels," Kel says quietly, eyes on his computer, and Effie's face gets impossibly hotter with the realization that he can hear everything from across the counter. "But they don't hold a candle to the men's clothes you wore last night."

Her mom doesn't hear him, but Effie is so flustered she completely misses what her mom says next. Before she can ask her to repeat it, her phone buzzes, and she pulls it from her ear to see a notification from Lance, saving her from the conversation. "I've gotta go, Mom—something just came up. We'll talk again soon, okay?"

"What is it, Elizabeth? Is something wrong?"

"No, no, Lance needs something."

"Well, alright. Call me back when you can, honey. We love you."

"Love you, too." Effie says a quick goodbye, hanging up and immediately opening her texts while she waits for the flush to leave her skin.

"I guess you can remove 'call Mom' from the list." Kel mops up the last bit of egg yolk with a piece of toast.

"You're lucky she didn't hear you or I'd remove *you* from the list," she retorts. "And you'd have to finish the rest of that phone call because I wouldn't be able to deal with her right now."

"Back up there, Blake. I made the list?"

And Effie's face goes red again, her left hand moving to cover up her right wrist, even though she'd washed the ink from both during her shower. She doesn't know how to explain that she taught herself to write with both hands so that more important things could go on her right wrist, because she doesn't know how to explain why she'd deemed him important. "I didn't want to forget your name," she says, hoping he'll let it rest there and pushing forward to more pressing matters. "Lance is going to be here soon. Help me go over what I'm supposed to tell him?"

3

1106 MDT//4d 8hr 3min after arrival

Lance drags his hands down his face, exhausted beyond measure. He's just finished sending off his report to the agency, hoping that they'll take him a little more seriously now that there are another two deaths on their hands. On *his* hands.

He's complicit in this.

Nausea burns in his stomach, and he fishes a roll of Tums from his pocket, popping a couple of the chalky, mint-flavored tabs into his mouth. If it weren't for the agency, he'd have called in help long before it ever reached this point, and he'd also be keeping people out of the mountains until they could get it sorted out.

At least he's headed home now. And the sun is shining, so good ol' 240 shouldn't be causing any more trouble for the next several hours.

He dials Danielle once he's in the car.

"Girls? Girls! Quiet down." Her voice is accompanied by high-pitched, off-tune singing that's probably closer to a screech. The singing drops a few decibels, but is still discernible in the background. "Sorry, babe. How's work?"

Despite the chaos, hearing his family has a soothing effect, and he can't help but chuckle. "Is that *The Lion King* I hear?"

"They're not even watching it, just taking turns being Simba and playing some strange version of the floor is lava," Danielle answers with a laugh, the noise in the background fading as she presumably relocates. "They're imaginative little hellions, I'll give them that."

"I'll run them around outside this afternoon to burn some of that energy off," he promises. "I might lose service in a bit; I just wanted to let you know I'm on the way home. Effie wants to talk when I get back, but I'll be in after that."

"Sounds good, honey. We'll see you soon."

"I love you."

"Love you, too."

They exchange goodbyes, and he ends the call, trying to hold on to that sense of warmth the rest of the drive.

He pulls into the driveway, barely having time to park and shut off the engine before Effie's front door opens. She tugs it closed, a hand running through her short blue hair before lowering to her mouth to chew at her pinky nail as she sets off across the yard.

They meet halfway, Lance resting his hands on his hips for lack of something better to do with them.

His cousin shifts on her feet for a moment before planting them firmly, and he can't help but feel like she's squaring up for a fight. When she lifts her eyes to his, a determined pull to her brow, he knows that's exactly what she's doing, and that pit in his gut yawns open again.

He holds his palms up, opening his mouth to speak, but Effie doesn't give him the chance.

"I know it's not a bear up there, Lance, and I think you do, too." She crosses her arms over her chest and tips her chin up, the glint in her hazel eyes daring him to counter her.

He keeps his expression even, gaze unwavering from hers. "I don't—"

"Nope," she interrupts. "Let me say it once more, with feeling: I *know* it's not a bear."

He sighs in resignation, dragging a hand down his beard. "Why couldn't you stay out of it, Eff?"

She pulls her gaze away, the combative set to her shoulders falling. "Nothing felt right about the situation, so I needed to look for myself. There's a ... a thing living up there, and I know how this is going to sound, but I SAW something fall from the sky and land in those mountains. If there's not an alien living up there, then whatever fell hit hard enough to wake up some sort of underground monster that no one has ever seen before. And I'm not stupid—I went to the ranger station in Norwood, but they won't listen. They won't listen and people are *dying*, and we could really use your help."

Everything Lance had been about to say blanks at her last sentence. "We?" He doesn't know whether to be thankful she was smart enough not to go alone or freak out that more people know. Did she go with Bethany? If Bethany knows, Griffin will know, and then it's only a matter of time before the whole department knows, and their families, and the town—but then he notices the giant white truck parked on the other side of her Jeep, unsure how he missed it before.

"Kel—Dr. Curtis. He's an astrophysicist and—"

"That kid who was at the trailhead the other day?" Relief floods Lance's veins even as irritation creeps up his neck. Of course no one knows how to listen to authority and mind their own business anymore.

Effie rolls her eyes, either at the interruption or the descriptor. "One and the same."

He grinds his teeth together, trying to figure out whether or not he needs to report this as a potential leak.

"And he's, like, thirty-two, so don't be a demeaning asshole. We're all adults here." She levels him with another glare, and he fights back the urge to snort, like age has anything to do with this shit.

A shadow flickers over them, and her head tilts back to follow the flight-path of the hawk over them. *Redtail?* He guesses distractedly, racking his brain for the right words to get her to leave it the fuck alone.

"Sharpie," she whispers the bird's identification, a hint of a smile twitching at the corner of her mouth. Then, she turns her gaze back to him and continues quietly, "It attacked me." And Lance is immediately focused on her and her alone. "We were in Gold King Basin. Kel was looking for signs of the meteorite, and it came over the ridge. I … It saw me, maybe too close to its home, I don't know, but it made this horrible noise, almost like the cry of a snowy egret, but deeper. Angrier." She shudders. "And then it ran at me. It moved over the rocks like … wrong? Just too smooth and all of its legs were out of sync. Kel saved me by shooting it with a flare, and it ran off into one of the old mines up there after that."

If Lance clenches his teeth any harder, they'll crack. His mind is spinning, weighing everything he knows and every commitment he's made. In the end, it's not the thought of that crunched up hatchback at the base of the waterfall and the deaths of the innocent that break him. It's the look on Effie's face, resolute in her knowledge, but backlit by a vulnerability that not many get to see, pleading with him to validate what she already knows. Effie, who's always been too smart and too stubborn for her own damn good, and never once had to question whether or not he would have her back when it came down to it.

It's that unwavering trust that he can't bring himself to break. Not when it's had twenty-eight years to take root, and not when his own daughters look up to her the same way she looks up to him.

He relaxes his jaw, an unexpected peace easing his mind now that a decision has been made. "Can we go inside?" he asks, gesturing to her casita.

She eyes him, equally wary and hopeful, before leading him across the yard. She pauses with her hand on the doorknob, looking back at him with an abashed smile. "Just so you know, Kel's here, too."

"Figured, because of that behemoth of a truck." He jerks his head in the direction of the vehicle.

"He's helping me. We're a team, at least until we can prove what we saw up there, and he's more qualified for this than I am."

Lance will *definitely* have to tell the agency about both of them. There are protocols for dealing with citizens who've seen things they aren't supposed to, for giving them incentives to keep quiet. But that's a worry for later. He nods, resigned to his lot, and follows Effie inside.

Kel is sitting at the breakfast bar and turns from his laptop when they enter.

"Kel, this is Lance," she introduces, turning to give Lance a pointed look. "If we want to get all official about it, he's Chief Deputy Sutherland. In which case, Lance, this is Dr. Curtis."

Standing, Kel pushes up his glasses and holds out his hand. "I believe we met the other morning, but it's a pleasure to be officially acquainted."

Lance shakes it. "Should we sit down and hash this out, then?"

Effie nods, leading the way to the living room. Lance raises a brow when she settles next to Kel on the couch, closer than strictly necessary. She raises hers back at him in a way that clearly communicates he can mind his own business.

Taking a seat in the armchair across from them, he can't help but feel like a line has been drawn, separating them as two opposing sides. He pushes away the notion, leaning forward with his elbows resting against his knees as he tries to think through how much information to spill. "I know about the Azathothlin," he starts.

"The what?" Effie asks.

Kel's eyes narrow in thought for a moment, and then he laughs. "Lovecraft. I like it."

Effie gives him a skeptical look. "Well, there's something un-predictable after all."

"It's sci-fi if you squint," he replies with a grin, then his eyes flash to Lance watching them, and he shifts uncomfortably.

Effie's lips quirk, but she turns back to Lance without com-ment. "Explain?"

"Azathothlin is the name they—" he physically bites his tongue, but Effie's brows have already shot up, and she leans forward.

"Lancelot Sutherland of the good king's round table, are you in on some secret squirrel shit?"

He places his palms together in front of his face, releasing a long breath before his gaze floats up to the ceiling. "Christ in a fucking Cracker Jack box." He drops his hands, knowing there's no turning back now. "There's an agency that knows about the creature you saw. This is the only one in our area, but they've seen others and have them well-monitored. They're convinced that it'll go underground soon and not come back out."

"There are others?" Effie's eyes grow wide.

Kel is frowning down at the carpet in a way that makes Lance uneasy.

"The point here is that they've told me there's nothing to worry about. I've brought up all of my concerns, I've reported every ... incident that I think is connected, and the official stance is that there is no cause for alarm."

"No cause for alarm?" Effie repeats with a scoff. "There are multiple of these creatures—these *aliens*—wandering around be-low us and there's no cause for alarm? They clearly eat peo-ple. They're dangerous. They could be reproducing by the hun-dreds—by the thousands, even, and—"

"Slow down, Eff," Lance interrupts. "Your concerns are valid, and trust me, I've already voiced them all myself. These things are all males, none of them has ever reproduced, and typically once they have one meal after arrival, they go underground and stay there. And before us, there's only been a handful of reports of human casualties."

"So why does ours keep popping back up to hunt?" she asks, almost pleading.

He opens his hands, palms up. He doesn't have an answer to that. "They have chips they use to track them. I sent one down into the mine today, so, if it comes back up, one of the techs at HQ will let me know. I'll go after it, kill it before it has a chance to do any more damage."

"And then what?" Effie crosses her arms, falling back into the cushions. "You just cover it up with a giant tarp? Nothing to see here? Does the agency come to collect it?"

Lance's brow furrows, and he shrugs. "I hadn't thought that far. I'll probably just throw it onto a trailer, take it up to the airport and have them come get it."

She snorts. "You have seen my runway, right? You can't land a cargo plane on it. It would roll right off the mountain trying to stop. Not to mention we're not rated for that kind of weight."

"Who said anything about a cargo plane?"

They look at each other in silence for a moment, both trying to figure the other out. "Are you planning to chop it up first, or ...?" Effie glances at Kel, but he's still working something out in his head.

"Chop it up?" Lance asks.

"That thing is fucking huge, dude," she says, exasperated. "You're not fitting it on a fucking citation."

Lance rolls his eyes. "They aren't *that* big."

Kel finally joins the conversation, then. "Ours is different," he says. "That's why it's not staying underground."

Lance scratches his head, trying to follow along. "You mean it's a different kind of alien?"

"No, no, that's highly improbable. I mean, if your people are saying that all of the Azathothlins that have come before are male, I think the one that landed here might be female."

4

1147 MDT//4d 8hr 44min after arrival

Effie is reeling from what Lance just told them, but Kel's addition, delivered so matter-of-factly, is another thing altogether. Before she can ask him to elaborate, he does, and she wants to roll her eyes at the theatrics of his timing except she suspects he doesn't even realize he's doing it, just sorting everything out in that methodically ordered brain of his.

"Let me guess," he starts. "You were told these things were roughly fifteen feet long, right?"

Lance's eyes narrow suspiciously. "Yeah."

Kel abruptly stands, grabbing his laptop from the breakfast bar. He clicks as he walks, dropping back down next to Effie and flipping it around so the screen faces them. "That's what wasn't making sense," he tells her, an excited light in his eyes that melts something inside of her. "Okay, there was a lot of this that wasn't making sense, so I should start from the beginning. I'll get back to the size, I promise, but bear with me.

"The day after I saw the Azathothlin fall, I had a colleague send me a bunch of different readings from satellites and telescopes, but there was absolutely no imagery. That threw me for a fucking loop, but it makes more sense now. If multiple of these things have found their way here, and this agency knows about them, presumably they've got plants in all parts of higher government."

Lance runs a hand through his hair with a bitter chuckle. "Not only did those bastards know it was coming, they figured out how to keep anyone else from tracking it or keeping a record of it."

Kel nods enthusiastically. "They'd have to have been. There's no indication of it going back at least several months. But the fact that even upon entry, not a single system registered it—"

"Fuck," Lance mutters, and something in his face twitches. "This whole thing goes so much deeper than I realized."

"I mean, yeah. If they not only have access to the satellite information but also the capability to alter what's recorded ... we're talking deep state levels of fuckery." There's a note in Kel's voice somewhere between awestruck and abhorrent.

Effie looks at Lance, an entirely new depth of unease blooming through her. "You've been working for them the whole time you've been here?"

"I was recruited before I was officially hired on, yeah." Lance meets her eyes, the sunlight through the window highlighting the silver hair at his temples. "They're not bad people, Eff. I saw how they're running things. These ... these creatures are under control; they're under constant monitoring. Keeping it all a secret is what's safest for the general public."

"Are you trying to convince me or yourself?" she asks evenly. She wants to be more accusatory, wants to ask how he could lie to her when she first told him her suspicions, but she can hardly muster a cohesive thought in this whirlwind of information.

"If your agency has been tracking this, then they already know what I'm about to tell you," Kel continues, breezing right past the emotional moment in the name of science. "Ours is much, *much* bigger."

Effie breaks eye contact with her cousin to look at the thermal image Kel is pointing to on the screen.

"As I said, they removed all of the imagery from every system I have access to, but when you look at thermal charts, you can see the way that this thing repels heat in the atmosphere. So I did the logical thing and tried to go back and look for other anomalies that matched, no images, just seemingly random repelled heat signatures." He flips the laptop around, clicking to a different window, then presents them with a spreadsheet filled with numbers and symbols that Effie recognizes from earlier.

"My colleague was able to find data going back a couple decades, but it's weird, because in every other instance, the signatures are all around fifteen feet long, when the one from Thursday measures at thirty-five." Kel looks from Effie to Lance expectantly. When neither speaks up, he pushes forward. "I'll admit I'm far from a biology expert, but I do have a few classes under my belt. The Azathothlins look pretty insectile in nature, and one almost universal fact about insects—"

"The females are bigger," Effie finishes, pressing her fingers against her mouth. "Gordon's a fucking female."

"You named it?" Lance gives her an unimpressed look.

"We didn't know someone had already had the pleasure of dubbing her an Aza-whatever." She shrugs, turning back to Kel. "You said that Lance's guys already know ours is bigger than theirs?"

Kel shrugs. "All things considered, there's no fucking way they missed it."

"No," says Lance. "No, no. They told me, just yesterday, they fucking *told* me that they're *always* male and they *always* go to ground, and that's why I don't have to worry."

Effie winces sympathetically. "I think you might've been lied to by the secret government agency."

Lance shoots her a withering look. "The sarcasm isn't necessary, thank you."

"As nifty as all this confirmation and extra information is, it still doesn't change anything. Not really," Kel interjects.

Lance looks between them both, brow furrowed. "What do you mean?"

Effie tilts her chin up, crossing her arms over her chest. "We're probably going to kill her."

"I'm sorry, what?" Lance snorts, and Effie bristles.

"Originally the plan was to just prove she exists, with the backup being destruction, but—" She meets Kel's gaze, and he nods, already on the same track as her. "This is clearly already a bigger conspiracy than we'd originally thought. *Your* people will probably keep word from getting out, so we may as well go full steam ahead with Plan B."

"You can't kill it," Lance insists.

"What, like we're not allowed to?" she scoffs.

Lance splutters a bit, holding his palms open, again.

"Are we supposed to wait for a male to come find her? For her to reproduce so her children can overrun the abandoned mines?" Kel asks. His voice is calm, but his eyes focus on Lance intently, as if willing him to look at it logically.

"If there was any risk of reproduction—" Lance starts, but then he falters, meeting Effie's gaze with a pained look. "They wouldn't be willing to put the world at risk like that. The whole point of their existence is to protect the public from these things and the chaos their confirmed existence would cause. I'm not working for the bad guys."

"Bad is almost always subjective," she points out, unwilling to deal with his emotions when she hasn't even had a chance to process her own. Kel opens his mouth, but she raises a hand to stop him, holding eye contact with the man across from her. "Regardless of what they told you or who you think you're working for, you know enough now to make an informed decision using your own metrics of right and wrong. Fuck their agenda; help us take this thing out before more people get hurt."

She watches the war of emotions cross his face as he strokes his beard, weighing the orders he's been given against everything he now knows. After what feels like an eternity, he clears his throat. "You've got a plan?"

Effie shoots a quick glance at Kel, then nods, lips pressed together.

Lance sits back, planting his hands on his knees. "Let's hear it, then."

5

1231 MDT//4d 9hr 28min after arrival

The conversation goes better than expected. Kel lays out their plan, answering all of Lance's questions without missing a beat. He leaves out the part about looking for any DNA to collect, figuring it's both irrelevant and not something the officer will condone. "So, basically," he concludes, "we can take her out without ever getting near her."

Lance looks impressed, even if begrudgingly so, but when Kel shoots a glance over at Effie, she's got this faraway look on her face. The tips of her fingers are pressed over her mouth, only half hiding her thoughtful frown. She notices his gaze and shoots him a little thumbs up, forcing a grin.

He wonders if maybe she's second-guessing their plan, if hearing it in the light of day has made her doubt it or change her mind about trying to take on the monster that attacked her only the day before.

Lance looks at her, and she straightens up and drops her hands into her lap in a semblance of professionalism. "Are you comfortable enough using bird bangers to ensure accuracy? Isn't wildlife control more of airfield operations' job than yours?"

She gives him a withering look. "It's a 15mm with no kick. Regardless, accuracy won't matter when the target is as big as we'll have." The bite in her voice helps everything click into place for Kel. Regardless of her accepting his help, Effie is mad at Lance.

"We watched a few YouTube videos about them last night, too, before deciding to bring them," Kel intercedes. "They're just an extra precaution, anyway. The bottles will get the job done."

The chief works his jaw, glaring at the floor for a moment. The prolonged silence starts to set Kel on edge, and he begins to doubt the wisdom of roping the man hired by the secret government agency in on their plan.

"I have some ANFO you can use."

The statement comes from so far out of left field that Kel takes a moment to decipher it. Then he blinks. "What?"

"Huh?" Effie echoes, but for a different reason, based on the confused scrunch of her nose.

"Explosive," Lance tells her before further explaining. "The city was doing a sewer construction project and bought some to help break apart the granite in the mountain. They didn't want to leave it sitting around with all the other random chemicals and fuel over at public works, so we offered to hold on to it for them. I still have the leftovers."

"Dude, that would be so fucking helpful," Kel gushes, sitting forward. Having access to a pre-made, high-grade ammonium nitrate would make the whole ordeal so much easier, not to mention safer. It isn't until Effie snorts, choking on a laugh, that he remembers he's addressing the chief deputy sheriff.

Lance doesn't seem to mind, though, and actually looks mildly amused. "You guys get the rest of everything we need. I've got to talk to Danielle and let her know I won't be around for dinner and then reach out to the agency for an update. Be back here by 5:45 and we can head up together to take care of this thing once and for all."

Effie frowns, all traces of humor doused by suspicion. "Why the agency?"

He rubs his hand over the back of his neck, breaking eye contact. "There were more deaths this morning. In light of my visit yesterday, I just need to see if there's been any response to that report."

Effie doesn't look convinced, but she nods anyway. "We'll meet you back here, then."

They all stand, and Lance rests a hand on his hip, the other running over his beard. "You two have no responsibility in this. You can back out of it—you *should* back out of it. I'll make sure it gets taken care of." He meets Effie's gaze with the last statement, something earnest and pleading in his eyes—a browner hazel than hers.

She glances at Kel, already shaking her head. "No, we're in this now. We're going to see it through. In and out before she comes back, Lance. Perfectly safe." She points her thumb at Kel. "And he's a physicist. Who out of all of us is more qualified to handle explosive chemicals?"

Lance gives him yet another appraising look, and Kel shoves his hands into his pockets, unsure exactly what the older man is hoping to see, but not too bothered about meeting the unknown expectation. Finally, the chief sighs. "I don't like this."

Effie shrugs, offering a stiff smile, and something unspoken passing between the cousins, like they've had similar conversations in the past. "You don't have to."

"You're a brat, you know that?"

"Oh, absolutely." She holds Lance's gaze, the look full of a self-assured confidence that Kel is insanely attracted to.

Lance just shakes his head, resigned, a small smile on his lips. He claps Kel on the shoulder as he makes his way out the door. It's unexpected, and Kel is just glad not to flinch.

When the door closes behind Lance, Effie steps closer to him, tipping her head forward to rest on his shoulder with a heavy sigh. "Well."

"Well," he repeats, inhaling the fresh apple scent of her shampoo. "You okay?"

She collapses into him, and his arms go around her shoulders. "It's not that I can't get around him having some high clearance job, I get why he couldn't just come out and admit that aliens exist, it's just ... I told him I saw something and he still tried to blow me off."

Kel has never experienced any of the dynamic that seems to exist between Effie and her family, but based on the differences in her interactions with her mother and with Lance, he knows that the relationship between her and her cousin is fundamental to her life. And he's seen enough to trust her intuition, even if she wants to start overthinking things now. "He was probably trying to keep you safe," he offers. "And he did eventually tell you. That's worth something, right?"

She makes a mumbled noise to the affirmative. "That could have gone a lot worse … and at least now we don't have to hodgepodge our own explosives."

"I guess we should restructure our shopping list."

She looks up at him with a smile that cracks his chest. Her earlier hesitation, whatever anxiety had dimmed the light in her eyes, has been forcefully extinguished. Her teeth sink into her lower lip, and she bounces a few steps backward. "I'll drive while you work out the specifics," she decides, moving to the door and slipping into a pair of sandals.

Kel packs up his laptop as she grabs her bag and scoops her keys from a ceramic bowl. He follows her out, stowing his own bag in his truck before joining her in the Jeep and pulling up their document on his phone.

"Bangers and screamers will still be smart," he says, as she backs down the drive.

"We'll pick them up on the way back." She pulls out her phone to select a playlist.

Kel nods, moving through the rest of the list and reorganizing things. With construction-grade ANFO on the table, he also feels confident in downsizing the amount of pyrotechnics he'd estimated last night, and begins running a few more calculations to figure out how much to remove. He's lost in his math when movement catches his eye, and he glances over to see Effie chewing on the side of her pinky nail. "What are you thinking about?" he asks.

She frowns, glancing down at her fingers for a brief moment

and shrugging. "Just the fact that there are more of these things out there—that there have been for years, and people know. Lance knows. And here we are cocky enough to think we can not only take out an alien but also squeak past an agency that has roots deep enough to alter satellite data?"

"Don't worry about them," he assures her. "You told me this morning that you trust Lance, and that includes trusting that he isn't going to let you be hunted down, right? So maybe it's a good thing we have an inside source. Besides, Plan A—capture evidence—is still the top priority. They won't be able to control the entire scientific community once we share this discovery." He reaches out to grab her hand, gently pulling it away from her mouth and giving it a squeeze before releasing her. "Team Curtis-Blake is about to be a household name."

"Gonna let me share your big moment, huh?" She grips the wheel with both hands to keep from chewing at her cuticles, shooting him a wry grin.

"We've only faced Gordon together. Seems like bad luck to pretend otherwise," he tells her, surprised by how fully he means it. Being around people isn't something that comes naturally to him; company almost always means a heightened awareness of himself, his interactions, his responses. Yet for how different they are, Effie's presence feels ... effortless. He's somehow forgotten that they were strangers little more than a day ago.

A Panic! At the Disco song starts playing through the speakers, breaking through his thoughts, and his head tips to the side in vague recognition of the tune.

Effie seems to catch the shift in attention, because she turns the volume up a couple clicks and informs him, "I never really left my emo phase in terms of music."

"I never had an emo phase," he replies.

She glances at him sidelong with a perfunctory nod. "This makes sense for you."

"Does it?"

"I think I've got you pretty well pinned now, Kel the Science Man."

"That's a bit long for a middle name."

"I'll strike it off the list." She opens her cell and hands it over. "Add a battle anthem to queue. I bet I can guess it."

He raises an eyebrow at the challenge, and she shoots him a look. "Don't go out-of-pocket to prove a point. First instinct song to get hyped for a face-off with Gordon."

After taking a moment to consider, he loads a song into queue and hands the phone back, which she places into a cup holder.

"Are you ready to be amazed, Kelvin Predictable-as-fuck Curtis?" she asks, wiggling her eyebrows in his direction.

A bark of laughter escapes his chest. "I don't think they let you put curse words on official documents, but go ahead." He waves his hand in front of him in invitation.

"The song you picked is 'Danger Zone,'" she proclaims with utter confidence, skipping to the next song.

Kel folds his arms across his chest, watching her with a smug smile as the beginning chords of "Highway to Hell" filter through the car. "Your brain is too stuck on aviation, my dear Elizabeth."

Her brow pulls low as she shoots him a suspicious look.

"*Top Gun*, right?" he asks, with a self-assured smirk.

"That's just a lucky guess," she grumbles.

"FE: Fucking Easy-to-predict Blake," he says with a pitying shake of his head, and her following laughter warms him from the inside out.

6

After lunch with Danielle and the girls, which was altogether too short, Lance goes back to the office to get things prepared for the night and check in with the agency.

He works his jaw to keep from clenching it, the joints already sore, and spits nicotine-laced saliva into an empty Coke bottle. There's not an inch of him that's not riddled with anxiety, questioning his every move since he'd told Effie about the Azathothlins.

But the bottom line remains the same. This is his home, and his biggest priority is making sure his family and the people he's sworn to protect are safe. And he can't do that if the agency is leaving him out of the loop at every turn, which is why he'd sent a text to Mr. Phillips as soon as he'd left home, demanding a phone call.

He struggles to rein in his anxiety-shortened temper when the phone finally rings.

"Sorry about the wait, Sutherland," Mr. Phillips says without preamble. "I understand you've got a little trouble on your hands, but don't you worry—"

Lance cuts him off. "Did you know? When I was up there yesterday, walking around with my thumb up my ass, did you know?"

Phillips sighs. "I forgive you the language, but there is no reason to be so crass. Just what is it that I'm supposed to have known?"

"That it's fucking *female*," Lance growls.

Phillips *tsks*, and Lance could swear his vision goes red for a moment. "I will advise you one more time, Mr. Sutherland, to watch your tone. If you want to be treated like a professional, show a little dignity."

Lance lets out a slow breath, lips pressed together. "Forgive me, Mr. Phillips, if I'm a little upset. As we established yesterday, people are *dying*, yet I'm being fed a bowl of fu—I'm being lied to when trying to ask for help and follow proper protocol."

"I'm sorry you feel that way, but our intention was never to lie to you. While it's true we knew there was a possibility 240 would be different due to its size, there was no way to do anything more than hypothesize. You seem pretty confident in your accusation, though. How exactly did you come to that conclusion?"

Shit, okay. Lance had known this was a likelihood when he decided to confront Phillips, but it doesn't keep his heart rate from speeding up. "Two civilians saw it come down, then later encountered it and brought their concerns to me."

There's a long silence on the other end.

"One of them had access to some sort of radar or satellite data and was able to see that this one is larger than the others. Having encountered it and seen its bug-like qualities, he came to the conclusion on his own. Considering how strange it's been acting based on what you know as normal ... It makes sense."

Phillips lets out a long sigh. "That's still nothing more than hypothesizing, Sutherland. As far as you're aware, it's only the two civilians who have seen specimen 240, correct?"

"Yes." Lance fights to keep the answer from coming out clipped.

"Names?"

He spits into his bottle, heart thudding in his chest. "Kelvin Curtis and Elizabeth Blake." It's not a betrayal. The agency was going to find out about their involvement eventually. *It's not a betrayal.*

"Standby, please." Phillips puts him on hold, and Lance spends the next few minutes reminding himself that this was standard protocol, that doing things by the book made sense because there was a reason things were written there to begin with. Besides, he's still on their side. He still intends to help, but if there was a chance that any of this would spur the agency to action, he needed to take it.

"All right, we'll need both Miss Blake and Dr. Curtis to sign an NDA, which I'll have forwarded to you shortly," Phillips comes back on the line without preamble. "Bring them both into the station as soon as possible. Now, I see Blake is working in our control tower, so there are no problems there, but Dr. Curtis is a liability. We'll be offering him an employment contract, which you need to persuade him to take."

This catches Lance off guard, and he hesitates, unsure of what to say. "Mr. Phillips," he starts, trying to figure out the most diplomatic way to word his hesitations. "I don't know him well, but even so, I'm not sure Dr. Curtis is onboard with the agency's mission."

There's a long pause before the other man answers. "Like I said, *persuade* him. You know this kind of information isn't safe for the public. Get him to see the wisdom in secrecy—hell, once he's signed the NDA, tell him about the complex, the other scientists you met. Appeal to his passions or something. I'm sure you can figure it out."

Lance spits into the bottle again before digging the nicotine pouch from his cheek and tossing it into the trash. "He thinks the Azathothlin is dangerous."

"Convince him it's not."

"How am I supposed to do that when I don't even believe it myself?" Lance sits back in his chair, irritation crawling beneath his skin with renewed heat. "My community hasn't been safe since it landed. I have five deaths on my conscience already, and if this thing is female, I'm supposed to just tell him we want to wait around for it to lay some eggs and overrun us? You know I understand the importance of keeping classified information from the public, but, sir, there are lines that I'm unable to cross." Lance is proud of how even his voice comes out, his emotions finally held in check.

There's silence from the other end of the line for an awkwardly long time. "Sit tight, Sutherland. I'm heading your way. Get ahold of the doctor and bring him into the station so we can have a chat ... We'll get everything worked out," Phillips grits out, his voice low and tight.

"Wait, you're coming tonight?" Lance straightens in alarm.

"Yes, I'll be there by this evening. Find those civilians." And then he hangs up.

Lance tosses his cellphone to his desk and runs his hands through his hair, willing his brain to slow down and accurately process everything that's happening. "Fuck fuck fuck fuck fuck." He sits up, drumming his fingers on his desktop. "*Fuck.*" Then he picks his phone back up and dials Effie.

"Hey," she answers.

"Are you still out?"

"Yeah, still in Montrose, why?"

"Good, don't come back through Telluride. There's been a change of plans."

"You'd better elaborate on that, Lancelot, or you're gonna worry me."

"We'll need to postpone the mines."

"What? Why?"

"My contact from the agency is coming in this evening. I'll be tied up dealing with him."

"Kel and I can still go," Effie insists after a short pause. "I'll even bring a radio for more reliable communication. We can let you know when Gordon leaves, keep you updated on everything that's happening."

Lance rakes his fingers through his beard, debating. "I don't know, Eff. Even a radio won't work in the mines."

"It will for a bit if it's a straight shot," she says. "We'll at least be able to let you know when we're out."

Lance presses his lips together. "I don't like it. We need to wait."

"You think this thing is dangerous, right?"

"Yes, but—"

"No," she interrupts. "That was a yes or no question. I asked for your help because I trust you. You're either on our side or you're not."

"I'm on your side, you know that, but—"

"What will waiting accomplish?" She isn't raising her voice, but there's a steel edge to it that gives him pause.

"I ..." He doesn't have a real answer. The agency won't agree to killing 240, not unless more people are at risk of finding out about her existence. Even with them finally taking his concerns seriously, how many more casualties is he willing to add to his conscience while they decide she's a big enough threat to exterminate? As much as he can appreciate wanting to study these creatures and use them to further human's understanding of the universe, the thought of Katie and Izzy growing up with a potential breeding alien under their feet makes him nauseous. "If you wait for me, I can keep you safe."

"I'm not a kid anymore, Lance," she says. "Regardless, is there really a way you can protect me from an alien that I can't? Or Kel? We're going up there tonight, and if you can't help anymore, that's fine, but I need to know now so we can make sure we're prepared."

She's right, he knows. She'd made up her mind before he was even involved, and his stepping back isn't going to deter her at all. "Okay," he agrees, quickly formulating a new plan. "We move forward as planned then, subbing a radio for me. But you both should stay out of town until it's taken care of."

"Why?"

Lance doesn't know how to tell her that they're aware that she and Kel know. The thought of her reaction, of not having time to explain his thinking, makes him sick. But he's always been quick on his feet. "On the off-chance they try to quarantine the area or implement some sort of shut down to keep people out. Just … trust me. Take Ophir back, stay at Kel's campsite, and go directly up to the mine tonight."

"We'll need to at least run by home. I have to change, and I'm in sandals."

"That's fine, but take the back way in."

"Got it. How are you gonna bring us the stuff?" Effie asks.

"It'll be in Griffin's cruiser. I'll make sure he's on shift when you head up." The deputy has enough of a relationship with Effie that Lance feels it possible to rope in his help without having to divulge everything that's happening. And there's no way he'll be able to sneak away once Phillips arrives.

"Got it."

Lance nods, running everything through once again in his mind. "You got the plan on lock?"

"Every detail," she confirms.

"Good. Griffin will be there at six o'clock. Radio me once you're on the way up, okay?"

"Wilco. Thanks for the heads up, Chief."

"Stay safe out there, kid."

After hanging up, Lance deletes the call from his phone log and calls Deputy Griffin, asking him to meet at the station.

With a fresh pouch tucked into his cheek, he gathers everything he needs and begins going over what exactly to tell the deputy, and even feels mildly prepared for the night by the time Griffin arrives.

"What do you need, Chief?"

"A favor," Lance begins, flexing his hands to work out some of the nervous energy. "And your discretion."

Griffin perks up, listening intently as Lance lays out the task ahead.

7

1723 MDT//4d 12hr 20 min after arrival

Bethany Cayse has always been adventurous. Her parents used to worry about her, but over the years, they grew to understand that she knows her limits, and she knows when to push them and when to hold back.

This is also something that Derek learned very quickly once they started dating. She has never been someone who could be limited or contained, and she never will be.

He's working again tonight, which is nothing new considering he's a lower-ranking deputy in a small town, and after lounging around watching *Friends* for the majority of the afternoon, she feels just about ready to jump out of her skin with the need to move. She fires off a text to Effie, asking if she's free to join her for a quick evening ride, then heads outside.

There are two important rules to mountain biking that Bethany learned when taking up the sport: always check your gear and never underestimate the mountain. Once verifying that each part of her bike is clean, secure, and operable, she loads it onto the back of her car and makes sure all of her other gear is in the back seat.

Effie hasn't responded, and Bethany smirks, assuming she's still wrapped up with science-guy. If her friend has been with him this whole consecutive time, then he must be something different, and she can't wait to hear all about it.

Bethany has the whole gondola car to herself on the ride up the mountain and takes the time to do some warm-up stretches, tucking one heel up against her thigh and pushing the leg flat. The light burn in her muscles is delicious, and she savors it for a moment before switching sides and pulling out her phone, sending a text to Derek letting him know she's in town and asking if there's anything he needs her to pick up.

Then she reaches the top and hops out, unloading her bike and walking it out from under the cover of the platform and off to the side of the main road to gear up. Straddling the bike, she inserts one earbud and selects a conspiracy podcast on her phone before tucking it into the side pocket of her backpack and buckling it across her waist and chest. Finally, she clips her helmet under her chin and pushes off.

Her phone vibrates with an incoming message, but she

doesn't feel it as she pedals across the dirt trail, and the text goes unread.

> **Derek: Don't stay in town, late, okay? If you can't make it home by sunset, head to the station. I think there's something wrong.**

8

1800 MDT//4d 14hr 57min after arrival

After getting back from the city, Effie swung by home for Kel's truck and a change of clothes, and then they'd holed up in his camper the rest of the afternoon.

They pull up at the Alta turnoff right at six. Derek is leaning against his cruiser, already waiting, and pushes off as soon as he sees Effie's Jeep.

She pulls up next to him, leaving it running while she gets out. "Hey," she greets, offering a smile that feels flat and unconvincing.

"You know what's out there?" He doesn't beat around the bush.

"What has Lance told you?"

He looks to the side, lips pressed in a thin line. "He said he couldn't explain, but you would know what to do."

She wets her lips, wondering if Lance had meant to leave this up to her discretion. His ties to the agency keep him morally obligated not to offer up information; barring certain death, her cousin would never go back on an agreement. But she and Kel have made no such promises. "It's not a bear that's been killing people."

There's no surprise in his face, just resolute understanding. "But you know how to kill it?"

"We're gonna give it our best damn shot."

"Let's get you armed up, then. We'll have time to talk after." He leads them to the back of the cruiser, and Effie is grateful he's not asking a barrage of questions she doesn't know how to answer. The three of them transfer a few boxes of bird bangers, a sack of ANFO, and a canister of kerosene from one vehicle to the other, and Derek gives her a handheld radio. "Use channel five," he instructs. "That'll keep you off dispatch, so only the Chief'll hear you."

"Channel five," she repeats.

And then Derek steps forward, enveloping her in a tight hug that betrays how uneasy he is. When he steps back, he looks over her shoulder at Kel. "Keep her safe."

Effie wants to protest that she's more than capable of looking out for herself, but Derek levels her with a look that reminds her just how much reckless shit he's watched her do.

"Will do," Kel answers, and they get back in the Jeep and head up the trail.

As she drives, she turns on the handheld to check in with Lance. "Radio check." Despite what Derek told her, she's unsure who might be monitoring.

"Line clear," Lance answers shortly. "Did you get everything okay?"

"Affirmative. We're en route now. I'll let you know when we're in place."

"Roger, I'll be monitoring. Just in case, double click before the first transmission. If it's safe, I'll reply."

"Copy." She sets the radio in a cup holder, and, aside from the music filtering through her speakers, they make the rest of the drive in silence. There's something about being handed a bag of explosive prills that makes it impossible to ignore what comes next, and she's struggling to brush off the nerves coiled tight in her gut.

Effie parks just around the bend from Gold King Basin, where the Jeep will be concealed from the mine, and turns off the ignition. The radio doesn't shut off with the car, though, and the beginning measures of Fall Out Boy's "My Songs Know What You Did in the Dark" start to play, causing her to burst into a fit of giggles, breaking the tense atmosphere.

"What?" Kel asks, half a smile pulling at his mouth.

She shakes her head, pointing at the radio. "The song," she says. "It's kind of pointed, don't you think?"

He tips his head to the side, pushing his glasses up with a knuckle as he listens, then it finally clicks into place. *Light 'em up up up.* "Well, shit. Let's fucking go."

"Nothing like a good battle anthem to shatter the nerves." Her eyes lock with his, and butterflies shoot through her entire torso. She sinks her teeth into her lower lip to keep from asking him to tell her that they're going to make it through this alive. Because it's not fair that she only got three days with him.

A lump forms in her throat with the thought, and she wants to roll her eyes at herself. *Not the time, ma'am.*

But Kel is giving her that stupidly charming grin, and his hair is peeking out from beneath the closure of his backward hat, and the truth is, she's never felt more inadequately prepared for a task in her life. So she lurches forward in her seat, grabbing the collar of his shirt, and presses her lips to his.

His hand slides up her neck, cupping the back of her head as he pulls her closer, deepening the kiss, his tongue sliding against hers in a rhythm that isn't frantic or needy or desperate, but the slow confidence of a promise meant to be fulfilled later. His thumb brushes across her cheek as he breaks the kiss, resting his forehead against hers.

They sit like that for a moment, Kel still touching her face, Effie still gripping his shirt until she realizes she's probably stretching the material and releases it, pressing her palm to his chest.

"Let's try to stop Gordon," he whispers, and goosebumps raise on her arms at the simplicity of the statement. How achievable it sounds. How his words ghost across her skin.

"Light 'em up," she whispers back, in time with the song. Then she pulls away, music abruptly cutting off as she opens the door.

9

1916 MDT//4d 16hr 13min after arrival

"This is getting ridiculous," Phillips says, steepling his fingers in front of his face and using them to push his glasses back up the bridge of his nose. "Where are they?" He'd arrived roughly forty minutes ago and had been impatiently sitting in Lance's office since.

Lance furrows his brow, looking down at the phone on his desk. "I don't know. They haven't come back through town." The agency's resources were clearly vast, which made the decision to disclose his personal ties to Effie an easy one. They'd make the connection either way, and rather he be able to truthfully state that she and Kel had left town for the day than waste resources having his officers scour town for her or show up at his house looking for her and worry Danielle and the girls.

Phillips narrows his eyes, watching him, but he doesn't squirm under the scrutiny. "You're sure they didn't use a different road?"

Lance chuckles, pointing to the map of Telluride on the wall next to them. "How else are they supposed to come through? If they were going to enter from the south, they'd have had to take 550 all the way down to Durango and over, which would also make it impossible for them to be back by now unless they weren't following a single speed limit."

The older man huffs, unsatisfied, but his eyes study the map, resigning himself to the chief's logic. "Call her again."

Lance nods, picking up his phone and dialing Effie. While the reception around Alta can be good enough to get a text through, a call takes significantly more data. As expected, it goes straight to voicemail. "Hey, Eff, me again. You guys okay out there? Give me a call when you can. It's important." Then he hangs up, slapping the phone into his palm for a moment before looking up at Phillips. "I don't know what to tell you, sir. But I've got a deputy stationed on the road into town, and he'll let me know the second they're in sight."

Phillips nods, tapping something out on his phone.

Lance clears his throat, bringing the man's attention back to him. "I'm still concerned about this Azathothlin," he begins, adjusting his posture in his seat. "There hasn't been a single night it hasn't hunted, and there's only so much I can do before people will start to question what's happening. Not to mention that these are people I'm sworn to protect. I don't know how many more innocent lives my conscience can take, to be quite honest with you."

Phillips glances back down at his phone, looking somewhere between bored and annoyed, and Lance doesn't know if it's with him or whatever conversation is taking place on the side. "Our tech gave you a tracker, correct?"

"Yes, but I don't know if it took the bait or not."

Phillips again taps something into his phone, scrolling for a moment before frowning. "It doesn't look like it's moving, but it is under the mountain."

"The chip is, at least," Lance reiterates. "And the sun is still up, so that tells us nothing. Doesn't it bother you that people might die?"

Phillips sighs heavily, as if Lance's conscience is a burden he isn't paid enough to deal with. "You're the chief deputy here, Sutherland. Actually, it's acting sheriff currently, right? You have authority for a reason. Put the town under curfew if you feel so inclined."

Lance opens his mouth to retort, then snaps it shut, wondering why he hadn't thought of it sooner himself. At this point, he's much more worried about protecting the public than about them figuring out that something is cataclysmically wrong.

With Phillips in tow, he heads down the road into downtown, radioing the rest of the department to let them know to start getting everyone off the streets and asking shops to close up before dark.

But enforcing a last-minute curfew in a popular mountain town during peak tourist season isn't easy.

After half an hour of trying to corral people, Lance runs a hand through his hair, gripping at the roots and pulling. "We appreciate your enthusiasm and willingness to help, Mr. Pritchard, but please stay indoors."

Pritchard, who used to be on the force before he medically retired from a back injury, scoffs, propping his hands on his hips. "I've been hunting for longer than you've been alive, Sutherland. And this is my home. I want to defend it."

Lance resists the urge to roll his eyes. The man is, at most, fifteen years older than him. "I understand that. And, again, I appreciate it," he repeats. "But you've got to understand that due to the nature of what's been going on, this is now the feds' territory, and having a civilian running around is a liability they won't allow, no matter how qualified we know you are."

Pritchard's face pinches together in solemn thought before he finally nods, clapping his hand to Lance's shoulder. "You're right. Those boys get pretty dicey about their jurisdiction, don't they?" he says sympathetically.

Lance gives him a look of conspiratorial exasperation. "They sure do. Maybe if they can't find this thing by tonight, I can talk to them about letting you and some of the others out in the field to help track it."

"That's why I like you, Chief. I tell everyone, 'Y'know that Chief Sutherland? He's one of the good ones, got a good head on his shoulders.' I'll check in with you tomorrow if there's no report." With that, Mr. Pritchard heads down the street in the direction of home.

He watches for a moment, then turns, jumping when he sees Phillips standing right behind him.

"Getting everything under control?" he asks, tucking his phone into the front pocket of his sports coat.

"Yes, sir." Lance rests his hands on his utility belt, hoping to look like he hadn't just been scared out of his skin. "Listen, I know what typical policy is, but if 240 does come back down tonight, I think we should talk about an extermination plan."

Phillips' expression becomes something similar to what Lance wears when he's trying to re-explain to Izzy why she can't climb the bookshelves even though, yes, they do look similar to a ladder. "We've talked about this, Sutherland. These things aren't like bears that get a little too curious. We can't just take them out or move them to a zoo to try and repopulate."

Lance blinks at the absurdity of the statement, his jaw actually dropping open as he realizes what's happening. "You're … you're hoping they reproduce," he says quietly, finally allowing himself to acknowledge that, while the agency's base motive may be the betterment and safety of humanity, that didn't mean casualties weren't an expectation.

Phillips gives him a tight smile, splaying his hands out, and Lance has never wanted to slug someone in the face so badly.

"The typical response to an invasive species is a swift and total eradication, not repopulation," he says, managing to keep his fists to himself. "Or haven't you hired any biologists? Because anything without a natural predator is bad news for the ecosystem."

"We're not killing it," Phillips grits through his teeth, all pretense of a friendly demeanor gone. "We don't know enough about them yet, and the board has decided they're not a threat. If this one does happen to be female, we could be on the cusp of a breakthrough, and—" he cuts himself off before he can reveal anything higher than Lance's clearance level. "Anyway, as long as you keep everyone off the streets, everything will be fine."

"Yeah," Lance replies, voice clipped. "I'll keep working on that." And then he moves off, intent on getting away from the man.

10

To the surprise of literally nobody, Bethany ends up staying out much longer than originally intended. Her podcast is captivating, and the mountain is being her friend, at least as much as an uphill trail can be. She stands, shifting gears and throwing her weight into a particularly steep portion.

She's above the treeline now, and coasts on the flatter area at the crest of the mountain for a bit before pedaling past the base of a ski lift and over to a ski patrol shed, both closed for the season. Dismounting, she rests her bike against the side of the shed and stretches out her limbs as she hydrates.

The air here—well above 12,000 feet—is crisp and thin, and she sucks it into her lungs greedily, resting her hands on top of her helmet as she looks out over the valley.

She tilts her face into the wind sweeping across the peak, letting it blow loose curls from her face and dry the sweat pearling across her skin. Goosebumps break out over her neck and arms at the change in temperature.

The sun is angled low over the mountains so that most of the trail is in shadow, and it's not until she steps into a patch of sunlight to warm up that she realizes how much time has gone by.

"Oh, shit," she mumbles, sliding her backpack off to grab her phone and confirm the time. Derek has sent her five texts and called her twice. The calls didn't go through due to lack of reception on the trail, but she opens the texts, anxiety knotting in her belly at his urgency.

> **Derek: Don't stay in town, late, okay? If you can't make it home by sunset, head to the station. I think there's something wrong.**

> **Derek: Are you home?**

> **Derek: Let me know when you get this. You need to head home soon if you're not already there.**

> **Derek: Call me please.**

> **Derek: Did you go for a ride? You need to make it home before dark.**

Her stomach turns, nauseous with dread as she dials him, raising the phone to her ear before remembering the earbud.

It rings once, and then he answers.

"Bethany, thank Christ. Are you home?" The worry in his voice is thick, his words spilling out frantically, and she can no longer pretend like the tightness in her chest is anything but fear.

"N-no, I'm up by the Gold Hill run. I didn't get any of your texts until now. What's wrong?"

Derek curses under his breath, but when he speaks, his tone is more controlled than before. "You need to head down *now*. Chief put out a curfew for town: no one out after dark. Head to the gondola first—they might still be open."

"What's happening? Is this because of that bear?"

"No, it's—yes. It's dangerous to be out."

Her fear is manifesting as frustration, and her feet feel rooted to the mountaintop. "Which is it, Derek? No or yes? What's going on?"

"It is the bear," he says with a frustrated sigh. "Only I don't think it ever was a bear. I think it's something ... I don't know. Chief didn't give me any details, but he sent me to get pyrotechnics for Effie. Whatever is out there, I think they're planning to kill it."

Bethany's brows pull together, but her feet unfreeze from the mountain, and she moves back toward her bike at a clipped pace. "Effie? Why would—this doesn't make any sense." She shakes her head, stuffing the phone back into her backpack and clipping it back on.

"I didn't ask. She and this physicist who was poking around out here the other day are wrapped up in this somehow. I just—baby, you need to get off the mountain."

Bethany blinks, pausing for a moment before she swings her leg over her bike. *Kel the science man?* "I'm headed down now. Beeline for the gondola ... roughly ten minutes?"

"Let me know you made it safe, okay? I love you."

Bethany nods, even though he can't see her. "Love you, too. I will."

He hangs up, and she pushes off, the podcast resuming in her ear. Downhill is a breeze, and it's easy to go fast.

But fast on this terrain, especially at dusk, is dangerous, and Bethany knows her limits. Knows better than to test the mountain.

There's an old story that Telluride got its name from the treacherous trails to and from the mines, and it's that old phrase that plays in her head on a stunted loop: *to hell you ride.*

So she keeps pressure on her brakes and her eyes on the trail ahead, watching her shadow stretch out long in front of her, then disappear altogether as the sun dips lower beneath the peaks, fear icing her veins the entire way.

11

2017 MDT//4d 17hr 14min after arrival

After parking, Kel and Effie had packed their backpacks full of incendiary materials and set up behind one of the broken-down structures in Gold King Basin to watch the entrance to Gordon's mine, waiting for her to head out on a hunt.

Kel can feel Effie's warmth pressing into him through the fabric of his hoodie and takes comfort from her presence and seemingly unwavering confidence. He's been on the verge of freaking out all day, panic buzzing restlessly just below his skin. For all his lifelong daydreaming about outer space, never once did he think he'd be facing off with an actual alien, and the full breadth of the situation hadn't truly hit him before this morning. That sense of surreality stuck with him throughout the day, nothing feeling quite like it was actually happening to him. *There is just no way this is real, right?*

And then there's Effie, who is entirely unshakeable by comparison. She faces down every situation they come across with a gleam in those hazel eyes like she finds the audacity vaguely amusing.

When she'd kissed him in the car, he could have sworn she knew he was stuck in his head, trying to convince himself that everything would be okay, that they'd worked through all of the possibilities and would make it out alive, that that was the only option. As soon as her lips had touched his, the panic sizzling beneath his skin settled, his mind latching on to the fact that, yes, this was happening, and there were only two outcomes. Either he would make it out alive, or he would die trying. No sense worrying about it now.

So he'd kissed her back, enjoying the warmth of her, the softness of her lips, the taste of her that made him weak in the knees with hunger. He'd let himself enjoy it, knowing it would either be the last of his life or the potential beginning of something more, and he was at peace with either result.

Now, huddled behind an old mining dredge, Effie shifts, peering over his shoulder to the last light of day quickly blending into darkness behind the mountains. "Gordon should be making her appearance any time now," she whispers, her words almost snatched away by the wind blowing into the basin. Then she meets his eyes, trying to read something in his face. "Tell me one more time how confident you are in physics and formulas?"

Kel shoots her a lopsided smile despite the way his stomach is churning with nerves. "I didn't earn a PhD for the gold star, Blake, and math doesn't lie. We can take her down."

She lets out a heavy breath, puffing her cheeks out as she nods and turns back to the mine. "Well, if I'd known gold stars were involved, maybe I would've gone to college."

"You never went to college?" He can't keep the surprise from his voice.

"That a deal breaker for you?" She gives him a sideways glance, eyebrow raised in amusement.

"Not at all. I just wouldn't have guessed it."

"Good to know my lack of formal education isn't obvious," she laughs. "But, no, Air Force, remember? There're two main reasons people join: education and escape. Sometimes both, but I was only after the latter."

"And now look at you, living in your own fortress of trees and granite," he teases, knocking his shoulder into hers.

She smirks, keeping her gaze on the mine across the Basin. "And look at you, teaming up against your career's most significant discovery with a girl who took the first opportunity to leave home with nothing but a highschool diploma and the clothes on her back."

"There's not a single other person on this planet more qualified to be on team Curtis-Blake," he says, and she leans into him. "Of course, now that I know there's life on *other* planets ..."

"Easy there, Kelvin Alien-watch, or I might just leave you up here," she threatens with a playful glare.

They settle back into a silence that would be comfortable were it not for the fact that they're waiting for an alien to crawl from under the mountain and hopefully not notice their presence.

As the moments tick by, Effie hums under her breath, fingers tapping against the toes of her shoes to a tune he can't quite place. He shifts, stretching one leg out in front of him, an ache in his knee from crouching for so long.

He's just pulled it back under him when Effie grabs his forearm in a vise-like grip and goes completely silent. His eyes dart to the mouth of the mine, and he sees Gordon's head poking from the dark maw, fuzzy antennae waving about, testing the air. Her four eyes glitter in the moonlight as she eases further into the open.

Kel's breath stills in his chest, all of his focus on the alien slowly appearing across the basin. She pulls herself out on those impossibly sharp legs, and when she's free, her whole body seems to stretch, abdomen expanding and legs lengthening, holding her higher above the ground. She shakes herself, the motion so similar to the way a dog might after waking up and stretching from a long nap, and a series of soft clicks echoes through the basin.

Then she starts the climb up the mountain, her legs moving independently, and a chill of trepidation runs up his spine. She's barely disturbing the scree, like she was made to traverse this terrain. Gordon is a deadly fucking predator, and calling her Gordon is doing nothing to dampen the fear that has his brow breaking out in a cold sweat.

She disappears over the ridge, and they wait, neither moving a muscle for several long heartbeats. Then Effie releases his arm to pick up the radio, double-clicking and waiting for the responding click. "She's on the move."

"Get in and get out," Lance replies. "I'll try to head up as soon as I've got things covered here."

"Don't worry about us; we've got this. Keep your higher-ups engaged and out of our way." Effie's voice is steady and full of confidence.

There's a pause, long enough for Kel to wonder if Lance is going to try to argue with her, but finally the handheld crackles to life with his reply. "Copy. Stay safe, and let me know when you're out."

"Wilco." Effie stands, rolling her neck on her shoulders and clipping the radio back to her belt. Kel follows suit, trying to force his muscles into submission against the apprehension that threatens to root him to the spot. Every fiber of his being is on high alert, terrified of what the rest of this night will hold now that it's time for action.

But Effie just looks in the direction Gordon went, reaching up to tighten her ponytail before dropping her hands to her sides, gaze narrowed. "These are my mountains, alien bitch. And you're no longer welcome."

12

2030 MDT//4d 17hr 27min after arrival

The night sky is clear, completely devoid of clouds, and lights twinkle in the distance, lighting Telluride up against the dark of the surrounding mountains.

The Azathothlin queen is no longer starving or exhausted or irritated. She's taken the time she needs to acclimate to this new place, has slept, regained her strength, and let the others know that she is here. She has explored, learned the area around her nest, and become comfortable with the terrain.

And now she intends to dominate. To truly, fully claim this territory as her own.

Gordon crawls over the mountains, the wind breaking easily over the hard, curved planes of her body as she heads toward the concentrated settlement of humans that is closest to her nest.

She knows, of course, that it isn't the only one. There is a small town just to the south, and another to the west of that and over the mountains. But they either aren't as populated or as close, and she has learned from experience how to gauge a potential threat and take it out early. These people will be the first to submit to her domain; the others will follow.

The Azathothlin moves through the trees, ignoring the cracking of bark as she carelessly pushes over trunks, carving her own path over the mountain. Now that she's back to full strength, there is no need to hide her presence.

What is going to harm her?

She is the only queen on this planet, and when the others she has borne hatch and grow, they will move out to territories of their own.

Something ticks in the back of her skull, an inkling of danger, and this irritates her. Because she isn't used to the kind of survival instincts that keep other creatures timid and wary, watching from the shadows for threats instead of for the thrill of the hunt.

But the weak spot in the plating across her chest seems to almost itch with the reminder that this prey may be more cunning than what she's used to. She clicks from deep in her throat, accepting the challenge.

If they want to put up a fight, that just means more fun for her.

13

2021 MDT//4d 17hr 18min after arrival

Bethany makes it to the gondola, choking down a sob when she sees it's still moving. Her legs are shaking, both with exertion and adrenaline, and she struggles to get her breathing under control as she dismounts.

There are quite a few people milling about for how late it is, a few other bikers, some tourists heading back down from Mountain Village, and their easy meandering loosens the anxiety squeezing her chest.

She's fine. Everything's fine. It's all going to be okay.

With equally shaky fingers, Bethany removes her helmet and hangs it from the handlebars before walking over to the bathroom. She's been out for a while, and the bumpy ride down did nothing to help the fullness of her bladder. Parking her bike outside of the restrooms, she unclips the waist and chest straps of her backpack, sliding one arm free to pull out her phone and text Derek that she made it to the gondola.

After finishing her business, she walks her bike onto the loading dock and focuses on her breathing, trying to get her heart rate to settle while she waits in line. When it's finally her turn, she loads her bike onto the back of the car and scoots inside. Just as she's about to toss her bag and helmet onto the seat across from her, two parents with a small child enter, and she sets her gear down next to her instead, offering them a polite smile as she shifts around to try to stretch her leg muscles.

The podcast is still playing in her ear, and she pulls out her phone to check for a message from Derek, but all is silent. She tips her head back against the window, folding her arms in front of her stomach and trying to force herself to relax as the podcaster talks about a cannibal New York cop in the 2010s.

Funnily enough, the description of mutilated women does nothing to settle her nerves, and she turns the podcast off, pulling the earbud from her ear.

"Look, Mama! Issa kwaaab!" The toddler across from her shrieks excitedly, pointing out of the window behind Bethany.

The mother smiles fondly at her child, gently pulling her hand down and shaking her head. "No, honey, there are no crabs in the—oh my God, Jonathan, what the hell is that?!"

Bethany turns to look over her shoulder at the same time Jonathan looks up from his phone.

"Jesus Christ," says Jonathan.

Bethany doesn't say anything. All sound gets caught in her throat along with her breath as she involuntarily leans closer to the glass, straining to see better in the dark, willing her brain to make sense of the image her eyes are sending it.

From the crest of the mountain, carelessly pushing its way through pines and aspens, is a monster. Its shell is a mottled gray-blue that blends eerily well with the rocks, but contrasts starkly against the vibrant green aspen leaves showering down around it. By the way the trees bend and snap against it, it's easy to guess that the shell is hard and unyielding. Its legs move independently of one another, long, jointed, and thick, the front two lined with spines.

While Bethany can see the similarities to a crab, its body is slimmer and segmented, but she doesn't place what exactly it reminds her of until it passes a gap in the trees, and she sees its triangular head.

It looks like a praying mantis. The thought somehow snaps her out of her stasis, urgency dumping adrenaline into her bloodstream.

Bethany scrambles for her phone, fine motor skills nowhere to be found as she struggles to get her fingers to cooperate, to unlock her screen and type a name into the search bar of her contacts.

The couple across from her don't seem to be sharing her struggles. The mother has the toddler wrangled into her lap, huddling as far back against the seat as she can, while Jonathan holds his phone landscape, trying to video the creature crawling through the growing darkness.

"The lighting is terrible," he grumbles to no one, or possibly to all of them. "I can hardly get anything on screen."

"What is it? Will it hurt us?" the mother whimpers, struggling to hold on to her squirming child.

Jonathan only answers the last question he hears. "Nah, we're way up here," he says confidently, standing to try to get a better view.

Bethany finally manages to dial out, sliding across the bench to give the man room as he rests a knee next to her.

"Pardon me," he mentions after the fact.

She ignores him, clutching the phone to her face as it rings.

"Chief Sutherland."

"It's Bethany," she says, taking one final breath before blurting everything else without stopping. "I'm on the gondola and there's something in the woods I don't know what but it's not normal and Derek said that you and Effie know things but he doesn't know what but that it wasn't safe and now there's a monster and it's huge and it's headed for town and I don't know what to do."

There's silence for two terribly long heartbeats before Lance replies, and thank fuck his voice is calm and void of panic because Bethany is holding her shit together with a soggy tortilla, and it's about to rip. "You said you're on the gondola? Do you still have eyes on it?"

Bethany swallows and rises from her seat, ignoring Jonathan's startled protests as she elbows him out of the way to get a better view. Twilight has come and gone, but between the lights on the gondola and the almost-full moon, she can follow the unnatural movement of the trees, now almost parallel with her car. "It's a few hundred feet up from where Easy Out first crosses under the gondola," she says, naming the road they're steadily approaching.

"Fuck. Okay. Listen, when you get down, stay in the station. Find any staff and get them to help you get the doors closed. You all need to stay inside and be as quiet as possible."

"Doors closed. Stay quiet," Bethany repeats, eyes glued to the break in the trees, even though she desperately doesn't want to see whatever comes out of them.

"I've gotta take care of things down here. Stay safe, Beth. Thanks for the heads up."

"Yeah, you too," she replies, hanging up as the creature appears from the trees. Moonlight glitters in its eyes and reflects off the smooth plates of its back, but what sends a shiver down her spine are the fuzzy antennae protruding from its mouth, barely visible in the dark but unmistakable once her mind has recognized them.

Despite her proclivity for adrenaline-inducing activities, Bethany always thought she had a strong sense of self-preservation, but instead of backing away from the monster, trying to hide in the depths of the gondola car, she leans further forward, unaware of her actions until her nose bumps up against the glass.

"Hey, you ruined my shot," Jonathan complains.

The creature disappears into the trees again, swallowed by shadows, and Bethany pulls away from the window, giving the man an uninterested look before turning to the woman. "I'm Bethany," she tells her.

"Ava," the woman replies, clutching the child tighter to her chest.

"Listen, Ava, I know you have no reason to trust me, but I was just on the phone with the chief deputy sheriff—"

"The sheriff? How do you know the sheriff?" Jonathan interrupts.

"—who's somewhat of a family friend," she continues, without acknowledging him. "Authorities are aware of the situation, and when we get down to the ground, we've been instructed to stay indoors. We'll close and lock the station doors until we get the all clear. I'll need your help to spread the word, to try to keep things from getting chaotic."

"But what about the baby?" Ava asks, eyes wide.

Bethany blinks, looking down at the child in confusion. "What about the baby?"

"If that thing is headed for town, we've got to get her out of here," Jonathan answers, moving over to Ava and taking the child from her.

Bethany finally turns to him, hands on her hips. "Didn't you hear me? We're not supposed to go outside. We have to stay in the station where we're out of sight. It's the safest place to be."

"And we're just supposed to believe that you know the police chief?" he asks skeptically.

"Chief deputy sheriff," Bethany corrects, lashes fluttering with the effort of keeping from rolling her eyes. "I'm asking for help so that we all make it through this safely. Do you really want to take your kid out into the open with that thing? Do you want to subject her to mass panic and hysteria when we get down there and no one knows what's going on or what to do?"

"Jonny ..." Ava pleads. "I'm scared. Maybe we should listen. There's a *monster* out there."

Jonathan looks behind him, one hand running down the back of the toddler's head, smoothing down the fine hairs. Then he nods as though coming to an important decision, and hands the child back to Ava. "You take the baby. Find somewhere safe to hide while I help get everyone else rounded up."

Ava nods, and the child squirms, holding her arms back out toward Jonathan. "Want Daddy!" she cries. Ava holds her closer, rocking back and forth with soft shushing sounds while Jonathan turns back to the window, watching the trees pass below with an air of self importance.

"When we get down there," he says to Bethany, "You find the staff and alert them to the situation, I'll round up the other visitors."

Bethany doesn't know if it's bad karma to hope that a giant crab-mantis eats the father of a young child, but it doesn't keep the thought from running a few loops around her mind as she watches his back incredulously for a moment. "Sounds like a plan," she agrees flatly.

Within minutes, they're lowering to the ground, and Bethany rises to unsteady feet, slinging her backpack over her shoulders and setting her helmet back on her head to keep her hands free, buckling it out of muscle memory. Jonathan looks at her, giving one last nod of acknowledgement before bending down to kiss Ava on the temple and pat his daughter on the head.

Bethany considers thanking him for his help, but then the doors are open, and she steps off, making eye contact with one of the staff and hurrying over.

"Ma'am, is that your bike?" he asks, pointing over her shoulder.

"I need your help. There's something dangerous out there, and we need to get the gondola stopped and these doors closed." Bethany doesn't break eye contact with him, doing her best to sound calm and collected.

"Stop the gondola? What are you talking about?"

"Radio to the top and tell them not to let any more passengers board. Something came down from the mountain, and we need to keep everyone inside and try not to attract attention."

He can't be any older than twenty-one, but already Bethany feels more safe with him than she did with Jonathan. Even though his brow is still furrowed in confusion, he nods, clicking the handset clipped to his collar and speaking into it, his eyes darting behind her to the operator booth across the station. "Stop the gondola. We might have a situation down here." The lift comes to a halt with a pneumatic hiss, and he looks back to Bethany. "What do you mean, something came down from the mountain?"

A piercing wail of terror breaks through the night, and Bethany's heart lurches into her throat. "We have to get those doors closed *now*."

The kid nods, waving over the operator for help and running for the set of exit doors. Bethany sprints for the entrance to assist as chaos breaks loose.

What starts as a few scattered screams quickly devolves into a cacophony of blind, unified terror. Someone knocks into Bethany's shoulder, and she stumbles to the side with a yelp. The inside of the station has erupted into movement, and she struggles against the disorganized wave of bodies. She whips her head around as more people bump into her, some clambering to get inside while others push toward the exit.

Her eyes land on the staff member she'd talked to, watching as he reaches up to unlock the metal hinge on one of the doors and push it closed.

"They're locking us in!" someone shrieks, and suddenly the disorganized stream of people finds a common goal, and they all surge toward the exit points.

Bethany is spun around by the force of people frantically trying to escape the building, but not before she sees the poor kid pulled away from the door, hands flailing as people push past. Then he's knocked to the ground, and she loses sight of him as she fights her way perpendicular to the crowd, trying to reach the wall.

A sob is lodged in her throat, her heart thundering frantically as she tries to push her way through.

Someone kicks her foot out from under her, and she sprawls forward. Her knees hit the concrete with a jarring thud seconds before her palms, skin scraping as they skid forward. Tears blur her vision as she struggles to get her feet back under her, thankful for her helmet as a knee smacks into her head. Just when she's about to stand, pain blooms from her side as someone's foot catches the base of her ribs, and they trip over her with a hoarse cry of surprise.

She turns her head, flinching when their face smacks into the ground, blood instantly erupting from their nose, and then a shriek of agony rips from her own throat as her fingers are crushed.

The thick tread of a hiking boot catches the nail of her middle finger, twisting it free from its bed, and Bethany's entire arm lights up with the pain of it, her stomach flipping in protest as she cries out.

Then the pressure is gone, and she manages to pull her feet back under her and force her way through the throng of people. She hits the metal wall hard enough to knock the breath from her lungs, then presses herself flat against it, clutching her hand to her chest as tears stream down her face, eyes wrenched shut as she listens to the continued sounds of chaos and terror that filter in from outside, all of it punctuated with a strange, otherworldly clicking.

14

Effie is scared shitless. In fact, she's never been more scared in her life, not even that time she almost rolled her Jeep off the side of Black Bear Pass when some asshat on a dirt bike came roaring around a switchback going the wrong way.

Granted, she'd screamed then, and she wasn't screaming now, but she could feel one waiting, curled somewhere between her gut and her throat, just waiting for the right moment to rip free.

For now, she hoists her backpack onto her shoulders, gripping the straps and turning to Kel. He's taken off his hat, smoothing his hair back before replacing it, then fitting a headlamp over it. He adjusts his glasses, resitting them on the bridge of his nose, and something in the gesture is so commonplace, so very *Kel*, that it settles a few of the nerves rattling around in her chest. "You ready to do this?" he asks.

She digs her own headlamp from her pocket, chewing on the inside of her cheek as her throat suddenly tightens. *No, I'm not ready. I want to go home. I want to curl up under a soft, fuzzy blanket and eat a bowl of cereal and watch TV and not know that any of this is happening.* "Born ready," she answers, forcing a grin as she slips the band around her head and pulls her ponytail free.

And as she walks with him to the mine, she realizes that her initial response was wrong. She doesn't want to be in the dark about all of this. It's terrifying, and it's dangerous, and she feels so underqualified, but there's something about knowing, about getting to see all this for herself and take action that's ...

exhilarating.

Effie holds on to that emotion, wrapping it around herself like her previously wished-for fuzzy blanket and letting it keep her together.

They stop in front of the entrance, clicking on their headlamps, and the tunnel is flooded with light. "After you," she tells Kel, sweeping her arm out.

He gives her a suspicious look. "You'd better not just be using this as an opportunity to look at my ass."

She rolls her eyes with a laugh. "You've found me out. Now be a gentleman and don't deprive a girl during her possible final moments."

Her heart flutters against her ribcage as she becomes encased in granite. Their footsteps are loud in the enclosed space, and she strains to hear anything else from up ahead. The air smells damp, cold, and mineral. She knows the entrance is no more than a few yards behind her, but she glances over her shoulder to make sure just the same.

You need to calm down, she chastises herself. With a conscious effort, she relaxes the tension that's wound through her muscles, shifting her shoulders against the weight on her back and shaking out her hands while Kel gets a few steps ahead.

She wraps her fingers around the straps of her pack as she follows, head tilting this way and that to examine the tunnel. The walls and ceiling are crudely hewn, carved out of the mountain by pick and dynamite. The ground is flatter, packed down by countless boots and mine carts over years. The track the carts ran on has been mostly covered by fallen debris and dirt, but it's still visible, gleaming dully in the light of her lamp.

"You having a party back there?" Kel asks. "Your light is bouncing all over the place."

"You spelunk your way; I'll spelunk mine," she tells him, quickening her steps to close the distance that's grown between them.

"This isn't spelunking so much as breaking and entering."

"Is it breaking and entering if there's no breaking? Entering doesn't sound nearly as prosecutable." She carefully steps over a section of broken track sticking up from the ground.

"You do like your connotations, don't you?" He glances back at her.

"It's the beauty of language." She gives him an impish grin and spreads her hands in front of her. "How far in do you think she's made her nest?" Another glance behind her shows they're far enough in that the light from the entrance is almost indiscernible. It's so dark outside, and her headlamp is too bright for the distant stars to compete with.

Kel shrugs, his backpack rising up and dropping with his shoulders. "These tunnels don't go that far. Most of these mines don't cut in any more than a mile before the shafts drop down."

Effie swallows, very aware of that scream lodged high in her chest and determined to keep it there. "Do you know how much potential for 'down' there is way up here?" Her voice sounds small in her ears, tinny against the solid black that surrounds them.

"More than is probably smart to think about." His attempt at humor is admirable, but falls flat. "Hey, does it look like the tunnel might branch off up ahead?"

Effie peers around his shoulder. "I don't ... maybe?" The way their lights bounce off the rock, throwing shadows, makes it hard to tell.

"Should it do that?" Kel asks.

They're both stationary, staring at the gaping shadow up ahead. "I don't know." But intuition tells her no.

Kel nods, light bobbing, then steps forward. As he does, the pile of fallen rocks—much fresher than the rest of the debris they've seen—becomes more visible. "I think we know where her nest is."

Effie follows him through the new tunnel, only a few yards long, before opening up into a large cave. "Holy shit," she whispers, stepping past Kel, her head tilted back to view the full expanse of the cavern.

The walls and ceilings glitter with veins of uncut gemstone that she can't accurately identify. But there's probably a literal ton of it, just sitting below the mountain. The floor is smooth and damp, carved out through erosion long before the miners ever blew into the mountain.

"How has this stayed hidden so long?" he asks. "How did no one see this when they were mapping the mountain from the original claim?"

Effie gives an unnecessary shrug, her head tipping to the side as she takes it all in, eyes wide and almost unblinking with wonder.

"This is ..." Kel places his hands on his head with a disbelieving chuckle. "This is insane. What is ... I can't ..." He shakes his head again.

"Does this count as spelunking yet?" she jokes.

"We didn't file proper permits for that," he answers, finally looking at her.

It could be the glare of her headlamp on his glasses, but he looks a little crazed, like it's all getting a little too real for him.

"Hey, stay with me, science-man." She moves next to him and grabs his hand. His fingers are warm against hers, which she takes as a good sign.

"It's just a lot to take in, is all." He swallows, glancing down at their clasped hands. "The things I've seen with a high-powered telescope while not ever thinking there was stuff just as amazing, undiscovered and waiting for an alien to break through and open it to the world ..."

"I guess there's one thing about invasive species," Effie agrees. "They essentially come with a guarantee to fuck with the local environment." Her hair tickles her neck and she shivers, glancing over her shoulder.

"What is it?" Kel asks, back on high alert.

"Does the air feel less stagnant to you?" She drops his hand to walk toward the back wall of the cavern, moving around columns and stalagmites. Another tunnel comes into view, and her stomach flips like she's on a rollercoaster. "Go mark the entrance where we came in," she calls behind her.

Kel's footsteps create a soft scuffle that fills the cave, followed by a rustling as he reaches into his backpack to grab a roll of reflective tape. Thank God for that foresight. The sound of him tearing a strip free echoes around her, but she doesn't pull her eyes from the tunnel ahead, afraid that the moment she does, something will spring free.

No, that's ridiculous. We saw Gordon leave, and Lance said there aren't any others around here. She still presses her back against the column behind her as she turns to survey the cave, making sure there's no movement before she focuses on Kel, who's sticking a final strip to the arrow he's affixed to the upper wall of the tunnel, pointing the way out.

"You found another?" he asks when he's finished, hurrying over.

She nods, her fingers digging for purchase against the smooth, surprisingly damp surface behind her. Her mind flashes to the time her family went to Carlsbad Caverns when she was younger. The tour guide told them the fine for touching any of the rock formations in the cave was thousands of dollars, that the oil left from a single fingerprint could change the way the formation grew for hundreds of years to come.

The entirety of both of her palms are pressed to this one, and she fights the urge to giggle at the absurdity as she pushes free from the column, set in the knowledge that she's about to do a lot more damage to this cave system than simply leaving a few fingerprints behind.

Kel tapes another arrow to the top of this tunnel, pointing toward the first, before they walk through. The ground is sloping so gently that Effie doesn't even notice it at first. "How many pounds of rock do you think are above us right now?"

"Enough to squash a Gordon."

"We're only a tad more fragile than she is." She wipes clammy palms against her leggings

"You're not wrong there." Kel rips off another strip of tape when they reach the end of the tunnel, the tear of it echoing through the cave opening up in front of them.

As he completes another arrow, Effie steps forward into a cavern much less open than the previous. Rock formations clutter the space, and her eyes roam up to the ceiling, taking in the vast amount of stalactites, like hardening icicles, just waiting for something to jar them loose so they can plummet into her skull.

Jesus Christ, Eff. She shakes off the dark train of thought, then yelps as her foot smacks something, sending her off balance as it rolls beneath her.

She careens forward, striking her shin against the object and landing on her hands and the opposite knee. A sharp sting radiates from her palms as they scrape against the rough ground, paired with a jolting ache from her knee and shin, both no doubt bruised.

Whatever she hit is *hard.*

With a sharp hiss, she rolls over, brushing gravel from her palms before reaching out to inspect the thing she'd stumbled over.

The scream—the one that's been tucked and waiting, ready to go since she stepped foot into the mine—tries its damndest to crawl up her throat, but her whole body has frozen, wedging it in place.

"Eff!" calls Kel, his hurried footsteps a disorienting echo around the cavern. "Are you okay? Where are you?"

Her body unlocks, and she's able to swallow down the cry and look over her shoulder, shining her light around the expanse of rock she's hidden behind. "Over here."

"Shit, are you hurt?" He carefully but quickly makes his way to her side.

She shakes her head, sliding her backpack from her shoulders and letting him help her stand. "Gordon's a female," she tells him in a small voice.

"Well, yeah, we already—*fuck.*" Kel's gaze follows hers to the pile of white, oblong shapes shining in the lamplight.

Effie's voice feels like it's coming from somewhere far away as she forces the words out, turning them into reality. "She's laid eggs."

15

Lance grips his phone so tight it starts to creak before dropping it back in his pocket and dragging a hand through his hair.

They're out of time, and the only priority now is keeping people safe.

"All units remain on high alert. Watch for a threat coming down the mountains by the gondola. Priority one is getting citizens to safety." Even as he speaks the words into the handset clipped to his shoulder, he can feel Phillips's angry gaze burning into his cheek. But he ignores the other man, checking over his weapons and walking to his cruiser to get the megaphone. He has to get people off of the streets.

"Your guns won't be enough to pierce her exoskeleton, you know," Phillips says haughtily, right on his heels. "You're just going to make her mad and cause even more problems for yourself."

Lance grips the frame of his cruiser door, willing himself to breathe, to think. He's got to keep 240 away from town, away from people, but how is he supposed to lure an alien away from an all-you-can-eat buffet? What is more essential to a predator than food?

"I'm going to have to report this," Phillips prattles on. "Not only have you failed to secure an NDA from two civilians before disclosing information about the Azathothlin, but now you've put your entire force on alert, acknowledging all but publicly that something strange has made its way here."

What is more essential to a predator than food? Lance turns the question around in his mind slowly, testing the edges, feeling like there's an answer he knows, that the key to everything is just out of reach.

"Your actions are in direct violation of—"

"Will you shut the fuck up? I'm trying to fucking *think*," Lance damn-near snarls.

Phillips plants his hands on his hips. "I beg your pardon, Mr. Suth—"

"It's *Chief*," Lance interrupts, and it's *definitely* a snarl. "And no, you will not get my pardon. Unless you're going to throw out ideas for how we can keep this thing from running apeshit through *my* town, keep your useless fucking piehole shut."

Phillips's jaw drops in utter disbelief, but Lance has no time to baby the man. "Predators," he mumbles to himself. *Predators hate competition—threats to their livelihood.* It's an answer, but he doesn't know what he's supposed to do with it.

Tucking it to the back of his mind, he leans down into the vehicle, switching on the PA system and grabbing the handset. He straightens, scanning the dark shadow of the mountain, but buildings obstruct too much of his vision even if he would some-how be able to see something in the dark.

"Attention citizens," he begins, and then all hell breaks loose.

It starts with a few screams filtering through the night, sharp and punctuated, and then those screams are joined by more, until, like a wave, a chorus of terror-filled cries sweeps through Telluride.

"Get off the streets. Find your way indoors and shelter in place." He can tell that mania already has too strong of a hold over the people for a broadcast to work at all, and he tosses the mic back into the cruiser with a curse. "We're doing this the old-fashioned way, then."

Slamming the car door shut, he begins jogging toward the

nearest group of tourists, looking around wide-eyed like they aren't quite sure if this is all some sort of special event. "You folks need to get inside. Now."

"What's going on?"

"Is something wrong?"

Lance doesn't have time for their questions, and begins ushering them up the walkway of whichever shop is closest. "You're in danger out here; everyone needs to get indoors."

"Our hotel is just up the road," one of them protests, balking against his attempt to herd them.

A piercing scream cuts through the night, and they all freeze momentarily. "It's off this street?" Lance verifies. When one of them nods, he steps out of their way, gesturing behind him. "Go, and hurry."

The report of a gunshot bounces off the mountains, giving the group the only convincing they need to run off in the direction of their hotel, and Lance moves forward to the next group of civilians, and the next, trying to keep people from blindly stampeding while getting as many inside as possible.

"McCurdy responding to gunshots near South Oak and San Juan," Lance's radio chirps.

"Roger. Sutherland on Colorado, between Fir and Aspen, I'm rounding up civilians. Any eyes on the disturbance?"

"Negative from Gorsky. I'm at Colorado and Willow doing the same, Chief."

McCurdy comes back over the radio, a tremor in his voice. "There's something ... dammit, I can't get through the crowd. I'm abandoning the car to pursue on foot. There's something out here, some fucking creature from hell."

"Do not engage on foot!" Lance orders as soon as the line is clear. "Focus on crowd control. Get people indoors and away from that thing."

He waits, fingers and teeth buzzing with the adrenaline in his veins.

"Copy that."

He knows there aren't enough of them on the streets to keep everyone safe, and there's still the greater problem of how to fucking lure 240 out of—

"This is the crash team up at KTEX. Do you need us to respond?"

The airport. It's far enough outside of town to minimize casualties, has its own supply of pyrotechnics, and the aircraft rescue and firefighting team stationed there will be able to make sure the whole mountain doesn't catch fire from the wind.

"Stay put, Crash. We'll keep you posted."

"Roger."

Lance stops in the middle of the street, scraping his fingers through his beard and trying to come up with a way to get 240 to chase him to the airport without condemning himself to certain death.

Snowy fucking egrets.

It slams into him out of nowhere, so suddenly that he stumbles a few steps before turning and sprinting for his cruiser.

Almost like the cry of a snowy egret, just louder. Has it really only been hours since Effie told him? Because it feels like a lifetime ago.

It shouldn't surprise Lance to find Phillips huddling behind the hood of the SUV, pale-faced and trembling, but it does, if only for the fact that he'd managed to somehow forget about the man in the short time since chaos broke loose.

"What's happening?" Phillips asks.

"Get in the car," Lance barks, ripping open the driver's side door and cranking the ignition. He throws on lights and sirens and stomps on the gas, momentum slamming Phillips's door shut for him as the man yelps in surprise. "You got a phone?"

The cruiser practically drifts through a traffic circle, and Phillips's shoulder slams into the door, eliciting another yelp. "Where the hell are we going?"

"PHONE," Lance repeats.

Phillips digs it from his pocket. "Jesus, yes, no need to yell. You're act—"

"Get me an audio clip of a snowy egret." His eyes dart down to the speedometer, watching it inch past 70mph, and the engine catches, automatically shifting gears as the RPMs jump into the 5,000s. His grip is tight on the wheel, the vehicle shuddering as it opens up to speeds it's never driven, not on the winding mountain roads. Luckily, the majority of where they're headed is a straight shot.

"Pardon. An audio clip?" Phillips asks, tone pinched yet polite in his confusion.

"Google a snowy egret call," Lance repeats, glancing back down to see they've topped 100mph. An almost giddy surge of adrenaline flips his stomach, and he watches the road carefully, well aware that neither he nor his passenger is buckled in and too worried about losing control of the vehicle to fix that for himself now.

"Why?" Phillips asks, but a quick glance is enough for Lance to tell that he's at least doing what he's told.

"We're going to lure her out of town."

"How is a bird call supposed to help with that?"

Lance shifts his grip on the wheel, hoping the half-formed plan in his brain is enough, that he didn't just abandon the town in a moment of crisis for nothing. "Gonna hope she thinks it's another Azzie."

Phillips makes a disgruntled sound, reaching over his shoulder to buckle his seatbelt. Then a YouTube ad filters from his phone's speaker, and he skips it forward. Long, low notes that sound like shredding paper fill the cab, raising goosebumps along Lance's arms and neck.

"Holy Mary, Mother of God," Phillips marks himself with the sign of the cross.

Lance shoots him a concerned look. "What is it?"

"It sounds so similar to them," he whispers in awe. "Not their normal communication, but when they're angry."

Relief is a heady feeling, sweeping through Lance strongly enough to make his teeth buzz. "Let's hope it's enough to make her give chase, then."

He slows, throwing on his blinker out of habit as he takes a side road up the hill toward the airport. When they reach the top, he parks by an airfield gate at the crest, cranking up the volume on the PA system. "Still have any reservations about killing our visitor?" he asks.

Phillips shakes his head, wiping nervous sweat from his brow.

"Great. I need you to operate the PA. Any idea how fast these things can move?"

"It's, um," Phillips clears his throat, nervously toying with his phone. "It's hard to say because of how tight things are underground. Our best estimation is maybe around forty miles per hour at top speed."

"Shit." Lance runs a hand through his hair and hands the PA mic to Phillips. "It's push to talk. Keep that egret playing."

Phillips holds his phone up to the handset, and the egret's call blares out over the valley. "So, uh, what's the plan here, Chief?" Phillips holds his hands dramatically to the side to avoid his voice being picked up on the speaker.

Lance opens up the center console and grabs a small pair of binoculars. "Once we know she's heard us and is giving chase," he starts, removing the caps from the lenses, "we're going to move onto the airfield. I'm going to run inside the main building, grab as many bangers and screamers as I can, and hope for the best." He keeps the window rolled up to prevent major feedback from the PA, raises the binoculars, and trains his gaze out of the window.

Though the speaker attached to the SUV is loud, Gordon's answering call still manages to reach them, and a cold shiver runs down Lance's spine.

A low whimper comes from Phillips. "Keep that audio going," Lance reminds him, keeping his eyes on the town.

16

2042 MDT // 4d 17hr 39min after arrival

Terror has swept the streets of Telluride. A pretzel cart has been knocked over, and frenzied feet stomp through the pale yellow cheese dip congealing on the sidewalk without notice. Parents snatch up their children in an attempt to keep them from harm's way, but there is no sense of order, and those with no direction in mind are pushed over or knocked into buildings as others race toward perceived safety.

The tang of warm blood paired with the sour stench of fear overtakes the Azathothlin's senses, and it is nothing short of electrifying. She clicks happily from deep in her throat, the sound ringing out over the cries of terror that fill the night.

This isn't a hunt; this is a show of power.

Gordon lunges after a group of people, one raptorial foreleg snapping forward to spear through a man's back. She brings him to her mouth, mandibles locking around his shoulder before she pulls her head back.

A short, wet rip vibrates through her as her leg partially tears through his lower torso before the socket finally gives with a satisfying *pop*, and she shakes his body off, flinging it across the road where it hits a building with a solid *thwack*, blood spurting from the stump of his arm and a roll of leaking intestines shooting from the wound in his gut. Both body and organs land with a wet smack against the sidewalk, accompanied by a loud crunch as she cracks his arm in her jaws, warmth flooding her mouth as blood and marrow spurt down her throat.

Still chewing, working on grinding down the larger bone fragments into more manageable pieces, she moves through town, reveling in the way the humans scatter before her. Weak, fragile, clumsy little things.

Warm, meaty, and tasty, too.

A loud crack cuts through the screams, and something smacks into her side. As she turns her head back to inspect it, another crack echoes, resulting in another ping against her armor.

Her antennae sweep over her shell, finding two dents in the carapace, both smelling of something metallic and acrid. She lifts her head, a lower, more threatening sound shredding from her throat as she scans the street.

One human stands watching her, arms raised and clasping a gun while everyone around him runs. She rushes toward him, and more cracks rent the air, the weapon in his hands flashing with each sound. She's pelted with bullets, but though their impact registers, they don't pierce her exoskeleton.

After nine shots, the magazine is empty, and she screams at him, the sound low and ripping and loud enough to make him stumble backward. But she lunges forward before he can fall, clamping her mouth around his shoulder and whipping her head back to send him flying into the air.

Both his bladder and bowels loosen as he flies, and she smells the stink of him before she raises one forelimb to snatch him from the air and swing him down against the ground with enough force to pop his head free, sending it rolling down the road. It bounces off a curve, leaving a bloody trail of gore in its wake.

Gordon doesn't wait to see where it stops, dropping his body and continuing through town, kicking over cars, punching through glass windows, and snatching up any person too slow to avoid her.

Lamplight reflects in the blood that coats her face, chest, and legs. A few more brave citizens have tried to shoot her, but nothing has pierced her shell, and now they are all dead, scattered in ragged parts down Main Street.

A group of people huddle inside a building, and she lowers her head to peer through the glass to watch them, her antennae dancing across the smooth surface. The window shatters easily beneath the tip of her leg, and she lowers her chest to the ground to reach inside when she hears her own call—an Azathothlin call—echo across the valley.

Gordon pauses, pulling back from the building and standing to her full height as it rings out again.

It's slightly garbled and tinny, but it is unmistakably a cry of anger. Rage. Power.

It's a cry of dominance, and her eyes focus on its origin, on top of a hill behind the town, where red lights blink on top of a tall tower.

Rising up on her back six legs, she answers with a tearing, ripping cry of her own. Then she drops onto all of her limbs and runs forward, stomping through the roofs of buildings and knocking over telephone poles as she heads directly for whatever has dared to challenge her.

17

2056 MDT//4d 17hr 53min after arrival

Anticipation swirls heavily in Lance's gut as he methodically scans the horizon. He has to remind himself to keep breathing, wanting to hold his breath on impulse.

Then he sees her, not so much crawling over buildings as post-holing through them, moonlight reflecting off her sleek back and the four glittering orbs of her eyes. She lifts her head, letting out another shredding cry, and Lance drops the binoculars into his lap, slamming the transmission into drive and cranking the wheel to avoid the airfield fence.

He grits his teeth as the cruiser bounces over a rut before returning to the road and flying toward the parking lot.

Phillips releases the button on the mic at the piercing shriek of metal against concrete when Lance turns the corner too sharply, clipping a barrier.

The chief whips his head toward him, and Phillips mumbles an apology, pressing his thumb back over the button, and the audio goes live again. The tires squeal against asphalt when Lance slams on the brakes, stopping just inches from the gate leading onto the airfield.

"Comeon comeon comeon comeon," he mutters, tapping his thumbs against the steering wheel impatiently while he waits for the RFID reader to detect the patch stuck to his windshield.

"What the hell are we doing?" Phillips hisses nervously, glancing toward the crest of the hill obstructing their view of town.

The beeps Lance knows to expect from the automatic gate aren't audible over the PA, but the gate shudders before sliding open, and Lance pulls the car through, whipping it around to the entrance of the passenger terminal that doubles as airport operations. "I'll be back," he says to Phillips, throwing the car door open.

His eardrums are immediately assaulted by the egret call blaring from the speaker on the roof of the car, and he slams his hands over his ears as he runs into the building.

There's a door down a short hallway, posted with a sign reading RESTRICTED AREA. AIRPORT PERSONNEL ONLY. Lance skids to a halt, bringing his hand up to the keypad as his eyes dart back and forth, his mind blanking in the moment of crisis. "No emergencies," he murmurs, pressing in 0911, the code given to the sheriff's department. He's used it every now and then to bring Effie things she forgot on her way in—snacks, Red Bull, a phone charger—but today is the first time he's ever come in with cause.

He sprints through the main office to the door leading to the garage bays where all the pyrotechnics are locked away and slides to another halt, running back the opposite direction.

"Can I help you?"

Lance's heart leaps into his throat in shock, then settles as he sees the person sitting up from behind the tall counter. Even when the tower is closed, airport operations stay manned twenty-four seven. "I need the key to the garage locker," he gasps out.

The man behind the counter stands, wiping his hands on his pants as he moves to a key box on the wall behind him. "Is there something wrong? One of the deputies came by earlier and took a bunch of bangers and screamers. Those things are expensive, and they're specifically meant for bird dispersal. I don't think we can just be handing out—"

"An alien has attacked the city, and it's being lured up here to minimize collateral damage," he interrupts, and the man drops the keys to the floor. "You need to stay inside, wherever your shelter-in-place point is, and keep anyone else in the passenger terminal inside as well."

The man hands the key over, fumbling around for a logbook to sign them out. "I'll bring them right back, I promise." Lance runs out to the garage without waiting for acknowledgment.

He wastes no time gathering what he thinks he might need and then a bit extra, then heads back through the building. When he places the key on the counter, he holds his palm over it long enough to make sure the man is paying attention to him. "Once you make sure everyone is sheltering, call the ARFF team. Let them know to stay indoors, out of sight, but on standby, until the situation is under control. We'll need them to manage a fire." Then he's back out the door and racing for the cruiser.

"Jesus fuck, that thing is loud," he laments once he's back in the driver's seat, dumping his haul carelessly over his lap and the center console. He begins loading a round of blanks into a magazine. "You ever shot a gun before?" he asks.

Phillips watches him, swallowing nervously. "Not for a few years."

Lance nods, loading the clip and holding the firearm up. "This is a 308. It's loaded with ten blank rounds." He opens a box of pyrotechnics, pulling out a red cardboard tube about half the size of a roll of pennies. "This is going to fly roughly fifty to seventy-five feet before it explodes. You'll need a new one after each shot. Black tip out, just push it right into the barrel." He demonstrates, sliding the pyrotechnic into the end of the small pistol before replacing it in the box and setting both weapon and ammunition in Phillips's lap. The intent of a bird banger is to scare away flocks of birds from the noise of the cartridge exploding, but he's hopeful that the Azathothlin is a big enough target for the explosion to make contact.

"You—you want *me* to fight it?" he stutters.

Lance is loading another magazine, which he sets in a cup holder, and then another. "I want your help, yes. I know fire hurts her, but one of these is not going to be anywhere near powerful enough to put her down. We're going to need—" he pauses, his mind finally turning at full capacity now that he's actively working through a plan. "Something more powerful," he finishes, setting the half-filled clip on the dash and turning up the volume on the radio. The air is silent for now, so he keys up. "Griffin, you on freq?"

"Griffin up; go ahead."

Now that a plan has fully formed in his mind, Lance is almost afraid to ask the question. He closes his eyes, holding his breath. "Do you have any ANFO left?"

"Affirmative, a couple bags."

A gust of wind buffets the cruiser, and he can't tell if he's dizzy with relief or if the SUV is actually swaying. "Get up to the airport, and expedite it."

"Wilco, Chief."

Just as Lance feels the first real assurance of victory settle over him, Phillips lets go of the PA mic. But before he can say anything, the older man unbuckles his seatbelt. "It's here," he whispers hoarsely, then pops the car door open, leaning out to vomit.

The world seems to slow as the chief turns to look at the alien at the far end of the airfield. It's the first time he's ever laid eyes on her, and goosebumps ripple across his body, the hair on the back of his neck standing on end. She's huge and imposing in the dark, her strong, tapered legs and the underside of her body highlighted by the runway lights. "Shit." He grabs the half-filled magazine from the dash, his fingers shaking so hard he fumbles the ammunition, dropping the small metal casings all over his lap.

"What do we do?" Phillips asks, wiping his shirtsleeve over his mouth.

The question somehow grounds Lance, and he stops for a moment, arching an eyebrow. "Isn't that supposed to be your fucking area of expertise?" He doesn't wait for an answer, turning his attention back to his hands to finish loading.

The Azathothlin bellows angrily, the sound deep and resonating enough to vibrate the car, and Lance risks another glance over his shoulder to see her crawling slowly up the runway, scanning for her competitor.

In the seat next to him, Phillips does a quick series of inhales and exhales, all from the mouth, and Lance is worried he might be hyperventilating. Then the man steps out, raising his arms over the roof of the SUV, and fires.

Lance flinches at the unexpected shot, the report like thunder in his ears, and he whips his head around to watch the cartridge sail through the air before exploding with a flash of light, followed heartbeats later by a resounding BANG.

240 zeroes in on the sound and moves forward.

Phillips fumbles for another cartridge, a low keening sound issuing from his throat.

"She's still way out of range," Lance snaps, shoving a handful of bangers into his pocket and throwing his door open seconds before Phillips fires off another shot.

This one, too, falls several yards short of her location and is blown sideways by the wind, but this time, 240 has seen where it came from and narrows her eyes at them. Her antennae extend, waving through the air as moonlight glints off of something silvery dripping from her mouth to the asphalt.

Oh, God ... is she drooling? Lance can't tell if he's spoken the thought aloud, because she lets loose another tearing roar before charging toward them.

Even with years of experience under his belt, Lance's bowels threaten to liquify and everything in his stomach turns sour, attempting to rush up his throat. But he stands, keeping his eyes locked on the approaching predator, and slips a banger into the muzzle of his weapon before aiming it in her direction at a slight pitch.

He waits, watching the area where Phillips's previous shots exploded, waiting for her to get within range even as every muscle in his legs tenses, instinct telling him to run from the monster ahead of him.

Phillips, apparently, isn't quite as adept at overcoming his baser instincts, and screams, firing blindly behind him as he takes off for the terminal.

The cartridge hits the tarmac and tumbles wildly for a few feet before exploding. The Azathothlin's focus locks on Phillips, and Lance risks taking his eyes from her to watch the other man's retreat.

It's clear fear has him in a terrorizing grip. He runs toward the entrance, but instead of grabbing the handle when he reaches the doors, he slaps his palms against the glass, screaming hysterically. "HELP ME! PLEASE HELP ME!"

Lance doesn't have to worry about turning back to the alien, because she's already on Phillips, one of her front legs shooting out and grabbing him around the waist just as he seems to remember how door handles work. "No!" he wails. "No, it's not fair! I made it—NO!" His fingers slip from the handle as she pulls him up into the air, his feet flailing as she raises him to her face. Phillips manages to pry one arm free, raising the gun and firing point blank.

The shot echoes off the building, but there was no cartridge loaded into the muzzle.

Lance shoots, watching as the red cartridge taps her side and bounces free, landing at her feet before exploding.

"Shit." She's too close.

The flash of heat beneath her gets her attention though, and she must assume it came from Phillips, because she roars in his face, spittle flying from her mouth as he shoots off round after round of blanks, screaming the entire time.

The sound of constant firing almost covers up the synchronized, wet crunch as she snaps his ribcage, but his agonized wail and the darkening patch on his shirt are enough to prove it happened.

Lance pulls his sidearm free and fires off a couple of shots that hit, but don't seem to harm the alien.

They do, however, pull her attention away from Phillips, and her gaze levels on him, all four eyes narrowing into an unmistakable glare.

Lance's mouth goes dry, and he drops back into the driver's seat, slamming the door shut just as she throws Phillips in his direction.

The man's scream is abruptly cut off as his body collides with the car, the entire frame rocking on impact. His back bends over the roof, snapping his spine and smacking his head hard enough to dent the metal.

He could just be unconscious, Lance tells himself, his foot already slammed against the gas. The tires spin with a squeal before catching, and he lurches away from the building, Phillips tumbling onto the tarmac.

Lance glances in his rearview as 240 gives chase, picking up Phillips and lobbing him toward the vehicle again. Lance winces, angling the car onto the runway as Phillips's body collides with the back of the SUV, crumpling unnaturally. *Definitely dead, then.*

Once on the runway, speeding into a relative headwind, he holds the wheel steady with a knee and loads another cartridge, then rolls down the window, reaching over with his right hand to aim behind him. He releases some of the pressure on the pedal, giving 240 a chance to catch up, his eyes darting between the rearview mirror and the quickly disappearing runway ahead.

When he estimates she's around sixty feet behind, he turns his head to look at her and fires, quickly turning back around. In the rearview, he watches the banger explode just in front of her chest, and she bellows at him, lowering her head and picking up speed.

He quickly reloads, letting her gain a small bit of ground and firing again.

He's shoving another cartridge into the muzzle when this one hits, exploding against the side of her face. As she slows, shaking her head with an elevated, tearing cry that shreds the air, he slows, too, firing another.

The flame is gone, but one of her mandibles is still smoking when the next flies over her head, going off against the back of her neck.

Lance doesn't give himself time to deliberate whether or not it caught or was just enough to flash the heat against her. He just keeps reloading banger after banger, some hitting, others flying wild, his ears ringing from the endless assault of noise.

And then he crosses the runway threshold into the overrun.

In a move he hasn't pulled since he was a dumbass nineteen-year-old, he drifts, letting the back end slide in front, lifting up onto two tires for a heartbeat that feels like an eternity, and then comes to a stop, front bumper facing an alien that's absolutely, without a doubt, *pissed.*

"Come and get me, girl," he whispers, trying to figure out if his cruiser is fast enough to squeeze past her if she's distracted. He grabs his handset. "What's your ETA, Griffin?"

"Pulling onto Last Dollar now, Chief."

"Copy that." His last transmission is almost drowned out as 240 bellows her anger at him again, stomping a few steps closer, the tips of her legs indenting the asphalt, breaking free little chunks. *Effie's gonna kill me for that spall.*

He grabs the fully loaded clip from the cup holder and loads it into his firearm, shoving another banger into the muzzle and leveling it out the window.

There's no blood in his veins, just pure adrenaline laced with a healthy dose of fear and a burning will to survive. He can do this.

The Azathothlin takes a few steps closer, locking eyes with him, and lowers her head. A low, menacing tone not punctuated enough to be called a growl rolls across the runway, and he steels himself.

Then her back raises in two perfectly split halves, angling out from her shoulders as dark, smooth wings unfurl like a sail behind her into the night, catching the wind and snapping open.

18

2105 MDT//4d 18hr 2min after arrival

Kel's head is buzzing, and Effie's words sound like they're coming to him from an entirely different room. He stares, head slowly tipping to the side as his mind tries to wrap around this additional level to an already beyond-fucked situation.

And then he starts to laugh. Loud, hysterical, uncontrollable laughter.

Because he's smarter than this, and the fact that he could be so near-sighted, so unable to piece together the simplest fucking puzzle of his life ... he'll cry if he doesn't laugh.

"Kel?" Effie's voice is small as she touches his arm, no longer self-assured. The fact that this has grown bigger than even her confidence can bolster is enough to snap him out of his stupor, and he slaps his hands over his mouth, swallowing down the rest of the mania.

"I'm sorry," he says, wiping tears from beneath his glasses. "I just—*fuck*, dude. How did we not expect there to be eggs? We know there are males here. What other logical reason would there be than for them to arrive first, build a hive network, and wait for females? What do we know about every apex predator? Their first and strongest instinct is survival. And what three things are necessary for survival of a species? Food, shelter, and fucking *procreation.*" He's rambling, gesturing wildly at the pile of eggs in front of them, so he doesn't know that all the blood has drained from Effie's face until her grip tightens on his arm and he turns to look at her.

She licks her lips, swallowing hard. "What was that you said?"

"About apex predators and survival?"

"No, about the males arriving first." She bites into the side of her thumbnail, her eyes darting around the cave in front of them. "About a network."

And even though his brain has laid the facts out in front of him, all lined up in a neat little row, what they mean hasn't hit until now. "The males will have found a way here. She wouldn't have made a nest where they can't reach her."

Effie sinks down to her heels, fingers digging into her knees. "What the fuck are we supposed to do, Kel? How do we fight this?" Her voice is tight, with fear or tears or probably both, and something about her losing it makes him calmer, his mind clearing. He can be the expert here.

"We do exactly what we planned," he tells her, crouching down to her level. "We can't map this shit out. We don't even know how many of them are out there. But we can take care of Gordon, and we can take care of this clutch. And then we bring our evidence to the authorities—away from Lance's agency—to people who will actually help. And if they won't, then we go public until someone who knows what they're doing can come in and eradicate the entire colony." Her arms are wrapped around her knees, all of her prior bravado leeched in the face of what this means, but her eyes have lost the blank stare. Instead, she's looking at him, holding on to his every word like they're anchoring her in reality. "Nothing has changed. We just stop Gordon."

"We just stop Gordon," she whispers back with a nod, pushing herself to stand, hands on her hips. "Then we make someone else deal with the rest." One more affirmative nod, then she takes out her phone, snapping a few pictures of the eggs. Chewing on her edge of her thumbnail again, she glances at Kel. "Wanna pick one up? For scale."

"Not really." But he does anyway. The surface of the egg is cool and slick. Not slimy, just … incredibly smooth. He picks it up, stuck between cradling it like a baby or holding it out like a fish. It's maybe a foot and a half long and weighs at least a few pounds.

Effie snaps pictures the whole time he's examining it. "That's golden. The candid ones will look less photoshopped."

"Should we … take one?"

Her nose scrunches up as she considers. "Not alive. If Lance's people got their hands on it, there's no telling what they'd do with it. But we can break it. Did you bring any collection stuff? We can save a bit of whatever is inside."

"Yeah, good idea."

Kel drops his pack, digging out a bag of pliers and baggies and vials. Effie turns her camera to video, hitting record as he finds a shard of rock to crack the shell.

He drives the sharp edge downward, but it glances off. He frowns, and Effie reaches to her belt, pulling her knife free and offering it to him hilt first. "Watch your fingers," she cautions.

He nods, focussing on the task at hand. He plunges the knife into the egg, and after initial resistance, it sinks in to the hilt. Holding one side of the shell, he pulls the knife down, and it feels almost like slicing into a cantaloupe, just a little firmer. A goopy, yellow-green liquid is seeping from the line he's cut into the shell, and he rotates the egg, continuing the rough incision.

Eventually, he's able to crack it in half, exposing the innards. The creature inside is curled up in a ball, an almost perfect miniature of Gordon. He pokes it with the tip of the knife, and the metal sinks into it with almost no resistance. It's already been cut in two by his opening the egg, but a wave of sympathy turns his stomach.

It's an adolescent monster, not a baby, he tells himself, lifting apart its curled limbs with the edge of the knife. Still, dissecting it here in this cave feels wrong in a way he can't shake. He settles for scraping up some of the amniotic fluid, depositing it in a vial before collecting remnants of the shell. His stomach turns again, but he scrapes up some of the thing's guts that spilled onto the rock, then carves off a bit of what would have been its exoskeleton. Turning a gallon-sized ziplock inside out, he scoops up half of the embryo.

"Okay," he says, wiping the knife clean on the leg of his pants before handing it back to Effie. "That should be enough biology for the evening."

She stops recording, taking the knife when he offers it. "I wish I didn't know that these will all grow up to wreak complete chaos on the world. Destroying live eggs just feels … icky."

"These things … they don't belong here. If they grow into another Gordon," Kel starts, storing the samples in his backpack.

"I know." She gives him a wan smile. "Light 'em up?"

He nods. "Think of them like a black widow clutch. You ever hesitated to squash one of those?"

A visible shiver travels down her spine. "Okay, empathy evaporated." She tucks her phone into a jacket pocket.

Kel walks around the clutch, trying to figure out the best approach. "What if fire doesn't penetrate the shells?" he asks, not really expecting an answer, because he knows what he should do.

"There are hundreds of them. Do we have the time to sit around and crack them all open?" Effie asks, following his line of thought.

He checks his watch, weighing their options. "We'll have to." He takes the knife back, systematically stabbing all of the shells while Effie prepares the flammables. He doesn't need to open them all the way, just ensure the fire has a place to penetrate. They've figured out a pretty good system, Effie placing small piles of ANFO in his wake, making pretty quick work of the job.

Before they're finished, though, a low, commanding voice cuts through the cavern. "Stop what you're doing. Put your hands up and turn around slowly."

19

2123 MDT // 4d 18hr 20min after arrival

Those wings might just be the most terrifying things Lance has ever seen. They almost seem to shimmer in the moonlight, waving in the wind as they fully extend, their proportion to 240's body no different than that of a butterfly's.

She's stopped advancing, but he needs her moving if he has any hope of getting around her. He fires the banger, and one of those wings curls over the front of her body. The force of the explosion is repelled by the smooth, darkly iridescent surface, heat and light fizzling harmlessly over it. He can see her through it, all four eyes watching him with a simmering anger.

He grabs his sidearm and fires at her, but the bullet actually ricochets off her wing, skidding against the runway a few yards away with a flash of sparks before lodging in the dirt off the shoulder.

The Azathothlin tilts her head, and Lance could almost swear she's laughing at him as a series of clicks works its way up her throat.

"Fuck you," he scoffs, loading up another pyrotechnic. His eyes drop to the boxes scattered across his floorboards, and he quickly changes tactics, leaning over to pick up a green box. He pulls the red cartridge out of the muzzle, replacing it with a green one, and fires. Reloads, and fires.

When these cartridges explode, they scream, whistling in whatever direction the wind takes them with piercing shrieks.

They do what he hopes, and 240 turns her head in the direction of the sound. He fires off three more in rapid succession.

The alien's wing flaps back as she bellows her fury, and in the cacophony, Lance slams his foot on the gas, sending up a silent prayer that the distraction is enough.

She whips back to him as he approaches, and he fires off another banger, aiming low.

It explodes beneath her, against her belly, and both wings snap around her so quickly Lance can feel the displaced air buffet the cruiser. Her legs draw up as the wings form together in a cocoon that covers her entire body, their edges pressed together and wrapped in a way that leaves no identifiable seams.

The pedal is already against the floorboard, but Lance still presses into it with all of his weight as he passes her, the engine redlining.

Once she's behind him, he sees a flash of red and blue ahead, and a hoarse chuckle of utter relief fills his chest. The cruiser starts to shudder with his speed, and he slows just enough to feel confident in keeping it under control, driving a straight line with his knee while he refills the magazine mostly by feel.

The Azathothlin has unwrapped herself, another shredding roar filling the night as she turns toward him, wings folding back up and sliding beneath the carapace that covers them.

"Where do you need me?" Griffin asks over the radio as Lance reloads the gun and guides the vehicle onto the taxiway, back toward the base of the tower.

He swallows, checking the rearview mirror to see 240 scuttling after him. He's not even positive he has a plan at this point. They just need to get her over the ANFO without those wings deployed.

"I'm headed your way, hold on."

A shot cuts through the night, and Lance scans the tarmac in front of the terminal, but he doesn't see anyone.

Avoiding Phillips's body and the blood seeping into the concrete beneath it, Lance pulls up next to the building as Griffin drives onto the airfield and comes to a stop next to him, opening his door and standing behind it with his sidearm raised.

Lance has to give the kid some credit. Even though his face is ashen and a little green around the edges, he holds steady, not a tremor in his arms as they rest over the door.

Another shot rings out, and Lance curses, grabbing another few handfuls of bangers and screamers and running to meet up with Griffin. But it wasn't the deputy who shot, his face tipping up to the tower in confusion as Lance sprints around the back of the cruiser.

The Azathothlin's attention also moves upward with another ground-shaking bellow.

"Bullets don't hurt her," Lance pants. "They just piss her off."

Griffin swallows audibly. "How many people are in that terminal, Chief? I've got a trunk full of explosives, and I think I might be about to shit my pants."

Another shot, and Lance looks up at the tower. Some yahoo is out there on the catwalk with a rifle. He can't be sure in the dark, but he'll bet anything it's the ops personnel, having grabbed one of the wildlife mitigation tools kept on hand for the occasional larger animal that may wander onto the airfield and present a hazard. And now he's armed himself and is playing sniper.

"He's going to get himself killed," Lance mutters.

"What are we doing with the ANFO?" Griffin prompts, mind latched onto the details like always.

Lance takes one quick survey around the airfield, mind racing, and nods. "I'll take it into the field between here and the runway. You head inside, make sure everyone is away from doors and windows."

"But—" Griffin starts to argue.

"This doesn't need to be a two-person job. You can help more by keeping those civilians calm, especially once that stuff blows."

"But what about—"

"That was an order." Lance cuts him off.

Griffin nods, tucking his sidearm into his belt and sprinting for the terminal while the alien is occupied with the man taking shots at her.

Lance climbs into the deputy's cruiser and speeds off just as she launches herself at the control tower. Watching in his side mirror, his blood runs cold as she lands on the side of the structure, the entire thing shuddering beneath her.

The man at the top cries out in alarm, dropping the weapon. It hits one of 240's legs on the way down, spinning it before it clatters against the concrete below and splits into several parts.

Lance pulls to a stop in the sod, knowing he has very limited time, knowing he needs to take advantage of her distraction, but he can't pull his focus away from 240.

Even as he gets out of the car, stepping down into the sparse grass, burned from the heat of the sun all summer, he watches her legs grip the sides of the tower and climb with an ease and speed that make all of his muscles tense, threatening to freeze in the face of abject terror.

One foreleg snaps around the man as he races for the door back into the tower cab, catching him in its spines.

Lance unloads the ANFO, taking a bag and dumping small piles all around the ground, then splashing everything with what's probably a too-healthy dose of kerosene, preoccupied watching 240 pull herself on top of the tower.

One corner of it buckles slightly under her weight, sending a shower of plaster and glass to the ground.

Lance climbs back into the vehicle, buckling himself in and driving across the runway. Turning around so that he's facing the alien, the spread of explosives between them, he loads another pyrotechnic and shifts the transmission to neutral.

From the top of the control tower, 240 seems to find his gaze, then drops the man.

He screams the entire way down, arms and legs flailing, and hits the concrete with a wet slap that Lance can hear from across the airfield, becoming no more than a lump of shadow on the ground.

Lance raises his eyes to find 240 still staring at him, and then she jumps down, one leg spearing through the man's remains as she lands in a crouch.

The alien faces him with an ear-piercing shriek, raising her mantis-like arms. When she lowers her head, he swears she's glaring at him, rage glittering in those black eyes.

She plants her two front legs firmly into the ground, and unfurls those giant, translucent wings.

Lance watches, slack-jawed, as the alien slams its back legs into the base of the control tower. All 110 feet of concrete and reinforced steel, built to withstand sustained winds over 60mph, shakes with the impact.

He swallows, holding steady, and she roars, all four eyes locked on him and shining in the light of the moon as she kicks at the tower again and again and again.

Her cry rings out across the mountain, loud and reverberating with indignation, and almost drowns out the rumbling cracks and low whine of bending metal that precede the entire control tower crumbling to the ground.

Lance watches in stunned silence as concrete, metal, and other debris rain down onto the Azathothlin. A huge cloud of dust obscures his vision, but only for a moment. Even as the wind blows it away, 240 rustles her wings, sending chunks of the tower flying across the ramp.

"You're fucking joking," he says, adjusting his grip on the firearm in his hand as she pushes away the rest of the dust with a great flap of her wings and locks eyes with him across the airfield.

Movement by the terminal door catches his eye, and his focus zeroes in on Griffin, stealthily making a dash for the weapon Phillips dropped before his demise and creeping toward the plaster-and-concrete-covered cruiser, to search for ammunition. "Go back inside, kid," Lance mutters, heart clenching in his chest. But Griffin loads a cartridge into the muzzle of the gun and takes a stance behind the door, too dedicated to leave Lance without backup.

Determined to keep 240's attention, Lance lays on the horn.

"Keep your freak eyes on me, bitch. I'm the one you want," he mutters, even as her laser-focused attention chills him to the bone.

20

Effie's heart leaps into her throat at the unexpected voice, and she raises her eyes to Kel, watching him comply. His Adam's apple bobs, his focus over her shoulder as he takes a step closer to her.

"Don't move!" barks the voice, and Kel stills, flicking his gaze to Effie. He's still holding the knife in one hand, both raised over his head as he watches her with wide, sad eyes.

His expression confuses her, which does nothing to settle her fear as she slowly sets her supplies on the ground and stands, lifting her hands. Her mouth goes dry when she turns around to see three men, clad entirely in black and sporting night vision goggles. All of them are wearing large tanks on their backs, connected to long nozzles that she identifies as flame throwers with a cold certainty. But the first has his nozzle hooked to his belt and is holding her and Kel at gunpoint.

"Drop the weapon," the gun-wielder orders, and she hears the knife clatter to the ground behind her.

"Who are you?" Effie demands, unsure where the bravado is coming from, but latching onto it regardless.

The lead man chuckles, a taunting, dangerous sound. "Don't

worry about who we are, Miss Blake. Worry about how much trouble you're in now that we've found you."

The direct address cuts clean through her, and she knows. These men are from the agency. Betrayal sears through her with a bitter sting. There's only one way the agency would know to come after her and Kel—Lance. Whether intentional or not, his misplaced trust has ruined their chance to stop this.

Her hands drop as the world seems to spin around her, all that bluster dissipating in the wake of her reeling emotions. But before she can get sucked into the vacuum left behind her shattered trust, the warm glow of anger stirs in her chest. She latches onto it, setting her feet and lifting her chin. "It's too late. We've killed them all."

"We'll determine that," the agency man answers flatly, snapping his fingers and holding a hand out to the side. One of the others hands him two pairs of flex cuffs, which he tosses across the cave to Effie's feet. "If you cooperate, nobody has to get hurt."

"We're not tying ourselves up," she spits indignantly, calling the bluff of the weapon pointed at her chest. If he'd meant to kill them, he would have done it when their backs were turned.

The leader shrugs, a cruel smirk ticking at one corner of his mouth. "Any interest in corralling the lady, Doctor?" The muzzle of his gun swings to Kel and back to her in a questioning manner.

"Go fuck yourself," Kel responds coolly, taking another step that puts him even at Effie's side.

"I was hoping you'd make this fun." He holsters the sidearm, which seems to be a signal for the other two, who immediately spring forward.

Kel darts backward for the knife, and Effie reaches for the closest weapon she can find—hefting an egg over her head and launching it toward the nearest attacker. It smacks against his shoulder, and he stumbles with a grunt, but is otherwise unde-terred.

Despite the bulk of the tanks on their backs, both of the men are fast and limber, and one of them is on Effie before she has the chance to grab another egg. His arms wrap around her, trapping hers at her sides, and she screams, throwing her weight back and kicking out with her feet. Her head knocks into his chin, his teeth snapping together with an audible click, and one of her heels catches his shin.

Kel manages to nick the other with the hunting knife, but the man is able to catch hold of his wrist, placing a solid blow to his solar plexus and wrenching his arm behind his back. His face screws up in pain, and he drops the knife with a gasp.

Effie screams again, attempting to drive her heel down onto her assailant's toes, but his arms tighten around her, and he tilts back, lifting her and dragging her toward the leader. She thrashes in panic, but even though she kicks at his legs, she's unable to get any real power behind the blows. Her chest hurts where his arms are crushing her breasts, and tears spring from the corners of her eyes.

The leader walks up to her, spinning a pair of flex cuffs on his finger. "Thanks for that. That was the most action we've seen since the incident at—"

A series of low clicks reverberate through the cave, inter-rupting the monologue, and all five of them still.

The hive system.

A wave of helplessness crashes over her, lodging in her throat as another series of clicks echoes around them. Without warning, the pressure around her torso disappears, and she's thrown to the floor. Her shoulder slams into the ground, and she grits her teeth against a yelp.

The man who'd been holding her has the nozzle of his flamethrower back in his hands and is looking wildly around the cave. "Fucking thing was supposed to be in town." His voice is pitched high in fear.

The leader also has his firing shaft in hand, scanning more methodically around them, trying to pinpoint the sound.

Effie rolls to her knees, lifting her eyes to meet Kel's.

There's a startled yell accompanied by a *fwump*, and then a flash of heat at her back. Everything after that happens almost too quickly for her to process.

An ear-splitting roar shreds the air, and Kel is released so his captor can arm himself. As soon as his wrists are free, Kel turns off his headlamp and sprints to Effie. He shuts off her light and grabs her by the arms, pulling her to her feet. Spurts of flame give her just enough light to see by as she follows Kel, stumbling but kept upright by his remaining grip on one of her arms as he darts behind a column.

As soon as her back touches the rock, he releases her, but his body is still pressed to hers, and she can feel his breath against her temple. She takes a deep breath, the smell of laundry detergent mixing with the acrid, burnt-rubber of napalm from the flamethrowers.

Effie peeks out from around the formation, watching as the three men ward off two Azatholins with staggered bursts of flame. The two males, much smaller than Gordon but still more than intimidating, roar at them, darting forward and then leaping back. It looks like the agency men are cornering them, slowly spreading out and advancing. A confusing sense of hope flits through her despite the physical ache lingering in her ribs from how tightly she'd been squeezed.

But then a flash of mottled gray flies from the side of the

cave, knocking into one of the men, and both go rolling. The man screams, a sound of pure, panic-laced terror, and then the sound is cut off as a leg spears through his chest, a spray of blood silhouetted in the air when the limb is yanked free.

The Azathothlin launches itself toward the others, only to be met with a stream of fire. The shredding bellow of the burning creature makes the whole cave tremble, and one of the remaining men drops his gun to slam his hands over his ears.

An Azathothlin immediately lunges for him, and the remaining man sends out a blast of flame, but it flies off target as he's knocked to the side by the remaining alien, and then all light in the cave goes out.

Effie pulls back behind the column, her eyes squeezed shut as the roar of the dying Azathothlin fades out. When the faint ringing in her ears subsides, she hears nothing but the wet tearing of flesh and the snap of bones as the agency men are devoured. It's loud and graphic, and her entire body is trembling as she tries to keep from gagging. Her stomach lurches dangerously, and her fingers curl into Kel's sweatshirt, pulling him closer so she can bury her face against his chest.

Tears leak from her eyes, and she struggles to swallow them down, struggles to block out the splat of meat being dropped to the ground and ripped apart, struggles against the horrible realization that she was so incredibly naïve to think that she could face one of these creatures.

Those men had known what they'd be up against, had been trained, had come equipped with fucking *flamethrowers* and still ended up dead. The whole fight had taken less than two minutes, and while the echo of helpless terror and anger from the man's arms around her still lingered, it was nothing compared to the terror of waiting, trapped in complete and utter darkness, for the monsters to find her.

21

2134 MDT//4d 18hr 31min after arrival

Kel can feel Effie's frantic heartbeat against his own chest, even after the tremors wracking her body subside. The look in her eyes when she'd glanced up at him from the ground is seared into his brain—desolate, helpless, an understanding that she was in way over her head and no longer expected to see the other side of this.

The arrival of the agency men had the opposite effect on him, though. The fact that people had been sent to stop him only spurs him further to make sure the job is finished.

Even if they can't kill Gordon, he *will* get the samples out of this mine and into the hands of the right people.

He squeezes his eyes shut, and the sound of his own heartbeat seems to grow louder, thumping steadily in his ears, until he realizes that the horrid, messy sounds of consumption have stopped.

One series of throaty clicks echoes around him, followed by a solid, rhythmic tapping. Then there's a frantic scuttling, and Kel knows in his gut that the Azathothlins have somehow seen them.

It's strange how time seems to slow so drastically when adrenaline is dumped so heavily into a person's bloodstream. Within the span of a single heartbeat, Kel has figured out that these creatures can see without light. He's also recognized that, aside from the single shot flare gun at his hip, all of their weapons are sitting in front of that egg pile—the one he must destroy.

Simultaneously with all of that, the fresh apple smell of Effie's shampoo fills his whole head, and he knows he has a chance to save her and kill these things in one go, and he's going to take it.

"Stay here," he breathes against her hair, and then he's moving.

Lunging into the open, he turns on his headlamp with one hand while the other reaches for the flare gun. The light is blinding, but it also appears to startle the Azathothlin closest to him, who shakes his head and bellows out a sound of tearing paper. Kel stops only long enough to steady his aim and fire, the shriek of the flare reverberating off the cave walls piercing his ears. Then he's running again before waiting to see it hit its mark.

His ears are ringing, but not enough to block out the sound of the alien as it tries to dislodge the fire melting its exoskeleton. It curls in on itself, raking its forearms across its chest as it shrieks.

Cold shivers course up his spine as he plucks his bag from the floor, reaching in with one hand for the can of kerosene.

His fingers grasp it, ripping it free, and another light joins his as Effie runs for the other backpack, but he doesn't stop to monitor her as he splashes fuel over the clutch.

Another shot rings out through the cave, and he spares a glance over his shoulder to see Effie reloading the small pistol—another round, another bird banger. She flinches when the first goes off, the sound bouncing from the cave walls.

The excess of noise seems to disorient the second Azathothlin as much as it angers him, and he roars, tossing his head and almost pawing at the air with his forelegs as he turns his attention from Kel. Effie fires the second banger, and smooth, dark wings ripple free from his back, wrapping around himself protectively.

Taking advantage of the creatures' distress, Kel picks up his backpack and dashes over to Effie. "Take this and head back to the entrance," he tells her, shoving it into her hands and taking the newly reloaded firearm from her. "It's got the samples of everything, we can't lose it!"

She holds the backpack in front of her with two hands, eyes wide as she shakes her head, but the agonized cry of the first alien has stopped, and he knows they're running out of time.

"I've got this," he insists. "Go!"

Her eyes narrow into a glare that has one corner of his mouth lifting up. Somehow, he knows her well enough to have expected the look. "You'd fucking better be right behind me," she chokes out. Without giving him a chance to reply, she turns and runs, slinging the pack over her shoulder as she races for the tunnel to connect them to the first cave.

The reflective tape they'd pasted next to the entrance is an actual God-send. He could kiss her for having the foresight to buy it.

Just gotta make it out of here first.

Kel shoots off another banger to keep the aliens distracted as he takes a quick inventory of the situation. Even collapsing this next cavern, he's saved enough explosive to take out the main tunnel. Making sure none of those eggs make it to gestation is the new top priority.

He drops to one knee next to the backpack Effie left, pocketing a few cartridges and a handful of 6mm blanks before reloading the pistol. As he works, he gauges the distance between himself and the nest, working out how far he should run before launching the banger at the eggs. Everything is technically too close, but if he can get the trajectory right and have it ricochet from the ceiling ...

Sliding the backpack onto a shoulder, he moves.

"Duck!" Effie screams, her head poking from the tunnel.

Kel drops, whipping his head from her to look around the cave.

While he'd been busy keeping an eye on the first Azathothlin, the second had thrown back its wings and launched itself at him.

What would have been a powerful hit to his head misses thanks to Effie's warning and his quick follow through, but the tip of the alien's leg still shreds through his thigh. He cries out as the creature seems to stumble from the lost momentum, knocking into him with enough force to send him tumbling.

The backpack is lost as he rolls, and stars explode across his vision when his head smacks against rock. Then he collides with a stalagmite, feeling something snap in his chest, and agony rips through his body, starting in his ribs and rippling outward. He can feel it in the roots of his teeth, and his toes curl as his stomach flips.

He gasps, unable to breathe past the pain that blocks out everything else around him.

Wait, no. He's just unable to breathe, period.

The pain in his chest is bright and hot, and his lungs refuse to pull in air, something grating in his chest each time he tries.

His headlamp is no longer attached to his head, but has luckily landed facing outward, so he can see the Azathothlins approaching him. Throughout it all, he'd managed to keep his grip on the gun, and he fires. A loud pop echoes throughout the cave, but nothing else happens.

The banger cartridge was knocked free from the muzzle in his tumble.

His vision goes dark along the edges as he fumbles in his pocket for more ammunition to reload, rolling onto his back and pushing with one foot against the stone floor to scramble backward as he works the weapon. The other leg is a warm, sopping mess, sluggishly pumping blood to the ground beneath him as a hot throb radiates from his thigh. Bile rushes up his throat, the pain radiating from his chest so intense his fingers tremble. Finally, he has another round ready to go, and rolls over onto his uninjured side to try to settle himself.

A bang, followed by a high, whistling shriek, distracts the aliens. Effie has shot a screamer across the cave to try to pull them away from him, or at least disorient them for a moment.

It gives him the time he needs. Gritting his jaw, breath sawing through his teeth in shallow bursts, he pulls his knee up and rolls onto it, holding one hand across his abdomen as he stands. He can't get fully upright, but he doesn't waste the energy trying, just backs up toward Effie, keeping her light behind him as he raises his other arm and fires.

Trusting the cartridge to hit the ceiling and fall into the nest, he turns as soon as he's shot it, not waiting to watch. "Get back!" He waves his hand and tries to scream at Effie, but it comes out in a choked wheeze, and the taste of pennies coats his tongue. She dips back into the tunnel, though, and he forces his legs to run after her, each step shooting fire from his thigh and jarring something in his chest, the pain taking him so far out of his mind that he feels he's watching from some place far away.

The banger goes off, and his foot hits the tunnel entrance.

Effie grabs his sweatshirt, pulling him down to the ground as an explosion shakes the mountain beneath their feet. Rocks pelt Kel's back, and the angry, agonized bellows of the aliens are abruptly cut off, one and then the other, as sections of the roof cave in on top of them.

22

The Azathothlin watches the man, an acute anger filling her entire body. He has hurt her. He has challenged her for this territory. And she *hates* him.

Wind catches in her wings, and she holds them level, refusing to wrap them around herself again. He is no threat to her. She will not show weakness—*cowardice*—by protecting herself within them.

Those small fires he uses to bite through her armor are no match for her, and this time, she will end him.

Gordon has put together that the contraption he houses himself within is capable of moving faster than she can, but its flimsy shell will not provide protection once she catches him. And this time, he will not get away.

Lowering her body closer to the ground, sacrificing range for speed and making herself a smaller target, she launches herself in his direction with a fearsome, challenging cry.

He remains still, which is unexpected, and she wonders if he thinks that he is safe within his metal confines or perhaps he plans to attempt to evade her at the last moment. Maybe there is a trap behind him and he plans to use her momentum against her.

She snaps her wings out, self-preservation demanding she keep them at the ready in case she needs to shield herself, and continues forward.

There's another pop that sends ripples across her vision, and she braces for the biting impact of the fireball against her chest. But he's aimed too low, and she knows it will land beneath her.

At the same time Gordon realizes his fault, the wind shifts, and she is assaulted by an acrid smell. It's the same smell that permeates the dark, smooth surface of the grounds here, burning and sharp and *wrong*, that made her retract her antennae, trying not to let it overwhelm her senses. But now it covers the grass and dirt beneath her.

The projectile lands between her front legs, and her survival instincts light up across every nerve in her body.

It explodes as she wraps herself within her wings, but whatever substance covers the earth catches before she's able to complete the cocoon.

The explosion of the projectile jars her, the sound disrupting her vision, but whatever it caught on fire detonates with a sound that cuts through her entire being.

The placement of her wings catches some of the initial blast force, but then they are forced violently back from her body.

Heat and immense pressure tear through her chest and pulse across her exoskeleton, but Gordon doesn't even have time to cry out before her body is ripped apart. There is only a distinct feeling of disconnection, and then there is nothing.

23

Effie's hands tremble with adrenaline, bile creeping up from her stomach as she crouches over Kel. *Don't fucking puke on him,* she tells herself, swallowing against the burn in her throat that matches the smoky smell of the air. It's unsettling how tantalizing the scent of the burning eggs is, almost like a barbeque, just a bit more acrid.

"You gotta wake up, Kel." She brushes her fingers over his face, drawing them through the blood that dribbles down his temple. The wound there looks worse than it is. After a quick examination, she can tell it's not that deep. His pants, however, are drenched in blood, and there's no tricking herself into thinking that's not a problem. "Fuck." Her hands shake as she strips off her jacket, pressing it against his leg to stanch the flow of blood. "Oh, fuck." Keeping pressure on the gaping wound with one hand, she fumbles for his belt with the other, tugging it free and wrapping it around the top of his thigh. She pulls it as tight as she can, then folds the extra back over, looping it the other way around his leg to help hold the pressure before securing it.

Her stomach lurches when she moves her jacket away from his leg. Too much of the inside of his leg is visible, and she leans with her palms pressed against the rocky ground for several heartbeats as she struggles to regain composure. With a shaky breath, she arranges her jacket over the wound, wrapping the arms around his thigh and tying them together.

"Okay, we're gonna be okay," she whispers hoarsely once the field dressing is complete, gently lifting one of his eyelids open to see if his pupil contracts.

It doesn't, the black center blown wide and eating up most of the gray. She's mildly certain that means he's concussed, but has no clue what to do with the information. At least he's still breathing, though it's shallow and … wet.

Why is it wet? Breathing shouldn't be wet.

Effie moves her hands to her knees, digging her nails in and breathing out heavily as she blinks away the tears lining her eyes. Equal parts smoke and dust and emotion, probably. She's got to hold it the fuck together.

"Eff," Kel mumbles, eyelids fluttering for a moment before falling closed.

Her hands immediately go back to his face, flitting around like a useless mother hen. "Oh, thank God."

He tries to sit up on an elbow and sucks in a sharp breath that makes him cough. A low moan pulls from his chest, and one hand drifts up to his ribcage. "You gotta get out of here, Blake."

"*We* gotta get out of here, asshole," she corrects him, trying to haul him up by his shoulders.

What starts as a hiss becomes a garbled cry as she lifts him to sitting, and his breathing hitches. With the backpack of alien proof on one shoulder, she hoists Kel under the other and struggles to her feet, gripping him around the waist and trying not to worry about the clammy feel of his skin. He grunts and coughs again, and even though he tries to hide it, she sees the blood that coats his lips.

With a stride that feels painfully short and much too slow, she walks with him toward the surface. His one foot drags along the ground with each step, and his breathing is a disjointed wheeze that she does her best to ignore. Because if she thinks about it too much, if she gives herself a moment to consider how much of his weight is on her and how the iron smell of blood is following them through the tunnel, she'll lose her mind.

It feels as though hours have passed, each heartbeat pulsing loudly in her ears, her thighs and calves burning with the exertion of moving uphill and dragging Kel beside her. But she knows it can't have been more than mere minutes.

Sweat drips down her spine, the light from her headlamp bouncing across the walls with each step, and she focuses on their tandem rhythm.

Step-bob. thump thump thump. step-bob. thump thump thump.

Then Kel lets out a strangled moan and pitches forward. Effie lunges to halt his momentum, her foot landing awkwardly on the edge of a rock and her ankle rolling beneath her. She collapses with a startled yelp, landing heavily on her knees but managing to keep hold of him so that he doesn't slam face-first into the ground. A sob of pain and frustration lodges in her throat, her eyes burning with unshed tears as she struggles to her feet, falling to the ground twice before letting out a frantic wail.

Effie pants roughly, refusing to cry but allowing herself to have this moment on the ground as she listens to her own voice echo down the tunnel to either side. Setting Kel on the ground as gently as she can, she rolls onto her backside and stretches her legs out in front of her, tipping her head back in an attempt to staunch the tears that want so desperately to fall.

"There's no time for fucking dramatics," she grumbles, a searing flash of self-pity cutting through her chest. With the back of a hand, she attempts to wipe the sweat from her brow, her skin gritty with dust and ash. Readjusting her headlamp and the strap of the bag over her shoulder, she scoots next to Kel, resting his head in her lap. "You gotta wake up, Dr. Curtis," she tells him, lightly slapping at one cold, clammy cheek.

His eyelids flutter with a gurgling breath, but he remains otherwise unresponsive.

"I can't carry you, Kel." The pitch of her voice rises with the plea, tears edging the words.

A deep, shredding call drifts through the tunnel, raising every hair on Effie's body as goosebumps cover her skin.

She didn't know it was possible, but her system is flushed with another dose of adrenaline, and she's on her feet before having time to think about it. Ignoring the protesting throb in her ankle, she drops the backpack in Kel's lap and squats down behind him, looping her arms under his shoulders to drag him backward through the mine.

It's impossible to tell how far away the Azathothlin is with the way the cave system throws its angry cries, but for how much the sound bounces around, it's scarily easy to tell when the call of one becomes the call of two.

Effie swallows against a rise of panic, shuffling backward faster until her feet hit a pile of rubble and she almost falls over.

She's reached the main mine shaft, and the draft of fresh air that brushes across her face, barely perceptible if it weren't for the stagnancy of the inner tunnels, is almost enough to bring her to her knees.

With a deep breath and renewed spirits, she pulls Kel over the rocks and into the main shaft. Her quads are burning from her squatted position, and her legs tremble, but she grits her teeth and pushes through it.

Once she's backed Kel away from the branching opening, she lowers him to the ground and grabs the bag from his lap. Returning to the opening, she takes out the remaining ANFO and spreads it in a line across the mine shaft, traveling back toward the entrance to the inner cave system and leaving a big pile among the rubble there. Then she dumps the entire can of kerosene, soaking the ANFO and the ground around it before returning to Kel.

Effie finally cries when she picks him up again, her muscles threatening to lock up, and a pained whimper leaves his lips that simultaneously deflates her and fills her with hope. He's in rough shape, and she's probably doing nothing to help with how she's dragging him across the ground, but he's alive enough to protest, and that means something. It has to.

"Just hang on," she grunts, shuffling backward. His hair tickles her chin when she huffs out a breath, and it's only then that it registers he's lost his hat. Of all the things to happen tonight, that's the one that feels like some sort of defeat. He lost his hat, and she lost her unwavering faith in Lance.

But the cries of the Azothothlins are definitely getting louder, and she can no longer afford the energy for self-pity. With tears cutting silent tracks down her cheeks, she hauls Kel backward, not pausing even when she feels a breeze at her back, but waiting until the ground shifts beneath her feet, hard-packed earth and granite turning to looser shale, and she cranes her neck over her shoulder to check her footing on the downward slope, pulling him onto the barely-there ruts of the road that used to be used to access the mine before finally setting him down.

Then she rummages through the pack, shoving a flare gun into her back pocket before grabbing a banger and the pistol. She fumbles with the small cap round, dropping one in her haste before finally slotting it into place and running back toward the mouth of the mine.

The light from her headlamp reflects off the little hairs of an Azathothlin's antennae where the tunnel branches out a hundred yards down the shaft, and without thinking, she takes a single step forward and discharges the weapon.

The crack of the gun echoes loudly around her, and the banger hits the ceiling, ricocheting to the ground and rolling a few yards before exploding with a bang.

But it's several yards short of its target, and the Azathothlin pokes his head free of the branching tunnel, his forelegs wrapping around the entrance as he pulls himself through. Even from this distance, his eyes glitter in the lamplight, and his mandibles part as he roars down the tunnel at her.

Dropping the empty firearm, Effie grabs the flare gun and points it down the tunnel. She screams back at him as she fires, every pent up emotion, all the compartmentalized pain, tearing through her vocal cords as a searing burst of light rockets down the mine shaft at the alien crawling toward her.

It collides, embedding in his chest, and he scrambles backward, trying to angle his legs in the tight space. He manages to bat the flare free with a foreleg, dropping it to the ground beneath him. His eyes meet Effie's with a singular, animalistic rage.

And then there's a soft *fwump* as the flare hits a patch of kerosene-soaked dirt, and a blue flash of fire licks along the trail of fuel before the ANFO ignites with a thundering boom that shakes the mountain, knocking Effie off her feet.

A wave of blistering heat shoots from the tunnel, and Effie throws her arms in front of her face as a ball of fire explodes outward into the night, barreling her over. The mine shaft collapses a heartbeat after, pelting her with rubble.

24

In his distraction, Lance had dumped way too much prill onto the grass, and the force of the explosion hits the cruiser hard enough to set off the airbag and send the car rolling backward. Heat pours in through the open window, singeing Lance's arm, and he's grateful for the face full of polyester that protects the rest of him from the blast.

He feels parts of the Azathothlin hit the car without hearing them, his ears ringing from repeated exposure to gunfire and absolutely shot from the sound of the ANFO going off. When the tires roll off the back of the runway, the surface beneath him turning bumpy, he pumps the brakes and bats down the deflating airbag.

There's no sound when his hands make impact, just the constant ringing over a muffled drone, like hearing underwater.

His field of vision clears, and he stares out at the destruction before him.

A giant crater is blown into the sod on the opposite side of the runway, the world cast in an eerie orange glow as dry grass burns. Lights flicker behind the blaze, and Lance realizes the guy from airfield ops must have at least talked to the ARFF team before surrendering his life to the stupidity of heroism, because the one engine on duty is rolling across the tarmac to put out the fire.

Lance presses the gas, but the cruiser does nothing but vibrate harder, and his brow furrows as he looks to his side view mirrors in confusion, wondering if his tires are caught or somehow blown. Then he realizes the vehicle is still in neutral, and shifts into drive.

The runway and taxiway are dotted with chunks of dirt, granite, and alien, and he tries to avoid any larger pieces as he makes his way toward the terminal, stopping by the fire engine and getting out.

His legs almost buckle beneath him, jittery with the adrenaline coursing through his system, and he shakes them out before approaching.

One of the firefighters says something to him, but Lance can't hear anything past that infernal ringing, and he shakes his head and shrugs, pointing to his ear. "I can't hear anything," he says. The faint sound of his own voice rattles beneath the ringing, and he takes this as a good sign that the hearing loss isn't permanent.

The firefighter gestures to his own nose, and Lance raises a hand to his face, startled to touch a wet warmth over his mouth that can only be blood. Now that his fingers have acknowledged it, he can definitely feel the stickiness of it against his skin, and his nose throbs painfully.

Though still extremely muffled, sounds start to become audible in one ear.

"You good, there, Chief?" The firefighter asks, handing Lance a towel he retrieved from the truck.

"Damn explosion just about took my hearing out," Lance explains, raising a tentative hand to his left ear, the one with more direct exposure and still no auditory response. A fluid drips slowly from his left ear canal, and Lance drops his hand before he starts focusing too much on it, wiping his fingers on his pants without looking. "What were you saying?"

"We stayed put like you wanted, but we saw most of it from the cameras. What the hell was that thing?"

Lance accepts the towel, wiping the blood from his beard

and mustache. Most of the fire has been put out, the entire area covered in a thick foam that glows in the moonlight, undulating in the wind in an eerie way that makes him shiver. "I …" He stops, running a hand through his hair.

"My bet is that it's like Godzilla and came from underground," a second firefighter calls, stepping up to them. "I've been trying to tell these guys for years that the hollow Earth theory is more than just a conspiracy."

"I've gotta check in with dispatch," Lance cuts in before they can try to suck him into the conversation, giving them a perfunctory nod and turning back toward his cruiser.

No, *Griffin's* cruiser. His is still parked on the ramp, and he looks in that direction and breaks out into a sprint when he sees a figure lying prone next to the debris-battered vehicle.

He floats away from his body as he drops to his knees next to Griffin. The deputy's torso is bleeding in multiple places, cut by sharp-edged chunks of 240's exoskeleton or shards of granite. The bottom tip of one of her legs rests less than a yard from Griffin's head, covered in blood and pulp.

From above, Lance watches as he presses two fingers to the younger man's neck, careful not to touch the section of skull that was sheared away and is now leaking blood and brain matter onto the tarmac. He watches as his hand raises from throat to brush eyelids closed over blankly staring brown eyes. And then he's sucked back down into his body, pinned to the Earth by the unbearable weight of grief and guilt.

He presses his hand to Griffin's chest, swallowing hard. *You shouldn't have come back out.*

I should have protected you.

Tears prick his eyes. "You did a good job tonight, kid. Stayed calm under pressure. Kept everyone safe … I'm proud of you," he chokes out, removing his jacket and draping it over Griffin's face. Then he forces himself to stand, moving to his cruiser to radio in to dispatch. There's still plenty of unrest in town, but it sounds like they've mostly got things handled, so he keys up the other channel. "Effie, are you there?" He waits, seconds ticking by. "Check in, Eff." Still no response, and though he's uneasy, he hopes that she's just already back on the road home, radio turned off.

Until she calls in, Lance is left to figure out how to deal with the alien corpse strewn about the airfield.

Between the hole in the sod and the crumbled tower, debris is everywhere, and he kicks at a chunk of cinder block with the toe of his boot. His left ear rings incessantly, but his right ear seems to be recuperating. Sounds are still muffled, and the strange pressure is still there, but he'll take it.

Now that the immediate danger is gone, the weight of everything starts to settle in. He looks around at the utter destruction spread across the airport: the parts of the corpse visible beneath the wreckage of the tower, the strange, bright blue blood and bits of carapace that are scattered across the airfield. Walking over to survey the gaping hole in the ground, a glimmer of moonlight across the taxiway catches his eye.

He jogs over, his nose throbbing with each step, and stops when he reaches the edge of the grass. It's a wonder none of it caught, but he realizes now that it was covered.

One of 240's wings is stretched across the turf.

Squatting down, he reaches out a hand toward the dark, shimmering surface. His lips part in shock at the complete neutrality of the feel of it. He expected it to be cool, like glass, or possibly warm from the lingering heat of the fire, but though there is resistance against his fingers, the wing feels like *nothing*.

Curiously, he presses against it, and the resistance moves beneath his touch, bending and dipping with ease as he draws his fingers over the surface. *What the hell kind of* ... His thought fades off because he doesn't even know what to call it. Material? Surface? Membrane? Whatever this wing is made of, he's certain there is no other substance like it on Earth.

Not counting the other 239-odd Azathothlins, of course.

Lance gulps, once again wondering how much the agency knows about these creatures, wondering what they might be able to do with the knowledge to be gained from examining them more thoroughly. His gaze travels the full, unbelievably large expanse of the wing, and he remembers how the banger's explosion had hit it without leaving a mark, the way she wrapped them around herself like a shield.

He stands there for a while, alone and lost in thought as his mind and body settle from the exhaustive events of the night, of the past few days. Fresh worry for Effie threads together with the pain of Griffin's death, emotion washing over him until he's adrift, numb to the world as his system clears itself of adrenaline.

It takes a moment for him to register that the muffled thumping that slowly overtakes the ringing in his ears is the chop of rotor blades, and he turns to look over his shoulder. Tracing the source of the sound is almost impossible in this state, but the rhythmic blink of red taillights against the dark expanse of the sky is unmistakable.

He brings an arm in front of his face to protect himself from the debris blowing across the field as three helicopters touch down on the runway, their landing lights showing the surface painted in bright blue gore.

As the rotors slow, the whine of the chopper engines dropping to a pitch he can't currently hear, the door of the first slides open and bodies spill forward, boots splashing through the ichor.

Lance squints, taking slow steps forward and trying to get a read on the uniforms, but he can't see so much as a name tape on the black canvas, much less a patch or indication of status. They're all carrying rifles, too, low port with the muzzles pointed toward the ground.

A Black man in a suit steps out, meeting Lance's gaze almost immediately and beelining toward him. Two of the men dressed in tactical gear flank him, and the rest spread out. Lance notices a couple of others that don't look dressed for combat, but he loses them in the commotion as the other man nears.

Lance runs a hand through his windblown hair, attempting to smooth it back and out of his eyes even as the rotor wash continues to buffet him. He sees the suited man's mouth open, but he's got no chance of hearing anything in these conditions, and shakes his head, pointing to his ears.

The man says something to one of the ... soldiers? guards? One of the black-clad men behind him, who then raises his hand to his headgear to relay a message. When the group of three gets within a few yards of Lance, he holds a hand up in a wave and calls out, "Can I help you?"

The man closes the distance between them, holding out his hand to shake. He's tall, bald, and seemingly unphased by the destruction around him. "The very man I was looking for. I was coming to ask you the same question, Chief Sutherland, but it looks like you've done just fine without our help." His deep voice is also raised above the whine of the helicopters, engines now slowly shutting down. "I'm Vice Director Clarence Howard, very pleased to meet you."

Lance's mouth drops open in surprised confusion, and he shakes the man's hand firmly. "Vice Director, I—" he stops, unsure what to say.

Mr. Howard offers an understanding smile, and there's a quiet grace in his eyes that somehow puts Lance at ease despite everything. "I'm sure you must have a lot of questions, Chief. I'm here to answer what I can and help you navigate everything that comes next."

Lance blinks at him, his surprise quickly fading as righteous anger floods his veins. "With all due respect," he bites out in a tone indicating the opposite, "it's a little too late for help. Help should have come the first time I brought up concerns. It should have come when I asked for answers. It should have come—" His voice breaks, and he swallows, tears stinging his eyes. "It should have come fucking four days ago and not now, when my cousin is out there in the mountains because she had the gumption to do something about it, when one of my deputies lost his *life* trying to make sure that I wasn't facing 240 alone!"

Mr. Howard surprises Lance by nodding. "I know, and I apologize that you weren't listened to. Rest assured that Mr. Phillips will be reprimanded for his part. Things never should have gotten this far, and that's why I came down personally to do what I can to help right the wrongs of how your situation was handled. "

This is the furthest thing from what Lance had expected to hear, and he has no other words except for a flat, "Phillips is dead."

"Fuck," Mr. Howard mutters, reaching out to clasp a large hand on Lance's shoulder. "I'm so sorry for everything you've been through tonight and for everything you've had to witness. I know there's nothing I can do to fix the mistakes that led to this point, but I hope I can at least give you a little bit of peace in telling you that your cousin is safe. A team was sent ahead of myself to make sure that she and Dr. Curtis made it out of the mine."

No, *that* is the furthest thing from what Lance expected to hear. "What do you mean? How … how did you know where she would be?"

The other man drops his hand from Lance's shoulder. "It wasn't hard to put two and two together, Chief. They knew where the Azathothlin was hiding, and you made it pretty clear to Mr. Phillips that Dr. Curtis was of an … opposite mindset to ours. Seemed safest to send in a team just in case."

"Did they find her? Is she okay?" Lance can't keep the worry from his voice.

"They haven't checked in yet, but I'll let you know the moment they do. Now, we have a long night ahead of us. Let's head inside and start getting things settled," Howard suggests, gesturing to the terminal.

With the adrenaline faded and the danger over, Lance's world once again expands outside of the fight and 240. He needs to call or at least text Danielle and let her know that everything is alright, and his hand moves to the holster on his belt that holds his phone. He looks around at the teams that came from the other helicopters, the airport suddenly swarming with people, flashing camera lights, and a low drone of noise as people talk, record, and begin cleaning up. "Yes, sir. If it's alright, I have to make a quick phone call, and then I'll be right in."

Howard assesses him for a moment, his gaze calculating.

"I need to check on my wife and kids."

"Yes, of course. Come in when you're done." Howard gives him one final look before heading inside the building, two guards still flanking him.

Dialing Danielle, Lance runs a shaky hand through his hair. After making sure that she and the girls are okay, he would try to call Effie again. In spite of Howard's assurances, he knows he won't be able to focus properly until he's sure his family is okay.

25

2236 MDT//4d 19hr 33min after arrival

Effie throws her hands out, halting her tumble and scrambling away from the heat until she's even with where she left Kel. She drops to the ground next to him, every part of her body aching, but that's all mostly quieted by the shrieking burn of her skin. It's tender, it's hot, and it feels too tight for her body.

She brushes a strand of hair back from her face, hoping that it's sticking due to sweat and not raw skin or blood. The fire coming from the mine shaft reflects in her eyes, turning the hazel an almost liquid gold. A bead of sweat rolls down her temple, dripping from her chin onto the raw skin of her arm, and she hisses at the sting of salt. But she can't bring herself to move, can't tear her eyes away from the fire slowly burning out as it eats up whatever fuel is under the mountain.

There's a helicopter parked in the basin, its presence shocking until she remembers the three agency men who'd shown up. And with their memory comes that flash of betrayal—*how had they known to stop her?* But she pushes the thought away.

Kel coughs, and she scoots closer, brushing his hair back from his face. "You pulled me out," he rasps.

She smiles wearily. "You've got a major scientific discovery to claim, Dr. Curtis. You don't get to die before that happens."

He coughs again, wincing in pain and wiping blood from his

mouth. Everything he does is feeble. "That's yet to be seen. You've still got to get me off of this mountain."

She glares at him. "Don't fucking talk like that. The hard part's over. We're both making it out of here alive now." She's still shaking with adrenaline, the chemical marginally quieting the constant scream of the burns along her cheeks and neck and *God*, her arms hurt so bad she doesn't even want to look at them.

The radio, she remembers. She can call for help, make sure someone is ready to get Kel the medical attention he needs. Frantically, she pats around her waistline, but the radio is gone, fallen from her belt at some point in the mine and now buried beneath the mountain. She pulls out her phone, but it shows no service, doing nothing but droning at her when she tries to dial 911. The spark of hope sputters in her chest, but she refuses to feel defeat this close to the finish line. "Come on," she tells Kel. "Let's get out of here."

It takes three tries for her to get to her feet, supporting most of his weight. His breaths come in ragged gasps through gritted teeth, and a fresh sweat has broken out along his forehead as he fights against pain and blood loss.

Effie wants to laugh, both of them trying to spare the other from the truth of their own agony. Her ankle throbs with every step, and Kel's shirt rubbing against the raw skin of her arm makes her stomach turn. It's a slow shuffle to the Jeep, and Effie has never been more thankful that she never put a lift on it. The thought of trying to throw Kel up into his truck actually does pull the laugh from her, and she collapses against the passenger side, hysterical giggles quickly turning into sobs. She helps him into the back seat, his knees bent to make him fit as he lays across the bench.

"Maybe—" a gasping breath "—I should—" another inhale that

shouldn't take so much effort "—drive," he jokes.

She wipes tears from her cheeks, gripping his calf since it's one of the only places she thinks won't hurt him. "Always with the jokes, Kelvin Alien-watch."

"Is that—" slow inhale "—what we're—" slow inhale "—sticking with?"

She chokes on another sob, too many emotions and chemicals running through her. "I hope you like it. We're actually foregoing the hospital to head right to social security and make it official."

"Per ... fect."

She tries not to stress about the rattling way he's breathing as she limps around to the front of the vehicle. Has it really only been four hours since she parked?

Turning the ignition, she releases the parking brake and starts a slow crawl down the mountain, avoiding as many potholes as she can, but the road is still bumpy.

The closest hospital is over an hour away, and she doubts Kel can make it that long. Her phone still shows no service, and she curses quietly, dragging her palm over her cheeks to clear the tears there. They refuse to stop falling, and she sits straight in her seat, throwing constant, nervous glances at the rearview mirror to keep an eye on Kel as she descends the mountain.

Derek's cruiser is missing from the base of the trail, and sour dread creeps through her bones at the potential of what that means. She sucks in a ragged breath, blinking through the cloud of tears, pain, and exhaustion fogging her vision when the trill of a ringing phone pours through the Jeep's speakers.

She flinches at the noise, foot pressing against the brake as she answers.

"Effie, thank God, are you okay? Are you guys okay?"

She swallows hard as Lance's voice fills the vehicle, the familiar timbre and cadence an instant comfort, and decides then and there that she doesn't want to know how the agency found her and Kel. Choosing to believe her cousin had accidentally, carelessly let something slip is easier than possibly confirming that he'd deliberately sold them out. The latter isn't a reality she would know how to live with.

"We need help." Her voice is quiet, choked, and she tries again. "Kel is hurt; he needs a hospital."

"Where are you?" Lance asks immediately.

"The turnout for Alta."

"Hold on." Then, from further away, like he's taken the phone away from his face, Lance says, "Requesting medevac for two civilians from highway 145 at the Alta Lakes access road."

"Roger that, Chief, standby."

"What are the injuries, Eff? Is he conscious?" Lance's voice is back to normal volume.

Effie turns to look at Kel, his face deathly pale in the dark, and shakes her head before remembering she has to talk. "N-no. No, he's not awake, and he's not breathing well. His thigh, too—I put a tourniquet on it."

"Okay, you're doing great. I'm sending help, so just hang on. What about you? Are you hurt?"

"Just m-my ankle. And I got burned," she stutters out. "It hurts," she adds quietly, gingerly tucking her throbbing arms to her chest.

A faint radio call filters through. "Chief? There's a bird on the way, ETA thirty minutes."

"Copy. Let them know we've got one unconscious, possible internal bleeding and lung damage with a tourniquet on one leg and another with burns," Lance replies over the radio, then back into the phone. "Did you catch that, Eff? They're coming. Half an hour. You've just gotta hang on a little bit longer."

Effie's hands are shaking so badly she barely manages to throw the transmission into park before collapsing into her seat, and she stops working so hard to keep her vision from unfocusing.

"Talk to me, Effie. You gotta let me know you're still with me." Lance's voice is tight, just on the verge of a tremor.

She blinks, flexing her fingers, which are very cold in contrast to the heat radiating from the rest of her skin and don't want to listen easily. "I'm … I'm here," she says, quiet but unable to find the mental stamina to repeat it louder.

"Good, that's good. I need you to stay awake, okay, Eff? Keep your eyes open and keep talking to me." The tears are now audible in his voice, and a smile twitches on Effie's lips. She wants to tease him about it.

Instead, she frowns, glancing down at her hands in her lap. "I'm so c-cold. And everything's … nothing wants to f-focus."

"It's okay. Can you lie down? Tip your seat back so your blood doesn't have such a hard time getting to your head."

With great effort, she hauls her hand to the side of the seat, hissing as the raw skin on her arm brushes the door. Her fingers numbly fumble for the release, then she's suddenly thrown back, drawing a weak yelp of surprise from her mouth.

"Did you get it? Are you okay?"

Her eyes slide closed, and she forces them open with a surge of panic, knowing that's not what she's supposed to do. "Yeah … I got it."

"Keep your breathing even. Just a few more minutes and someone will be there to help you, okay?"

"Lance?" Effie says, trying to listen but unable to get her

body to obey her. Her side feels wet. Had she been bleeding? No, probably just Kel's blood soaking through her clothes. "I'm s-so t-tired." Her tongue is thick in her mouth, and she can't tell if she's enunciating enough to be understood.

"I know." Is Lance ... crying? It definitely sounds like he's crying, and that scares Effie. "I know, but you've gotta stay awake, just for a little bit longer. Don't stop talking to me."

The command annoys her. She wants him to leave her alone, and she can't fully remember why she called him in the first place. She's about to muster up the strength to tell him to fuck off when it comes rushing back in a burst of clarity, her heart rate spiking. "Did you ... Gordon. Where is Gordon?"

Lance lets out a laugh, wet with tears. "We got her, Eff. She's dead."

Every part of her body feels exceptionally heavy, but she smiles. "Good." Then either the moon and stars start to dim, or her vision clouds over, but the world goes dark.

26

2311 MDT//4d 20hr 8min after arrival

Bethany sits on the floor of the gondola's operator station, knees pulled up to her chest. Her finger, wrapped in a paper towel, throbs dully, and her side aches where she was kicked, but she knows she fared much better than others.

Gina, the gondola operator, had been nice enough to share her shelter once chaos broke loose, and is tucked on the floor across from Bethany.

The wail of sirens cuts through the night, raising the hair on Bethany's arms as apprehension swirls through her in a nauseating wave. But she recognizes the cadence growing closer. It's an ambulance.

Moments after the siren cuts off, instructions are called out, muffled by the walls and garbled by a loudspeaker. "Anyone requiring first aid, please form a line. We'll take care of as many people as possible, but until more help arrives, please let those with greater injuries such as head wounds, broken bones, and chest pains go first. If anyone has any experience administering first aid, please come see us, and we'll set you up with some supplies to help treat minor injuries."

Gina chokes on a sob and leans forward to throw her arms around Bethany, and the two women cry together, relieved to have made it through. Though they'd been strangers only a couple hours before, that time spent together on the floor of the operator's box has bonded them. They've survived this night of terror together.

They separate after a moment, and Bethany wipes the back of her hand across her cheeks. Though they've been told the coast is clear, neither woman stands, both of them knowing what still faces them outside of their little box.

The worker who'd tried to help Bethany close the doors had been trampled to death, his body left broken and bleeding on the concrete. Neither Bethany nor Gina is eager to see that carnage again, and God only knows what awaits them outside the relative safety of the station.

Bethany meets Gina's eyes, and she nods, reaching out to grab Bethany's uninjured hand. Bethany keeps her eyes down as she leaves the operator's box and heads toward the exit, and assumes Gina does the same based on how tight her hand is being squeezed.

Despite her best efforts, Bethany's eyes drift of their own accord, and she sees the boy's blood-soaked shoes. Once she gets to the white shard of bone poking through his leg, she jerks her eyes back forward and rushes outside, dragging Gina behind her.

There are throngs of people in the street and the courtyard area, but though many are hurt and still scared, it's nowhere near the blind mania from earlier.

"I'm going to go look for my girlfriend and kid," Gina tells her, giving her hand a final squeeze before dropping it.

"Good luck," Bethany smiles, genuine but tired, watching her weave her way through the crowd. When she loses sight of her, she steps forward, wondering if there's anything she can do to help. She had basic first aid training in the military, but that's been years ago now, and she wonders if she would be better off just staying out of the way.

A flash of blue and red catches her eye, and she immediately moves toward it, hoping it's Derek, but willing to talk to anyone in the sheriff's department at this point.

Before she makes it through the crowd to the cruiser, a rush of motion from up the road distracts her and everyone else. Men clad all in black enter the street and begin setting up a cordon.

The FBI? Bethany thinks, taking another faltering step forward. After watching the strange team for a few moments, she trains her attention back on the cruiser. It's good that these other people are here. *All help is good help, and this just means we'll all be better taken care of,* she decides.

Lyndsey: Hey, hey, hey! Welcome back to another episode of Off the Beaten Path. If you're new here, we're just a couple of van-life weirdos who love road trips, adventure, and talking about all of it. Today we're recording in the Uncompahgre Mountains of Colorado, and oh *boy*, do we have a mystery for you.

Mark: If you've been following any of the typical conspiracy sites, then you heard that something strange happened out in Telluride back in August. People died, the town was destroyed, but no one can confirm what really happened.

Lyndsey: Here's the thing, there are no official records about that weekend at all. Outside of a couple of news articles about localized wild animal attacks, you can't find a single statement stating that anything out of the ordinary happened. A whole entire air traffic control tower got wiped out, but you wouldn't even know it unless you did some heavy digging.

Mark: Some locals and tourists who were in town on the night of August 27th have claimed that a monster came out of the mountains, but some quite a few groups of truth-seekers have gone out there since, and none reported seeing anything at all.

Lyndsey: Not only have no outsiders found any evidence of a creature, but no witness has been able to provide any photo or video evidence, either.

Mark: That's not quite true. There was a video uploaded to Facebook that made the rounds. It was taken from one of the gondola cars, and there is indeed some sort of shadow that people can see moving through the forest. But, the lighting is shit, and the quality is even shittier. Some people have claimed they see something like Godzilla, others claim Mothman, and most agree that it's creepy, but impossible to say with certainty that there is anything actually there.

Lyndsey: And that's what's wild, right? Something like 2,500 people live in Telluride, not counting tourists, but how did no one get any sort of photo or video when everything hit the fan?

Mark: One popular conspiracy is that a bunch of secret agents showed up and wiped everyone's phones.

Lyndsey: Mmm, well, we're here to deep dive into all the local lore, and throughout the next hour, we'll take you on a step-by-step journey on what purportedly happened that fateful night.

Day 5

Monday, 28 August 2023

1

0003 MDT//4d 20hrs after arrival

Effie's eyes flutter open, the world dim and blurry. A sense of her body comes next, dull pain blooming across her skin, tight and hot where it burned, but something cold runs through her veins, and she has enough cognition to find it ironic that her body is warming up. Her fingers regain feeling and she flexes them, then her toes. When she wiggles the latter, a muted twinge of pain rolls from her left ankle.

It's only moments after that that her hearing starts to return, slowly at first, muffled in her head, then clearly. There's a rhythmic beeping from her left, and she jolts upward in a panic, suddenly realizing she has no idea where she is.

There's just enough light coming through the window for her to make out the hospital room, another woman sleeping soundly in the bed next to her. Vague memories of the medevac flight flicker back to her, but nothing clear.

She'd come to when the helicopter arrived, but faded in and out throughout the ride, unable to focus or carry on a conversation. They asked her questions and told her what they were doing, but she wouldn't be able to say whether or not she responded. At the hospital, her wounds had been treated, and pain meds had been administered. With that throbbing, fiery ache finally quieted, she'd slipped back under.

Now, she looks around the room, noticing her clothes folded on a chair next to her, and, finally, her phone on a table next to the bed. A soft knock at the door interrupts her reach for it, and she looks up with a wide, startled stare.

"Hey, welcome back," a nurse greets, stepping into the room. "It's good to see you awake. Mind if I turn on the light?"

Effie shakes her head, swallowing against the fuzzy dryness she's just noticed in her mouth. "Where's Kel?"

The bright fluorescents over her side of the room temporarily blind her as the nurse tugs the curtain between the beds further closed before moving to the foot of the bed to read her chart. "He's in surgery right now, but don't worry too much. You made sure he made it to us in one piece." She smiles encouragingly. "Looks like you went into shock on your way over and haven't been very lucid since. I'm gonna ask you a few cursory questions just to see how you're doing now. Do you know your name?"

"Effie," she answers, realizing there's a cup of water next to her phone and downing the whole thing. "Elizabeth Blake," she reiterates, realizing they probably pulled her info from her ID.

"How many fingers am I holding up, Effie?"

"Two."

"And do you remember where you were when we picked you up?"

"The turnoff ... for Alta Lakes."

"Excellent." The nurse marks something down in her chart and replaces it at the foot of the bed. "You're on a basic saline drip right now, just replenishing some fluids and electrolytes, and it looks like we have you on tramadol for those burns—lots of first degree there, but a few patches of second as well. I'll go grab the doctor so she can give you a full brief, but do you have any questions in the meantime?"

Effie picks at her cuticles, absorbing the information and fighting against the overwhelming urge to cry. "When will I be able to see Kel—after he's out of surgery, I mean. Am I ... How long do I have to stay in this room?"

"That'll be up to the doctor, really, but now that you're awake and doing better, I'm sure she'll be fine with getting you out of here. I can't see a reason to keep you admitted. Now you just sit tight, and I'll go see what we can do about getting you out of here, okay?"

Effie nods, offering the nurse a small smile. When she's alone again, she grabs her phone and sends texts checking in with both Lance and Bethany, then gnaws on the edge of her thumbnail, letting her eyes wander around the bright, sterile room.

She tries not to think of Kel, not when she can't ask any questions, so instead she focuses on the dull warmth of her burns underneath their ointment-treated bandages and the fact that they made it out of there—*both* of them. She'd killed the monster at the end, but she *isn't* a final girl. She isn't the sole survivor. She can't be.

2

It's past one in the morning before Lance is able to step away again, leaving the force under the lead of Captain Gorsky while he meets with Mr. Howard in the command tent that had been set up in Oak Street Plaza.

"Ah, please, Chief, have a seat," Howard says when he enters, gesturing to a chair across the table from him. "I appreciate you prioritizing this chat. Telluride has been through a great deal tonight, and the next few days are bound to be just as much of a whirlwind."

Lance nods, unsure where to carry the conversation, but brimming with questions just the same.

Before he can voice any of them, Howard continues. "How are your wife and children?"

"Safe. We live outside of town, so my daughters aren't even aware that anything happened tonight."

"That's wonderful to hear. And Elizabeth?"

Apprehension blooms anew through his veins. The night's stress can't be good for his blood pressure, and his fingers twitch with the urge to dig a nicotine pouch from his pocket. "She let me know when they arrived at the hospital. She's stable at least, but Kel is in critical condition."

"It's very upsetting that our rescue attempt failed. I can't imagine the horrors she's faced tonight, and I'm thankful to know she and Dr. Curtis made it out alive," Howard tells him with a serious frown. "I know this probably seems like it's all happening very fast, but you have to understand that it's important to get out in front of these things to prevent mass panic. First things first, I assume you or your wife is planning to go to the hospital at some point today to be with Elizabeth, perhaps bring her back home?"

He fights the urge to drag his hands down his face in weariness. *Today*, meaning it's somehow already Monday. "Yes, as soon as I'm sure things are settled here, I'm going to get cleaned up, check in on Danielle and the girls, and then go see Effie."

Howard nods, sliding a business card across the table. "We understand she's been through quite an ordeal, which is why we aren't yet reaching out directly from the agency. Please give her this number if she has any questions—it's my direct office line—but we think she might be a bit more receptive and feel less bombarded if you were to act as our liaison. Now, we will, of course, be covering all of her medical bills as well as compensating for any damage done to personal property as well as mental and emotional hardship, within reason. But we will need her to sign an NDA as well as give us a formal debrief of the events during and following arrival as she remembers them. The brief can take place over video call, preferably from your office, where we can ensure a secure connection, but we would appreciate that it happen as soon as possible, just to make sure the details are all fresh."

Lance is silent, once again completely caught off guard and unsure how to respond. His interactions with the vice director have been so much more transparent and forthcoming than what he'd grown used to with Patrick.

Howard doesn't seem to mind the lack of response, and continues. "We'll also be doing the same for Dr. Curtis, with one exception, of course—"

"You still want him to work for you." Lance finally finds his voice.

Howard sighs. "I trust your discretion not to repeat this conversation, Chief Sutherland, but yes. We must insist on it, I'm afraid. Our hope is that he trusts you for the fact that Elizabeth trusts you, and that whatever rapport that's in place between you will help you broach the subject with him. Make sure he understands how amazing this opportunity is for him. Make it seem like something he logically can't refuse."

Lance holds back a scoff. "Because he *can't* refuse."

"I know it may seem harsh, but you understand where our hands are tied. He's in a unique position that allows him the means to undermine everything we've been working toward for decades. He may think that the world needs to know about these creatures, but we've run multiple models of what might happen if the greater public had access to this information, and it's cata-strophic every time. I've no doubts that once he's privy to the full breadth of our operation, he will see things our way."

Having no real response to this, Lance just nods.

"Now, before you get back out there, I want to prepare you to deal with the media and the community, as you'll be handling everything on your own as soon as we're finished here," the vice director continues.

A frown pulls at Lance's brow. "How long do you expect to be here?"

Howard looks at his wristwatch. "Oh, we should be able to have our part of everything finished up within the next hour or so." He seems amused by the shocked expression on Lance's face, and elaborates, "We're only here to clean up any non-native mat-ter and ensure that none of the electronics in the area were able to capture or otherwise save any evidence of the Azathothlin's existence. Once our part is done, we'll be out of your hair just as fast as we came, thus my need to brief you on how to handle the media."

It's all overwhelming, but Lance manages to listen as Howard instructs him on what he's allowed to tell reporters or concerned citizens that ask about the night's events and how to plant seeds of doubt that make any extraterrestrial or otherwise outlandish claims seem unfounded and impossible. The low timbre of Howard's voice is both calming and commanding, and Lance finds himself strangely placated, understanding the agency's point of view where the public is concerned.

After coaching him through the most probable scenarios, Howard gives him an encouraging smile. "You'll do just fine, Chief. Just try to stay out of the news as much as possible and remember to divert any attention you can to the community's efforts to rebuild. After we've got Elizabeth's statement, take a couple weeks. Spend time with your family. We'll have a new assignment for you soon enough."

"Wait." Lance holds a hand up, searching Howard's face. "You're moving me?"

"Well, yes. There's no longer an Azathothlin in this area, nor are we expecting there to be any time soon."

Lance was sure there would be some form of repercussion for what he'd shared with Effie and Kel. For conspiring to kill 240. But they have her body now, and soon, they'd have Kel. Maybe that was worth all the trouble. He blows out a breath, raking a hand through his hair as a headache begins to pulse behind his temples.

"Have I lost you, Chief?" Howard cuts through Lance's train of thought.

"Sorry, sir. I'm just surprised, is all. I'd sort of figured after what a mess this turned out to be, that ... well, that I'd be let go," he states simply.

The other man meets his gaze evenly, sucking his teeth before speaking. "I'm going to level with you—there's a lot about what happened with SCP38-1875-240 that was not standard protocol. But, as you know, 240 herself wasn't standard. What happened here was an unfortunate tragedy. I understand that you brought concerns to Mr. Phillips multiple times without being heeded, and we're going to remedy that.

"We recruited you based on character. You're a loyal man, Sutherland. You're committed, and you play by the rules. However, you're also intelligent enough to know how to respond and think on your feet when shit hits the fan. You've got a level head, and that's worth more than gold. There's no telling how many lives you saved tonight with your quick thinking getting 240 away from town—nor how much time, money, and headache you saved the agency as well. We plan to learn from our mistakes here, and we need you on board to help us reassess our protocols and procedures. Rest assured, whatever new position we find you will be coming with a pay raise to reflect how much we appreciate your continued service and discretion."

I can do good for the world. I can keep people safe. Hasn't that always been what he's wanted out of life? Wasn't that why he'd started working in law enforcement in the first place? The agency was unconventional, and there would always be things he didn't know, but ... here was the vice director himself assuring him that he could make a difference. What Effie and Kel went through, the havoc in town, the lives lost ... Griffin ... He can prevent all of that from happening again. And if he can help another town, keep them safe when another inevitably falls, that's *good*. That's the right thing. Right?

They're not the bad guys.

The thought settles inside him. Even if he doesn't fully believe it in this moment, eventually, he will. "Thank you, Director Howard," he says, reaching out to shake the man's hand.

"It's a pleasure to have you on our side, Chief. Give me a call once you have an update." Howard clasps his hand firmly, and Lance exits the tent, mind reeling and still too drained from the night to properly sort through everything that's just been dumped in his lap.

3

0303 MDT//5d after arrival

Kel can't get a full breath in—hasn't been able to since that little fucker kicked him. It had felt like he'd been torn apart and broken open, but he'd somehow been able to keep moving. Adrenaline is a hell of a drug.

So is whatever must be pumping through his veins. He knows the pain is there, lying beneath the wave of numbness that engulfs his entire being, but he can't quite bring himself to care.

He thinks of being twelve and showing his dad an article on Spirit and Opportunity, two rovers NASA landed on Mars. Little Kel had been filled with pure, childish excitement imagining the ancient civilizations that might be uncovered. His dad had ruffled his hair and told him not to fantasize, pushed him to think about things more logically—figure out how the rovers had been built, how NASA had figured out how to get them safely to the surface. His dad's face narrows and elongates, his mouth splitting open sideways until the head of an Azathothlin sits on his shoulders.

Kel catches the faint scent of apples, or maybe that's just his brain trying to supply something pleasant. Either way, it makes him think of Effie, and he turns away from the altered memory.

Somewhere, in the recesses of his mind, he knows that her face was streaked with dirt and tears the last time he saw her, her hazel eyes clouded with fear. But the image his mind conjures is of her in his bed, hair a blue halo across the pillow and a soft smile on her lips as she talks about ... what had she been talking about?

He wants to reach out and touch her, but not a single one of his muscles responds to the request, and that wave of complete and utter numbness rises higher, sweeping him along with it.

4

0316 MDT//5d 13min after arrival

Lance has never been more exhausted in his life, but he's far from tired. He goes home to shower, where he stands there for longer than necessary, hot water pounding against his head and shoulders as he watches grime and blood and ash travel slowly down the drain.

Danielle comes in, wrapping her arms around his middle and holding him, her body pressed against his.

"I feel so lost," he whispers, and then he starts to cry, because he doesn't know if he's made the right decision. He doesn't know what this means, what kind of man he is.

"I'm here, baby," Danielle's lips brush against his skin. "No matter what, I'm here." Her arms tighten around him. "I love you, Lance Sutherland. You are *good*, and I am so, so proud to be your wife and to call you the father of my children."

He turns to her, then, losing himself in her completely, and when that is over, he stands there holding her, forehead pressed to hers long after the water at his back has grown cold. But he's resolute now, knowing he's doing what's right.

After, he sits in his car, driving away from her—away from Katie and Izzy, whose foreheads he'd kissed before quietly slipping out—because there's one more person he has to see before all of this can finally feel settled.

Effie is in the hospital in Montrose, and he's ready to bring her home.

It's been a few hours since they last spoke, and he calls her now to let her know he's on his way.

"Hey," she answers, her voice tired but otherwise steady.

"How you holdin' up, kid?" he asks, unprepared for the lump that forms in his throat with the words.

She chuckles. "A little banged up, but otherwise fine. They gave me pain meds for the burns and wrapped up my ankle. It's just a bad sprain. I've got some gnarly bruising pretty much everywhere, but it's all been surface level, luckily. They did a CT scan, too, since I passed out, but I didn't hit my head or anything, and it all looks fine."

"That's good. I'm so glad you're okay. What about Kel?"

Effie pauses, and there's a rustling sound, like maybe her hand went over the microphone, but she's back a second later. "He's ... he's still in surgery. It looks like his leg will heal, but he broke a rib and punctured his lung."

"Fuck ... he's strong, Eff. He'll pull through," Lance puts as much conviction into his voice as he can muster.

Effie sniffles. "If you hadn't called when you did ... If I'd kept driving and passed out ..."

"Hey, don't even think about that, okay? It didn't happen."

"Yeah, you're right. I just ... it's been a fucking long few days." She laughs harshly.

"I can't argue with you there," Lance says. "Are they discharging you?"

"Yeah. I have a dermatology follow-up to schedule, but other than that, I'm clear."

"I'm on the way; be there in maybe forty-five. If Kel's still not awake yet, I'll wait with you."

"Okay." There's a pause, and when she speaks again, her voice is tight. "Lance? Thank you."

His chest aches, and his mind turns back to when she was a feral little kid, always climbing trees or running off into the desert. Every time she'd fallen or gotten scraped up, he was there to help her back to her feet. Will she understand why he has to stay with the agency? Why he'll go wherever they intend to send him if it means ensuring that history doesn't repeat itself? "Of course," he answers. "I'll be there soon, kiddo. I love you."

"Love you, too."

As he drives, he replays his debrief with Vice Director Howard in his mind, knowing he'll have to explain everything soon enough and needing to remind himself that he's made the best decision for his family. Effie isn't going to be happy about it. She fucking loves these mountains. Maybe she'll end up moving in with Bethany? But will she even want to stay after everything that's happened? Will she still feel safe?

By the time he pulls into the hospital parking lot, he feels more settled and sure of himself. If not quite eager for the next steps, he is ready to move forward. Effie texted him a floor and room number, and the relief he feels when he discovers it's just a waiting room is so strong it makes his legs weak.

He pushes the door open, immediately spotting her.

Her head shoots up, and she stands when she sees him, rushing over with tears in her eyes. She slams into him, and he holds her tight, not loosening his hold until he feels her start to let go.

She tips her face up, delicately wiping tears from under her eyes, her skin red and angry with burns. "I'm really glad to see you." She gives him a watery smile, lips pressed together. "It's been …"

"I know," he squeezes her shoulder, giving her a once over. Her leggings are filthy, and there's a damp spot on her shirt where it looks like she tried to wash some blood out. The undersides of both her forearms are bandaged, but her face is clean, and the parts of her that aren't burned have a healthy color. "You scared the shit out of me passing out like that."

"Apologies, Chief. I'll keep it under control next time." Her sarcastic answer further settles the relief in his chest, but the mention of next time tightens it all over again.

He looks over her shoulder to the people sitting in the far corner of the waiting room, then guides her out into the hallway. "They want to talk to you about everything that's happened," he tells her softly, watching her for any adverse reaction. "They'll need you to sign an NDA, too. But they're going to cover all of your medical bills and offer you a settlement. I know that doesn't make up for everything that's happened, but they want to help in any way they can."

Effie scoffs, leaning against the wall. "A settlement, huh? Enough for me to quit controlling air traffic so I never accidentally see an alien fall from the sky again?"

"Eff ... the tower's gone."

She blinks. "What?"

He glances around the hallway, keeping his voice low. "The Azathothlin knocked it down."

Her jaw drops. "Bitch move."

Lance's lips quirk up. "Payment for destroying her nest, I guess." His smile falls, questioning. With everything that's happened, he never learned what went on in the basin. "Did you destroy her nest?"

"Yeah, it's buried under a metric fuck-ton of rock," she assures with a tired smirk.

They stand in silence for a while, Effie's head resting against the wall, eyes vacant as she chews at the side of her thumbnail.

"You don't have any qualms? About signing the NDA, I mean. The interview can wait until you've had time to rest and process everything, of course." Lance shoves his hands deep in his pockets, uncomfortable with pushing her. Lord help him when he has to try to convince Kel to join the side of government conspiracy.

Effie pulls her hand down, lightly folding her arms across her chest to not aggravate her skin any further than necessary, and studies him for a moment. He resists the urge to pull his gaze away, unsure what she's looking for in it. "You're staying with them?"

He nods, running a hand through his hair, the gray at his temples stark in the harsh hospital lighting. "They're gonna move me. But now that I know what these things are capable of, it's the right thing for me to do. They asked me to help them revamp some protocols so that something like this doesn't happen again. I'll be prepared. I can help people." His voice is low, but strong with conviction.

She looks away, lips pursed, then her expression clears, and she meets his eyes again. Her face looks sad in a way that Lance can't explain, a glimmer in the green-flecked hazel of her eyes that almost looks like disappointment, and the bare beginnings of a wobble in her chin. "Yeah," she says, her voice cracking just slightly. She swallows. "I'll sign it."

Lance feels his shoulders droop, and he tries for an encouraging smile. "How's Kel doing? Any update?"

Her gaze drops to her feet, her head dipping so that her face is concealed by a short blue curtain of hair. Her fingers twist into her shirt, and then she tips her head back up to look at him. "He didn't make it."

Tears flood her eyes, and Lance pulls her close, letting her lean on him for support. "Oh, Effie," he whispers, his own throat tight. "I'm so sorry."

"Terror in Telluride? Reports have come out of San Miguel County that Telluride was terrorized late Sunday night by what many are claiming to be a monster. With a confirmed death toll of eleven, over thirty injured, and an estimated $4.5 million in damages—including the complete destruction of Telluride Regional Airport's control tower—it's undeniable that *something* happened last night, but there are no clear reports as to what. Out in the field right now, we have Jameson, ready to patch in and give us a report directly from ground zero. Over to you, Jameson."

"Thank you, Jessica. As you can see around me, the usually bustling streets of Telluride are about as empty as can be, with most of the town's residents choosing to stay indoors and the tourists packing up early to head home. I have, however, found a few people that are willing to share their account of what happened last night."

Gloria King, visitor and eyewitness: "I was hanging out in the plaza, buying funnel cake for my children when out of nowhere a giant crab came out of the forest! It started snatching people up and eating them, and everyone was running and screaming—it was utter chaos. No, I didn't get any photos or videos. I was too busy trying to get my babies to safety and out of the way of that horrible creature! What was it? Well, like I told you, it was a giant crab, but it didn't have any claws, just these horrible, spiked legs that it used to grab people. I don't know where it came from, but I'm betting you it was some kind of cryptid, like Bigfoot."

Stanley Pritchard, resident and eyewitness: "Yeah, I saw that monster start running rampant through the town. You won't find nobody with any proof, though. Feds came by as soon as it was all over with and cleaned everything up, walked around with these devices and wiped everyone's phones. How do I know they were feds? Well, who else but the government would be trying to keep all these science experiments a secret? I'm retired from the sheriff's department, you know, and I'll tell you right now that there are things out in these mountains that The Man doesn't want you to know about. Bears and Bigfoot are the least of your worries."

Margaret Atwood, resident: "Oh, what happened last night was such a tragedy. All those poor lives lost! I was already in bed by the time the riot broke out, but I just feel so sorry for the poor souls who got caught up in it all. I'm collecting donations for a memorial service, you know. We really do need to band together during these times and pay our respects. What was that? The riot? Well, what else would it have been? You don't really believe in monsters, do you? No, people just got spooked and you know what happens in a crowd. Hysteria catches like wildfire, and before you know it, you're helping eleven grieving families plan premature funerals."

Lance Sutherland, San Miguel County Chief Deputy Sheriff: "No, I can't tell you exactly what happened. I wasn't on scene when chaos broke loose, but I can tell you how proud I am of how our department handled it all and ushered everyone to safety. The folks on duty did right by their community. What happened up at the airport seems to be an unrelated event. There are people pulling blueprints and contracts for that tower, but what appears to have happened was a structural issue. I'm no engineer, but to my understanding, it was a combination of wind and a faulty foundation that brought it down. No, I don't put any weight behind claims of there being any sort of monster in these mountains, but there are quite a few apex predators that live out here and can cause a great deal of harm. We do our best to mitigate, but unfortunately, it's their territory that we've made our home in. This community suffered a tragedy, but the people here are strong and resilient, and they've already banded together to heal and come back even stronger."

Day 6

Tuesday, 29 August 2023

1

Lance stands at his kitchen window sipping a cup of coffee while cartoons play in the background. An arm slips around his waist, and without even thinking about it, his own moves around his wife's shoulders, pulling her into his side.

"How are they doing? Do you want to go bring them breakfast?" Danielle asks, and Lance realizes that he's been staring at the casita while lost in thought.

"They headed out earlier this morning."

Bethany had come by yesterday shortly after he and Effie got back home and stayed through the night. He'd left them alone and made sure the girls didn't go bug them, either. It was good that they had each other; neither should have to grieve alone. He ignores the little scratch at the back of his mind that warns him it's not good for Effie to be around anyone when she still hasn't signed the NDA, when the agency still needs her statement. Her well-being is more important.

"Maybe they went back to Bethany and Derek's," Danielle muses. "I'm sure Beth doesn't want to be there alone so soon.

Those poor girls. I can't even imagine." She squeezes him before moving away to prepare her own coffee.

There's a knock on the door, and he looks over his shoulder to Danielle, curious who would be there so early.

"I'll get it!" Izzy calls, jumping up from the couch and running to the foyer with Katie on her heels. Danielle sets a mug underneath the coffee maker before following.

His daughters' soft chatter carries down the hall, then a quick patter of feet as they run toward the kitchen, Katie holding a box up above her line of sight. Lance steps over to halt her before she smacks into the table.

"It's for Effie!" Izzie tells him excitedly. "Can we take it to her?"

"Maybe later, bug." Lance takes the package from Katie and sets it on the counter. "She's gone for now."

2

1119 MDT//6d 8hr 16min after arrival

Effie has completely forgotten about the bike seat her dad sent her only five days ago, but it's the very least of her worries now. A burning itch coats both of her arms, her skin slowly healing, but it seems a small agony compared to the ache that spreads through her chest as she watches the trees race past, and she tightens her grip on the steering wheel. She's going to miss these mountains more than she wants to admit.

"You okay?"

She pulls her eyes away from the road for just a moment to

look at Kel. His black alien eyes hat was lost to the mines, so Effie gifted him one of her favorites until he can replace it. It's hot pink canvas and white mesh, a bright blue Colorado "C" patch sewed to the front. He's got it on backward, holding his curls off his face. If it weren't for the bags under his eyes and the scabbed-over abrasion on his cheekbone, it would be impossible to tell that just yesterday he'd been on the brink of death.

She gives him a reassuring smile, turning back to the road. "Losing faith in me already?"

Kel had done his best to hide how nervous he was about Effie towing the fifth wheel. He'd guided her through tear-down and hook-up, then laboriously climbed into the passenger seat before she drove off.

Effie will never admit it to him—not for a good long while, anyway—but she had also been extremely nervous to tow something so big through the winding mountain roads. There was no way Kel could drive, though, not with a few broken ribs and unable to even lift his arms without his face going white with the pain.

"Never." Kel smiles back, but it comes out as more of a grimace, and he gingerly shifts around to try to get more comfortable, lifting his shredded thigh with his hands to reposition it. Beneath his pants, the leg is covered in gauze and sutures, and he needs a cane to walk while it heals. But he'd kept it, and with time, he should regain full use of it.

"You should've stayed in the hospital for another day like they offered," Effie tells him, keeping her eyes on the road.

Kel just wrinkles his nose, unable to shrug or wave her off. "I can rest just as well in the passenger seat as I can in a hospital bed," he insists. "Plus, why give those squirrelly fucks a chance to come harass me?"

Effie sighs, slipping the transmission into second gear as the road dips into a decline. "They've probably found out you're alive by now, anyway."

"Good luck trying to chase us down," he jokes. Between his broken ribs and the weight of the camper behind them, Effie refuses to let the speedometer pass fifty-five miles per hour.

For all of the physical trauma Kel had been through on the journey out of the mine and down the mountain, the puncture in his lung could have been a lot worse. Surgery had taken only a couple of hours, and he'd woken up not long after that. When Lance had called, Kel had asked her not to mention that he was awake yet, unsure where her cousin stood with the agency after everything that had happened.

Should it become clear that Lance was still with them, Kel had told Effie to let the agency think he'd died instead of trying to argue the refusal of an NDA and harbor the existence of hard evidence from a sick bed.

She'd rolled her eyes at the melodramatics, but went along with the plan, knowing it was probably the safest way to ensure they had a chance to prove the Azathothlins' presence.

She hadn't meant to cry when she told Lance, but she'd been so exhausted—mentally, physically, emotionally—and that final lie had broken her. Because that lie meant that, for the first time she could remember, she and Lance were on opposite sides.

But just as she knows he thinks he's doing the right thing, she's equally sure that she's made the right choice.

She glances at Bethany in the rearview mirror, and heart cracks. Bethany's head is propped on a pillow against the window, dark curls tumbling over her shoulders as she rests, her eyes closed. Effie doubts she's slept more than a handful of hours since Sunday morning.

As soon as Bethany told her that Derek was dead, Effie resolved to tell her the full truth about everything. She deserved to know. Derek had deserved to know before giving up his life.

In the early hours of the morning yesterday, Bethany had gone out to Effie's Jeep to grab the backpack that held all of their irrefutable proof and kept it safe until Effie's return. Then Effie spilled everything she knew, and the two had spent the rest of the day talking, grieving, and planning their next moves. When Effie could no longer fight her exhaustion, Bethany had stayed awake. By the time she woke up that morning, Bethany had told her she was going with them. If Effie and Kel were fighting the agency and these creatures, Bethany wanted to, too.

As soon as Kel had confirmed he was approved to be discharged, Effie and Bethany had driven up to Montrose to collect him.

Just like that, team Curtis-Blake, party of three, is on the way to California so Kel can hand-deliver the alien substances he collected, with their first stop being a FedEx in Cortez. Effie had made her own scientific connections when stationed in Arizona, and is going to overnight a portion of the samples to a friend in the biology program at Northern Arizona University, adding another reputable source to the list of people who have irrefutable evidence.

If the agency hasn't already figured out that Kel faked his death to avoid them, they'll sure as hell find out then.

"How'd you keep Lance from hounding you about the NDA?" Kel asks, breaking her out of her thoughts.

She presses her lips together with a little shrug, shifting back into third as the road levels out. "He thinks you *died.* The agency may be heartless, but he's not. He wasn't about to hound me about anything, certainly not right after bringing me home all exhausted, beaten-up, and cried-out."

Kel turns his head to face her, carefully reaching out with his left arm to poke at her across the center console. "Elizabeth Catherine Blake, are you saying you *like* me? Oh my stars, how *embarrassing*."

She laughs, easily swatting him away. "You're going to make me run off the road if you don't watch it, Kelvin Alien-watch."

He pulls his hand back with a chuckle that cuts off into a wince.

"That's right. Don't dish it if you can't take it," she teases.

The road straightens out, and Effie turns up the volume on the music.

There's still a lot that will need to be worked out. With the destruction of the control tower, Effie no longer has a job. But she does have her GI bill, and that conversation with her mom that feels like a lifetime before has been turning slowly in the back of her mind. Maybe she will go to college. Conservation—with an emphasis on the study of invasive species—might be worth considering. And then there's Kel, who's essentially about to pick a fight with a secret entity of the American government.

But those are all problems for the future. For now, they have a plan to tell the world about the aliens living under their feet, and they have each other.

Weirdly enough, that last little tidbit eases something within her, and she realizes it's not just nervous anticipation that's knotted in her stomach, but also excitement for whatever comes next.

3

1428 MDT//6d 11hr 25min after arrival

An Azathothlin crawls through the Earth.

His journey has been long and arduous, moving from tunnel to cave system, sometimes chipping through rock to continue on, and once even dropping into a cold, swift, underground river that carried him for a ways.

But, finally, he knows he can rest.

The tunnels he and his kind have lived in since their earliest arrival have always been completely uninhabited. They've been working ever-so-diligently to connect the tunnels and make it easier to travel back and forth, extending their hive from the central point outward.

In the event that they stumble upon a tunnel system that isn't vacant, they take care of it, snatching away whatever living creatures that enter and feasting on them in the dark, leaving nothing behind but any inorganic matter that is often buried too far beneath the Earth's surface for anyone to find.

It will take several years yet before all points are connected and easily traversable, but that's no matter. They're diligent creatures, the Azathothlins, and while they have no true understanding of time, they do know that when they're done, they'll have everything they need to grow their colony, to keep it safe and fed and thriving on this planet, much like the planet they traveled from, now far too populated to properly support them all.

And so they're sent to Earth, where there is plenty of space and resources to sustain them.

The ground vibrates beneath him, allowing him to clearly see the tunnel ahead despite the utter lack of light. His antennae slide forward, caressing the object he's held delicately in his spined forelegs throughout the journey. The air in this tunnel is acrid with the scent of burned fuel and chemicals, but it's stale, quickly fading once the shock of the initial assault on his senses fades. Laced along with those smells is the one of warmth and blood and flesh that he knows means *humans*.

The vibrations come from the humans, too. He's been on this planet long enough to know the sounds that come from the machines they use to scrape minerals from the Earth's crust. They're still active here, which is good.

The new queen will be hungry when she hatches.

The Azathothlin chips away at the rock wall with the hard, pointed tip of one leg, creating a small alcove where he gently, almost tenderly, lays the egg he's carried.

He settles down on the ground beside it, tucking his legs beneath him and resting his chin on the floor.

The other eggs were destroyed, and he knows not what happened to the queen who laid them. But this one still pulses with life, and he knows the scent it left behind will lead others to it.

They will feed her and protect her while she grows, and then she will establish their colony on this planet, truly claiming it as their own.

Acknowledgements

Horror has been my most coveted, long-standing escape since I was a kid. From sneaking horror books into my library hauls, to my first scary movie, to writing short stories filled with violence and gore and terror—horror was my first love, one of the first parts of me that was truly my own. Keeping with that theme, I gave this book everything else I loved, too, and filled it with all of my favorite things.

Thank you, reader. Writing wouldn't be half as much fun without you here to read it. Time is such a finite thing. Thank you for spending yours with me. It means the world.

To the people behind the making of this book, who helped me with plotting and opinions and vibe checks and every other little thing that turns a clump of words into a book, I'm so fucking lucky to have you all in my life. Mursiel, my soul twin, this book quite literally wouldn't exist without you and our vibes-only, no-planning-required road trips. I can't fucking wait to take it back to Telly with you. Taylor, knowing you'll never be afraid to tell me to kill off a character or put a little more depth behind something is just the cherry on top of your ever-reliable book recs and chaotic messages about *Survivor*, *Criminal Minds*, and the most despicable horror. Sarah, my voice of reason and empathy meter, I don't know where I would be without you to question the emotional validity of a character's actions or question my ability to perform simple math. Cass, you were the first person to read Telly in its entirety, and the way you devoured even that early draft was so validating. Rachel, Kelsey, Sarah, and Elle, I know I say it every time, but I'm so, so grateful for the time and energy y'all put into helping me polish these stories. Thank you all for being here with me.

To my parents, who gave me the autonomy to be myself whenever possible. Mom, when you noticed my interests were starting to take a dip toward something darker than *Warriors*, you stayed up with me to watch *Criminal Minds*, bought me a box of Stephen King books for Christmas, and took me and my friends to see horror movies for my birthday. Thank you for seeing me, in the midst of everything else, and giving me every opportunity to enjoy the things I loved. Dad, thank you for helping me cultivate my sense of adventure, for teaching me the art of taking dirt roads with no destination other than adventure and for listening to me ramble about whatever book I was reading while doing so.

Josh, your constant love and support is invaluable throughout this process. You're my favorite hype man. I love you, and I love doing life with you.

And to Telluride, thank you for the best nature and all the camping trips. You're part of why Colorado feels like home.

Until next time. Thanks again for being here.

—Car

About the Author

Carissa Hardcastle is a lifelong adventurer and bookworm who will never turn down fast food, still listens to 2000s pop punk, and always greets wildlife that crosses her path. Though fiction has been her passion since she was young, she also spent seven years as an air traffic controller in the Air Force, where she cultivated a love for all things aviation. Carissa grew up exploring the Sierra Nevadas of California, but now lives in Colorado with her husband. Mountains are her happy place, and much of her writing pulls inspiration from the grandeur and magic of the Rockies. When not writing or out finding adventure, she enjoys consuming horror and fantasy in any medium available.

For more information and updates, check out www.carissa hardcastlebooks.com

www.ingramcontent.com/pod-product-compliance
Lightning Source LLC
Chambersburg PA
CBHW022011310726
48972CB00006B/1598